AFTER DECEMBER

AFTER DECEMBER

KASIE WHITENER

Chrysalis Press
Columbia, SC

This is a work of fiction.

Chrysalis Press, an imprint of Kat Biggie Press
katbiggiepress.com/cp

Publisher's Cataloging-In-Publication Data
(Prepared by The Donohue Group, Inc.)

Names: Whitener, Kasie, author.
Title: After December / Kasie Whitener.
Description: [Blythewood, South Carolina] :
      Chrysalis Press, an imprint of Kat Biggie
      Press, [2019]
Identifiers: ISBN 9781948604536 | ISBN 9781948604550
      (ebook)
Subjects: LCSH: Friendship--Fiction. | Forgiveness--
      Fiction. | Generation X--Fiction. | Suicide--
      Fiction.
Classification: LCC PS3623.H58459 A48 2019 (print) |
LCC PS3623.H58459 (ebook) | DDC 813/.6--dc23

Library of Congress Control Number: 2019952673

Cover Design by Melissa Williams Design

Interior Formatting by Melissa Williams Design

"With candles, with flowers
He was one of ours
One of ours."

"River" by Natalie Merchant
Indian Love Bride, 1995

TUESDAY

"I'm sorry, Brian." Dad expelled a long stream of air, pushing the words across the country, popping static through the cordless phone.

I doubled over on the edge of the bed, pressing elbows into knees.

"Mac said he'd been struggling."

The room swelled with afternoon sunlight. One secondhand chest of drawers. One ladderback chair. One large bay window.

"He was alone." More static and Dad's grief then, "Your flight's at eight-thirty. I'll call Joel to get you."

"Don't. I'll take a cab." I pressed the heel of my hand into my eye.

There was a long pause and I expected him to apologize again. But he didn't.

"Don't forget your keys." Then he hung up.

I felt the shift of weight behind me as Meli sat up in bed. When I looked up, the sun blinded me and I closed my eyes into the brightness of the window, pressing my palms down onto the sheets. Two minutes since he'd said it.

I could feel Meli touching me, both of us naked in the golden light. Her voice, the one that said, "Do you love me?" just before the phone rang, completely replaced by Dad's long-distance tenor.

The words echoed in my ears, the conversation on repeat in my head. Three minutes since he'd said it. Then I said it.

"Tony killed himself last night."

Meli laid her cheek against my shoulder. I felt the wetness of her earliest tears and the softness of her hair over my back. Her fingers wrapped around my arm.

I threw the phone across the room. It hit the door frame and clattered into unsatisfying pieces on the wood floor.

The safety of my confinement was over. I had to go back to Virginia.

Pulling myself out of Meli's grasp, I stood up and stared out over the rooftops to the Pacific Ocean, shimmering and sultry, begging the sun toward the horizon.

WEDNESDAY

It's February and it's too soon to be going back. This is the time of year they usually suggest coming to California. If I asked, they would be on a plane in minutes to be with me. At least that's what they say. But they don't come. We say things like, "When will you be home again?" and mean Herndon, Virginia. Half of my life is there. Two parents. One ex-girlfriend. Four best friends. Well, three now. Tony is dead.

Sixteen hours and thirty-two minutes after being told, I took my window seat. Eight-nineteen on a Wednesday morning. Just another guy on a plane.

Forty-five minutes since my last cigarette and barely fifteen seconds since I'd thought about a smoke. The cabin door closed with a thud. I pressed my temple to the airtight window and squeezed my eyes shut.

Six weeks since New Year's Day. Me shoving clothes into my bag. Tony still dirty and hungover from the night before.

"You just left her?" he had demanded.

"What was I supposed to do?"

"Work it out. Forgive her. I don't know. Give her a chance at least. This isn't you." He had his coat on, the zipper hanging open with a ski lift ticket on it, a burgundy ball cap on his head with a yellow script R.

"It's been over for a while now."

He stood in the corner of my old bedroom, watching me move from dresser to bed. Under his coat a buttoned-up flannel, a t-shirt beneath that, still wrinkled because he'd slept in it. The same Tony as every other day for our whole lives.

"Have you even thought about what you're doing?" He sounded frustrated but didn't step any closer to me. Angry but not able to raise his voice. Hoarse with the thickness of too many cigarettes. Weak from no sleep. High.

I tugged the zipper around the edge of the bag.

"I didn't do this to us," I said.

"Didn't you?" Tony who'd always known me best. But I was different. Changed by the events of the last fourteen hours. Sick and tired of them all.

"Time to leave?" he had asked, one eyebrow raised, eyes milky, lips dry.

"Seems like it's always time to leave." I hoisted the bag onto my shoulder.

That wasn't how it was supposed to go. That shouldn't have been the last time we were in the same room. Not fighting about Kacie of all damned things. I wrote that scene. Captured our dialogue and his posture and my bravado and the suffocating tension. I wrote it in a spiral notebook in pencil on the return flight. But I didn't know it was our last scene together.

I didn't know anything then. Not really.

Fucking Virginia with its ambitions and requirements and expectations. I keep all that shit in a box. I open the flaps on school holidays and vacations. I let myself peek inside when Tony calls me in the middle of the night. Sometimes I even crawl inside for a week or two. In Virginia, I was a winner. Swim team record holder, X Games qualifying skateboarder. A champion.

Except every time I go back, I feel melted, disfigured, like the wax of a well-used candle, unfit for anything. So mostly I just keep the medals and newspaper clippings and pictures of me holding trophies in the boxes against the wall under the window sill of my San Francisco apartment, and let them collect dust.

When the plane finally made its approach to Dulles International Airport it was four forty-nine Eastern Standard Time. Exactly twenty-eight hours and six minutes since my father had called me. I startled when the flight attendant touched my shoulder and instructed me to bring my chair to its fully upright position. We descended into Dulles airport and I changed my watch from Pacific Time to Eastern as the landscape grew bigger in the window.

I had made excuses to stay away over Thanksgiving but gave in and went home for Christmas break. Nine days of it anyway. And now I was back in Virginia. Carrying those memories, that baggage, the confusion and hurt and anger of New Year's. *Tony is dead*, I thought, for the millionth time. Five twenty-seven p.m. I descended into baggage claim.

She stood alone by a vacant rental car counter. Kacie had come for me. As expected.

We'd met in a high school creative writing class sophomore year. She was new and she wrote poetry and I wrote skateboard action scenes. Tony said she was pretty and I told him she would be mine before spring break. On our first date, we drove around looking at Christmas lights and she tucked her hand into the pocket of my suit jacket. In my parents' living room with the Disney animated *Beauty and the Beast* on VHS, we snuggled close and I could smell her vanilla body lotion. When the credits rolled, that tender Celine Dion song came on and I drew her off the couch and into my arms and we slow danced and she sang softly in my ear.

Baggage claim was crowded with arrivals and greeters

5

embracing, pressing their faces into one another's necks, their intimacy resonating from them like careless echoes thrown against cave walls.

Kacie's elbows pressed into her ribs, a white rose perched in front of her. I once gave her five roses: one for each of my senses she'd enchanted. She had her hair pulled back into a cloth band and her skin was pale. She had gained weight and her cheeks were still red from the air outside as if, like me, she'd only just arrived. She wore a black pea coat with large brass buttons, fake vintage from Banana Republic.

I walked slowly, deafened and disoriented, as if underwater.

Before she could speak, I wrapped my arms around her and pulled her against me. Her arms slipped behind my neck and her hot cheek pressed against mine. I smelled her shampoo, her skin, that vanilla lotion, and the tears I'd been holding back swelled into my eyes.

"Brian." Her murmur tickled my ear and I turned my face to press my lips against hers but she pulled away. "Brian," she said again, putting me away from her. The smell of outside broke between us.

I squeezed my eyes shut and swallowed back the tears. Turning away and shoving a fist into my eye, I said, "Did Joel send you?"

"I asked him to let me come." She touched my sleeve but I couldn't meet her gaze. "I hope you brought a coat," she said, looking at the fleece and my empty hands and wrapping her arms around herself. "It's cold."

Pulling slowly away, I blinked a few times to force my vision to focus. I nodded and wandered toward the baggage carousel.

She followed me and stood a few feet away as we waited for the buzzer and the bags and the frenzy of people staring and grabbing and inspecting and muttering. A honking noise warned the arrivals of its motion, a red light flashed. A family with a stroller. One elderly couple. Three businessmen in black wool coats. One folding a stick of gum into his mouth.

"The rose was a nice touch," I said over my shoulder.

"A man gave it to me when I walked in." She waved it toward the entrance where a concrete hill ascended toward the pick-up zone and an airport worker pushed a man in a wheelchair up the ramp while a lady followed dragging a rolling suitcase.

"It was supposed to remind me of POWs and soldiers missing in action."

"Did it?"

"No," she said, looking a little ashamed. "It reminded me of Christmas lights."

I didn't know before I went that California would give me the box in which to conceal and store my East Coast life. Spirals of scenes, pencil scratches on college-ruled pages, buried under copies of dog-eared Hemingway novels. Pictures with curled edges, summer league blue ribbons, and notes folded into tucked origami shapes. I didn't know before I went that I wanted to forget. But when I got there and forgetting became so easy, I did what I've always done: I got really good at it. I told myself that Herndon, Virginia, even in its box, is just a collection of used-up things.

The baggage carousel turned slowly. A well-traveled khaki-and-leather bag rode down the chute, landed between two black suitcases, one with a yellow string. The carousel brought it closer. My dad's hand-me-down folding luggage, the one with my suit in it, the suit I would wear to bury Tony, packed with t-shirts and flannels, boxers, socks, and too much extra space. I grabbed it, checked the tag just to be sure, then opened the front pocket and tugged out a heavier coat. I re-zipped the bag, lifted the strap over my shoulder, and nodded toward the exit.

"I tried to call you," she said, the words spilling out almost involuntarily.

"When?"

"Yesterday. After I heard. Were you home?"

I stared at her face. Those green eyes glistened and I thought maybe she wanted to cry, too. I thought about yesterday, being naked with Meli, her telling me she loved me, and glanced away, a passing stranger carrying my gaze. When I looked back again, Kacie was glaring at me.

"Right," she said, as if she'd seen my thoughts. She turned her back on me. "Let's go." I followed her toward the parking lot signage. She dropped the white rose in a round trash receptacle beneath a tall advertisement for insurance.

A phone rang, a voice on the announcement system called someone's name but it wasn't mine. We descended the concrete hill toward short-term parking, the gritted floor providing traction despite the glisten of dirty snow that had been trudged in and melted. The glass doors at the bottom of the ramp slid open as we approached and the cold air rushed in. We walked through the tunnel, passed the taxis and hotel vans, and emerged into the open air. The sun had set and the Virginia sky bore evening like a bruise. I pulled my jacket closer to me and tucked my chin to my chest, trying to shield my face from the wind.

The first time I left, I'd been gone for eleven weeks, from the first of September to the Wednesday before Thanksgiving. The plane had been full and the airport packed when I came through the gate. Kacie had been hopping up and down and pushed past several other travelers to throw herself into my arms. I dropped my carry-on at our feet and buried my face in her neck, kissed her skin, her ear, her jaw, her lips. I remember breathing her in and suddenly realizing how homesick I had really been.

It got easier, though. We kept up the routine: a dramatic reunion, a desperate hug, playing for the crowd like two severed halves of a whole. I wrote those scenes, too. Tight arms, shared breath, the taste of her cherry lip gloss. But each time I left, it was easier to say goodbye and each time I returned, it was easier to break the hug.

The last time I came home, I'd been gone seventeen weeks. She met me at the curb outside of baggage claim. She didn't even get out of the car, only leaned across the center console for me to peck her on the cheek. It was Christmas Eve and the flight attendant had worn a Santa hat for the entire trip. I'd had four beers and the last one was free. If Kacie smelled them on me, she didn't let on. She hadn't said anything, just drove me home. Eight weeks had passed since then.

Kacie stopped at the sidewalk and waited for a break in oncoming traffic. Then she charged across the street and I followed her and she weaved through a couple of rows of dirty cars. With a loud, familiar beep-beep she disarmed the car alarm on her old grey Toyota, the one that took us to Ocean City for beach week and to Baltimore for the Orioles' games and down to Virginia Tech that weekend for the state meet. The lights blinked like fireflies.

I tossed my bag in the backseat while she shoved the keys into the steering column. Dropping into the front seat, I pulled the door closed, cracked the window and lit a cigarette. She did the same. The inside wasn't nearly as cold as outside confirming she had just recently arrived. The heat blew loudly from the dashboard and the windshield fogged up. It was five forty-seven p.m. Eastern Standard Time. Twenty-nine hours and three minutes since my father called.

The first two drags of the cigarette were desperate and unsatisfying but the third one was hot and full and I closed my eyes for just a moment, reminded myself where I was, and exhaled slowly toward the crack in the window. When I opened my eyes again the windshield had cleared but she still hadn't put the car in gear.

"We really should talk about New Year's."

"Leave it alone, Kace," I said, shortening her name as if I

still had the right to do so. She backed down. I knew she would. I knew everything she would do. I hadn't bothered to look for Joel in baggage claim; I knew she'd be there. I had spent my taxi cash on beers on the plane, so sure Kacie would be waiting and I wouldn't need a Dulles Flyer. This was like every other arrival. Except it wasn't. Not even close.

Kacie's parents bought the Toyota when we were all in high school. It was dingy and abused the way things are when they're taken for granted. A persistent cigarette smell and faded interior accompanied a rattle as the engine tried to pick up speed leaving the payment booth. The Toyota closed the distance to my parents' house. Dave Matthews Band sang "Crush" on the radio and Kacie leaned forward to turn it up. I listened to see if she'd start singing. She didn't. I finished my cigarette and threw the butt out the window, then rolled the glass back up and held my palm in front of the vent for warm air. The song ended.

"This isn't exactly the time to ask for forgiveness," I said, rubbing my hands together and glancing over at her.

"Who's asking?" She finished her cigarette, too, tossed the butt and rolled up the window. The music seemed to swell with the wind gone.

"You could have called or something." I turned the volume knob down. "Weeks ago."

"Would you have been alone?" She looked over at me and then at the radio. Pressed the knob so the sound went off completely. "I wanted to see you in person," she added.

"Oh, well, good thing this happened then, huh?"

We were silent long enough to get off the highway, following the mass of rush hour traffic off the exit ramp and up on to Reston Parkway. After two rotations of the light at Sunset Hills, the Toyota climbed slowly up the hill in front of Reston Town Center. I looked up to the Hyatt which loomed above the shopping plaza and parking garage. The ice-skating rink between the Hyatt and Clyde's would be open but mostly vacant until the weekend.

We passed what used to be Hechinger's but was now some corporate hardware store and the county soccer fields and the town houses where Kacie's sister rented a place. We drove by the grocery store strip mall where Chris had worked at Baskin Robbins. We'd already passed Worldgate Athletic Club with the movie theater where Tony and I saw *Teenage Mutant Ninja Turtles* in our first drop-off-by-ourselves movie trip and the office park with the manicured courtyard into which Kacie and I used to sneak after dark until the hired security chased us away.

Kacie turned left onto one of the few two-lane roads still snaking its way through that area. Then she dug into her purse and extracted lip balm. I turned my face to the window as she smeared her lips with it. I heard it drop back into her bag. Smelled the faint cherry scent.

Finally, with a deep breath I later recognized as an attempt at patience, she said, "This isn't easy for me, Brian."

"I know," I said, but it was barely audible. Being here wasn't easy for me, either, not to ride by all those memories, not to share the same air with her and certainly not to think about the last time I'd been here. The geography was fucking with me and I had to squeeze my eyes shut to blacken the familiarity of it all. I remembered thinking over New Year's that it wasn't my fault. That none of it was my fault. I still believed that, less than a foot from her, riding home from the airport in February. It was too soon. The wounds were still too raw.

Nearly home. She pulled into the drive. I reached for the release to my seatbelt. She laid her hand on mine. I jerked away.

"Brian, please." She faced me now, those pink lips glistening.

"Tony killed himself." The second time I'd said it out loud.

She winced. Her eyes filled with tears and she turned back to the steering wheel, staring out the windshield, waiting for me.

"Nothing else matters." I stepped out of the car and slammed the door. Opened the back door and pulled my bag out then slammed that door, too. I stormed up the walk, unable to resist stomping, refusing to give her another glance despite hearing the car back out of the driveway.

In the baggage claim at Dulles, I had reached for her just like the morning I learned I'd gotten accepted to Cal State, the day I broke the state record in the 200 IM, like leaving for the X Games, like coming home without a medal. All the times I'd held her and she'd held me.

But there had never been anything like this. This time she'd pulled away because the last time I reached for her had been different. I was different. Changed by what she'd told me, I had crushed her lips to mine. I had been unforgiving and unmerciful. I couldn't reach for her again.

Tony is dead, I reminded myself, the phrase thicker now, with my unshed tears choking me. I wanted to shout it at the retreating car, like a storm. I wanted thunder in my ears and rain pounding my flesh, smearing the tears I hadn't yet cried. I would welcome the punishment of it. I felt singed, smoldering, like the way I felt after we'd dosed.

I should have let her go when I let myself forget.

Guilt flooded me on the steps of my parents' house. I turned the key and pushed the door open, admitting myself and my bag.

It hasn't always been this way. I haven't always been this way. I loved her more than I ever thought possible. For a long time, I did everything I could to let her know how much she meant to me. I used to go to her house at night and leave flowers and poetry on her car. I used to call her just as she went to sleep and read to her over the phone. I quoted Shakespearean sonnets to her, made pledges of my fidelity, described how I would kiss her when I saw her again. I told her anything that made her smile into the phone when she said my name. I used to tell her how beautiful she was. I meant it, too.

Then I went to California.

I walked through the hallway of my parents' house and decided not to think about her anymore. I turned the corner and flipped on the light.

The kitchen spans the back of the house and has tall, honey-colored wood cabinets and ceramic countertops. The stove and refrigerator are beige as are the backsplash tiles and the wall. Over the corner sink is a framed cross-stitch that says, "The kitchen is the heart of the home," but it didn't fill the space so Mom hung sand dollars we'd collected at Nag's Head around it. A wallpaper border wraps around the top of the walls and bears the pale blue wisps of waves and sky.

Mom always communicated via magnet-note on the top freezer door.

"Dinner is fend for yourself."

"Get your clothes out of the dryer."

"Back late. Get homework done."

On Wednesday, she'd left a note saying she would be home around seven. I pulled it out from under the *Ski Wisp!* magnet and let it flutter to the counter. Then I took one of Dad's beers out of the crisper, opened it, and stood over the large counter island in the middle of the room.

The back wall has a wide bay window with fat wood blinds. I could see myself in the reflection of the lighted room. I walked around the kitchen table, approached the bay window, and stared out through the slats. Reaching for the pull, I dragged the blinds all the way up and stared past my image to the lawn.

There is a tree in the middle of the yard. I could just make out the shape of the naked limbs in the glow cast by the kitchen window. As kids Tony and I used to jump off the bus and race to that tree, climbing up it as fast as we could. It's much bigger now but I remembered when my hands could wrap all the way around the branches. I would straddle the topmost limb, turn, and look down to watch Tony following behind.

He was a skinny kid, his adult teeth were too big for his mouth and he always had some scrape or bruise on his chin or jaw. He smiled a lot, though. He laughed a lot, too. He told the dumbest jokes, the ones uncles tell you at family reunions and to a kid they're hilarious.

"A mushroom walks into a bar," he'd say and laugh already, "The bartender says, 'We don't serve your kind here'. The mushroom says, 'Why not? I'm a fungi.'"

There was a cat in the neighborhood we used to chase out from under the deck with sticks. We would tie a rope to the back of my bike and take turns pulling each other on the skateboard behind it. Once, Tony and I took Dad's hammer, whatever nails we could find, the extra wood under the deck, and built a go-cart on my old wagon wheels.

Back then our neighborhood was considered out in the woods, but by now Northern Virginia has no woods left. The whole place is carved up with parkways and subdivisions. Every new home has that one spindly tree in the front yard that the developers plant but it never grows into much at all. The houses have aluminum siding and shutters that match the door. The cul-de-sac my parents live on has mostly older couples with grown children. The house Tony's parents used to live in is now owned by a retired military officer and his wife. The Williams moved into a newer development when Tony and I were in high school. I doubt Mac and Rhonda have been to the cul-de-sac since my parents had a cookout on graduation day.

The neighborhood has a pool and a swim team. I swam for

it. Still hold a few records. I coached there for a while, too. Then I was nineteen and couldn't swim in the summer league anymore so I quit. I remember summers as a pool rat, though. Tony and I went to the pool for early practice and then stayed all day until it was suppertime. At ten-till-the-top-of-the-hour the guards would whistle a long, slow alert that it was break. During break you could only stay in the water if you were over sixteen. We'd sit on the concrete with our feet in the water waiting for the whistle to blow so we could go back in. By the time we were old enough to swim during break, we were the lifeguards. Teenage summers meant girls in bikinis and deciding what music would play on the loudspeaker. Lying around the guardroom with a beaten copy of Atlas Shrugged, sunglasses, and Budweiser beach towels, feeling grown up. Then the hangovers and wondering if the swim lesson moms could smell the booze on us.

How did I get here? My parents' kitchen. *Tony is dead.* I took a long drink from the bottle. Focused again on my reflection in the glass. Took another drink.

The phone rang. I dropped the blinds back down and turned away from the window. The cordless phone cradle hung on the wall in a built-in desk between the kitchen and living room. I pulled it to me, pressed the "talk" button and said, "Hello?"

"So your plane did land?"

"Hi, Meli. Sorry. I was getting ready to call."

"It's fine. You're safe."

"Home."

"Did she come?"

I flipped the light switch off and walked over to the table, pulled a chair away and sat down.

"Yeah," I said. "Yeah, she came."

Silence on the line. Three thousand miles and all those unsaid things.

"I thought it would be Joel," I said. "And she's not here now."

"You're okay?" she asked.

"It is what it is," I said. "Waiting for my mom to get home."

"And then?"

I shrugged and said, "Then probably hang out with the Crew."

"And Kacie."

I didn't answer. I lifted the beer bottle to my lips and drained the contents.

"Call me later?" I could hear her breath in the receiver. Wanted to feel it on my cheek.

I closed my eyes. "Meli?"

"Yeah?"

"I wish you coulda come with me."

"Me, too. Call me later."

She hung up first. I held the phone in my fingers, pressed them tightly to the edges of it, the tips turned white, the silence almost broke me.

At some point we traded tree-climbing and bike-riding for skateboarding and smoking weed. We first got high in eighth grade. Tony stole some marijuana from his brother. He paid for it with a black eye but after that we bought it from Gavin and he was cool about it. Gavin was in and out of juvenile hall and Tony could get away with pretty much anything as long as it wasn't as bad as the shit Gavin pulled.

We tripped on acid a few times freshman year. We did some cocaine junior year, mushrooms and some more acid. I stayed away from heroin for the most part, the only time I did it I threw up. Kacie was afraid of needles but she had a helluva blow habit when she went back to UVA after last summer. I suspected she'd been fucking around for a couple of years, but all that shit stayed in Charlottesville so I didn't accuse her of anything. She and Tony used to get high together over the phone and when she hung up and went out, he'd call me and tell me about their date. Kacie and I never had long distance dates but Tony and I did. By four a.m. his time, I was the only one still awake. So, he'd call all slurry and complaining of a headache and I'd listen and smoke.

Tony stayed in Herndon. He always said he was going to transfer from the community college to Madison or Tech but he never did. We all left except him.

Joel went to Pittsburgh where he met Tabby. She was a serious girl, quiet at first but then she and Kacie got pretty tight over a couple of breaks and Tabby's bossy-older-sister side emerged. Every time we were together, she made sure we ate more than we drank, didn't break anything irreplaceable, and had rides home. I think Kacie was glad to no longer be the only girl in our group even if she did roll her eyes a few times at Tabby's condescending tone.

Jason, Joel's twin, went to Frostburg on a hockey scholarship but left after two years to play minors in Michigan, a Red Wings farm team.

Chris barely got out of high school and moved to Atlanta to live with his mom. He went to community college and planned to transfer. Whenever he came home he stayed with his father who was remarried with two much younger children. Chris called them "thing one and thing two" affectionately. I never met his step mom but Tony said she was hot.

We had all been gone since 1995, coming home with some regularity when there was nowhere else to go. But Tony stayed and worked and said he would get his own place. But he didn't. He lived in his parents' basement. He delivered pizzas for a while, waited tables for a while, and bartended for a while.

He'd always say, "Hey, guess who I saw last night?" and it would be someone we knew in high school.

I never said that. I always acted surprised when he told me. He had friends where he worked and knew all of the bartenders in town but no one really knew Tony but me, Joel, Jason, Chris, and Kacie.

I was still holding the phone when it rang again. It startled me and took me a second to realize what was happening. On the second ring, I answered. It was Joel.

"Jason's getting in tonight and we thought we'd have everyone over to the house. Have you been to Tony's?"

"Nah, just got home."

"Cab from the airport?" he asked.

"You told her to come, Joel. You gave her all of the flight information." I pinned the phone between my shoulder and ear and stood up.

Joel coughed a bit through the line. "Ya pissed at me?"

I crossed the room, yanked the fridge open, and reached for another beer.

"Kacie and I cannot be salvaged, all right?" I said, popping the top off another bottle. I waited for him to respond. He didn't. Finally, I said, "What time are people coming over?" and lifted the bottle to my lips.

"Around nine."

I swallowed a very large gulp. "K. I'll see you then."

"Call Chris?"

"Yeah, man."

There was another strange silence for just a moment and he said, "It's good to hear you, man."

"Yeah," I said, "Sure is." I pressed the 'talk' button and walked over to the cradle. I hung the receiver back up and stood for a moment, looking into the darkness of my parents' living room. I tipped the beer bottle back against my lips, drained half the contents, and sat back down at the table.

Joel and Jason's father had abused their mother for seven years. That was how far back they could remember it, anyway. Maybe that's only as long as they'd known it was happening. In high school, we never hung out at their place. Our first year in college, their dad put Mrs. Lincrest in the hospital and the twins had him arrested. For the violence, he'd have served a few months but the police investigated him and found not everything was on the up-and-up with his business. The IRS got involved and the FBI and not long after their mother got her divorce, everything but the house was seized to pay back taxes. He was still in prison when I saw them at New Year's and might as well have been, he'd have nothing but the clothes on his back when he was released which was more, the twins said, than he deserved.

Mrs. Lincrest's dad had died a week before Christmas and the week of New Year's she was still in Nannyglow, Pennsylvania with her mother. We didn't see much of the twins during the two weeks I was home but the New Year's Eve party had been at their house. It occurred to me I hadn't heard Joel's voice since he'd asked me to leave that night.

My mother arrived and found me in the dark kitchen with two empty beer bottles and a third one freshly opened. She put her purse and keys on the counter and came to the chair I was sitting in. Her hand went to my forehead where she pushed my hair out of the way and kissed the top of my head.

"Hi."

I reached up and took hold of her arm. "Hi," I said.

We stayed like that for a moment, listening to each other breathing and feeling a sense of unexpected relief. I was glad she was there. She was glad I was alive.

"You okay?" she asked finally.

"I think so," I said.

"Wanna talk about it?"

"Not really."

Then we were quiet again in the darkness for a minute. She drifted away from me, turned on the light and got herself a beer from the crisper. She sat in the chair next to mine and we both stared through the slats of the blinds to our reflection in the light in the window, and past it, to the dark, snowy backyard.

"The funeral is Friday," she said. "Rhonda called to see if you would be coming home today. She would like for you to come by the house tomorrow."

"We all will."

"Did everyone come?"

"Joel and Tabby are here, Jason gets in tonight. I gotta call Chris. Kacie drove up this morning." The third beer was empty now. I wanted another one.

Mom took a small drink from her bottle.

"Have you seen her?" She was trying to be casual, trying to relate. I could smell the faintest trace of her perfume, the fabric softener on her clothes. I wanted to hug her again.

"She came to the airport."

Mom picked at the label on her beer bottle. "Joel said he was going."

"She's been meeting me at the airport for three and a half years." I looked down at my hands. "He called her."

"But I thought you didn't want to see her."

"I didn't." I gripped the bottle with my fingertips, pressed them so they turned white and then released them. "Couldn't avoid it all weekend."

"No, I guess not." My mom is a very pretty woman. She has short blonde-brown hair like mine and green eyes she wears circle glasses over. She wears very little make-up and she smiles a lot. She's smart, too, I think that's part of it.

"Would you like to have dinner with us tonight?"

"Sure. How was work?"

"Work is work," she said, which was the response I had gotten from her all of my life. She couldn't tell me about most of the things that went on there. I wasn't even sure where the building was. I had never been to her office. That day in school when everyone went to work with their parents, I stayed in the library all day reading books and writing stories about my parents fighting the evil forces of communism from their secret lair. When we were in sixth grade, Tony had his dad call mine and ask if I could come to work with them the next day.

My dad had said, "Why?" Mac explained the tradition of take-your-kid-to-work-day, and my dad and I had a serious father-son chat.

"Why didn't I know about this?" he asked me.

"Can I go to work with you?"

"Well, no, son, you know my work is very secret."

"That's why I didn't tell you," I had said, very adult-like for my eleven years. "No reason to ask when I couldn't go with you. Besides, I'm gonna be a writer not a secret agent."

I remembered that day clearly sitting in the same chair at the same table with my mother twelve years later. The look on my father's face registered guilt. I had become the sacrifice he and my mother made in order to have successful careers. Worse, I knew it. I knew, at eleven years old, that work was more important to them than me. I often wondered if I really hated them for that or if it was just an excuse to misbehave.

I looked at my mother, waiting patiently for me to confide in her.

It was just an excuse.

"What are you thinking about?" she asked me.

"Career day. Sixth grade. Mac took Tony and me to his office in the old Honeywell building in Tyson's Corner. It was cool." Mac was an architect and had a great drawing table, a gigantic window that looked out over the capital beltway, and lots of markers, pens, and colored pencils.

"We just colored for a while and he worked. We got to eat lunch in a conference room and roll around on his chair." I smiled, relating the memory to her. "It seems like forever ago."

"Half a lifetime," she said. "When you're twenty-two, ten years is half a lifetime." She sighed then. "He was too young."

She had barely touched her beer and I reached across the table and took the bottle from her. She watched me take a long drink from it. I started to slide it back but she shook her head, so I kept it.

"Will you tell your father?"

"Tell him what?"

"He knows Tony was on heroin." She said the last word so quietly it was almost a whisper. "Will you tell him about you?"

"I don't do heroin."

"I meant the other."

"The cocaine? I should tell him about that?" I looked at her when I asked but then quickly looked away. "It's over now," I said. Then I watched my fingers tear at the label on the bottle. "I don't want to worry him," I added, but it was a lie.

"And if he asks?"

"He won't. He doesn't want to know."

Dad had a lower rank than Mom in the clandestine service and so he was the one who'd met the bus when I was little and took me to swim practice every morning until I was old enough to drive. That should have made us close but it didn't. I'd learned early not to call him from the nurse's office and ask him to come get me; he'd refuse. I learned not to be sick before school, and had more than once thrown up in the locker room after practice without telling him. He didn't show affection except in polite phrases and he didn't touch me other than to wipe something off or straighten some tuck or fold in my clothes.

"Give him more credit. He tries. You know he does," Mom said. "We both do. I wasn't exactly receptive, either. But we're better for it, you and me, aren't we?" There was the guilt I knew so well; the same guilt I'd seen on my father's face when I was eleven. She had taken my confession last summer in stride. I was only forced into it because of a particularly ugly incident she witnessed.

Without knowing Mom had come home, Kacie and I carried the fight we were having down the stairs. I was chasing her with it, and she was fleeing. She stumbled on the bottom steps, fell into the front door. I watched. She cried.

"If you're going to make it a big deal, just go," I said.

"I am." She stood back from the door, turned toward me, saw my mother down the hall and pulled her shoulders back, dashed tears from her cheeks.

I followed her eye line and saw Mom standing near the hidden secretary between the kitchen and living room. I turned back to Kacie who was digging in her purse for car keys.

"It's more than *that*," she said.

"It's more?" I asked.

She looked up at me. "You know it is." She turned away, ripped the door open, and fell through it. I closed it behind her, not bothering to watch her stumble across the yard. Standing at the closed door, I glanced through the side window and saw her jerk on her car handle. She was sobbing now. If I wanted to run to her, to apologize, and I like to think I did, I found a way to decide against it. I turned and found my mother standing in the hallway.

"Is she okay to drive?" she had asked.

She knew a good bit of what had gone on, but not everything. Not by any stretch of the imagination. I told her enough to explain why Kacie had been upset, why she had appeared drunk, why she had to leave. I told her Kacie had accused me of sleeping with Meli. I told her that was ridiculous. I didn't tell her I knew Kacie had been fucking around at UVA, too. That we had a "don't ask, don't tell" arrangement and she'd broken it by demanding the truth. I didn't tell her the part about Kacie and I being naked twenty minutes earlier. I didn't tell her Kacie's lips had been swollen by my kisses or that her eyes were wet and red with tears. I told her Kacie was on drugs.

Mom had listened, had accepted the story. She had tried to trust me because of that guilt, the guilt I saw in her eyes two days after Tony killed himself. The guilt over working when I had parents' breakfasts at school, swim meets, even the X Games. She carried guilt over the nights she disappeared while I slept. She felt bad that she didn't reappear for days, that she never had an explanation. She felt guilty that she hadn't taken me shopping for school clothes, hadn't had a family portrait made since I was four, and had no idea what I had done to earn the scholarship to Cal State East Bay. I had been using that guilt against her for a long time. I knew it well. I knew it meant she was relieved Tony was dead and not me. And I knew she felt guilty for that, too.

"I'm going to lie down for a while," I said. "And we'll just take things as they come when Dad gets home, okay?"

"Okay," she said. "Only, that means you're going to smoke a cigarette, right?"

I smiled. "Yeah."

"We'll get better at this honesty thing," she said. "I promise."

I stood and left the kitchen, taking my beer with me and leaving the empties on the table. I heard her put them in the recycle bin before I even got to the staircase. I dragged my bag up the steps and down the darkened hallway to the left.

Since I left for California my bedroom had become a guest room. The bed was the same, but all of my trophies, books, and posters had been put away. I opened the closet and slung my hanging bag inside where it draped over a well-worn Santa Cruz Jeff Grosso board, the middle of the deck scrubbed out from rail slides. One picture of Kacie and me at junior prom sat on the desk, and my high school yearbooks were still on the shelves. There was an ashtray under the bed on the far side and I pulled it out and opened the window. The February air was cold but it felt good against my cheeks. I lit a cigarette and sat on the floor under the window.

The bed was in the center of the room and had a wooden headboard and a burgundy comforter. I stared at it for a long time remembering making love to Kacie in that bed. I never wrote those scenes, but I could have with the details I remembered. Her skin. Her scent. Her hair. Those curls. Green eyes that glistened. I remembered every glide into her. How warm and tight she was. She fit me. Perfectly. It was like worship being with her.

I took another drag of my cigarette.

"Say it," she had whispered.

"I don't know what you're talking about," I teased back.

She smiled. "Say it."

"No," I'd answered and rolled away from her.

She'd kissed my back and shoulders, her breath hot on my skin. Her hand slid down to my butt and she tickled it gently with her fingernails. "Say it," she whispered again.

"I missed you," I mumbled.

"What's that?" she asked, then pulled her hand from my skin.

I rolled over to her and laughed a little. "I missed you," I said, lying flat on my back, looking across at her.

"Me?" she had asked, propping herself up on her elbow. The sharp angle of her cheek swelled against the heel of her hand. Her face flushed, her green eyes narrowed, those long lashes fluttering against one another. Then she kissed my chest, propped her chin on me, stared up at me. I went cross-eyed, looking at her.

With my fingers under her chin, I gently lifted her face to mine and kissed her.

"There is nowhere," I said, "Unless you're there."

The day I'd confessed to my mother wasn't the last time I'd touched Kacie that way. The last time was New Year's at her sister's place. But I hadn't told her I loved her then.

Since I'd moved to California, we stole moments whenever we could get them. It was still like high school: the driveway, the parking garage at Town Center, her sister's bed, a hotel room in

Vienna, even the pool deck at Tony's parents' house after he'd gone inside to get high. When Kacie and I ran out of things to say, we fucked. By this past summer that was all we were doing. Fucking and getting high.

Another drag and the cigarette glowed in the darkened room. "Nowhere," I mumbled into the cold air seeping in through the open window, "unless you're there."

Instead of coming home for Thanksgiving I had gone to Meli's parents' house. They lived in Sacramento, somewhere I'd never been. The red haired girl everyone in her before-Brian life knew as "Melissa" met me right after I moved to California. In line to register for classes, she sported a Van Halen Balance t-shirt and I asked if she'd seen the tour. Our first conversation was about Sammy Hagar.

She could sing every Beatles song ever recorded in its entirety, chewed her fingernails without shame, and had long red hair that hung flat and straight around her shoulders. When she wore low-rise jeans, her hip bones poked out. Everyone in her family had waterbeds, had for as long as she could remember. Her father, Frank, was a jeweler, owned a mine in Montana and a store in old town Sacramento. Her mother, Marie, was a semi-retired massage therapist who fostered cats for the SPCA. We didn't sleep in her water bed; I stayed on the couch. Frank and Marie told me they were happy to see Melissa had found someone she really liked. I really liked her, too, but I hadn't said much about her to anyone in Virginia.

Except Tony who knew her as Meli. Like how you rebrand something you've claimed. He'd named her 'Meli' in their first introduction. After Scarlett O'Hara's nemesis.

"I'm nothing like Melanie Hamilton," she had argued, "I'm not good like that. Not loyal or forgiving or honorable. Not really."

He'd just grinned and said, "You're a perfect you. From now on, 'Meli' shall be synonymous with being the perfect *you*."

"A poet," I'd added, "A songwriter. A singer."

"A good time. A redhead," Tony had said. And it stuck. Like so many inside jokes, allusions, and secrets. Things between us that remained vivid and earned, like shiny maize leaves on autumn trees.

Used to be I told him everything. Midnight phone calls were his specialty.

"I don't know how you do it, Listo. Long distance things are hard."

Two months after Christmas, my first year in San Francisco, and I was standing outside of the dorm in flannel pants and Ugg boots. There was an overhang that sheltered me while I smoked a cigarette.

"I love her, man," I had answered, meaning Kacie.

"I know you do. She knows you do." Tony laughed then. He was fucked up. "I can't get this incense to light and I've been trying for like an hour," he complained. "Wait, there, there it goes." He laughed again and exhaled dramatically. "Where was I?"

"Who knows?"

"I know you, man," he'd said, "better than anyone, better than Kacie."

"No argument here. So?"

"So that's how I know." He paused for what I guessed was a drink and finished, "I know there's a woman in your bed right now. Who is she?"

I stood quietly on the concrete in front of a dormitory three thousand miles from his warm, dark room in his parents' basement. I smoked. It wasn't the first time this girl had been here. She dated my roommate. He was out at some fraternity thing for the weekend and she was all mine. She had been the first but when I realized how easy it was, there were others. Tony knew about all of them and he kept that secret. He kept it because cheating on Kacie like that, daily sometimes, made me a real fucking asshole and he didn't want anyone to know what an asshole I was. And I trusted him with that secret from the very beginning. I trusted him until I believed that I wasn't really an asshole. But I was.

"Monica," I said finally. "Her name is Monica. She's my roommate's girlfriend."

"Not the best way to make friends," he scolded mockingly.

"I already got all the friends I need," I had said and meant it, at the time.

I finished my cigarette under the window in my old bedroom and reached for the phone on the bedside table. I called Chris, taking a second over the glowing buttons to summon his dad's phone number from my memory.

"When'd you get in?" I asked.

"About an hour ago," he said. "Long fuckin' drive." He was still living in Atlanta, but his dad had given him a car two years ago to replace the Eclipse he'd bought when we were in high school. He'd paid for the Eclipse by working at the movie theater and it earned him "Best Car" in senior superlatives. Tony fucking loved that picture: Chris on his black Eclipse and this wispy blonde girl, Heather something-or-other, on her white Honda del Sol. Tony called it "Salt and Pepper" which made Chris roll his eyes.

"For real," Tony had said when we got our yearbooks. "Could they find a whiter white girl to pair with you?"

I think the Eclipse had just died or something. One time he picked me up in it and then the next visit he came over in a Honda Civic. I couldn't remember what color the Civic was.

"We going out tonight?" Chris asked.

"Over to the twins'. Gotta get some beer."

"I can come get you," he offered. "Food first?"

"Gonna eat with my folks. Come around nine?"

"See ya then."

And we hung up. I looked at my watch. Seven forty-five. The garage door rumbled below me. Dad was home. I turned on the lamp, shut the window, and headed into the bathroom.

Nothing had been moved since the last time I was home. The tile was clean, the tub unused but the shampoo and soap sat where I had left them, waiting, it seemed, for my return. I tugged the fleece over my head and threw it aside. Grabbing the bottom of both shirts, I peeled them off as one and dropped them on the floor in a heap. A string of hemp tied around my neck bore a seashell and a black string looped under it with three silver charms. I left them both on, always did, and stepped out of my jeans and shorts and into the stream of steaming water. I showered quickly, the water feeling better than it should have, feeling like it could replace the flood of memories, feeling like it could actually clean me.

My mother played a classical music soundtrack during dinner. I liked the music but now all classical music makes me hungry. That makes elevators awkward and symphony concerts unbearable. My father was setting the table when I walked into the kitchen. Mom looked up, Dad turned around, and I waited for them to say something.

Dad looked sort of anxious. He's a handsome guy, brown eyes and long, narrow cheeks. He keeps his hair trim but he has a full head of it, thick like mine. I was spared his curls and color, that rich black that bore glints of silver but no sign of thinning. He's the same height as me and when we both stand tall, we are eye to eye.

"Hungry?" he asked, his eyebrows arching toward his hairline.

"Not really," I said, standing in the doorway, watching him shuffle the silverware in his hands. I wondered if he'd hug me. He didn't.

His frame is narrower than mine, but he's still fit and lean. He swims five thousand yards daily, at five a.m., before the world is awake. There's a precision to him that permeates everything he does.

He glanced at Mom and back at me. Then turned around to the table and laid the remaining forks and knives by his plate and mine.

"Let's eat something," Mom said. "Sit down, okay?"

So I did. I sat in my chair, at the middle of the table. Mom was on the left end with a glass of white wine. Dad sat on the right end with a beer in a cold glass. I had a glass of wine and a bottle of beer in front of my plate. All I wanted, though, was water.

Mom said a quick blessing. I wondered if Dad listened when I wasn't home. He always pretended to when I was there. She spooned some pasta onto my plate and Dad laid a slice of salmon on his.

"How's San Francisco?" Dad said.

"Fine."

"And Melissa? Is she well?" Mom asked.

"She's fine."

"Finding any work out there?" Dad asked.

"Not really," I said.

And it went like that, they asked the questions and I gave some answers, nothing that would require me to think about it too much. It always felt like being on stage for like the twenty-fifth show in a thirty-show run: not nervous or creative, not directed or polished, but recitation and repetition. I sometimes envisioned the stage lights high above, hot beams falling through red or blue or green filters to tinge and tweak the scene as I performed.

Mom finished her wine and got another glass, refilling mine as she did so. I worked on the beer and Dad said, "Thinking about an MBA?"

"No," I said. "Don't have the pre-reqs."

"Still avoiding the real world?"

"Why not a Masters in English? Or a PhD?" Mom suggested.

"And be a professor?" I asked as if the thought had never occurred to me. She smiled and I smiled back.

"Prettiest places in the world, golf courses and college campuses," Dad said.

"Did your PGA tour card come?" Mom asked, winking at me. I've never swung a golf club in my life.

"It's in the mail," I said. "Should have it by graduation in May."

"Have you been to the Williams' house?" Dad asked. He pressed the side of his fork into the flakes of the salmon, separated a bite from the hunk. The scrape of the fork on the plate had an unexpected volume. He raised the bite to his mouth. I could see a greasy sheen on his chin. I watched him chew.

"Not yet," I said, waiting for him to meet my eyes.

"Damn shame about that." He worked the fork into another bite of salmon, pinning one long fettuccine noodle with it. "Still I say you mess with fire." He raised the bite to his mouth.

"Honestly," Mom said, her own fork poised over her plate, nothing skewered on it. She didn't have the fish oil sheen on her chin, but her lips were wet. She was staring at him, not her plate.

"What?" They made eye contact across the table. "What did I do wrong? Brian knows. He knows that's not the way to go, don't you?" he prompted. He left his fork on the side of his plate and reached for his beer. He lifted the napkin out of his lap, wiped his chin, took a drink, a practiced balance between right hand and left, a dinner adjustment, familiarity. He looked at me. Finally. I met his gaze. The classical music was building toward crescendo.

"Sure," I said, not looking away.

"Not smart to mess with that stuff and Brian knows it," he reiterated, tilting the beer glass toward me and then Mom. He was convincing, even if he was only convincing himself. "I'm sorry about Tony, son," he added, setting the glass down and picking up his fork again. "That kind of thing is nothing but a tragedy."

"I know, Dad." The music settled down. We were all quiet for a few minutes. Forks to plates, salmon past lips, more fish oil wiped by napkins. I pushed food around my plate, a few bites. The window beyond the table mirrored it all in the glare of the lamp.

Then my mother said, "And Kacie?"

"And?"

"Has she?"

"Killed herself? No, Mom, she hasn't."

Mom's fork fell to the plate with a clatter. She said, "I meant has she quit all of that stuff?" and took a drink of wine.

"Kacie was involved?" Dad stared at my forehead as I stared at my food.

Classical music swelled between us again. Mom had teed up the conversation she wanted us to have. I wanted to be mad but mostly I was thinking this had gone too far to turn back now.

I said, "We all were, Dad."

I'd never told Mom the full truth and just then I couldn't remember what I had and had not previously disclosed. I wondered if saying anything might put me in danger of saying too much. I had a quick flash of college, my flat in San Francisco, and knew I had betrayed the people who were paying for those things. It's a strange sort of loyalty we feel to those who have provided for us, and how we conceal the things that may upset them so as not to lose the support we still need. Kacie's parents still didn't know we'd gone to Virginia Tech that weekend in 1994

and Tony's parents had no idea he'd been fired from three different jobs. I think my parents would have taken a high school road
trip or me getting fired better than what I could tell them.

"Brian?" Mom asked.

"Yeah, Mom?"

"Would you like to tell us what's been going on?"

I shrugged and took another bite of my dinner. "Which
part?" I said.

Then Dad said, "The part where one of your friends takes so
many drugs he cuts his wrists?"

It was raw, still, and I felt tears in the back of my throat.

I lifted my beer and drained it. "No, I don't think that I would
like to tell you," I said, each word slow, clear, quiet. I placed the
empty bottle back on the table.

"Why not?" That was Mom, hurt that I hadn't told her everything like she thought I had.

"I don't see what it matters. I don't do drugs anymore and we
never had any major family dysfunction so let's be thankful we
came out unscathed, okay?" I stabbed the salmon, took a bite.
Tried to wait them out.

I remembered listening to fights at Tony's house. The yelling
woke us up one night when I'd slept over. Tony had bunk beds
and he always let me sleep on top. I leaned over the edge and
made eye contact with him in the dark. Mac was yelling at Gavin,
deep throaty frustration, like the growls of a bear. I watched as
Tony slipped out of bed and crept to the door. He pulled it open
just a bit and we heard Mac threaten to send Gavin to military
school. We heard Rhonda weeping and asking how could Gavin
do this to them. Then we heard Mac order Gavin to his room
and the pounding of his sixteen-year-old feet on the stairs. Tony
closed the door quietly and climbed up the ladder on the end of
the bunks. He crawled over the blankets to lie down beside me.

"You okay?" I whispered.

He nodded but didn't say anything. After a while the house was quiet and Tony was, too, and we slept.

Another time they fought, we snuck out of Tony's house and into mine. My parents never fought like that. When we woke up the next morning it was to Dad confirming to Mac over the phone that, yes, Tony and I were sleeping in my room. I was grounded for scaring the shit out of our parents but Mr. and Mrs. Williams apologized to both Tony and me for fighting loud enough we had to run away. We didn't tell my parents that Tony's parents had apologized or why we'd come to my house in the first place. They already knew Gavin was driving Mac and Rhonda crazy.

Dad shifted in his chair. He'd been pressed up against the table, elbows on either side of his plate, shoulders forward, chin down. Now he leaned back, crossed one leg over the other in a figure four, held his shin in his hand. He was watching me. He was baiting me.

"We used to be close, Brian," he said. "We went fishing."

"We went once when I was eight, Dad. Don't say it like it was our weekend thing."

"What about the trip to Arkansas?"

The third time I got caught skipping, Dad decided it was as good a time as any to take me home to see my grandmother in Arkansas. She hated Mom so we usually just let Dad go on the yearly visit alone. This time, though, I was being punished. Instead of a local skating exposition where there was a rookie competition I was sure to win, I was off to Eureka Springs with Dad.

"The trip where you showed me how dismal my life would be if I didn't quit skipping school? Hardly a bonding trip."

"What about swimming?" The examples came like fast pitches and I kept swinging at them but most of them were in the dirt.

"I don't swim anymore," I said.

"There are other things." His face, so like mine, his expression one of practiced concern. Like he was trying to sell me something.

"Do you think if you'd spent time with me I wouldn't have gotten high? Ever?" I pulled my napkin from my lap and dropped it on my plate. I shoved away from the table and copied his posture, ankle over knee and a figure four. "A few ball games, a souvenir photo taken on some bridge somewhere and Brian's clean and sober, right?"

"What happened, Brian?" Mom. Still sitting up straight. Watching us watch each other. "What is this really about?"

"I started swimming and I was good and then good wasn't good enough." The words just fell out. "Then I started writing and I was good and then good wasn't good enough. I skateboarded and I was good until," a little slurred, a little sauced. I was angry now, but only a little. "I mean, I almost made the X Games," I said, but it sounded kinda like a whine.

A minute elapsed before I realized I'd said all that aloud. I had had this fight in my head a hundred times. Used it to rationalize just about every hit I'd ever taken, every puff, every snort, every square dissolved on my tongue, even a needle in my arm once.

My dad didn't know this fight. His brown eyes widened, the bushy eyebrows arched above them, reaching toward his receding hair line. His thin lips tightened, the color sucked out of them but still glistening from the oil off the salmon. His hand gripped his leg, he tried to stay reclined.

"This is about the drugs," he said. His voice was tight, controlled. Quiet but firm.

I could see myself in the window, through the open blinds, my reflection smug, my posture careless. I didn't think I gave a fuck.

"With as much money as we have I was offered seven

scholarships and I took one. But the one I took wasn't good enough, was it?"

Dad's foot came down on the floor then, and he leaned toward me. I kept my posture, tried to look relaxed.

"*We* don't have a lot of money." That quiet voice he used for the deepest of sins. "Your *mother* does. You and I are just living on it."

Out of the corner of my eye I saw Mom wince.

Dad sat back again, seemed to compose himself, crossed his arms over his chest.

"You want to know about the drugs," I said. "That's when they started."

"I don't understand," my mother said. "You told me it started last year."

"He told you about this?"

"Because Kacie was mixed up and he was going to break up with her last summer." Mom got up to refill her wine glass. She took mine, too, even though I hadn't touched it.

My father pulled his napkin from his lap and tossed it onto his plate. "Go on, Brian, tell me how I've wronged you," he said.

"That's it, that's all of it. Nothing was good enough for you, so I set out to please myself. And I did and my friends did and the drugs did and that's it." I smiled because I could but he didn't. I knew my smugness was getting to him by the twitch in his eyebrow.

"Your friends." He sneered. "Kacie. Tony. Who else? Some damn suburban sex and drug ring? Plenty of joints and STDs?"

"What were we supposed to do?" I asked. "Home alone every day, left to ourselves and each other. What the fuck did you think was going on?"

He glared at me and I wasn't sure if it was the confession or the cussing.

"I mean, come on, Dad," I dropped my foot to the floor and

shifted my weight to the right, toward him. "Did you think I was reading Shakespeare and taking SAT prep tests? I never even had a damn job."

"Swimming was your damn job."

"Alan, enough. Brian, tell the truth."

"It is the truth. It started in eighth grade." I sat up, shifted back toward Mom's side of the table, both of my feet on the ground, my arms out to either side. I shrugged with them, a big gesture indicating the house, the emptiness, the aloneness. Trying to explain the hours I spent without them. "You left me twenty dollars a day. For what? What kid needs twenty bucks a day?"

I looked over at Mom. She dropped her head to her chest, and I felt a stab of guilt. She had known. Of course she had known. I looked back at my father trying to figure out what he had known.

He was glaring at me. I could see the rage and him trying to control it. I smiled again.

"Brian," Mom said softly.

"It's okay, Mom. He's mad. I get it."

"And he's drunk," Dad said. "But we paid for that, too."

"Relax, Dad," I said. "I'm fine now. No more drugs. Not really."

"Not really?" Mom repeated.

"That makes it better?" A shout. From my father. As he stood up from the table, shoved his chair toward it. "You're fine?" He turned toward the window, pushing a hand through his hair, staring out past our reflections in the window to that tree in the yard, the one I'd counted the branches on earlier. I wondered for a second if he saw Tony and me as kids hanging like monkeys from that tree. I wondered if he remembered when we were just kids.

"Dad, listen."

"There is a boy dead and you talk about drugs like they're

nothing." He turned to me, looked me in the eye. "Mac is burying his son and it could have been . . ."

"Me?"

"Yes!"

He slammed his hand on the table and it echoed in the room. The move brought him close to me, leaning over me. Then he said, too quietly, "But it wasn't. You lucky shit." He straightened up. Looked at Mom over my head, then looked back at me. His eyes were glistening.

"When you look at Tony's dead body, remember how lucky you are." He turned away from me and started out of the kitchen.

"Alan, wait."

"Thanks, Joan." Dad left the room.

"Brian," Mom whispered. "What are you doing?"

Here's the thing about Kacie. I understand that I cheated first and more frequently. I know for three years I went off to San Francisco and came back and moved on her like I'd not even looked at another girl. I know that. I understand the complications of high fidelity, of thinking that I can do it and she can't, I'm a hypocrite, I know that. Every time I thought of her underneath someone else, anyone else, accepting anyone the way she took me, I felt sick.

But I had a mantra for dealing with it: We were a high school thing, not true love. We were never meant to last and she could fuck whomever she wanted. Except someone we knew.

There are unwritten rules about this kind of thing and she'd been breaking them since the summer. I had thus far made a big show of being the injured party and that position had the most stability, though it was a complete farce given what I'd done to

Kacie. I decided to stick with it, blame her, hate her, as I waited for Chris on the porch, not entirely sure if the Crew would let me get away it. What I knew for sure was one dramatic confession was enough for the night and I couldn't be more ready to escape my parents' house. I stood smoking in the soft yellow porch light, running over everything that had already happened; I felt like I'd been here forever.

When Chris pulled into the driveway I took my cigarette with me and climbed into the passenger seat. But he handed me a bowl and I smashed the cigarette on the driveway, closed the door, and we headed to the Lincrests' house. When we arrived I was suitably stoned. I clasped hands with Joel when he opened the door to let us in and we exchanged a quick semi-hug with a clap on the back. Chris hugged him for real and we walked toward the kitchen on the back of the house. Tabby was mixing a drink and had her back to us. Kacie stood next to her and stopped talking when we entered. I threw Kacie a fierce glare. She rolled her eyes.

Chris moved to both of them and they exchanged hugs. Kacie closed her eyes into his shoulder while I hung my coat on the back of a chair.

"You've lost weight," Tabby said, hugging Chris. She's really pretty, with black hair she kept pulled back from her face and a warm brown color to her skin. She's Filipino, tiny, narrow, and seems to match Joel perfectly like a predestined pair. He met her in their second year at college. She waited tables in the bar where he poured drinks. Her humor is mean-funny, bordering on brutal, and she can hold her own in a debate or a wager.

"Hi, Brian," she said, looking me in the eye but making no move to hug me.

I didn't step toward her either.

Then Jason came in and moved past me, hugged Chris, and stood near Kacie with his back to me. They didn't touch. He must have said something quietly because she shook her head so slightly her curls barely bounced. The noise from the television in the living room sizzled between us like carbonation and the bottles in the six packs we'd brought clinked like chains.

I looked out the back window to the deck. In the center was a round glass table where we'd played cards every summer. The umbrella had been put away and the bottom of the pole stuck up through the center like an ominous pike. Beyond the table, the railing and a short staircase to the yard. I remembered jumping over the railing in pursuit of Tony after he'd ripped my hat off my head and taken off. The table had erupted, everyone yelling. I hadn't even thought of it, just leapt over the rail and caught him in the grass. We were sixteen. My eyes glazed with the memory and I felt untouched, detached, unforgiven.

Chris stepped closer to me, clapped his hand on my shoulder and leaned into me. I took a breath and nodded.

Joel went to the refrigerator and shoved the six packs Chris and I had brought inside. He returned with a bottle for each of us and we followed him into the living room. The TV glowed with a hockey game. Joel jabbed the remote control at it and lowered the volume.

Nine fifty-two. Wednesday. Twelve hours ago, I was leaving California. I was waking up, packing my shit, trying to smoke, trying not to sob, whispering to Meli that I was ready to go. Ten hours ago, I was in an airtight flying coffin with the aisle guy, pretending I didn't want to borrow his *Sports Illustrated* with Scottie Pippen on the cover. Four hours ago, I looked out the window as we descended. So much happened. I smoked out the window of the car her parents gave her in high school, she touched me, a few beers, a few phone calls, a shower. Two hours ago, all I wanted was a glass of water. So much happened. More beer, more talking, a parting of something. And now here. Where we had been once to celebrate. Where that celebration had disintegrated. And now again.

Joel and Tabby sat on the loveseat by the sliding glass door. Chris took a corner of the couch, Kacie sat in the middle, Jason sat next to her, I stood. I pretended I didn't want to sit. I pretended I didn't care he was sitting next to her. I pretended I'd forgotten New Year's Eve happened but I hadn't and nobody else had, either. I watched hockey like I fucking cared who was playing and drank beer like Tony was there but he wasn't. And if he had been I'd have told him I remembered. But I didn't tell anyone. I didn't say anything.

"Did you get that class?" Tabby asked Chris.

"Yeah, I lucked out. Some idiot failed his exam and didn't have the pre-req, so I showed up on day one and the professor added me. So I'll be done in May, like I'd hoped," Chris said. He was smiling and his words were slow but he sounded clear and focused.

"That's great," Joel said.

Chris nodded. "Yeah, *lucky* and great."

"I'm glad for you." Tabby is beautiful and Joel knows it. He looks at her like he's amazed by it. She smiled at him. I remembered those smiles. The "I can't believe you love me" smiles.

"I'm going to smoke," I said.

"I'll come," Chris agreed, and he and I headed out to the back deck.

It was colder than it had been when we arrived and I tugged the collar of my pullover up around my ears and chin; I'd left my coat over the kitchen chair. Chris lit his cigarette, I lit mine, and we stood quiet for a few moments.

"Got anything to say?" he finally asked.

"I'm stoned."

"It's good weed."

I smoked and thought about how cold it was and about my coat just beyond the door, past the couch, past her, in the kitchen. Then I hated the East Coast weather and wondered why it couldn't be as warm here as San Francisco even though the latter hadn't been very warm as of late. But that was hard to remember when I was trying to find things wrong with Herndon, Virginia. So I believed as I always did while home that San Francisco was so much warmer and just better all around.

"It doesn't seem real," Chris said. "I keep expecting him to walk in the door."

"But he won't."

"No." He shook his head.

I wondered how Tony had felt the last time we were all home. It couldn't have been easy for him to have us all invade his life for a few weeks and then leave again. We treated him like a vacation house we didn't think of off-season except to brag about it and check on it now and then. But when we returned we occupied it fully and then we left again, boarding it up for the winter, so to speak. I feel sad thinking that but I didn't think that at that time. At that time, I was thinking there were so many places I would have rather been. Baja for one.

Then Jason came outside.

Puerto Rico.

And Chris went inside.

Jamaica.

And we were alone.

Alaska.

"Can I bum a smoke?"

I gave him one. Siberia.

He lit it. "We should talk." He handed my lighter back to me.

"About what?"

"About Kacie."

The moon.

Jason is bigger than me and the coat he wore was leather and didn't hide his size a bit. He was tough, too, and had a cut over his eye. I asked him about it, trying to be casual.

"Practice. It doesn't hurt."

"You practice getting cut?" It was a dumb thing to say and I wanted to take it back. But he didn't respond to it and I knew that he knew that I was high.

"Brian, about Kacie."

London.

"She doesn't deserve this."

Bosnia.

"She wasn't trying to hurt you. Now it's all kinds of weird and New Year's was and now again." He took a drag. I took a drag. He exhaled. I blew a cloud of smoke out that chased his over the deck rail and then the cold air was all there was until he spoke again. "After Tony. I don't know. Chris told me to just. Fuck. I'm dyin' here, dude, help me out." He looked at me then, straight in the eye.

"What does she deserve?" I asked.

"What?"

"You must have some idea," I said, "of what she deserves."

"Brian, I only mean that she's hurting." He tossed the cigarette away, over the deck. I thought about him bumming one and then barely smoking it. Wasting it.

"Kacie and I are over. We were before you happened." I finished my cigarette and tossed it after his. It wasn't so cold now and I figured I was just numb.

Jason shoved his hands in the pockets of his coat. "You'll forgive her?"

"Whatever," I said. "Let's not deal with that this weekend. We have heavier things, ya know?"

"I know, man, Tony. Jesus, what a blow." Jason was awkward with words and I thought I used to catch him responding to things the way a movie script would, not how he would. It feels fake to write it down but to hear it sounded worse.

"Yeah," I just said.

"The last time I talked to him was bad."

"What time?"

"About four in the morning on a Tuesday. Must've been two weeks ago I guess. I called because he'd emailed me right then and I wanted to talk, you know, no online chat bull shit but talk." He shook his head. Jason has sharp cheekbones and tanned skin and his lips looked swollen from biting. But they're always like that.

"What'd he say?"

"Hi. He just emailed me and said 'hi' and I called and he said 'hi' and he sat there for a minute and he said 'do you remember Mrs. Tanner?' and I said that I did."

"Mrs. Who?"

"Our English teacher in tenth grade. He said she told him to be somebody. But she never told him who to be and he was pissed at her now for not explaining." Jason shrugged. It wasn't a dramatic movement but he seemed satisfied by it.

We didn't talk after that. We went inside and Tabby brought another round of beers for Joel and Chris and handed one to Jason but not me. She didn't look at me. Kacie was missing from the room. I walked past Tabby and into the kitchen.

The familiarity of the house insulated us all. The deep blue of the couch, the heavy wood entertainment stand, slightly dusty and decorated with framed photos. Joel and Jason graduating, Joel and Jason at the beach as kids, Joel and Tabby at a football game, Jason in his hockey uniform, Mrs. Lincrest flanked by the boys at her fiftieth birthday party last summer.

I waited in the kitchen for Kacie to return but she didn't and after a couple of minutes I grabbed my coat off the back of the kitchen chair and went in search of her. I found her on the front porch, smoking, and she was shivering.

"Come inside," I said.

She didn't say anything so I stepped outside. She wore a pink ski coat and it puffed up around her ears, making her shoulders appear padded. She had one arm tucked tightly around her and the other folded, the wrist bending toward her lips to hold her cigarette in place. She took a drag, her lips glistened with saliva, her cheeks flushed red. She stood with her legs tight together, the knees bending, rubbing, trying to warm each other through her jeans.

The Lincrests live near enough to Dulles Airport to see approaching planes and the control tower lights. A high beacon alternates white and green, a long sweep across a plane about four stories above us. When we were kids we would lie at the bottom of their front yard slope and play freeze tag with that light. When it was green you could run, but when it was white, you had to drop to your belly. We called it Russian freeze tag because it reminded us of some of those Cold War movies like *Red Dawn* and *War Games* for some reason.

"What do you want, Brian?" she asked finally.

"He's dead, Kace," I said, shortening her name to a syllable. I choked and didn't say, "I want him to come up the sidewalk under that beacon. White. Green. White. Green." I felt crazy.

A car went by on the street, its headlights flooding the front yard and then turning away as it followed the pavement around to the left. Blue house. Yellow house. Brick house. The taillights faded down the street. I tried to count the houses. Some snow remained on the curbs where a plow had piled it and the mound had iced over. Then I turned and watched her. She smoked and stared out at the neighbor's yard.

"Can we call a truce?"

"Why?" she asked.

"Because I don't need this shit this weekend," I said, the words strung together in a single exhalation.

"Sorry to inconvenience you. Maybe I'll just leave."

Would she? Never in a million years.

"Say it," she said. She was looking at me now.

"What?"

"Say what you're thinking."

"No."

"You're hoping I'll leave."

"I know you won't. You have to be here to comfort your new boyfriend."

"Fuck you, Brian."

"Not me, Kace. You're not fucking me." I felt mean. When I thought about her she was usually naked and when I saw her here I could see her with him and I felt mean and crazy.

She sort of laughed and took another drag. "I deserve this?" she asked.

I shrugged.

"Then I'll earn it. Stay away from me this week, you hear me?" She dropped her cigarette and turned to go inside.

I grabbed her arm though I had no right and she looked at me again. Our faces were close, our breath mingled in puffs of steam between us. Her eyes were wild, they searched mine but I couldn't keep up. I looked away and let her arm go. She put her hand on the door knob. Then she said to the door, "He wouldn't like this. Us at each other's throats."

It occurred to me that was why I had grabbed her arm. I wanted to agree with her but before I could she said, "But he's not here, is he?" and went inside.

Tony always wanted everyone around him to be happy. He had this diplomatic way of making the peace and there was always peace to be made. High school can be very dramatic and some relationships go on longer than they should. We were never very good at letting go, not any of us. We'd known each other practically our whole lives. Chris was the newest and we met him in seventh grade.

The worst of our drama was the drugs. We'd been smoking reefer since middle school and stayed pretty light for years, just the occasional trip or shroom or X. It wasn't until Chris got a hold of some blow that we started using all the time. I feel nauseated thinking about all of the coke we did summer after senior year. I could have financed my entire education with the cash we blew. By then Joel had already declined anything worse than pot and Jason rarely even did that. But they stayed with us, drank plenty, kept skating, listening to music, inviting girls over. Jason played hockey, Joel studied more than the rest of us, but they were around even when we were too fucked up to notice.

Tony got wicked migraines and would sink into these moods whenever he felt the headache coming on. The people we knew used drugs to relax or entertain themselves but Tony was managing pain. He said the drugs helped him get out of bed, stay awake, and paint. Eventually getting stoned became what he did, part of his personality so much so that it was rare to see Tony when he wasn't fucked up. It became hard to tell when he was high and when he wasn't. Sometimes I didn't even know what he'd taken.

By New Year's there were two camps: the dids and the did nots. Joel and Tabby and Jason were the nots. Tony, me, Chris, and Kacie were the dids, though to what extent varied. Kacie insisted she only used when she was with me but that was only true until August. She wanted out but I kept bringing it with me when we were together. Then I left and quit and when we came back for New Year's, she had been using the stuff she got at UVA. Chris had backed off and was only smoking weed. Tony said there was no habit, but he was just hiding it from us all.

I considered them my family. We were everything to one

another. Until we weren't. Until we graduated and the world got a little bigger and then we were only together on holidays and then drugs changed us. Our family wasn't so tight anymore. It is a part of that influence that a user stops trusting people, but I mean I didn't speak to them at all. I talked to Tony. We all talked to Tony about how we weren't talking to each other. Joel and Jason said that Chris and I were pulling away and Tony said we weren't. They said there must be something wrong and Tony assured them it was nothing. Tony knew. He was with us. Joel and Jason knew but they pretended they didn't. Joel would ask Tony to ask me to call him. But I wouldn't and then Tony would bitch that Joel was bitching and then we all shut up and Tony tried desperately to keep us talking.

Jason and I lost touch first. Kacie used to talk to him and he'd email her and they'd hang out at UVA when he was in Virginia. She'd tell me what he was up to and at first it was good to hear. Then she was using it to fill the empty air between us and I didn't care. Then I knew we had nothing else to talk about and I fucking hated hearing about him. Finally I told her I hated it and she said she'd quit but she didn't. Then I quit talking all together. I quit listening, too. She would talk and I would watch *The Smurfs* and eat cereal. Then she fucked him. Then New Year's Eve happened and everybody knew about everything. And now no one's talked to anybody in a while. Except Tony. Who, apparently, talked to Jason just two weeks ago.

When I went back inside after smoking under the Russian freeze tag light on the Lincrests' porch, the hockey game had gone to intermission and everyone was listening to Tabby tell a story. I took my coat off, hung it over the back of the chair, and stepped into the living room.

Chris was on the end of the couch and he lifted his bottle toward me. I took it and opened my arms. Tabby was still talking and she ignored me, but Jason and Joel handed me their empty bottles, too.

I retreated to the kitchen. I could still hear the story and their laughing in response when I opened the fridge. As I gathered the new bottles, I felt the room shift. I stood and turned to see Joel and Chris step into the kitchen. I handed them each a beer. Then Jason followed them. They'd left the girls in the living room.

We stood around the center island and opened our beers, passing the church key between us. Each of us took a drink. Joel, like Jason, had high cheekbones and narrow brown eyes. His lips are thinner, though, and he managed to smile through them across the island at me.

"How's California?" he asked.

I shrugged. "Same, I guess, as it was a month ago."

"I dream of it sometimes," he said. "When it's cold as shit in Pittsburgh, I think, 'Why the fuck didn't I go to California with Brian?' We could open a surf shack on the beach, charge tourists for lessons, have bonfire parties."

Chris laughed. "I think that, too. And Atlanta doesn't even get that cold. But, man, bikinis and convertibles, Sex Wax and Ugg boots. Bring it."

"Wimps," Jason said. "Try Michigan."

"Fuck that," I said, and Chris and Joel said it, too.

"The Ugg boots are right," I said, "but add dreadlocks and corduroys. San Francisco's not that warm; not like L.A. or *Beverly Hills 90210*. It's more like Seattle, really."

"Don't tell me that," Joel said. "Sometimes the Brian I imagine is the one I like best." We made eye contact over the island counter and I looked away first.

"Anyway, it's the right place for you," Jason said. "To write. Or whatever." He took a long drink from his bottle and glanced over his shoulder toward the living room.

"Yeah," I said, following his eye line. "It's right for me."

"So the funeral is Friday?" Chris asked.

Joel nodded. "Yeah. I talked to Mac today, he said come over tomorrow."

"I can't believe it," I said. "It's like a nightmare."

"Yeah, it sucks," Joel said, "but it's not unbelievable. Seems more like about time." He was turning his bottle in his hand, slowly, as if reading the label, listening to the grind of the glass against the counter top.

"Who called you yesterday?" Chris asked.

"Mac called me," Joel said. "Asked me to get in touch with you and Kacie and Jason. He'd already talked to Brian's dad."

"You called Kacie?" I asked him. "Where was she?"

"No, after I called Jason, he called Kacie," Joel said, jerking his chin toward his twin.

I felt a surge of jealousy and then I remembered where I'd been when Dad called. I watched Jason take a long drink from his bottle and avoid eye contact with me. I tried to imagine Melissa naked, leaning against me, kissing my shoulder through her own tears.

"Then my dad called you," I said. "And you sent Kacie to meet me."

"Not exactly," Joel said, eyes narrow. "She asked me for the flight information when she got here today." His voice was low, just between us, but I heard the girls stop talking and wondered if they'd heard him, too.

"Everything okay?" Tabby called over the rail and into the kitchen.

"Everything's fine," Jason called back.

"Something to say?" I asked.

Joel shrugged.

"Fuck it." Chris drained his beer. "I'm beat. Let's go."

"Wait," Jason said. He shoved his twin's arm. "Don't start this shit tonight. Come on."

"Whatever," Joel said. "There's nothing to say."

"Sure, there is," I said. "He's not here to defend me."

"No," Chris said. "No, he's not here." He pushed his empty bottle across the counter.

"Stay," Jason said to Chris, across the island, right through mine and Joel's glare. "We're friends. We're all friends." He looked sideways at me, glanced back at his twin and finished, "It just hurts, that's all."

"That's all," I echoed.

Joel stepped back from the island, said, "I gotta piss," and left the room.

Chris and I were the first to leave Joel's, not right then, but after a while when we realized we had only one thing to talk about and no one wanted to talk about it. We left shortly after midnight but I didn't get home until three-thirty. We sat on the bleachers at the high school and got stoned again.

"Know what I miss?" Chris said.

"What?"

"Everything."

I nodded. I understood. I missed everything, too. Virginia, high school, skating, swimming, those easy afternoons when we lay around stoned, those late weekend nights when we didn't go home. It seemed sometimes that I missed it all so much it hurt and that everything that had happened since high school was a dream I was stuck in. If I could manage to wake up, there would be no San Francisco, no break up with Kacie, no Tony's suicide. We had our whole lives ahead of us, they told us. But our whole lives suck and I want to have that youth back, that innocence. I want to not fuck it up the next time.

"It feels wasted," I said.

"So much we can't get back," Chris said. "That's the kick in the balls of it. You think we should have paid more attention. I was in such a fucking hurry to get outta here." He looked around at the campus, the baseball field, the quad, the tennis courts, the parking lot, the sidewalk that led from the auto shop building to the main building, the gym entrance with its wide, covered entry.

"But out-of-here sucks."

"Yeah it does. And I can't get back in." Chris laughed then, stood up, one foot on the seat, one foot on the stair. A puff of air came out of his mouth and hung over me. He looked over the back of the bleachers' top rail, down to the concrete below, turning his back to me and the field, speaking into the distance from us to the dark school beyond the parking lot. "I'm not old," he said, "at least, not as old as I feel."

I hardly heard him. I was listing the things I wanted to feel again. Standing at the top of a half pipe before my turn, heavy rock music blaring out of the speakers, a PA system calling my name. The gritty feel of the blocks on my bare feet, the echo of the starting bleet, the splash of the water and the swirling silence below the surface. Pressing Kacie against the wall in her parents' house, her teeth in my neck, my hand under her skirt, and sliding up inside her without making a sound. I wanted that fervent, hungry sex back. I wanted the rush of not getting caught. I wanted passion again. I had replaced passion. With denial.

I was stoned and it was fucking cold. My fingers were numb and shaking, my ass hurt from the wood bench, my legs were frozen stiff. I said, "I want to memorize every feeling as I see it, as it happens so that years from now I'll remember what this was like."

"Let's go sit in the car," he said.

"Well, maybe not this," I said. "But I sure as hell wish I'd thought of this memorization thing before."

THURSDAY

I was hung over Thursday morning.

The phone rang at nine-thirty. Mom wanting to make sure I was up. The maids would be there any minute, don't let them find me in the shower. Besides, I was due at Tony's house and be sure to give Mac and Rhonda her best.

I managed to pry myself out of bed and get in the shower. I let the water pour directly onto my teeth, my lips, and my eyes. I turned it from hot to cold and ducked my head under the stream, letting the coolness wash over my back.

I dried off, dressed, and left with Chris about ten a.m. to go to Tony's parents' house. It was early but I knew they'd be receiving visitors all day. When we got to their house, though, there weren't very many cars and rather than feeling trapped there as a surviving witness of Tony's drug habit, I made an excuse about being hungry and Chris and I went for breakfast.

The Amphora Diner in Vienna stayed open all night. Half of the place was a pie-serving, coffee-pouring diner and the other half was a restaurant with tablecloths and food we could never afford like calamari. We used to sit on the diner side for hours just drinking coffee and smoking cigarettes. That was the only place we could legitimately loiter. After freshman year at San Francisco, though, we discovered they no longer allowed that type of time killing and forced patrons to have at least a ten-dollar meal tab per table. Vienna was about fifteen minutes away and the most direct roads were fast and wound around random houses rather than manufactured neighborhoods. We liked the drive as much as we liked sitting there.

Then they built an Amphora in Herndon. Same deal, diner on one side and restaurant on the other. It's chrome and shiny and stays open all night like the other place. Only, as we found out on Thursday, that place only lets you smoke at the diner counter during breakfast hours. We were the only people there but a rule is a rule apparently.

"Jason and Joel are there by now," Chris said.

"I know."

"I'm a pretty good friend for coming up here with you."

"I know," I said again.

Chris smiled. "Writing much lately?" he asked.

I shook my head.

"What's her name?" He stirred his coffee and pretended it was the most normal question ever.

"Melissa. But I call her Meli." I answered like I knew the question was coming.

Silence for a little while. Elevator music and the spoons against the porcelain coffee mugs. The tear of a Sweet-n-Low packet, the push of fingers through hair. Eyelashes clashing blink after blink.

"This 'Meli' the one Tony hooked up with that fall?"

"The very same."

Chris nodded. "How long's this been going on?"

I took a drink of my coffee. "Couple of weeks," I lied.

Chris made just about everything easy, even lying. "What's her situation?"

"What do you mean?"

"Well, you're graduating, right?"

"Yeah, in May."

"Well, when you come home," Chris asked, "will you leave her there?"

"I'm not coming back," I said though I hadn't really decided that yet.

"Oh?" Chris said, but I thought he didn't really seem surprised. "What will you do in California? Work?"

"Not sure if I'll stay in San Francisco. I have an opportunity to go to Spain for the summer. Might do that." I took another drink and pushed my plate of French toast away. "What are you going to do?"

"I changed majors and thought I would have another year," he said. "But it turns out I'll finish in May. Gonna come back here, find a job."

"What did you change to?" I asked, realizing that I didn't know.

"Finance." Chris looked at his watch.

"Really?"

"It's Georgia Tech. Most everyone is engineering. But there is a business school, too."

"Georgia Tech? I thought you were at UGA." We were supposed to be best friends and it occurred to me then that I hadn't talked to him, really talked to him, in such a long time.

He was finishing an omelet and looked up at me mid-bite. "Man, UGA isn't even in Atlanta." Then he seemed to decide not to bother explaining further and we sat quietly for a few minutes while he ate and I drank my coffee.

"How are your parents?" I asked.

"They're okay," he said, dropping his napkin on the empty plate and pushing it away. "I don't think my mom and Micah will stay down there much longer. It ain't easy being black in Atlanta."

"Why not?"

"You want me to list the reasons alphabetically? Or chronologically? We can begin with slavery if that'd help." He shook his head, but he was grinning.

I felt stupid. "How will it be having them all in the same town? I mean, with your dad and . . ." I fell silent.

"Angela," Chris said. "Should be fine. They've all pretty much got their own lives. Mom and Micah will more than likely get a town house, too small for me to live in, so Joel and I might get a place."

"Really? Joel?" I pushed the handle on the coffee mug, turning it in circles on the table. "Last night he seemed kind of uncool with . . . well, I mean, he's always hated us smoking weed." I stopped talking, not sure, really, how to talk about New Year's and the dos and the don'ts and the division we'd all become too comfortable with.

"Yeah, it's still a thing," Chris admitted. "But we'll get past it."

"What about Tabby?"

Chris shrugged. "Looks like she'll be another year in Pittsburgh. If Joel gets funding, he'll get an office. Until then he's working from wherever he can."

"Funding?"

"For his business."

"Joel has a business?"

Chris laughed at me. "You don't listen for shit, man, do you?"

"Guess not."

"Joel and his freshman roommate started an internet company." Chris flagged the waitress down and asked for a to-go cup. "They're looking for venture capital funding right now," he continued. "There's a ton of it here. Not so much in Pittsburgh."

The waitress returned with two to-go cups and we dumped our coffee into them. Then she topped the cups off from the pot in her hand, laid our check on the counter in front of us, and left again.

I took those few quiet minutes to absorb what Chris had told me, feeling certain I'd heard it all before and for some reason just hadn't held on to it. I knew some guys in San Francisco who were doing internet companies, but it seemed like some weird technical stuff that just bored the shit out of me.

Chris added sugar and cream to the Styrofoam cup, fastened the lid, peeled the tab up, and blew inside.

"Does Joel know stuff about computers?"

Chris laughed again. "A little bit, yeah," he said.

"Wait, I remember he had some job a while ago doing HTML coding or something, right?"

"Don't hurt yourself, man. It doesn't really matter." He took a drink and said, "Last night was weird."

"Fuck. Just gonna get weirder, too."

"Guess we oughta just get to it, then," he said. He shoved his arms into the coat hanging on the back of his chair.

I laid some cash on the check, lifted my cup, and reluctantly followed him out the door. I climbed into the passenger seat of the Civic. Maybe he'd need to stop for gas or more cigarettes. Maybe there would be a traffic jam or a construction detour. Maybe a plane would miss the runway at Dulles and make an emergency landing on Elden Street, trapping us in the Amphora parking lot.

Chris took the parkway, which was the long way, and we drank our coffee and smoked cigarettes and sat at thirteen stoplights.

Elden and Herndon Parkway where I'd turned left on a red light once because Kacie had her hand in my pants and there had been a break in oncoming traffic and I hadn't noticed my light hadn't turned.

The Parkway and Courts of Chandon, where I'd coached a summer league team when I was too young to know a thousand bucks for the whole summer worked out to less than six bucks an hour.

The Parkway and Van Buren Street which cut through to the post office and the Autohaus, a garage that serviced German cars. It always had several punchbugs in the lot. I used to tell Kacie to drive by there just so I could pummel Tony's arm shouting, "Punchbuggy blue! Punchbuggy red! Punchbuggy yellow!" We had elaborate rules related to points tallying but the slugging was the real win.

The Parkway and Spring Street with the Marriot Courtyard that we'd stayed at on prom night. Where I'd slowly and deliberately peeled Kacie's turquoise dress off her and the panty hose with the sparkles and the tiny matching thong with the little rhinestones on the hips. Where she stood in front of me wearing just that choker necklace and then we'd taken a shower without soap or shampoo just so we could be wet and naked together. I squeezed my eyes shut.

Chris turned right and took Sunset Hills parallel with the Toll Road for a while until Reston Parkway.

I listened to Pearl Jam coming through the radio. I tossed my cigarette out the window and rolled the glass back up. I reached into my pocket for a pack of gum I'd bought at the San Francisco airport.

Left onto Reston Parkway. Past Town Center, over Baron Cameron, past the rec fields and Kacie's sister's townhouse. Left into Bennington Woods.

Eleven-thirty and we were at the Williams' house and there were more people there, the driveway was full, so Chris parked on the street just beyond the house. We sat in the car for a minute. I held the gum out and he took it, unwrapped a piece, and shoved it in his mouth. Without looking at one another, we opened the car doors and stepped out.

I followed Chris up the walk but as we neared the porch, he stepped back and let me go ahead. I hesitated, my hand over the doorbell. My heart was pounding. I reached for the knob and turned it. With a shove, I opened the door and stepped into the foyer where Tony's dad, Mac, was closing the hall closet after putting someone's coat inside.

Mac is a big guy, about six feet five and two-eighty, and he hugs like a grizzly bear. He pulled me against him as soon as he saw me and I couldn't hold the tears at bay. His big hand was on the back of my head and I clutched at his shirt. I felt my chest heave, trying to get air, trying to expel everything I needed to tell him.

"I'm so sorry," I whispered into his armpit, feeling his deep breaths against my chest. I cried hard into him, the words failing me, and squeezed my eyes shut. After a minute, he let me go, pushed me out, arm's length, and held my shoulders. I forced myself to look up into his face. He was smiling kindly at me.

I choked on my gum, coughed, and swallowed. "I'm sorry," I said again.

"Is that Brian?" Tony's mom, Rhonda, is a China doll compared to her husband and she pulled me to her, face first, for a kiss below each of my eyes. "Brian, Brian, Brian," she said. I wrapped my arms around her and pressed her tiny frame to mine, wanting to squeeze as tight as I could but afraid to break her.

Chris was hugging Mac and I saw him wipe his eyes as they broke away.

In the summer, Tony's parents had pool parties and barbecues just about every weekend. It was usually our Crew and a rotation of Mac and Rhonda's friends. At one of these parties, Tony and I came inside carrying some dishes and his mother said to the two of us, out of nowhere, "You boys are so good to each other. You must always be. Always." She had nodded her head, laid a hand on each of our cheeks, and smiled. We were seventeen. I don't know what we did after that. The memory sort of ends with her walking back outside through the sliding glass door.

"You were so good to him," she said to me on Thursday when

I was twenty-two and he was dead. I closed my eyes and tried to memorize that moment.

We followed Rhonda past the closet and powder room, through the hallway and into the kitchen. I took my coat off and hung it on the back of a chair. There were some relatives there we had met before at graduation or Christmas or some other family thing and we all sort of whispered hello. Tony's parents asked me about San Francisco and I said something useless.

"Brian's a writer," she said to her sister. "Tony always said you were really good."

I managed a weak smile. Tony didn't know shit about writing. I listened to Rhonda and her sister talk about something I didn't really know anything about. Chris helped Mac pull the table apart so they could put an extension leaf in the middle. I watched them bend under the chandelier and shift the furniture around but didn't offer to help.

Then Rhonda stepped closer to me and said there was a book for me in Tony's room. Would I like to go and get it? Escaping to the basement sounded wonderful. I left Chris to wait on the twins who should have already been there but weren't.

Tony's room was the entire right side of the partially finished basement. He had a queen-sized bed and dozens of gigantic pillows. One wall was painted in swirls of red, yellow and orange like it was burning. Another wall was splattered from the easel projects that had sat in front of it. The ceiling was open rafters and draped between them were two tapestries he'd bought at some gypsy store in San Francisco, one of which matched the flames on the wall and one with water color angels whose wings were outstretched and palms were flat together in prayer. A sliding glass door was entry and exit into the backyard. It provided some natural light but not much and Tony had about six lamps to make up for the darkness. I turned on a few of them and sat on the edge of the bed.

Picking up the remote control off the sheets that had been carefully tucked in, probably Rhonda's doing, I turned the television on in the corner. It was tuned to a country music video station. I always knew Tony was a closet country fan. His compact disc collection occasionally stored a Garth Brooks or Faith Hill disc and he said Garth was cool and Faith was hot. I turned the TV off and turned the stereo on. Pink Floyd *The Wall* blared out of the speakers. Definitely pre-suicide music, I thought, and then ached with it but didn't turn it off.

Then I saw the book. Lying on the floor beneath the easel was his weathered copy of *The Catcher in the Rye*. On top was a post-it that read "Brian." That was it. Fucking ridiculous, really. Pink Floyd and *The Catcher in the Rye*?

"Come on, Tony," I said, "some originality, please."

I opened the book. Inside was a tightly creased piece of paper. Unfolding it, I saw the faded pencil marks of a note written years ago. It was a poem by Roy Croft, one I remembered being used for Tony's quote in the senior yearbook. He had copied it out of *Best Loved Poems of the American People*, a book he'd gotten from his grandfather. The book was full of some of the shittiest, most sentimental drivel in all of written work. But Tony loved it. Aside from Browning, Shelley, Kipling, and Byron, it had Longfellow, Keats, and Poe. But it wasn't the masters that Tony liked. It was the sentimental sing-songy rhymes that he gravitated to and this piece, a pledge from one friend to another.

"I love you," Croft's poem said. "Not only for what you are but for what I am when I am with you." I read these lines to myself, then tested my voice on them. It was shaky and stumbled through the syllables. "I love you, not only for what you have made of yourself but for what you are making of me."

My eyes filled and the words blurred and I looked up from the page, blinked and stood, refolded the paper, shoved it back in the book, and closed the cover. I dropped the book on the bed and crossed the room to the bathroom.

Closing my eyes, I imagined the scene like it would be in black and white on some movie screen. Blood on the sink, the toilet lid down. Tony, stumbling from the sink to the tub, sitting, folding over his knees. The light would be too bright for his eyes to take. Maybe a half-melted candle and a weary Roger Waters riff. I slid down the door to the clean white tile, pulling my knees to my chest.

"What are you going to do now?" he had asked me.

"School, I guess, try to write something."

"You could be really great," he said. He was grinning while he tried to light a candle. He'd melt the wax around the wick then peel it away with the edge of a pocketknife. Once he'd tugged the wick loose, he'd light the candle and set it down. The table next to his bed, the cabinet that held the stereo, the microwave table on which he'd set his TV and VCR, they were all covered in candles.

"What are you going to do?" I asked him.

He laughed. "Deliver pizzas. Get high. I dunno."

It was the day after the X Games qualifier, when I'd finished ninth and lost my sponsor and wasn't going to have a career riding my skateboard. I had failed.

"Come to California with me. I'll do school. We'll get a place. You can work out there same as here. It'll be good."

He laughed. "Nah, California's not for me. Plus Mac and Rhonda would lose their shit if I talked about going that far away. Rhonda's got a new shrink she wants me to see. Says he'll prescribe something for my headaches." He was working on another candle now. The daylight had faded out of the window and evening was coming.

"Medication?" I asked. "You think you need it?"

He shrugged. "Couldn't hurt." The flame caught on the

candle and he set it away from himself. The light gave his features some demon-like shadows that played and then disappeared. He looked up at me and smiled.

"Don't worry about me," he had said. "I'll figure something out."

I imagined his hands, covered in blood, pushing through his short-cropped hair, leaving sticky traces on the light brown strands. I imagined his blue eyes, maybe wide from realizing what he'd done, or narrow with a complete lack of understanding.

"Tony? Tony? Wake up, man," I had said, not bothering to whisper, though the house was dark and quiet. The moon shone off the surface of the pool. I had squinted in the glare of it and shoved the sliding glass door aside.

"What? Brian? What the fuck, man?" He was twisted up in a blanket, his pillow wedged between his cheek and the wall, his face smooshed in sleep.

"Tony!" I had said impatiently. "Wake up, fucker." I pushed the sliding glass door closed behind me and stepped closer to the bed.

"Dude, get out. What the fuck."

I ripped the pillow out from under him and threw it at his head.

"Wake up," I had said and sat down on the side of his bed. I reached for the lamp and turned it on. A yellow halo fell over the bed. I could feel him moving behind me, trying to get comfortable again, with me taking up half of his space.

"I think I fucked up," I said.

"Yeah? So?" His t-shirt stretched tight across his back.

"So wake up, man." I smacked his shoulder. "Help me."

He rolled over and blinked into the lamplight. Then he sat up and moved beside me. His feet hit the ground and he rubbed his face with his hands. I smelled his breath as he coughed.

"Jesus, dude, you fucking stink."

"Asshole," he said. He stood and went to the bathroom. I heard him piss and then run the water and brush his teeth.

"She knows."

He came around the corner, the toothbrush hanging out of his mouth.

"Someone told her."

He stepped back into the bathroom, spit, rinsed, and came out wiping his hands on a towel. He had socks on his feet, boxers and the wrinkled t-shirt on.

"Are you sure?" he had asked.

"Pretty sure."

"So, okay. Then you can break up. It's what you wanted." He looked past me at the clock, took a step toward it, and cussed.

"It's not what I wanted," I said, looking up at him.

"Then what the fuck, Brian? If you want to be with her, be with her. If not, then fucking break up with her. This shit is making us all fucking crazy." He threw the hand towel onto the counter, flipped the bathroom light off. Then he flopped back down on the bed behind me, in the yellow halo from the lamp, staring up at the tapestries on the ceiling.

"I'm not ready," I said and slid down to the floor, my head back on the edge of his bed. I pulled a cigarette out of my pocket and shoved it between my lips.

I started to light it and he said, "You're a dick. It's four a.m. Go home." He shifted on the bed, I heard the blankets move, the springs squeak. Then he reached for the lamp, turned it off and said, "Don't worry. I won't tell anyone."

"She already knows," I had said.

With my eyes closed I saw him sitting on the floor across from me. There wasn't room for both of us, but somehow we were both there. His knees were up, his arms across them, against his forehead maybe, his wrists were bleeding all over him. His chest was bare, his eyes were swollen. I imagined his shoulders shaking. I imagined him sobbing. In my mind, I was writing the scene, watching the final moments of his life, wondering if a ringing phone would have stopped the razor. I thought about the medication he'd tried, the cocktails of uppers and downers for mood control and attention span and sleeping too much or not sleeping enough.

Sixteen years we'd been friends. One hundred ninety-two months spent here, or my house, or his old house, the pool, the back yard, the tree, the bar, the skate ramps. Five thousand eight hundred forty-four days of getting up early, sleeping late, staying up, watching the rain through the window, sneaking in and out through the sliding glass door. One hundred forty thousand two hundred fifty-six hours with him in my life laughing, talking, getting high, knowing me better than anyone else.

I imagined him standing up, looking at himself in the mirror, seeing himself the way I sometimes did when I was fucked up: exaggerated, clown-like. Did he see his smile like elastic, his eyes like pennies, his stupid dog tags he'd gotten from the museum and wore everywhere, the glass earring he said looked just as good as a diamond but it didn't. The blood on his arms, smeared into his hair, on his eyebrow, his temple.

I could see him standing over me. I wanted to reach up and touch him. I dropped my head back against the wood and heard his mother say, "You two are good to each other," and then I cried.

When I left the basement, resurfacing in the kitchen, Kacie had arrived. She made eye contact with me and I felt a wave of shame. I walked past my friends, dragged my coat off the chair, made my way through the foyer and out to the front porch. Lighting a cigarette, I pulled my coat closer against me. Damn February. Damn Virginia.

I wasn't surprised when the door opened but I was surprised it wasn't Kacie. Chris stepped onto the porch. "You okay?" he asked.

"Fine," I murmured.

After a minute, he said, "I'm gonna head out."

I nodded, wanting to go with him.

"Joel said they'd bring you home."

I nodded again.

"This sucks." Chris sighed. He pulled his car keys from his pocket. I assumed he meant "this" the death of a friend and having to face his parents and not being high while doing it.

"I know" was all I could say. Then he left and I finished my cigarette and waited a little while before going back inside.

Mac was sitting in the formal living room, in a wingback chair by the front window. He was staring at his hands.

I walked down the step into the room and sat in the chair adjacent to his. He looked over at me and his face was crusted with dried tears. His blue eyes, Tony's eyes, were weary and worn. I didn't say anything because I couldn't think of anything and he didn't say anything I guess because he couldn't. So, we sat there, Mac and me, not sure of what to do but knowing we didn't want to feel any of this anymore.

I remembered Tony standing in the rain under a tree with no leaves, begging me to feel the relief the rain was giving to his burning skin. It felt good on my burning skin, too. I thought I felt it but mine was physical and his was so spiritual. I wanted to try again, right then in the Williams' living room. I wanted to stand under the tree and have Tony coach me through it again. I swore I would get it right this time. I didn't share that memory with Mac. He didn't need to know that heroin-induced desperation Tony and I had once participated in, Tony more recently than me. But I gritted my teeth at the thought of it anyway, held my tongue to the roof of my mouth, gripped the armrests of the chair and wondered what it felt like to want to die.

Jason came to the door of the living room. I knew it was him but I didn't look up. He sat on the step at the entrance. I could hear him breathe. None of us spoke. Mac was breathing. Jason was breathing. I guess I was, too, but none of us spoke. In a little while, Joel came in and sat on the step, too. We all watched the windows, everyone's gazes in different directions. Out to the dimness on the porch, the sunshine on the lawn, the trees across the street. Out. Away. Past here. Past now.

"When Tony was four," Mac said suddenly, "he got really sick. We had to take him to the ER. Flu and pneumonia. He couldn't breathe. Turned blue. And Rhonda . . . Rhonda was so scared. I don't think I've ever felt so useless." He smiled then. "She was such a great mom to those boys. In the ER that night she just held Tony's hand and Gavin in her lap and read book after book. Tony on the bed, IVs in his arms, Gavin sucking his thumb, his face in her neck. And I just sat across the room looking at her wondering when we would be allowed to fall apart."

I thought of Mac's big bear hugs that felt warm and safe, unlike my own father's rigid claps on the back. Thought about Tony telling me how great his dad was. Wondered how he could have done this to Mac.

"You can't keep them safe, can you?" Mac asked of no one in particular.

Kacie came in then. She was holding two books and she walked to me and stretched them out. I took them. One was *The Catcher in the Rye* but she'd left the Post-It with my name on it downstairs. The other was a green velvet notebook, not much wider than the paperback novel.

"What's in the book?" Mac asked.

I held up *The Catcher in the Rye* for them all to see.

"Any meaningful words underlined?" Joel asked.

"Es-ki-mo," Jason said, enunciating each syllable with a smirk.

I let myself laugh. Looking over at Mac I said, "Eskimo. Line from a movie we've probably seen a million times. *Heathers*."

"About teenage suicide," Kacie said, glaring at me and then, just for emphasis, glaring at Jason, too.

"It's okay, Kacie," Mac said. He smiled at her. "Tony probably would've said it first. He'd have thought it was funny."

She went to him and held his hand. "I feel so sad," she said quietly.

"I know, sweetheart," he said, squeezing her fingers.

I watched her swallow away her tears and thought about the fragments of life. The things you swore were gone that flooded back in an instant, and the things you wanted so desperately to retain that disappeared forever as if they'd never happened.

"What's in the book, Brian?" Mac asked again.

I opened it and took the page out. "It's the poem he copied and carried around with him."

"The one from the yearbook?" Joel had his legs folded up and his arms draped over his knees. His twin was in the same posture and I smiled seeing them there, identical in so many ways. I wondered where Tabby was, then realized I was glad she hadn't come. I was hopelessly outnumbered with her around and Tony gone. Thought about asking about her but I really didn't want to make Joel lie about her skipping the visit to Tony's parents. It felt like we'd left New Year's behind. Jumped over it or forgotten about it or forgiven it just because we were united in this grief. The swell of sadness in Tony's house had squeezed out the tension we'd choked on last night. There were words between us but we weren't afraid of them anymore.

"You remember that?" I asked.

Joel and Jason nodded.

"From that shitty poetry book," Jason said. Then he looked

at Mac, as if catching himself cussing, and blushed and dropped his head. "You called it that," he muttered.

I smiled. "Yeah, I did."

"Well, let's hear it," Mac said.

"Now?"

Voices moved from the kitchen toward the front of the house. Rhonda appeared, ushering an older couple toward the door.

"Pastor Don is leaving," she said to the room.

The twins turned and looked over their shoulders at the preacher and his wife. Mac let go of Kacie's hand and stood, walking toward them with his hand outstretched.

"Thanks for coming, Don," he said. The older man stepped down into the living room, took Mac's hand and walked him into a hug. Mac dwarfed him. The Mrs. Preacher hugged Rhonda, and murmured goodbyes followed them to the door and floated out with them.

I heard the grandfather clock chime. The sound was one I remembered from the first time I'd ever slept over at Tony's. All those weird noises that are a part of someone else's house so much so they hardly notice them, the ice maker, the clock ticking, the air conditioning rushing through the vents. They'd become a sort of symphony I knew as the melody of Tony's house. I stared at the clock face, not registering the time, just working to make sense of the fragments sliding around me and finding myself overwhelmed by the number and weight of thoughts and feelings.

I opened the green notebook and flipped to a random page. I read the lines quietly and then said aloud, "I can't remember all the times I tried to tell myself to hold on to these moments as they pass."

I leaned forward in the chair, elbows on knees, book cradled in my hands.

Then Kacie said, "And it's one more day up in the canyon,

and it's one more night in Hollywood." She knew the song, knew the verse, and she'd picked it up like the edge of a parachute. I imagined us all holding tightly to it, stretching it between us, bouncing it like in elementary school P.E. class. I looked at the twins and hoped they'd grab hold.

"If you think you might come to California," I said, "I wish you would."

Jason met my glance again and my eyes filled and my vision blurred. His jaw clenched.

Joel shifted a little and his right hand's grip on his left wrist tightened.

"I know," he said quietly.

Kacie faced the window onto the front lawn. Her hair fell in long curls down her back, I could just see the roll of her shoulder under her purple sweater, and the edge of her chin in profile. The daylight fell over her, illuminating the pale colors in her hair. I ached to touch her. When I turned back to Jason, he was looking at her, too.

The green book was Tony's collected song lyrics, poems, and quotes written in various pencil strokes and pen marks over eight years or more. It was one of the reasons he usually had a back-pack with him. When we skated, it had his pads in it, too, but he'd stopped carrying those a couple years ago. The book, some light-ers, an Ace bandage, his wallet, a change of clothes, a stick of deodorant, a few other odds and ends, and we called it his man purse and usually gave him all kinds of shit for carrying it around like a woman. But anyway, Counting Crows "Long December" was on the page I'd turned to, after the Roy Croft poem and before a few things he'd penned himself.

I held it up and said to Kacie, "Where'd you find it?"

"It had my name on it," she said with the slightest lift of her chin.

Mac came back into the living room but didn't ask about the

books again. Joel and Jason stood up as he entered and made some excuses about getting out of the way. It was one o'clock and I was starting to feel hungry. I stood with them and we all spoke quietly, said goodbye to Tony's parents, hugged them again, and walked out into the cool February day.

I remembered Tony's neighborhood as having smaller houses than my parents' and wondered just for a moment about when they'd made the move over here and why we hadn't thought about it then. I looked over to the driveway. Three blue cars, a silver car, two red cars, a mailbox, a lump of frozen snow near the curb, a passing car, and a few naked trees. I tugged the zipper up my chest.

"I'll take you home," Kacie offered.

"Thanks," I said.

"We'll see you later?" Joel asked.

I nodded. No extra hugs, no touching even between Jason and Kacie, and I simply followed her down the driveway and let them pass us to Jason's blue SUV parked behind her.

"What happened to, 'stay away from me this weekend'?" I asked her as we settled into her car.

"It's in the book," she said.

While she turned the engine on and backed the car out of the driveway, I opened the green notebook, flipping through the pages looking for whatever it was she was referring to. It was a note, it was addressed to both of us, and it was on the last page.

"Did you read this?" I asked.

"Of course I did," she said.

"Has anyone else?"

She shook her head. "Light me a smoke, will ya?"

I closed the book, pulled two cigarettes out of my box and lit them both. I handed her one and rolled the window down.

"Are you going to read it?" she asked.

"Can I wait?" I said.

She nodded and smoked quietly. A long pull in, a long stream out, toward the cracked window, one hand on the wheel, eyes on the road.

"I'm sorry, Kacie." That's when I turned away, looked out the window, counted the houses as we passed.

"Okay," she whispered.

"I don't know what else to say."

"There is nothing else to say."

That wasn't true. There were so many questions to answer, so many stories to tell, so many reasons I was wrong and hurtful and tortured and hateful. But right then I was just too sober for all of that. She was, too, apparently. And she let me off the hook.

We rode the rest of the way to my parents' house in silence. She let me out without trying to touch me and I took the books with me. I trudged up the walk without looking back and she drove away.

While you're there, you take time for granted. You assume that this moment is the first of many that will be your happy life. Then after it's over, the longer it's been since you felt it, the more perfect it seems and you wish so desperately to have it back. I think there are a lot of moments I want back. I want to remember the details of all the wonderful things that happened. I want my senses all opened, so that later, when I want it back, I can smell and see and hear and feel it all again. The scent of her perfume, the glow of her skin, the song that was playing, his laughter, the feel of his hug, passing smiles between us, all of us. I want to memorize it as it happens so I'll have it all when I need it some distant day. I didn't think I had any sense of it until then. I sat at my parents' kitchen table cursing myself for having slid through all of those years with Tony and never stopping to memorize any of it. I couldn't remember the sound of his voice and that realization made me crazy.

I heated a bowl of leftover pasta from last night's dinner and ate with the green velvet book open on the table. I read all the poems, the quotes he'd collected, the things he'd recorded. I started to hear him in the words of others. The song lyrics had faint tunes but it was his voice writing them down, reading them back to me, thinking through them, what they meant. Page after page, getting closer and closer to that last page but putting if off a little bit. When I did reach it, I saw it was written in the same tight, thoughtful script in which his own poems appeared. I saw there were places where he'd erased the pencil marks and then written over the smudges, getting the words just right. I listened to the page more than read it. I let Tony's voice say the words. It was short and delicate and something I'd already known but he often reminded me of things that mattered.

I read it twice. Considered turning the page and adding a response. Then closed the book and pushed it away.

I reached for the phone and called Melissa. The line in San Francisco rang and rang but she didn't answer. I waited for a machine to pick up but after five rings, I realized I didn't know what I would say and hung up just as the machine responded.

I wondered what I should do until it was time to go out and drink again. Then I decided to drink right then and went to the crisper for a beer. I stood across the room from the green book.

Everything used to be so simple, as far as I could tell. Life was automatic. I could go from here to there to there without having to worry about how I got there. I did what I was supposed to do, what I wanted to do, and what I shouldn't do in that order. Then thinking back, how easy it was, I felt miserable at all the work it seemed to be now. I wondered how much harder it could possibly get. And staring at that book on my parents' kitchen table, I thought it was the hardest it had ever been.

I finished my beer, cleaned up my dishes, poured a glass of water, grabbed the book, and went upstairs to smoke and take a nap. We weren't going out again until eight.

It was three thirty, though it looked much later; the sun that day was just as elusive as the day before. The snow on the ground was only leftover snow, the kind that hangs around a few days piled up into dirty clusters by snowplows and shovelers. That snow is hard, warm but unwilling to melt. There are pebbles and dust stuck on it so looks dirty and old. I looked across my parents' backyard, seeing snow in the shaded areas where no sun could have melted it away. It wasn't hard or dirty, just well hidden.

As I sat under the open window in my room, the phone rang. It was Meli.

"So, you went to his parents' house today?"

"Yeah."

"How was that?"

"Hard. His dad is so sad. I didn't know what to say."

"I'm sure that was hard."

I took a drag off my cigarette and a drink out of the glass of water. I heard Melissa moving around on the other end of the line.

"What are you doing?" I asked.

"Nothing. Moving stuff."

"What kind of stuff?"

"Nothing. It doesn't matter. Who else was at Tony's?"

I listened to her moving and breathing for a few seconds and then said, "Joel and Jason and Kacie and Chris."

"That must have made it easier," she said.

"A little, yeah."

Melissa didn't know about New Year's. I hadn't told her and

she hadn't asked and all she needed to know was Kacie and I were over and I'd assured her of that as long ago as Thanksgiving.

"Abby said Dr. Kittering asked if anyone had seen you." Abby was my classmate and Meli's best girlfriend on campus.

"What did she tell him?"

"Nothing."

"Did you tell her?"

"Of course I told her. She said to tell you she's sorry."

A twenty-two-cents-per-minute quiet stretched between us. I pictured her at my flat. Wondered if she'd fixed the phone so she could call on my long-distance bill instead of hers.

"It doesn't feel like I got here yesterday," I said finally.

"It doesn't feel like you left yesterday."

I smoked. She did whatever she was doing. I heard her grunt a little with the effort of something or the weight of something.

"So, what will you do tonight?" she asked.

"Go to Uno probably. It's where we usually drink." I'd told her the whole of Northern Virginia was corporate restaurants and that we'd hung out at Reston Town Center since we were in middle school. First loitering in the flimsy white patio chairs that sat around cheap metal tables all over the central plaza near a three-tiered waterfall foundtain, then walking the sidewalks around the outside rims of the place, or lying on the grassy hills between parking lots and streets. We used to skate on the top levels of the five-story garage and climb the stairwells of the ten-story Hyatt until we were run off by security. Lately, though, we'd been in the bars, Uno and Market Street, Bistro Bistro and Clyde's. Tony had known the bartenders and we usually got pretty decent rates as long as we stuck to draft beer.

"Everyone?"

"Everyone," I said.

"And last night?"

"She told me to stay away from her this week," I said.

"Why?"

"Because, Meli, we're done."

"I know that." The motion on the other end had stopped and she was quiet, thoughtful. "I didn't ask about her."

"But you wondered."

"I wondered," she conceded.

"Don't wonder. Don't worry. I'm not working on that shit this week. More important things. Tony's things. He left me a book and a page with a poem and I think they're going to expect me to say something tomorrow."

"Jesus, Brian, I'm sorry. I'm being stupid about the Kacie thing. Of course Tony is more important. I won't ask again."

I wanted to hold her then. I closed my eyes and thought about her hair in my fingers, her skin next to mine.

"Let me go. I'm going to nap. It's been a hard day."

"Okay. Call me later."

"Will do," I said. But I wouldn't.

We all knew that the next day was the next day, the funeral, and nothing would change that. We all knew that it would be gray and rainy and we would cry again and it would be the end of Tony, really the end of him, not like he didn't come to the bar tonight, not like he was all over some girl and so was avoiding us, but the end of him. That feeling stayed with me but it didn't seem to have stayed with anybody else.

In Uno, the bar is catty-corner to the entrance, it wraps to the right, leaving a small alley between the windows and the bar. We had a table by a window and it only sat four so the six of us crowded around it, Kacie, Tabby, and Joel seated and Jason, me, and Chris standing.

"Do you ever think about cartoons?" I asked Tabby, four beers into our evening of denial. She had volleyed the conversation around me since we'd arrived. But we were all softer now, four beers in, and I decided to dispel the tension between us.

"How so?" she asked, apparently sensing a benign subject we could discuss.

"Like the way they formed us into who we are."

"Give me an example," she said, lifting her glass and taking an imperceptible sip of her beer. She consumed it like one might a cognac, without actually swallowing.

"Take for instance, *The Smurfs*," I said. My legs were slightly spread and I was standing shorter than I usually am, eye-to-eye with her as she perched on the barstool. I had to look past Joel to her and I could feel him between us, waiting to see where the conversation would go.

"That was a communistic society at its best," I continued. "Every Smurf had his specialty. The Baker did all of the cooking for the entire village, Handy fixed everything for the village, Hefty was the strongest and therefore the hero for the village. Everyone knew his place. Don't you think that now we're all trying to learn our place?" I thought for a moment about what I had said, as I could see Tabby was doing. Before she could answer, though, Joel piped up.

"Like all the Smurfs must have already been in their thirties?" He laughed and I did, too. Then he said, "In every episode, the hole in the system was apparent. Like, in one of the shows every Smurf's pants might be ripped or worn out and Tailor would be overrun with work."

"And in stepped Papa to remind the others that Tailor was only one Smurf and they would have to be patient," I said.

"What about Vanity? What was his job?" Chris asked.

"Maybe he was the example of what vanity can do to a society," Jason volunteered. "Like, every time he was responsible for the Smurflings, they got into trouble. You couldn't depend on Vanity for anything."

"Jesus, the Smurflings. Nice pull." Chris grinned at Jason.

"The hardest working Smurfs were the laborers," Kacie said. "Handy and Hefty and Baker and Tailor."

"I wouldn't call Hefty a laborer," I argued. "He was more of the Olympic athlete type, like his job was to make the other Smurfs look up to him and want to realize their potential. He won every event in the Smurf Olympics, ya know."

"They had a Smurf Olympics?" Chris asked. "Did I miss that episode?"

This was the kind of philosophy we occupied ourselves with. "Take *The Simpsons* as another example," I said. "The cynicism of that show illustrates our entire generation."

"Is this a Gen-X rally or what?" Jason asked.

"Find your place in society," I said. "You are the barkeeper, the drunk, or the religious self-righteous."

"I'm the drunk," Chris said.

"Raging alcoholic," Kacie proclaimed, raising her hand slightly.

"No. Alcoholics go to meetings," Chris clarified. "I'm a drunk."

"Did anyone notice *The Smurfs* went off air right after the Berlin Wall came down?" Joel asked.

"They're on Cartoon Network every day at ten," I said. "I schedule my classes around them." Everyone laughed.

I remembered then all of the wonderful things about those times, the conversation, the smokes, the beers. I remembered how tall a beer glass was when I was eighteen and how small it seemed when I was twenty-two.

Our bartender came over to empty the ashtray and collect empty glasses. Chris and Kacie were talking about ACC basketball and Joel and Tabby were talking about spring break. Jason and I weren't talking and it didn't occur to me to start. Then Chris asked me to take a walk up to Clyde's, which I knew meant let's go to the car and get stoned. So we did.

When we got back, the bar had filled up and we'd lost a stool from our table to the crowd the next window over. Joel and Tabby were gone, and Jason and Kacie were sitting close to one another but staring at the TV overhead and not speaking.

"Where'd Joel go?" I asked.

"He and Tabby walked over to Bistro Bistro," Kacie said.

"To see anyone we know?" Chris asked.

"Hope not," Jason said.

Everyone I knew was accounted for, I thought. I said, "Order me another beer, will ya?" and excused myself to the men's room.

High as hell and a little drunk, I made my way through the crowd, passed the bar and headed to the right. The crowd opened up where the restaurant began, at the servers' station and kitchen entry. Uno's floor tiles were all black and white. I followed them down a narrow hall between the bar and the kitchen. The pay phone was on the left, the ladies' room first, and the men's just beyond it. The door was one of those old school building doors, heavy and with a big window of opaque glass. I pushed it open and stepped into an empty stall.

I didn't sit. I just closed the stall door, locked it and leaned against it. The metal was cool on my cheek. I stood like that for what seemed like forever. I thought about all of us standing around that table by the window, lifting our glasses to toast, sucking down shots and not thinking about tomorrow. I thought about glancing at the door a thousand times or so waiting for Tony to walk in. I remembered Tony talking to a dozen people I'd never seen before, people he knew from work or wherever, people he never introduced us to. I thought about the looks I got from people I probably should have recognized, people who probably knew Tony, and I thought about how I'd just looked away again and again. I thought about knowing him and knowing he wouldn't show up tonight.

I took a deep breath that smelled like bathroom cleaner and pulled a cigarette out of my breast pocket. I lit it and inhaled deeply. Someone came into the bathroom, used a urinal and left. I smoked quietly, hearing the music expand when the door opened and shrink back to beyond the walls when the door closed.

The next time the door opened someone said, "Brian?"

I didn't answer.

Joel stepped closer to the stall and put his hand on the door. It shifted a little bit but stayed closed.

"Brian?" he said again.

"Yeah?" I said and it came out weaker than I'd planned and so I said it again.

"You okay, buddy?"

I took another drag and exhaled toward the ceiling. "I guess," I said.

"Come out, will ya?"

I did. Joel stood against the far wall. I stared at myself in the mirror for a minute. I took another drag but watching yourself smoke is like poking a bruise so I looked away.

"Tony called me on Sunday," I said, exhaling a long stream of smoke.

"What did he say?"

"I wasn't home." I flicked the filter of my cigarette with my thumb, dislodging the ash which fluttered to the floor.

The door opened again. Joel put his hand up to keep it from hitting him. The music swelled. Chris entered, pushed the door closed behind him. The music stayed outside.

"Everything okay?" he asked. He stepped in front of the stall I'd just exited, stood across from the mirrors, glanced up at himself and then looked back at me.

"Fine," I said. "We're all fine, apparently."

"Look, Brian, you gotta let it go. She said it was only once, ya know?"

"What are you talking about?" Joel asked Chris.

"The Kacie and Jason thing."

They both looked at me.

"I don't give a fuck," I said. That was a lie.

"Oh, okay." Chris had on a button-down shirt, open, with a white t-shirt beneath it. His sleeves were rolled up, his shirts untucked, the collar unbuttoned, the breast pocket thick with a box of Newports. "So then, what's with hiding in the john?"

"Needed to think for a minute."

"Do my best thinking in the john," Joel said and then sort of laughed.

"Me too, come to think of it," Chris said, pulling the box out of his pocket.

Joel wore a blue button down, all but the top one fastened, the shirt tail tucked into his khakis. He reached out to Chris for a smoke. Chris handed it to him and then took one for himself. I finished my own cigarette and dropped it on the black-and-white tiled floor.

The noise beyond the bathroom pulsed. I couldn't hear my heartbeat from the bass in my ears. The mirror vibrated on the wall, used paper towels overflowed the trashcan, their edges shivering with the thuds. Chris shuffled his feet a little bit. Joel pinched something on the end of his tongue and brushed his hand on his pants.

"I didn't call him back," I said.

"Wonder what he wanted."

"Who?" Chris asked.

"Tony," Joel said.

"He called me Sunday," I said.

"I wonder what he wanted," Joel said again.

"For me to talk him out of it," I answered.

"You can't know that."

"But I can. I do. I know it inside of me like he was waiting for me to tell him not to do it. But I wasn't home." I put my left hand on the edge of the sink and shoved my right into my pocket.

Chris leaned against the stall I'd exited. Joel stepped away from the wall and kicked at a paper towel crumbled up at his feet. As he smoked his cigarette, his shoulders sagged.

"Why does a guy do a thing like that?" Chris asked.

"Who knows?" Joel said.

"I don't believe her that it was a one-time thing," I said.

"Why not?" Chris asked.

"Why should I?"

He shrugged.

The music pulsed beyond the opaque glass window in the schoolhouse door.

"You still have that roommate?" Joel asked me.

The answer was no. I lived alone. But I said, "Which one?"

"The one with the girlfriend."

Chris started laughing. "Tony told me you fucked that girl-friend."

"He said that?" I asked.

"Yeah, he said dude found out about it and went nuts."

"Wasn't like that." I edged closer to the sink, careful not to look at myself in the mirror. I spit into the basin and ran the water to wash it away. I thought about telling them. I wondered if Joel was still my friend or not.

"She was hot," I said, "so yeah, I fucked her. Roommate walked in; that was pretty awkward."

"Did he take a swing at you?" Chris asked.

"Nah. Called her a whore and left. Next day after class all of his shit was gone."

"Did you keep seeing her?"

I spit into the sink again. "Nah. Who wants to date a whore?"

Then I ran the water to wash it away and glanced at myself in the mirror.

Both of them laughed, Joel, too, and I guessed he was my friend. I can't remember when he had quit listening to stuff that Tabby wouldn't like to hear. But it seemed that I couldn't remember telling him anything like that before.

The door opened again, some guy we didn't know walked in.

None of us asked each other what time the funeral was the next day, though I was pretty sure Chris and I didn't know. We didn't talk about seeing Mac that morning, and I didn't tell them about the note in the back of the book. I did suppress a glimpse of Tony's bathroom that kept coming to mind.

Joel said something about his freshman roommate marrying the girl he'd dated since their first week at Pitt. I listened, realizing I didn't even know the roommate's name and Joel was in business with the guy. How did I not even know his name? I guessed Joel had never fucked his roommate's girlfriend and I just then felt bad about being the guy who had.

The stranger peed behind me. Then he left and Jason walked in.

"What's going on?" he asked.

None of us said anything.

"Private party?"

"Not really," I said.

"Everyone okay?"

"If feeling like I left a limb at home is okay then I'm okay," I said. "How about you, Joeler?"

He gave me a look that said he understood but he didn't answer the question.

"Come back to the table," Jason said. "I can't handle all those women by myself."

"There are only two," Chris said.

"I'm a little drunk." He stood up a little taller, pulled his shoulders back, managed to smile and added, "It's the best excuse I could come up with."

"In that case," Chris said, "lead the way."

"You can trust Jason," Joel said to me after the door closed behind them.

"With what?" I asked.

"She needed somebody."

"Charlottesville is full of somebodies, why didn't she fuck one of them?"

Joel shook his head. "That I don't know."

Then we left the bathroom and the pulsing music was all around us. Tonic, "Open Up Your Eyes," from Lemon Parade, a disc I'd worn out. That and Chalk Farm, Toad the Wet Sprocket, and the Empire Records soundtrack, the last one stolen from Melissa.

I stopped at the bar on the way back to the table. The bartender asked me what I wanted and I told her. She was cute, a little short for my taste, but cute. She had a cheerleader's smile. "On your tab?" she asked.

"Yeah, I'm at that table," I said and pointed toward the Crew. "With the blonde?"

"Not *with* her, but yeah." I smiled at the bartender, she smiled at me and I went back to my table. "Shots coming," I told them. The music was so loud now I had to shout.

The beer Chris had ordered for me sat on the table. I picked it up and drained half of it. I could feel Kacie watching me. I met the bartender's glance and smiled. When next I looked at Kacie, she glared.

This had been going on for years, me flirting with, lighting cigarettes for, and smiling at random girls. Kacie always said, "Brian's a flirt," and meant he's a cheater. She always knew. But she never asked me about it. Not directly. I didn't have any idea why.

The worst part is that I think she truly believed I would out-grow it. I think she truly believed I was only that way because I was nineteen, then twenty, then twenty-one. She said I liked to make sure everyone had a good time. She said I was social. She said she knew I went home with her. There were nights when she was leaning against a wall after Joel, Tabby, and Jason had left and Tony and I were talking to a couple of girls. Then Tony would ask her if she was okay and she would say yes. In the bathroom, she would stuff her pinky into a vial, shove that powder in her nose, and she would be okay.

There were nights when Kacie would stand on the bar, guzzling a tall boy and taking her five bucks from whatever guy she had bet. There were nights when she would skip across the parking lot, playing as I took her home, hanging her arm out the window as I drove, trying to touch a tree limb. Those were the nights when Kacie could party. She was so much like me then. We were synchronized, same-paged, meant to be. The fun, talented Kacie with the beautiful smile and the melodious laugh, the one who could kiss so gently it was like tasting a cloud. That one I missed.

But by the end of last summer and over New Year's she'd been reduced, shrunken into Kacie begging me to go home, Kacie falling asleep in the car, waking up disoriented and whiny. She wanted to fight. She was bitter and strung out. That Kacie was easy to leave.

The girl sitting next to Jason by the window on the night before we buried Tony was neither of the two Kacies I'd known. She was pale but not fragile, skin like porcelain, clear and fresh even in the smoky bar. She smiled genuinely and listened attentively. She sipped her beer and smoked her cigarettes, not taking the light Jason offered her, but reaching into her purse for her own. She said things like, "I know I brought it," and "it must be here somewhere," and "that's okay, I found it."

I watched her eyelids twitch over her eyes as she stared into her bag. I watched her lips press against the cigarette as she lit it. I suppressed the urge to want to know what she thought of the note from Tony. To ask her how she was handling all this, to tell her how sorry I was that I hadn't called Tony back on Sunday. Somewhere inside I knew I needed her to tell me that I couldn't have saved him. But I didn't ask her to. I didn't speak to her.

I was a fool that night. I finished beer after beer and accepted shots from the bartender. I flirted with her and she asked me to stay after hours. I told her Chris was my ride and she said he could stay, too. I ignored everything in me that wanted to get closer to Kacie. Everything that said Tony's note would have done it. I didn't even tell her I had read it. But she must have known.

When the bar closed we followed the crowd out the door, spilling onto the sidewalk pulling our coats up around us. I watched Kacie shove her fingers inside brown leather gloves. Jason offered Chris and me a ride home but in the hours since we were at Tony's, since we'd been in the bar and I'd gotten all fucked up, I'd renewed the division Kacie put between me and Jason and no way I was riding with him. I said so.

Chris said we'd take a cab, knowing he'd wait until they left, and then would drive us both home, extra careful of course.

Joel asked what time we'd be around in the morning, reminded us the time of the funeral and the guilt washed over me.

"Be at my house at nine?" he asked Chris.

Chris agreed.

I looked across the road at Kacie, standing close to Jason, ducking her head into his shoulder as the February wind blew.

My knees bent and I squatted where I stood in front of the window of the bar. I put my hands over my ears and closed my eyes tightly. Waves of nausea swept through me. I felt Chris's hand on my back. He was saying, "Brian, you okay?"

I felt tears clog my throat and shook my head.

Joel stood in front of me, his shoes toe-to-toe with mine.

Jason and Kacie were still freezing together under the lamppost across the street and Tabby was with them, waiting on Joel. But Joel and Chris were watching me and finally I looked up.

The wind, cold and fierce, blew the tears out of my eyes and they drizzled down my cheeks.

"Brian?" Joel asked.

"I'm okay," I said.

"We're all okay," Joel said quietly.

Chris grabbed my arm under the elbow and they helped me to stand. I wavered a bit and Joel pulled me against him in a great big hug that felt warm and old, like Tony's dad or winning used to feel.

"Joel, come on," Tabby called from across the street. "It's fucking cold."

Joel let me go and stepped back, raising a hand to his twin and his girlfriend. I looked across the road. Kacie and Tabby had very different expressions on their faces.

Chris assured Joel that he and I were both all right and Joel left with Tabby. Jason and Kacie trailed him through the parking lot.

I wished she would turn and look at me, but she didn't.

"What the fuck happens now?" Chris asked me. The sidewalk was emptying out and cars were leaving in all directions, headlights burning away the darkness around them.

"We go back inside," I said.

By now the florescent lights were on and everyone was paler than they had been. I found my bartender and smiled.

"Glad you decided to stay," she said.

Four shots in me and I said, "Me, too." At least I think that's what I said.

Chris stood next to me, wanting to know what the plan was.

"Are you partying?" I asked the bartender.

"Yeah, over at Jeff's." She motioned to a dark-haired guy that wore an Uno shirt. "You guys should come." She made sure to look at Chris.

"I don't know," Chris said.

"We have something to do really early in the morning," I said.

"What's that?" she asked.

"It's nothing," Chris said.

"We have to bury my best friend. He killed himself three days ago."

The pretty bartender stared at me. I smiled. Chris grabbed my arm, again, by the elbow and led me out of Uno. We went home without saying anything else.

FRIDAY

Five hours of drunken sleep later, an alarm went off and I hallucinated. Where the fuck was I? I opened my eyes trying to remember how I'd gotten here. A half-empty beer bottle sat on the floor under an open window. I still wore my shirt and jeans from last night, but my shoes and belt were on the floor. Why was the alarm blaring and where was the fucking clock? I raised my head; it throbbed. My room. My parents' house.

"Brian?" Mom's voice called from the hallway.

I reached for the snooze bar and pressed it down.

"Brian?"

"I'm up." I managed to press my hands into the bed, raise myself up, knees underneath me, and sit back on my heels. I shifted my hips and hung my legs over the side of the bed.

"I'm up," I said again and heard her retreat down the hall.

The clock read 7:30. I turned the alarm completely off. The sun hadn't come up yet but the sky outside of the open window was pale. I stood slowly, took a step to the window, and slammed it shut. Rolling the shirt up my belly and yanking it over my head, I faced the mirror above the dresser, tugged absently at the necklaces stacked at my throat and rubbed one eye with the knuckle of my left hand. I could smell the liquor and smoke on my skin.

My mouth tasted like ass and my lips were crusted with dried drool.

"You look like shit," Tony had said.

"Thanks, dick," I had replied.

"Did you bother to sleep?"

"Yes. Sort of." I had yawned and could smell the foulness of my own breath.

"Get a shower. I wanna take you somewhere."

I blinked several times into the mirror image. My bedroom. My parents' house. Trying to push the memory away, I walked out of the room, into the bathroom, and stepped into the shower, tired, still a little bit drunk and wishing I had had about three more hours to sleep. The water felt good on my skin, warm and clean. It washed away the sweat from the night before, reckless sleep and fitful dreams.

"Where are we going?" We were riding along Route 7 toward Leesburg in his dad's car. Tony let the radio play the oldies station and neither of us smoked. We'd stopped into 7 Eleven and gotten two bottles of water and two Cherry Coke Slurpees.

"I found this place last spring and it's amazing. I wanted to come back once the leaves changed," he said. "And I'm gonna share it with you." He grinned.

"Gee, thanks," I said.

It was Thanksgiving break and I had come home the Saturday before the holiday week. It was my third year away and last night we'd all been in Tony's basement getting drunk and playing cards until the twins left and Tony and Kacie and Chris and I got high. Kacie had taken me home, we'd messed around in my parents' driveway, but I'd been too stoned for sex. I'd staggered inside and up the stairs at around four a.m. Now it was ten-thirty and Tony had kidnapped me for some fucking mission out to Leesburg.

He drove for a while and at one point I thought I was gonna throw up and then it passed and then it happened again and we still weren't there. Then he turned off the road onto a gravel drive and we followed that, slowly, for a while as it wound its way up into the mountains. At the top, a crumbling stone wall and a tiny white wooden church. There were no cars, which was weird because it was Sunday, but there was no sign either and I realized it must be abandoned.

Tony was parking the car and then turning off the engine and getting out.

I opened my own door and stepped out, looking up at the steeple. I could see, now that we were closer, where the boards had broken and the paint was peeling, and there was moss and mold growing on the corners and the windows.

"Look," Tony said.

"I'm looking."

"No," he said, "Over here."

I backed up a bit, still watching the church, taking in the details of its decay and decimation, wondering about the people who'd once worshipped here, got married here, had funerals here. I surveyed the lawn, full of weeds and grave markers that had toppled over and crumbled. A sidewalk ran down the middle, from the front door to the road. I followed it, turning back toward Tony.

He was standing on top of the wall that separated the churchyard from the road. I walked up behind him, put one foot on the wall, made sure it was stable, and then climbed up beside him.

"Holy shit," I said.

In front of us was a break in the tree line maybe fifty yards wide and beyond that, the deepest valley I had ever seen. It was blanketed on both sides with trees dyed all the colors of autumn: gold, amber, auburn, and crimson. The trees rolled down the hill in front of us and up the hill on the other side. It was a massive rainbow of leaves and branches like I'd never seen before and have never seen since.

Tony and I had stood there, quietly, watching the sunlight

pour down from the early noon sky and bathe the valley in warmth. The chill of fall slipped past us and I shoved my hands in the pockets of my coat.

"Fucking magnificent," Tony had said. "It looks like it's burning."

The bathroom was filled with steam when I stepped from the shower. I grabbed a towel off of the toilet and put it to my face for a few seconds. It smelled like fabric softener. I dried off and wrapped the towel around my waist. Turned on the fan and let myself out of the bathroom, pulling the door shut behind me. Some idiot had installed the smoke detector outside of the bathroom door and escaping steam would set it off. I'd done it more times than I could count and every time we had visitors they did it, too.

My bedroom was cold, though the window had been closed for ten minutes or so. I sat dazed and damp on the end of the bed for a few minutes, trying to figure out what I was supposed to do next.

Mom knocked twice and entered. "Brian?" she asked, peeking in and then stepping through the doorway. "You okay?"

"Yeah," I said.

"What suit are you wearing?"

I pointed to my bag hanging in the closet and she went to it and unzipped it. Pulling the black striped suit from the inside she surveyed it briefly. "It looks wrinkled," she complained.

"Don't care," I mumbled.

She laid the suit on the bed and pulled the shirt out of the bag. "What tie?" she asked.

"It's in there."

She laid the ensemble together and looked from it to me.

"It fits?" she asked skeptically.

"Good enough."

"Brian, I know this is hard."

"It's okay, Mom," I said, even though it wasn't. "I'll be okay."

"Anything I can do?" She was still standing over my suit.

"No. I just need to get dressed."

"Do that." She headed for the door, stopping to kiss my forehead. Pushing my hair back with her hand, she tilted my face to look at hers. "It will be okay," she said. "I know it will be."

"It has to be."

She left and the room felt bigger without her in it. I stared at the mirror on the wall. "Dammit, Tony," I said. "What'd'ya go and do this for?"

My throat was thick with unshed tears and I wanted to rid myself of them before I left the house, but I didn't. I dressed in my suit, pulling my socks up and tucking my feet into shoes I hadn't worn since the last time I went to church. That had been a long time ago. Before Kacie's parents moved away, back when we were still pretending to hope they'd like me as if that would ever matter to us. Her mother was a Protestant minister's daughter and her dad was a congressman. They'd attended out of habit and duty, and Kacie attended out of guilt. I went because I wanted her to keep having sex with me and I didn't want to have to marry her to ensure that outcome. I expected to find the bulletin from the service we'd attended in the inside pocket but the suit had at least been cleaned, if not worn, since then.

Downstairs my father was drinking coffee and staring at the newspaper, but I don't think he was reading. He looked up when I came through the door.

"Good morning," he said.

"Good as any," I replied.

"You okay?"

"Would be if everyone would stop asking."

"I poured you some juice," Mom said, standing near the edge of the counter. She was wearing a dark blue suit with a cameo broach.

I took the glass she offered and gulped it down.

My father sipped his coffee. My mother watched me with a pitiful look.

"Thanks," I said, handing the glass back.

"Got in at three," Dad said.

"About there, yeah," I agreed.

"What were you doing?"

"Getting drunk," I answered.

"Have some more juice," Mom offered.

I took another glass.

"Brian," Dad said, "I think it's time."

"Not now, Alan," Mom interjected.

"Yes, now," he said. "I think it's time we talked about what happens in San Francisco."

"Okay," I said. "The trolley cars go up and down the street ringing their bells. The sun comes out around two o'clock to burn away the fog. The weather isn't as nice as it is on the post card and there are some wildly liberal politics in the news every day. That kind of stuff?"

"No," Dad said. "Are you planning to get a job?"

"No."

"Not ever?"

"Oh, Alan," Mom sighed.

"What?" he asked. "Can't I ask where our money is going?"

"Not today," she said.

"He doesn't know what else to say, Mom." I looked back at Dad. "Do you?"

The sunlight was pouring through the bay window, over his newspaper and coffee cup. He stared at the cup.

"Your mother and I are making plans."

I heard Mom draw in a deep breath. "Right now?" she said. "You want to talk about this now?" She turned away from me, ripped the refrigerator open, and shoved the juice inside.

"What's going on?"

"We've put the house on the market," Dad said. Mom's slamming of the fridge door punctuated the statement.

"You're selling the house?" I took in the counters, the cabinets, the windows, the carpet, all the things I knew so well as part of what I called home.

The expression on Mom's face was pained but I knew what he'd said was true when she didn't contradict it.

"We're moving," Dad said.

"Where? Ashburn? Alexandria? Tyson's?" I asked, naming off places nearby that had smaller homes, townhouses like the one Chris said his mom and Micah would probably get when they came back.

"Arizona," Dad said.

"Oro Valley," Mom added.

"What?"

"Your mother is eligible for retirement and so we're ready to go. We're selling the house and moving to Oro Valley, Arizona." Dad folded his newspaper and then drained his juice.

The room was so quiet I thought maybe we'd all stopped breathing. Then I took a breath and realized I was the only one who had stopped breathing.

"You're never here anyway," Mom said. "We'll be closer to you in California, if that's where you're going to stay, and the community we found is really nice. It's near where Kev and Deb live." My uncle worked for Raytheon and had relocated to Arizona a while back to work in the corporate headquarters. "There's this great house just across the way from them." She was rambling a bit but she seemed aware of it and stopped after a few words about patio homes and a swim club with a Masters team for Dad.

"It's a golf resort," Dad said.

"You don't play."

"We're going to." Mom grinned. "I'm getting a set of pink

clubs for my birthday, right, Alan? And your dad worked out with Kev's swim coach and really liked the team."

I could tell she was excited. She looked happy to be talking about their plans. I wondered why this was the first I'd heard of it and then I remembered our fight the other night. Chris had said his parents had their own lives. I wondered if this was what he meant.

"Are you hungry?" Mom said.

"No, thank you."

"Sorry to spring it on you," Dad said, "but I thought you should know as soon as we could tell you." He stood and stepped closer to where Mom and I were. "This house has been good to us. But it's time to move on." He stopped short of touching me, but I could feel him nearby and I wanted to turn to him. I wanted a hug.

Instead, I splayed my hands on the counter, locked my knees in the wrinkled pants of my old suit, blinked to try to keep from being nauseated, and thought about that graveyard high above the burning valley. Tony had spread his arms out to either side as if embracing the whole of the scene. The slight fall wind had swirled around us, but the trees barely shook. I felt again like I might throw up. I had that sense of weightlessness I get during take-off and thought I was looking down on the valley from beyond an airtight window. I felt distanced but Tony was in it. He was in the moment, in the trees, in the sunlight, in the morning, in the hilltop and the roll down into the center as much as if he had caught fire himself.

"Fucking magnificent," he had said. "It looks like it's burning."

In my parents' kitchen, some eighteen months later and for what would be one of the last times we would stand there as a family, I looked at my dad. His eyes were searching my face. I met them and clenched my jaw.

"It's okay," I told him. "It's going to be okay."

"It has to be," Mom said softly.

Everyone else was at Joel's when I got there. I parked Dad's car on the street and quieted the radio. Staring up at the house, counting the long windows on the second floor, five, and the downstairs windows with the blinds tilted away from the morning sun, four. I turned off the engine and stepped out, dragging a wool coat across the driver's seat.

The front door opened without my knocking and I entered through the foyer and crept into the kitchen. Tabby and Kacie sat at the table and Jason, Chris, and Joel stood by the refrigerator.

"How ya feeling?" Joel asked.

"Hung over."

The room was quiet. "Look, I'm sorry," I said. "It's really hard for me."

"To apologize?" Tabby snapped.

"Yes," I said.

"It's all good." Jason clapped his hand on my shoulder.

"Yeah," Joel agreed. "We're all feeling it."

Chris didn't say anything. He was staring at the counter and the half-empty plastic bottle of Gatorade on it.

"Who's driving?" Tabby asked, standing up and pushing the chair back under the table. She had on a short black dress, black stockings, and black high heeled shoes. Her hair was pulled back into a severe bun. Some red lipstick and she could have been one of the girls from Robert Palmer's "Simply Irresistible" video.

"Me and Chris," Joel said.

"Then let's go and get this over with," Tabby said.

I saw Joel wince. He took the glasses off the counter and turned toward the sink with them.

Tabby picked up her purse and Kacie stood up. She had on a black skirt and a dark red blouse that billowed around her arms and narrowed at the cuffs. Her hair was swept into a loose knot at the back of her neck. She raised a hand and brushed hair out of her face. It was a gentle, delicate movement that made me ache. She turned her face toward me and our eyes met. Hers were watery but she looked away before she could let any tears go.

Jason stepped between us and put a hand on Kacie's back. "You okay?" he asked her. She nodded.

Chris stepped closer to me, grabbing his bottle off the counter, and directed me toward the foyer. We exited ahead of everyone else. I heard them behind us as we shuffled down the stoop and front walk.

Joel drove his blue SUV that was just like Jason's. Tabby sat in the front, and Kacie and Jason got in the back. Chris and I followed them to the funeral home.

"Listen, dude, about last night," I began.

"It's all good," Chris said. "I feel the same. It's all so fucking sad." He reached over and opened the glove compartment. "At least I don't have to watch Jason comfort my ex-girlfriend. Here, take the edge off." He passed me his dugout and I stuffed it and lit the end, taking a puff.

"More like soften the nausea," I said, blowing the smoke out. I took another hit, then coughed hard into the sleeve of Dad's old wool coat Mom told me to wear over my suit. "Hurts like hell," I said, before another exhale. "I probably just need more fucking sleep." I pinched wool fuzz off my tongue and tried not to gag.

Chris laughed. "Ain't that the truth." He was already high, I realized, and so I put the one hitter away and closed the glove compartment over it.

Greene Funeral Home is located in downtown Herndon across the street from the old town hall. The road between them used to be a quiet little main street and is now a constant traffic jam. We parked in the side lot, near the bike path. It was ten a.m. and the building was surrounded by cars. Inside, the floor is covered with an indoor/outdoor carpet in soothing blends of rose red, beige, and three shades of green. The designs look like it couldn't decide whether to be paisley or flowers.

My eyes were bloodshot like I'd been crying, but I'd been getting high and the edge was gone but so was my sense of awareness. It was like watching the damned thing happen from above like some sort of movie; a sick movie where the dead guy's best friend is too stoned to mourn. But that was how I felt, numb and empty.

Jason, Kacie, Tabby, and Joel filed into the back of the room. The chairs in front of them were filled with people. Some I knew, some I didn't; mostly friends of Mac and Rhonda.

Everyone was whispering like we were in a library, trying to leave the mourners quiet with their thoughts, I guess. There were plants in the corner with clean and shiny leaves that caught the light. I wondered whose job it was to water them, to wipe them off so they weren't dusty. I wondered if the undertaker had ever considered putting poison ivy in those pots. Such a beautiful leafy plant with that reddish hue. It would have been distracting, adding a danger element that, quite frankly, the room could have used. Everyone was brushing by the plants as they walked around the chairs and their occupants. I counted the number of people who would be scratching by the time we reached the cemetery if only Greene had thought of the poison ivy play. Or oak, poison oak would have been okay, too.

In the front of the room was a cherry wood box with satin lining and the lid was partially open so that Tony's face would be visible if you got close enough to see inside. I decided not to get that close. There was soft music playing and Mac and Rhonda were speaking to a couple older than them.

Joel navigated through the crowd, past the plants, to Mac and Rhonda and hugged each of them and then pointed to the back of the room where we were all standing against the wall. Rhonda came toward us, hugging Tabby and Kacie, then Jason and Chris and finally me. She smelled like lavender, that damp towel smell that I remembered from the guard room, my swim bag, and the lawn chairs near Tony's backyard pool. I wanted to cry but I didn't. She did, on my shoulder a bit, then pulled away, smiled weakly, and excused herself.

I looked at Chris. I didn't think I could do this. Chris didn't look good.

"I have to go outside," he said.

"We just got here," Jason hissed.

"I can't." He looked at me.

"I know, man, go on."

"Thanks," he said.

Jason let go of Kacie's hand and followed Chris for a few steps, whispering some instruction to him after which Chris nodded, left, and Jason returned to Kacie's side.

Joel stepped up to the coffin, touching the edge of it slightly and then reaching out for Tabby's hand. Jason went forward and the three of them talked quietly in front of Tony. We couldn't hear what they said and then all of them left the room.

Kacie and I were still frozen behind all those chairs.

My parents entered and spoke briefly with Mac before finding me and walking over. Dad's navy-blue suit matched Mom's; each looked as if it had been tailored to be worn with the other, like his and hers mourning outfits. Mom's hair was combed back away from her face and she had pearls in her earlobes that matched the cream color of the cameo broach on her chest. She stepped in front of me, blocking my view of the coffin.

"You okay?" she asked but didn't wait for my response. "Hello, Kacie," she said softly.

"Hi, Mrs. Listo." Kacie shifted closer to me a bit, her shoulder behind mine as though giving me a wall to lean against.

"Kacie," my father said. He didn't look at me.

"There's Tony's grandmother," Mom said, and they walked away.

Casket. That's a word you don't think you'll hear very often. Especially not in relation to yourself or anyone near to you. Undertaker. Funeral. Burial. All of those words, out of context in normal conversation, like attrition or yolk or parchment. I rolled the words around in my head and imagined them on my tongue. I rhymed them with other words. I focused on them. Casket. Basket. Undertaker. Thundermaker. Bury. Surrey.

Finally my feet were moving and I brushed past the non-poisonous plants to the cherry wood box that held my best friend. The satin inside looked luxurious and soft. The picture frame on the top of the coffin held a snapshot taken of Tony and his family, Gavin, Mac and Rhonda, all smiling from the railing of Grand Canyon.

Then I looked at him.

I stared at that face I loved, that face I knew and wondered what had happened. What did it feel like to want to die? The swirls of red and yellow and orange on the walls of his room and the burning valley came to me. The music and the book and the poem.

"Tony," I whispered. "Wake up, asshole." He didn't move.

I looked up at the ceiling. The tears were hot on my eyeballs. I let them go, they streamed down my temples. How could he have done this? Then I looked back down at him and the tears fell off of my cheeks, onto the satin, turning the white to putty.

When we were nine, Tony's dog, Butterscotch, died. Goddamn, we loved that dog. I remember he had a full, deep gold coat, and he was so warm all the time. I remember how we played with him and ran with him and called him "Butts" until Rhonda told us to stop. Then how he got sick and wouldn't run anymore, then he wouldn't eat and then he went away. One day we came home after school and Butterscotch was just gone. Mac tried to explain it but we really didn't understand. We just cried.

"Tony?" I whispered. "Is Butterscotch with you?"

I didn't feel her step up beside me, but suddenly she was there. Kacie slid her hand into mine. She squeezed it gently. I felt her shoulder behind my own.

Then I said, "Will you bury me next to him?"

She pulled me to her and hugged me. I cried softly on her shoulder then breathed in her smell of vanilla and cried a little harder. She was crying, too, but her breathing remained steady. I felt her tears against my neck but her chest didn't contract like mine. I remembered what it was like to feel her cry. Standing over Tony's casket, in the funeral home, before the burial, there was no one else who could have held me. She knew it. At least, I think she must have.

It's not supposed to end. That's what makes everything so powerful at the time. I mean, in high school, with the classes and the drugs and the skating, you think, "Man, I can't wait to graduate," but when you finally do, it's like, "What the hell happened?"

I don't understand at what point things went from being so goddamned meaningful, from a look, or a kiss, to that thing you did or that thing she said. Now, it's like it means nothing. Now, it's like, why did I ever care about that? You get twenty-two years under your belt and you think, not much really matters in the long run. Like you've had a long run and you know the little stuff is little even if while it's happening it seems like a big fucking deal. Even if, while it's happening, you can't tell the difference between what matters and what doesn't.

Now, you're standing in the parking lot of some bar wishing she would look over his shoulder and want you back and then you're standing over a hole in the ground waiting for them to put your best friend in it forever.

And the truth is none of it really matters in the long run. There is no permanent record and memories of things like kisses and looks and highs on a weekday afternoon. Those memories fade and you're left with a half-empty photo album of things you've done whose details you can ill recall.

Then they put him in the ground.

That's how it went.

It was raining and the water slid down my cheeks despite the umbrellas and the tent and the handkerchief Kacie shoved in my hand. And I thought, "Why does Kacie have a handkerchief?" It wasn't like a Kleenex or a tissue. It was a lacy handkerchief like a prop from a play or something she might have inherited.

It was my turn to speak and I pulled the weathered copy of *The Catcher in the Rye* out of my coat pocket like some god-awful B-movie and stood in front of family and friends and strangers and said, "Tony was my best friend."

I held the book tightly in one hand, pulled the note out of it and tucked the book back into the inside breast pocket of my black coat. I felt awkward and cold, sad and alone. I looked around at all of the faces that mirrored the sadness in my own body and wished desperately for a cigarette.

"He was better than me in a million ways. He always forgave me." I hadn't prepared anything to say and just now felt a pang of anxiety over it, realizing I was supposed to be comforting and reassuring these people about Tony. My Tony, our Tony, the very same Tony that they all loved just as I had loved him and

I wondered if he loved them back. I wondered if he loved me back.

"He left me this." I waved the page a bit and said, "It's a poem. The part I think means the most goes, 'I love you for the part of me that you bring out; I love you for putting your hand into my heaped up heart and passing over all the foolish, weak things you can't help dimly seeing there, and for drawing out into the light all of the beautiful belongings that no one else had looked quite far enough to find.' Tony was like that for me, for all of us," I said, waving at Kacie and Jason and Chris and Joel and Tabby. "He saw only the best parts of us."

After a moment in which I decided I didn't want to be speaking anymore but didn't know how to get out of it, the minister from the day before stepped up to me, clapped my shoulder and murmured, "Thank you, Brian."

I looked at Mac and managed to say, "It shouldn't have happened, Mac. I'm sorry," before I took the preacher's hint and let myself be directed back to a seat.

Kacie stepped past me and I realized I hadn't known she planned to speak. She had a Bible in her hand and began to read without any preface.

"Preserve me, O God, for in thee I take refuge," she read. "I say to the Lord, 'Thou art my Lord; I have no good apart from Thee.' I bless the Lord who gives me counsel; in the night my heart also instructs me. I keep the Lord always before me; because he is at my right hand, I shall not be moved." She took a second to swallow and wipe a stray tear from her cheek. "Therefore my heart is glad and my soul rejoices."

I wasn't entirely sure why Kacie had chosen a scripture. I suspected it had something to do with habit or duty or guilt and I was skeptical.

Kacie added, "Tony has not gone to a place without God, but rather to God Himself."

I smiled at that thought and, as if she'd read my mind, Kacie said, "He's probably already painting the walls." Then she stared at that fucking box like there was something inside she really didn't want to bury.

We all felt that way, I think.

When the minister shooed her off with a gentle pat on the back, too, Kacie came to sit beside me and threaded her fingers through mine. The sky opened up and the rain came down harder and the faces around me began to blur with the mist of the storm. I glanced away from Tony's coffin and saw a red-headed girl I didn't know and a guy standing next to her I'd never seen. I figured they must have worked with Tony at TGI Friday's. They were on the fringe of the tent with an umbrella between them.

The preacher opened his Bible and said, "The Lord is my Shepherd, I shall not want; he makes me lie down in green pastures. He leads me beside still waters; he restores my soul."

I stopped listening. They would put him in the ground after we had all left the premises.

So, we left and Chris and I got high again in the car and the numbness soothed the edges where the hurt had been eating away at me.

Tony's dead, I thought again for the millionth time, trying to make it sink in. We were sitting in the living room at his parents' house, having already tried the kitchen, family room, and back deck.

The hardest part of all would be after we left that place, when we no longer got to wear the visible signs of such hurting and sadness. No one really knew at the time how much it would ultimately hurt. Even if it hurt then, it was that fake, teen-melodrama kind of hurt, that action hurt where we all sort of frowned and cried and pretended not to eat because we were too sad to be hungry.

Television programs, they show emotion like it is supposed

to be. They show people sad and lonely, but the truth is that's how we all behave because we're told that's how sorrow looks. I could go down into his bedroom and sit in his closet among all his clothes and his old skateboarding pads and helmet. I could flip through yearbooks and read notes that people had written to him when he was here among us with a future and decisions to make. I could stand on the stairwell and look at all the pictures of him growing up, remembering having a birthday party for Butterscotch, meeting Santa at the mall, and taking team photos in our Speedo bathing suits. I could do all those television and movie mourning scenes, but it wasn't going to get me there. It was all just fake sadness, surface sadness, the kind you can share with others.

True sorrow wouldn't find any of us, or at least not me, for a while. But on that Friday, I had no way of knowing this wasn't the real way it was going to be, I only knew that Tony could have appreciated that I was doing my best to make it sink in.

Tony is dead.

He's not going to walk in the door, come up from the basement, step out onto the porch, flop into the couch cushions beside me. No amount of moving around that house and remembering him in every place was going to get him back there, too. Eventually we settled into the formal living room under the grandfather clock listening to the symphony of sounds in Tony's house with the added murmurs of sympathizers and clink of dishes from the kitchen. Chris and Tabby filled a few plates and carried a few cups out of the kitchen.

Rhonda had gone upstairs to lie down. Mac was sitting in his recliner in the family room. Gavin lay in a lounge chair near the covered pool out back, his own friends around him. My parents left early and quietly, offering me a ride home which I declined saying I had to go back to Joel's to get Dad's car.

Jason and Joel sat on the step where they'd been yesterday.

Chris and Tabby handed out the food and drinks and then took up opposite corners of the velvet couch. Kacie and I sat in the wingback chairs. No one was touching. No one was making eye contact. We were all just breathing.

It hadn't yet sunk in despite the mantra and the visible way everyone looked so sad and the reminders of him everywhere. It hadn't sunk in and I just sipped punch and nibbled a cracker like I wasn't hungry. But I was starving.

When it is all drab and gray and raining, it's funeral weather, but when the sun comes out around two in the afternoon, and the air is crisp like football weather, it hardly feels like a funeral anymore.

The house had a few guests left. Tony's Aunt Stacey was helping Rhonda put away the casseroles and the half-eaten hors d'oeuvres. They stretched Saran Wrap over the dishes and ripped it at the end with those razors on the box. I escaped to the porch but Kacie wandered back into the kitchen, wanting to offer to help.

"How much longer you wanna stay?" Chris said, settling in beside me.

"Feels hard to leave." I took a drag off of my cigarette and counted the cars parked behind Joel's, along the curb, and across the street.

"Did you see Christian in the bar last night?" Christian Heilman was an old rival, one of those almost-had-her guys that followed Kacie around in high school. He played lacrosse back then and since had developed a nasty habit of chasing sluts and snorting blow. He'd been with the same girl all through school but had never hidden his obsession with Kacie from anyone.

"Did he go to college?" I asked.

Chris pulled another cigarette from his pack and held it between his fingers. "Tech for a while. He played lacrosse. Then he quit, moved back here about a year ago."

"Tony ever see him?"

"Who knows?"

"Did he ask about Tony last night?" I asked.

"Not me."

"Maybe Joel told him."

The wind had died down and the sun was warming the pavement and the legs of my pants. I moved my feet for a little circulation.

"Say, Chris? Think Tony's in heaven or something?"

"A five-year-old could ask that question better than you," he said.

I tried to laugh but nothing happened.

"Probably," he said after a while.

"Believe in that kind of stuff?"

"A little, I guess."

"Tony sure did," I said. "He used to get on me about it all the time. I'd say 'goddamn' and he'd scowl." I shook my head. "I don't know. What did he know anyway?"

"Not much I guess," Chris said.

The front door opened and Joel stepped out onto the porch.

"Gotta light?" He took the lighter I held out, put the flame to his cigarette, and then shoved both hands in his pockets, holding his cigarette between his teeth. "It's still cold," he hissed through pressed lips.

"Tony's board's downstairs," Chris said. "Maybe we skate some later?"

"How much later?" Joel said.

"I dunno. Before dark I guess."

"I'm freezin', man. I'm going inside." I dropped the butt of my cigarette onto the porch and went for the door.

"Did ya have to get high this morning, Brian?" Joel asked suddenly.

"Get right to it, Joel," Chris said.

"He's going inside and I wasn't going to say anything in front of Kacie."

"Like Kacie doesn't know," Chris said.

"Did you?" Joel was looking at me, straight at me, and it seemed like it had been a long time since he'd done that. His brown eyes had the penetrating glare of a cop.

I let my own grey eyes narrow, that feeling of being sick of the judgment crowding out the guilt; just like it had the last day I'd seen Tony.

"Yes." I went inside and straight to the bathroom, turned my back on the vanity mirror, and dropped to my knees in front of the toilet. I imagined the rain coming down on me like it should have, imagined everyone pulling their umbrellas closer to them, not allowing me shelter. I saw Tony lying in a box, not opening his eyes. Then I threw up every last cucumber sandwich I'd eaten. It could only have been five minutes later when I managed to stand over the sink and clean myself up but it felt like hours staring into the commode.

I rinsed my mouth with cupped hands full of water and patted my face with a towel like they do in the movies. I watched myself do all of this in the mirror thinking about what a wimp I had become. Narrating the action in my head as if I were writing the scene for someone else. Thinking about Tony getting high and kneeling beside the toilet. Thinking about Tony wanting to kill himself and wondering, again, what really wanting it felt like.

I checked the toilet to make sure the evidence of my weakness had been flushed away and then exited the bathroom. Lifting my eyes from the floor, I met Kacie's blank stare. Her green eyes were puffy and red and it seemed she was all out of strength.

"You okay?" I asked weakly.

"Should ask you that," she said.

"I'm fine."

"Just a little sick?"

"Yeah."

I sat down at the table near her but I didn't touch her. There was no one else in the kitchen.

"Where'd Rhonda go?"

"Aunt Stacey took her back upstairs to pack."

"They're leaving?"

Kacie nodded. "She is. Going to her sister's for a while."

"And Mac?"

"Haven't seen him."

Tony's kitchen, when it's quiet, sounds like the grind of the dishwasher by the pantry, the tinkling of wind chimes beyond the window, and the ticking of the clock above the sink. There used to be the dripping of the sink, too, but Mac fixed that two summers ago.

Kacie lay her head down on her folded arms, staring out the bay window into the back yard. I reached over and put my hand on her hair, stroking it gently. We sat that way for a few minutes before the front door opened and Joel and Chris came in.

"Where are Jason and Tabby?" Joel asked.

I took my hand from Kacie's hair. "Haven't seen them."

"In Tony's room," she said.

I held a blink a bit longer. Joel glanced at the door and stood still behind Kacie.

Chris said, "I'll go get them."

"Is it time to go?" Kacie asked Joel, lifting her head and looking up at him. I could see fresh tears on her cheeks, her lips shone with them. She wiped them away.

"Yeah, I think so. I think I want to rest at home or something."

"Yeah," Kacie agreed with Joel, "me too."

"Brian?"

"Hmm?"

"What are you going to do?" Joel asked.

"Oh, I don't know. I guess go home. Chris and I talked about skating."

Kacie looked at me for a minute and then said, "In your suit?"

Joel shook his head and helped Kacie to her feet. Her red blouse showed creases on the front and damp spots on the sleeves. She put on her coat and her scarf and Tabby and Jason and Chris came out of the basement.

"We'll catch up with you guys later?" Jason asked Chris.

"Yeah, sure," Chris said.

"Brian?" Jason said.

"What?" I asked, taking my gaze from the window.

"We'll hang out later?" he asked.

"Of course," I agreed.

Then they left, the four of them, out the front door, with Jason holding it open for Kacie and then opening her car door for her and she slid into the leather seat as he closed the door behind her and she would stare out the window, I knew, at Tony's house. And I would sit inside and narrate to myself how all of that went even though I wasn't there to see it happen.

Joel and Jason would take Kacie home and Jason would walk her to the door. But he wouldn't kiss her, that would be awkward. And she wouldn't hug him because she didn't want to be touched, not by him anyway. Or so I hoped.

Chris and I sat at the kitchen table in Tony's house until Mac came downstairs.

"What now?" he asked us. "What will you do now?"

"We'll drink," I said, "and mourn in our own adolescent ways."

"And when you have to go back to San Francisco, and

everyone goes back to school, what then?" He pulled a chair out from the table and sat down, heavily, in it.

"Then we forget any of this ever happened," I said bitterly.

Mac said, "I wish I could leave. Rhonda's going. Says she needs some space." We were all quiet for a few minutes.

"It wasn't easy for Tony, was it, Mac?" Chris asked.

"No. He wanted to leave every time you guys did." He laughed a little bit then. "He loved being in California."

"Why didn't he move out there with me?"

"That I don't know," Mac said. "I'm not sure why he came home at all. He was so happy visiting you and so unhappy here."

"Was this all a surprise, then?" Chris asked. "If you don't mind my asking," he added.

"No, I don't mind. I guess the policemen asked me the same things. I was surprised, of course, sad mostly and then." He stopped there.

Chris was watching Mac, and I was watching his hands on the table. He folded them and unfolded them while he spoke. Then he put his right thumb and index finger on either side of his wedding band and left them there. Chris and I watched Mac's face try to cry, and there were no tears left.

"Rhonda is devastated," he said tightly. "And I can't help her."

More silence and we all shifted gazes to the window and the world beyond it. The sunlight low in the west now cast long shadows over the backyard.

"Can I make you a drink, Mac?" Chris asked.

"Yes," he said immediately. "There's juice in the fridge and vodka."

"In the cabinet under the desk," I finished for him.

"Yes, that's right, under the desk," he said.

Chris stood and retrieved the bottles and poured himself and Mac each a screwdriver. He poured my vodka straight and sat it before me. Mac eyed the glass.

"Straight?" he asked.

"The juice gives me heartburn," I excused.

"Brian drinks all of his liquor straight except for bourbon," Chris said.

"That's the kind of thing Tony would know, right?" Mac shook his head and a small smile perked at the corner of his mouth.

"All of your friends know that kind of thing," Chris said.

"Tell me something about Tony his friends knew."

Chris and I exchanged a look and then he said, "Tony liked redheads."

"Why redheads?" Mac's big hands cupped the cocktail glass between them.

"Because the first girl to break his heart was a redhead and he was addicted to them after that," I answered.

"Who broke his heart?"

"Sheila Andrews," Chris and I said together.

"Ninth grade, he carried her poetry and flowers," Chris said.

"Bad poetry," I clarified.

"Right, bad poetry." Chris laughed a little and Mac smiled.

"What did he drink?"

"Captain and Coke," Chris said, "when he had money. And draft Miller Lite when he was broke."

I tried to remember Tony drinking, but mostly I kept seeing him getting high, being high, asking me if I wanted to get high.

"I thought he was on meds, Mac?" I said. "In therapy?"

Mac looked at me then. His face had aged in just the last two days. His blue eyes were deep with despair.

"He hadn't been to therapy for a while. Kept skipping appointments. I don't know about his prescriptions, seemed like he never got them filled. He said one drug made him ache and another made him feel too tired. Never could get the right one to . . ." He drifted off but I knew the end of the sentence was "fix him," and I knew there was no such drug.

I thought back to the last time Tony and I had talked about his therapy, treatment, meds, whatever he was doing to address what he always called his headaches. It had been a really long time. Maybe before the summer even. I couldn't remember what we'd been talking about instead but it was probably me.

"What about his paintings? What made him paint?" Mac asked.

I shrugged. "He told me he painted because he couldn't write." I thought about the burning valley, that sense of elation and awe he'd had standing on that broken stone wall.

"He told me once that he became someone else when he painted," Chris said. "Maybe he did it to be someone else." He had discarded his jacket and tie, and the button-down shirt sleeves were rolled up his forearms.

"Weird thing about that is that his paintings are more purely him than anything else in the world," I said.

"They are, aren't they?" Mac asked. Earlier, he'd changed out of his suit and into a sweater, something Rhonda had probably given him for some holiday or birthday.

I finished my vodka in a quick swallow and got up for another one. The chair pushed away from the table with a scrape on the floor. I looked down and Mac did, too, as if watching the chair leg scratch the surface, but the wood floor bore no mark. I didn't push the chair back in, only walked around it to the counter where Chris had left the vodka.

"Rhonda wanted to send Tony to an arts school when he was in sixth grade," Mac said. "Bet you didn't know that?" he asked, watching me move around the table with the bottle in one hand and my glass in the other.

"No," I admitted.

"He wouldn't go. Said he couldn't leave you." Mac shook his

head and I poured another shot. "Amazing the kind of loyalty that kid was capable of. Think he got his share of heart and more." Mac shoved his glass across the table.

I filled it. I hadn't brought the juice and when I looked up at him, he shook his head as if to wave it off.

Chris said, "First time Tony and I met he was rescuing some funny-looking kid from bullies. I can't remember his name. He was slow and the other kids picked on him. But Tony, he just walked up and told them all to leave that kid alone. The bullies, they were older than us, and Tony was so little, but he didn't care."

"No, he didn't care." I smiled, remembering Tony's eclectic group of acquaintances throughout high school. "People were drawn to him."

"He was kind," Mac said. "Said he wanted to love people like Jesus did."

"He tried," I said. "Forgave my ass for some pretty bad stuff."

"We were always so occupied with Gavin. What trouble he was causing, how to get him back on the right path. We never talked about what all that was doing to Tony." Mac sipped at the glass, his lips glistening with liquor.

Tony and I once heard Mac tell Gavin he was tearing the family apart.

"Look what you're doing to your mother! To your brother!" Mac had yelled.

I had stared at Tony in the darkness of the upstairs hallway. His blue eyes shone with tears. "I wish he would leave me out of it," he'd whispered. I wasn't sure if he meant his dad or Gavin. We were twelve. Not long after that, Tony found a pack of cigarettes in Gavin's room and broke every one of them. Gavin knew, of course, that Tony had done it and when he asked him about it, Tony told him to quit or he'd tell Mac and Rhonda. But he never told them anything he learned or knew or heard about Gavin.

The early evening shadows crossed the back yard and climbed up onto the deck. I could see the railing of the deck darkened by its own shadow and the pool beyond holding the long deep shadows of leafless trees. Gavin and his friends had gone and the lounge chairs were stacked by the diving board.

"Where did Tony get that poem?" Chris asked me.

"A book his grandfather gave him when he was seven," Mac answered. "An anthology of America's best-loved poetry. He had a hundred bookmarks in it and was always discovering a new 'best one.'" He smiled. "What did you call it?"

"The shittiest poetry in America," I said. "Sappy, cheesy stuff. But man, he loved it."

"He sure did," Mac said. "God, I'm gonna miss him." Mac's voice cracked a little and he raised his glass and downed the entire drink.

"Me, too," I said. Chris nodded. I finished another shot and poured a third. I pushed the bottle across the table. We heard Aunt Stacey come down the stairs. We heard the dishwasher change cycles and the icemaker drop another batch. We sat there with Mac for a while. Then we left.

All of those songs that build adolescent fantasies are lies. The love of a lifetime, the bed of roses, the end of the road, those songs that tell about a love that does not die, a love that engulfs a person, seduces a person, those are all lies. The truth as I have come to find out, is that the only love worth living for, worth dying for, is made for movies and sappy songs. And the people that write them want it as desperately as the rest of us. But none of us have it.

Then those who claim to have it are living those adolescent fantasies and have yet to find the truth, which is that love is less about what you do and more about who you are.

So, I loved her. I thought I did. Anyway, I loved her with all that I was then. But no such love really exists. If it does, it shouldn't leave and if it leaves, it wasn't real. The only thing real is the very real hole where that pretend love used to be, that very real emptiness where I had once filled myself with adolescent fantasy.

If ever I grew up and out of that pretend love I would wish that I hadn't lived so long in it and with it because it was never what it claimed to be. I'd have no one to blame on that account but myself. I knew that then, leaving Tony's house with a mild buzz after a conversation I never thought I'd have. I knew love had been defined for me long before the music, the sex, and the drugs had fucked it all up. I knew it was in the last page of that velvet book and I knew we'd put it in the ground that day.

Mac said Tony liked baseball when he was a kid and then had stopped liking it sometime between fifteen and nineteen.

I told him I thought Tony quit liking baseball when we were twelve and he threw up after too many hot dogs at the old Baltimore stadium. They built Camden Yards when we were in high school, but Joel and I could never get Tony to go up there with us.

Mac said he had forgotten about that throwing up thing. Chris asked why that would make Tony hate baseball. I told him that was just the way Tony was and Mac agreed. For Tony, nothing was independent of the circumstances that surrounded it. Sex was only good with certain lighting, people, and places. Music was only good with certain bands, in certain company, and under the right mind-altering drugs.

Tony liked Van Halen in the mornings, to get started. He liked the inspirational stuff like "Dreams" and "Right Now." He preferred to hear sacred songs like the Cure's "Lovesong" by himself. He liked 311 on acid and bar music like Fighting Gravity on Mary Jane.

I kept the latter part of this monologue to myself. Mac needn't know about his son's drug preferences. It seemed irrelevant at the kitchen table. But I narrated these things internally as I went home that day. Chris took me by the Lincrests' but we didn't go inside. I got into Dad's car and drove home.

Mom had gone back to work but Dad was there when I got there. He had changed clothes and was watching sports on television.

I sat down on the couch, staring out the back window through the sunroom toward the yard. The daylight was nearly gone and the room was dim with no lamps on. The television glowed, coverage of a golf tournament somewhere that was bright and sunny. The volume was so low I could barely hear the announcers, and, as I reached for the remote control, Dad looked at me.

"Tony once told me that he couldn't beat you at anything," he said.

"He couldn't."

"He was ten at the time and climbed out of the pool after a race. I was his timer, and when he saw you'd finished before him, he said to me, 'I can't beat him at anything'."

"What did you say?"

Dad thought for a moment. "I said 'you'll get him next time.' That's what I always said to him after you beat him. 'You'll get him next time' like he ever had a shot at it." He was staring at the television.

"Winning wasn't that important to Tony," I said.

"No, I guess it wasn't." He was looking at the TV but his gaze was far away as he said, "The worst part is I was always glad he'd lost to you."

I watched him breathe for a minute and then said, "Of course you were."

"You couldn't give him one win, could you?" he asked me, looking at me now.

"No, Dad, I couldn't," I said plainly.

The afternoon sun would have lit the room with soft maize but it was long gone and the evening's bruised purple blinked in and out of the TV's fluttering glow. The walls soaked the purple up hungrily. The picture frames wore shiny glares of the TV light, animated, and the mantle seemed taller in the shadows of the room. It would be full dark soon and another day would have come between me and Tony's death.

"Are you eating dinner here?" Dad asked.

"I guess so."

"What are we having?"

"I don't know."

"Why did you do it?" he asked me.

"Do what?"

"The drugs, why did you do it?"

"It's not like one random incident, Dad. It's not like failing a test or skipping a class."

"I don't know how to talk about this," he said, still staring, glassy-eyed, at the TV.

"Then let's don't." I pulled a pillow from behind me and laid it on the coffee table. I settled back deeper into the couch. My one foot pushed the shoe off the other and then I had only my socks on. I stretched my legs up to the coffee table and propped them on the pillow.

Silence again for a while before Dad said, "When I saw Mac, I didn't know what to say."

"I know."

"What did you say?"

I shrugged. "I told him that Tony hated baseball because he once threw up after too many hot dogs at an Orioles game."

"Is that true?" He was looking at me again.

"Sure it's true."

"What was the score of the game?"

"What game?"

"The game you were at when Tony threw up."

I could have pretended it was an odd question, but I knew my father well enough to know he cared about stuff like that.

"Dad, I was twelve. I went to hundreds of Orioles games."

"But that game."

"I honestly don't know," I said.

"You knew he threw up."

"I know a lot of things about Tony. I know he liked New Kids on the Block when we were in fifth grade. I know he played shortstop for the Sterling Wildcats for three games before faking a knee injury and riding the bench. I know he lost his virginity to a girl he'd met just two hours before he saw her naked. What does any of that mean now?" I shook my head and played with the tie I had removed a few hours ago, folded in my lap.

"The score of the game, Brian. What was the score of the game?"

"Five-one, Yankees."

I'd like to say that was one of the tickets Kacie had put in our scrapbook which she gave me for Christmas two years ago and that is why I remembered it. But that game was before Kacie. I knew the score because, as it turns out, I care about that stuff too.

Dad and I talked a little bit about the Yankees in the late 80's and early 90's and decided that if Steinbrenner was still interfering in daily baseball business, he was hiding it awfully well. Then we talked about the Super Bowl and where had I watched it and what did I think of the pass coverage and all that.

At last he said to me again, "Why did you do the drugs, Brian?"

"Because I could, Dad. Is that reason enough?"

"No."

"Yeah, I didn't think it would be."

"But you didn't get dead." My dad sighed a long, tired sigh that seemed like all of the air he had inside of him. Maybe he had been holding his breath the whole time.

"I can't punish you. You aren't dead. It was wrong of you to lie to your mother and me and put yourself at risk that way. Do you understand how stupid that stuff is?"

"I understood three months ago and quit."

"And this new girl, this Melissa, does she do any of that?"

"No. She's a just-say-no girl."

Dad nodded. "There is not much I can do, is there?"

"No," I said. We were quiet then, him staring at the TV and me watching the backyard disappear into the darkness, and the reflection of us in the family room taking over the glass door.

"Why are you moving?" I asked.

"Time for a change."

"I'm not ready."

"You will be."

"This is my home."

"This is a house," he said. "You'll always be home wherever we are."

I wanted to believe that, but I knew San Francisco hadn't ever felt like home and it was the only other place I'd ever lived besides Virginia. Instead of trusting him, I felt like my sense of home was lost somehow.

"So, we've talked about it." He collapsed his recliner and stood up. "I'm going to start dinner. Your mother will be home shortly."

I reached up to the lamp on the table between us and turned it on. The warm halo of light fell around me, illuminating me in the window reflection.

Dad stopped on his way out. "Brian?"

"Yeah, Dad?"

"Did you ever want to let Tony win?"

"Every race," I said.

"Thought so." And he left the room.

When we went to Uno that night I had every intention of letting large quantities of alcohol make me forget the day had ever happened.

As we walked in, the bar was packed and I could see over the crowd the pretty blonde bartender from the night before. She didn't see me and I wondered if I had made her feel sorry enough for me to comp my check.

I had fallen asleep on the couch after my talk with Dad. When Mom came in around eight to ask me if I wanted dinner, I had told her no, showered, and left for Uno with Chris. It was nine-thirty and I was high from the bowl we'd smoked on the way over. My stomach was growling so I took a menu from the hostess and carried it to the table with me.

Chris got us beers. Tabby and Joel already had a table, and Jason and Kacie were supposedly on their way.

Joel knew we were high, I think, when we walked in but he didn't say anything in front of Tabby. The Penguins were playing on television. It was the beginning of the second period and we were watching it because we didn't have anything deep or meaningful to say. Then Kacie and Jason arrived. Jason watched the game with us. Kacie and Tabby started talking about Kacie's sorority sister who was getting married and the weddings they had been to and which ones were more lavish than others and what things were essential to weddings and what things were just frivolous.

Chris and I were trading comments about the Caps, who played the night before, their captain, Adam Oates, and his inconsistency when Jason said that Oates was a good guy but he liked Gonchar better.

"Has three hat tricks already this season," Jason said.

"Two of them in the same week," Joel said and it all went on from there, all of us blah-blah-blahing as if, earlier, we hadn't been in the suits we only wore to church, as if we hadn't been hurting for days over something we couldn't have expected or prevented.

I needed to eat so I walked over to the bar. Glancing down the length of it, I saw a red-haired girl I thought I knew. When she smiled at me, I smiled back.

"Who's that?" Chris asked me as I rejoined the table. The restaurant was empty and the music had been turned up to night-bar level. He leaned in to me to be heard, and I looked over his shoulder at the group behind him.

"You don't know her?" I semi-shouted back.

"I don't think so."

"Thought we must, she's been looking this way," I said.

"She's looking at you," Chris said.

I shrugged and reached for my beer. Kacie and Tabby weren't talking now. Kacie had lit a cigarette and was staring out the window onto the street. I wanted to tell her I'd read the last page of the notebook. I decided after I ate, I would move around to her side of the table and tell her, just her. If she'd let me get that close.

I turned back around and saw the hockey game had gone to intermission. I glanced back over the crowd at the redhead to see if she was still looking at me. I thought about Meli and remembered I hadn't called her since yesterday. I wondered what she thought of that. I was still wondering about that when the redhead across the room slid off of her stool, and I could see clearly the guy she was sitting with. He was small in frame and had shaggy brown hair tucked behind his ears. She said something to him, he looked at me, and then she walked toward me.

"Hi," she said. "You don't know me, but I knew Tony."

I looked back to see if everyone at the table was listening. Kacie had stopped mid-sentence. Joel had leaned forward in his chair.

"Did you?" I asked.

"Only just. We met a few weeks ago." She was thin and small and wore a turtleneck sweater that seemed ready to swallow her head. Her hair was short, pixie cut, and she'd spiked it up in the back so it looked like a firework. She wore tiny clips in the front. She bit her lip like she had forgotten what else she came over to say, and I watched her pull the sleeves of her sweater down over the heels of her palms.

"I heard you speak today," she said, "and I wanted to tell you—all of you," she turned her eyes on each of my friends, "that I'm sorry about what happened." She had to shout the words and I wasn't sure how much everyone else heard.

I heard Kacie say, "Thank you."

The girl looked at me again and managed a weak smile. "He was a good person."

"Yes, he was," I agreed, a tightening in my chest ready to force a cough.

"Well, see ya." She turned around and walked toward the dining side of the restaurant. I watched her retreating back, saw her step down the three small stairs near the hostess stand, pull a coat off the rack and shove her arms into the sleeves. Then some people stepped between me and her, and I blinked and turned back to the table.

"Weird," Joel said.

"How do you think she knew him?" Tabby asked.

"Tony loved those redheads," Chris said with a faint smile.

"Brian?" Kacie asked.

I looked at her and she was asking me who that girl was, but neither of us spoke. I took another drink of my beer and looked back at the hockey game. It was still at intermission, though, and there was no escaping the conversation.

"What did she say her name was?" Tabby asked.

"She didn't," Jason said.

"Do you know her, Brian?" Kacie asked.

"No," I said.

"Maybe he worked with her," Chris suggested.

"He did just start that new job," Joel said.

"At Friday's," Kacie said. "He was working at Friday's."

"Maybe that's how she knew him," Tabby suggested.

"Probably," Jason agreed. "Anyone want a shot?"

"I'll get it," I said and walked over to the bar, having to push between a few people to reach the turned backs of the people on the stools.

It was ten-thirty and I'd had about four beers and the little bit of weed and one more shot before the one I ordered then. The bartender's name was Ashley, which I thought was very cheerleader-ish and cute. I apologized for my behavior the night before and she cocked her head to one side and said, "What do you mean?"

I thought that was a good way for her to handle it.

Just then my sandwich arrived so she handed it to me with a black napkin roll-up of silverware. I asked for shots and Ashley said she would bring the shots to the table since there were six of them. I went back to the group and in a few minutes she came from behind the bar with a tray.

"What's this?" Jason asked.

"What does it look like," I said.

"Jager," Kacie said distastefully.

"Right," I said.

"I don't want any, thanks," she said.

"Not even for a toast?" Joel asked.

"She doesn't drink it," Jason supplied.

"Not since high school when I got really sick on it and threw up for two days," Kacie said. "He knows that."

I shrugged. "Chris can have yours," I said and turned to look at Joel but caught Tabby's look instead. She was shaking her head and mumbled something I couldn't hear.

"Brian can have it," Kacie said. "You bought it."

"Oh, of course I did," I said and took the glass from in front of her.

She didn't look mad, just a little annoyed, and I thought maybe she hadn't really wanted a shot anyway, so this had saved her from having to decline. When she met my glance, I thought she was almost smiling but it passed as quickly as it had come. She reached toward my plate, took a French fry from it, and stuck it in her mouth. She leaned closer to Tabby, listened to what she had to say, but her face didn't change.

I was standing on the bar side of the table with Jason on one side and Joel on the other. Kacie and Tabby had the only chairs on the window side and Chris stood between Kacie and Jason. I looked over her shoulder to the window and could see the sidewalk and streetlamp outside. Then I focused on her again, but she had turned her attention back to Tabby.

"What should we drink to?" I asked. Everyone except Kacie reached into the center of the table and took a shot glass.

Chris said, "I propose that from now on, every time we buy a round of shots, we buy one for Tony."

"Let's," said Joel.

"So we'll always remember him," agreed Kacie.

"So we'll always remember him," repeated Jason.

"If he has a shot then we can't toast him," I said. "What would he toast?"

"Burning skies and angel's wings," Kacie said.

"Of course, to burning skies," said Joel, raising his shot in the center of the table. "And angel's wings," he finished and we all raised our own glasses.

I saw Tabby's lips move, saying, "What does that mean?" but she'd asked Joel so I ignored her. He pointed up; he must have been reminding her about the ceiling in Tony's room which she'd seen today for probably the first time.

"Salud," I said and we all drained our shot glasses and Kacie drank her beer.

"Who will take Tony's?" Chris asked.

"Why let a good shot go bad?" I asked.

"Take it, Brian," Joel said. "You did good today, take it."

So I drained the ghost Tony's shot, too, and looked across the room thinking maybe the game had started again but it hadn't yet. Then I saw the guy with the shaggy hair and he was looking at me. He stood up from his chair, the girl was gone now to some other place, and he walked toward me, leaving his beer behind. There was a crowd between us, and I don't think anyone else saw him until he arrived at the table.

"Brian?" he asked.

"Yes?" I turned and faced him, we stood toe-to-toe and he was a little taller than me so I looked up a bit.

"I'm Eric Waters."

"Okay," I said.

"I knew Tony."

"Okay," I said again.

"You were at the funeral today," Tabby said.

Eric Waters looked at her and said, "That's right."

"Can I help you with something?" I asked, feeling a bit like he was standing too close and looking a little too long at my Crew, my friends, our place.

"Just wanted to say I'm sorry for your loss and he was a good guy and all that shit," Eric Waters said. His voice was flat, devoid of sentiment in any of the words except *shit*.

"Yes, he was," Joel said for me because I didn't speak.

"How did you know Tony?" Tabby asked.

"Did you work together?" Kacie supplied.

"Haven't we met?" Eric Waters asked Kacie.

"No, I don't think so," she said and looked down.

Jason said, "Okay, thanks, man."

Eric Waters glanced at each of us. "Tony never mentioned you," he said to me.

"Never mentioned you either," I said.

"Did you go to Herndon?" Tabby asked.

"No," Joel said, "no, you didn't, did you?"

"I was a year behind you guys at South Lakes."

"And how did you say you knew Tony?" Tabby asked.

"He didn't," I said tightly.

"No," Eric Waters said, absently scratching the back of his neck. "I didn't."

"Here," Jason said, "the game's back on."

"Need a beer, Brian?" Chris asked, coming around from behind the table and standing to my right, next to Jason.

"Sure," I said faintly, still watching Eric Waters who was looking at the television, his eyes droopy like he was sleepy or bored or high.

Turning back to me, he said, "I was with him."

I didn't look this time. I knew everyone was paying attention.

Tabby said, "Did he just say he was with him?"

"Yes," Kacie hissed.

"With Tony?" Jason asked.

"When?" Joel demanded.

"On Monday."

Then it felt like the music stopped playing and the bar crowd shut up and not even Tabby had anything to say. I felt a deep silence like not breathing. I counted the days since Monday: Tuesday on the phone with my Dad, Wednesday on the airplane, Thursday in his bathroom, Friday beside his casket, Friday over his grave. Today. Today, earlier, hours ago, me in the rain, standing over the end of him.

"You saw him?" I asked.

"Yes," Eric Waters said. "We were in the bar and he said, 'Let's get high.' We went to his house and we cooked some. Got high."

"And then what?" Joel asked.

"And then I left."

I turned away from him slowly and pushed through the crowd. Stumbled down the three steps at the hostess stand, past the coat rack in the vestibule, and out into the fresh air of the February night. I fell out of the door of the bar and sucked that cool Northern Virginia air into my lungs, exhaling a long stream of steam into the night sky. Tipping my head back on my neck, I stared at the street lamp above and the stars beyond it but what I saw was the ceiling in Tony's bedroom full of burning skies and angels' wings.

"Brian?" said a voice, and it was the redhead. She stepped up the curb toward me. "What happened?" She looked into the window and apparently saw Eric Waters still talking to my friends because she said, "Did he say something to you?"

"He said he was there," I answered in more fragments and deep breaths than that.

"Only for a little while," she said quickly. "We all just got high and then . . ."

"You were there, too?" I asked.

"With Eric," she said. "Well, not *with* Eric, but he was my ride and when he left, I did, too." She had her hands shoved deep into the pockets of a grey coat. A purple scarf puffed up underneath her chin and a matching purple hat was pulled down low on her forehead.

Just then Joel came through the door with Eric Waters in tow.

"Tell him what you told me," he demanded. "Tell him!" he shouted when Eric Waters stalled. Joel shoved him forward. Eric looked at the redhead and then at me.

"Tony said he didn't think anyone would notice if he . . . if he . . ."

"If he died!" Joel burst. "Tony said he didn't think anyone would notice if he died. That sonovabitch." Joel left me there with those strangers and he went back into the bar. I could see him through the glass, talking to our Crew.

Kacie stood and started to come outside, but just then Chris returned from the bar with two fresh beers. He told her something before grabbing his coat and coming outside.

"I'm sorry," Eric Waters was saying. He had a coat in his hand and lifted it as he spoke, shaking it over his shoulders and shoving his arms into it.

"Me, too," said the redhead.

"Who are you?" I snapped at her.

"Veronica," she whispered, scared and more than a little fucked up.

"You have the last words of my best friend and *you're* trembling," I said harshly.

"It's cold," she whined.

"Did you fuck him?" I asked her.

"What? When?" she stammered.

"Asshole," said Eric Waters.

"Yeah, pretty much," I seethed.

Chris came outside then, looking from me to Eric and back at me. "Hey, man," he said softly. "Maybe you should come back inside."

"I didn't know," Eric Waters said, rubbing his chin where a few days of patchy stubble grew, "what to do," he finished lamely.

"Someone says that no one would notice if they died, and you didn't think anything weird about it?" I asked, incredulous.

"Man, I wasn't his shrink."

"No, you were his dealer."

"Man, look." Eric Waters held his hands up flat between us.

"Was it your stuff? Was it your stuff you cooked, or his?" I asked.

"Does it matter?"

"Just answer me," I said. "Was it your stuff?"

"Yeah, but—"

"And you're on it now, aren't you?" I asked.

"What?"

"You're on it now," I repeated. The idea of the same drug in his veins right now, still pumping blood, still breathing, infuriated me.

"Man, look," the guy said again. "I didn't know him that well. I only sold to him a few times and he was cool, you know, liked to party, always had cash, and he liked Veronica, so we hung out."

My hand reached out and grabbed him by the neck. I pushed him up against the glass at Uno and stared into his droopy eyes, which kept rolling from side to side like he was trying to stop the spins. He wasn't struggling. My forearms pinned his shoulders and our faces were so close he couldn't see anything but me.

"What are you up to now? Twice? Three times a day? How much does it take?" I pulled him toward me and then shoved him against the glass again. His head lolled back and struck the window. I had him at arm's length now but he still wasn't struggling.

"Look, dude, that was Tony's problem, not mine," he mumbled. "Tony didn't know when to say when, you know?"

I hit him. I cracked him with my right fist clear across the eye so that his face slammed the window to his right.

"Brian!" Chris said, pulling on my shoulder.

But I hit Eric Waters again, thinking about that first time and tying that rubber on Tony's arm and watching his veins throb in the crook of his elbow. I shoved my fist into his gut for the image of Tony's teeth gripping a syringe.

Then Jason came out of the bar, and he and Chris pulled me off of Eric Waters who slumped to the sidewalk in front of the window. I looked through and saw Kacie looking at me. I pressed my palm to the glass and leaned my weight into it.

"Brian, let's go." Jason pulled on my arm, turned me away from the building.

I stumbled a little trying to step over the crumbled Eric Waters. Then I looked at Veronica, who was still trembling and said, "Leave. Take him. I'll cover your bar tab." I followed Chris inside and saw Jason behind me helping Veronica get Eric Waters to his feet.

When I reached the bar, Ashley was pretending she hadn't seen me hit that guy until I said, "I keep making bad impressions on you," and managed a smile.

"I'll give you a chance to make it up to me before it's all over," she said. She gave me half of the contents of a silver shaker and poured the other half for herself. We took the shot and she gave me a bar towel full of ice for my hand.

"I'm going to cover their drinks," I said, indicating the window through which she'd seen Eric and Veronica on the sidewalk.

"Thanks," she said. "I'll just add it to yours?"

"No, let's settle it now." I tossed her a fifty-dollar bill and she handed me a twenty back. "Tip?" I asked.

"You'll get me later," she said and then went to speak with another customer, but not before dropping her eyelids low and giving me the sexiest look she had.

When I returned to the table, Kacie was gone. Tabby said she'd had a headache and Jason had taken her home.

"You okay?" Joel asked.

I shrugged. "Still hungry," I said, looking at my sandwich left sitting on the plate. Chris indicated the chair Kacie had vacated and slid the plate toward it.

"Sit and eat," he said.

I climbed up into the seat next to Tabby and felt her stiffen but she didn't say anything. Half of my fries were gone and that made me smile.

"The French fries didn't help her headache?" I said.

"The fight didn't help her headache," Tabby said.

"That got out of hand," I admitted, shoving half the sandwich in my mouth in one bite. It had cooled and the cheese was thick and rubbery but it was good anyway. I hadn't eaten since I'd puked at Tony's house. With the first bite, I realized how hungry I was.

"That guy fucking deserved it," Joel said.

"Seriously, what was that dude trying to prove?" Chris asked.

"What else could he have expected coming over here with that story?" Joel said.

I chewed and drank my beer and listened. My hand was swollen but I couldn't eat and keep Ashley's ice pack on it, so I'd put the ice pack aside.

I saw a glass of water in front of Tabby.

"Not drinking anymore?" I asked.

"Someone has to drive," she said shortly.

"Going to piss," Joel said in response, and walked down the

hall toward the men's room. Chris went, too, though without announcing it.

I looked at Tabby who was watching them walk away.

"What the fuck is wrong with you?" she said.

"Excuse me?"

"You're trouble, Brian."

"Okay. Guess you answered your own question then."

"But everyone worships you," she continued, as if I hadn't responded. "They defend you. They think you're some kind of goddamned hero."

"Except you."

She glared at me. I wanted to move away from her, but there was nowhere to go. My back was against the window and my food was in front of me. I looked down at the plate.

"Okay, Tabby. Say whatever it is. Now's your chance." I took another bite and looked up at the hockey game.

"You're selfish, Brian," she said. "You don't think about anyone except yourself. I don't understand why they all put up with it, but they do." She drank from her water, looked around like she wished someone else was there to interrupt. "Kacie's the worst. God, she's a mess. I told her not to go to the airport yesterday. She never fucking listens. But Joel, too. He says you're the Captain but he doesn't explain what that means other than it excuses your bad behavior."

I smiled at the Captain remark. When we'd all skated together, we'd been the Crew, and I was the Captain. This was around the time of *Dead Poets Society* in which Robin Williams played a rogue teacher at a boys' school who inspired his students to think beyond the predetermined scripts for their lives. He was fired for being subversive and they'd recited the Whitman poem, "O Captain, My Captain," to him in homage. Then, after we'd entered a contest and the organizers asked who our team captain was, the phrase stuck to me. Can't say I was ever really the right pick, but I was the best skater and I guess that was sufficient.

"You know I almost made the X Games," I said.

Another glare.

"True story. Qualifier in Miami. Went down, skated. Didn't make it. Terribly disappointed." I shoved a French fry in my mouth. "Still recovering." Then I took a long drink from my beer, which was nearly empty.

"Grow up, Brian," Tabby snapped.

I wiped my hands on my napkin, shifted the plate a little.

"I'm trying," I said.

She stared at me, her almond eyes narrowed. Seemed as if she was wondering if I was telling the truth. I'd seen that glare before. Arms folded, one over the other, on the edge of the table. Lips pressed tightly together. Disapproval.

"It's not easy," I admitted.

Her fingers clenched her elbows and she sat back in her chair. Then she said, "Try harder." And looked away again.

We stayed until the bar closed, Joel and me and Chris finishing the hockey game, Tabby patiently finishing two more waters. This time it was Joel who got loaded; he and Chris took several more shots. After I'd finished my food, though, I was less inclined.

When the florescent lights came on, we all filed out. I left Ashley a sizeable tip and promised to return the next night. She leaned over the bar and whispered something dirty in my ear about what she'd do for me later, but I told her that night wasn't the night. I took a rain check for Saturday and followed Chris and Tabby and a wobbly Joel out the door.

"Brian," Joel said, "Brian. I love you, man." He clasped me tightly in a hug and I hugged him back. "On New Year's, I was wrong."

"Don't worry about it," I said.

"No, dammit, listen," Joel said and it came out as a slurry stream of syllables. "I should have believed you."

"Joeler, dude, just go on home." I hugged him again and then opened the SUV door for him. I looked back at Chris. "It's been a while since we've seen him in this fine form," I said, helping Joel up into the passenger seat.

I stood between him and the open door. He looked down at me and his eyes were glassy. He smiled. "I love you, man," he said again.

"You're not wrong about me," I said quietly, so only he could hear. Then I backed up, clapped him on the shoulder, and stepped out of the way.

"It's been a while since he's been this way," Tabby said, closing the door for him and walking around the front end.

"Goodnight, Joeler!" Chris shouted through the passenger window. Joel lolled his head to the side and grinned stupidly at us. "Third shot of Jager?" Chris asked.

"Fifth," I said. "It was definitely the fifth one that did him in."

We were smiling at them even though Tabby seemed pretty pissed. Chris and I waved as their car pulled out of the lot, then sauntered toward my father's car sitting lonely on the edge of the parking lot under a tall street lamp. Because Chris had driven the two nights before, I had driven that night which gave me the freedom to decide where I was going rather than home.

I took Chris home and in his driveway I said, "Hey, man, do you think I'm trouble?"

"Yup."

"Seriously?"

He laughed. "Nah, man, not any more than any of the rest of us. But that fight tonight. Shit. That was outta hand."

"Yeah," I rubbed my knuckles, which had lost the swelling but had begun to bruise. "What about selfish? Do you think I'm selfish?"

Chris blew out a stream of air that sounded like, "pfffffft," and reeked of booze and I laughed.

"All right. So, I'm a little selfish."

He held up his hand, showed a pinch, and said, "A little. But look, man, it's cool. We know you don't mean anything by it. It's just you."

I thought about that for a second and said, "That doesn't make it okay."

Chris grinned. "Man, I'm fucked up. Lemme go. See ya tomorrow?"

"All right," I said.

He opened the car door and got out. Before he closed it, he leaned back inside and said, "Tell Kacie I hope she feels better."

"What? I wasn't even."

"We all know you, man." He closed the door then and I waited until he made it into his dad's house before pulling out of the driveway.

I wasn't ready to go home and Tony's basement wasn't an option. I walked through 7 Eleven in a fluorescent haze and emerged with two bottles of Gatorade, a bag of M&Ms, and a new box of cigarettes. Then, as predicted, I ended up at Kacie's sister's house which was where she always stayed when she came into town. Audrey's house was dark and empty, but open, so I entered, locked the door behind me, and took the stairs two-at-a-time to Audrey's room. That's where I found Kacie, sitting against the headboard, flipping through channels on the television. It was well after two a.m.

"Waiting for someone?" I asked her.

"Just you."

"Knew I'd come?" I asked.

"Everyone knew you would come."

"So Chris said. He also said to tell you he hopes you feel

better." I closed the door behind me and stood over the bed. "It's late," I said.

"I'm not sleeping much this week so it really doesn't matter." There was an empty tumbler on the nightstand and a bottle of Absolut on the floor next to the bed.

"Like your vodka straight?" I teased.

"Same as you," she said.

I tossed the bag of M&Ms at her, sat down on the ladderback chair in front of Audrey's desk, and hit a key on her computer so the screen would come alive. It did, in a bright splash of light and color over the keyboard, the desk, my lap and my hands, which, I noticed just then, were trembling. I took a swig of the Gatorade and screwed the cap back on.

Kacie hadn't touched the M&Ms; they were nestled in the comforter over her legs.

I clicked the computer mouse and found my way through Audrey's desktop to the solitaire program, changed the deck of cards to the fishes and began a game.

"Make yourself comfortable," Kacie said.

"You knew him, didn't you?" I asked.

"Who?"

"Eric Waters."

"I guess so," she said.

"You met him hanging out with Tony getting high." Red seven on black eight. Black six on red seven. Black eight on red nine. Click, click, click.

"I guess so," she said again.

"What does 'I guess so' mean?" Red ten on black jack. Black nine on red ten.

"It means I don't remember all that much about hanging out with Tony when we got high." She turned the volume up on the television now. The bed covers were bunched over her legs, one leg out and bare in the glow of the TV and computer screens.

Her skin looked blue and ghostly. "I don't remember all that much about the last six months at all."

"You remember Jason," I said immediately.

"Can we make this fight about one thing, Brian? I can't fight with you about all of it. Pick one thing and we can fight about it and then you can go." She shifted against the headboard, shoving at the pillow that was wedged behind her.

I smiled at the screen. Red three on black four. Ace of spades. Two of spades to the ace. Black four on red five. Red five on black six.

"Let's fight about your coke habit," I said.

"Okay, let's," she agreed. "It was all your fault."

"How?"

"You started with that stuff. I only did it because you were doing it."

"Free will, Kacie, free will. Please, that fight is weak."

"Okay, let's fight about your heroin use. 'I'll never do that, Kacie.' 'Needles weird me out, Kacie.' 'That stuff is dangerous, Kacie.'"

"And it is," I agreed.

"Oh, Brian, please. You think I don't know what you and Tony did last summer?"

"Pretty sure you don't know anything," I snapped.

"Fuck off, Brian."

I reached for the tumbler on her nightstand and she flinched. Lifting the bottle from the floor, I settled back at the desk and kept with the game on Audrey's computer. I waited for Kacie to ask me to leave, but she didn't. The sounds from TV simmered in the room but my back was to it so I stared into the computer screen and we just waited on one another to move. Black six on red seven. Ace of hearts. Two of hearts to the ace.

The room wasn't big and if I had turned, I would have been able to reach over to the television and turn it off. Instead, I leaned toward the lamp on the desk and turned it on. It splashed a warmer light into the room. I looked over at Kacie whose skin no longer looked blue.

"It's a good thing Tony didn't survive that dose," she said absently, "because I'd have killed him myself for taking it."

I glared at her but she wasn't looking at me yet. She was still staring, zombie-like, at the television at the foot of the bed.

"It wasn't an overdose," I said. "You get that, right?"

"The question is, do you get that?" Kacie demanded, finally looking at me. "How do you go around and praise him for his goodness and his honesty? How do you keep saying how wonderful he was, when he did the most selfish thing imaginable?" A tear escaped her eye and dripped down her cheek like melted wax overflowing a candle.

"He was my best friend," I said quietly.

"And you had no idea," she said. She looked away, back to the television, to the covers over her lap, fluffed them a little. "Some best friend," she said.

"So this is my fault?"

"Sure, Brian, it's your fault." Her tone was flat. She took a deep breath through tear-clogged nostrils. They could have been sniffles but sounded more like a bad cold.

I let go of the computer mouse and tipped the vodka bottle over the empty tumbler. In one shot, I emptied it again. Then I poured another one and offered it to Kacie. She tugged a tissue from a box of Kleenex sitting next to her and took the glass I offered. The lamplight showed crumpled tissues in her lap that had blended into the covers in the dimness of the TV light.

Kacie dropped her voice to a lower level than the television and said, "All you've been able to think about is what Tony meant to you."

"What am I supposed to think about?"

She sighed a little, took the vodka down with a gulp, and said,

"I don't know, Brian. Try thinking about Tony. Not your magical mystery Tony who took care of you and loved you but the one who got high by himself on weeknights and sold his prescriptions instead of taking them. Think about the one who dropped out of college continually and lived at home because he kept getting fired from jobs for not showing up." Kacie took a big breath and it sounded like a hiss through her teeth when she said, "Try thinking about the guy who loved one particular redhead, not all of them."

"Which redhead?" I took the glass from her hand and refilled it.

"The one you're fucking in San Francisco." She pinched the Kleenex to her nose and blew, hard, into it. Then she folded it over and pinched and blew again.

I looked away. After what we'd done today, I didn't think we had any tears left and I didn't really know who those tears were for. She acted like they were for Tony but I wasn't convinced.

"Don't bother lying to me, Brian," she continued, waving the snotty tissue in her right hand. "I know all about Melissa. I know all about Tony hanging out there for three months because of her and how you went with her to her parents' house over Thanksgiving and how you've been sleeping with her since the summertime. I know all about it." Kacie laughed, although I didn't think anything she'd said was funny. She glared at me and said, "I knew then."

I didn't have to ask her when. She had known about Melissa when she'd fucked Jason and she hadn't mentioned it until now, now when she knew I wouldn't bother defending myself against it. Now when I didn't have the energy to lie to her any longer.

"Fuck Tony," she said suddenly. "Fuck him for taking the easy way out and leaving us behind. Fuck all of his Christianity that said he wouldn't go to heaven if he killed himself so he did it anyway just to see. Fuck the headaches and the medication and the therapy and him saying he was getting better when he was really getting worse. Fuck all of that because he made us think it was real, and it wasn't, not any of it."

I sat back and sipped the vodka and watched what looked like a mad version of Kacie staring at the TV and babbling incoherently.

"He said he just wanted to love people like Jesus loved people, and he didn't want anyone to feel badly about him. Well, I do. I hate him." She was changing channels quickly now until she finally gave up, threw the remote down, and stared blankly at one that was just electronic snow.

"How can you hate him?" I asked her. "Tony was the only thing you and I have ever had in common."

"Did you love him?" she asked.

"Yes."

"Me, too. It's a shame that wasn't enough to make you faithful to me."

I stood then and walked to the window beyond the bed, standing side-by-side with the television.

"What happened to this fight being about one thing?" I wanted her to look at me, but she just kept staring at the TV. "I thought we had an agreement. I thought we understood one another." Finally, after waiting for her to speak again and not knowing what else I should say, after turning around to look at her and thinking she looked crazy and beautiful at once, I said, "I'm sorry."

"No, you're not," she said immediately. "You're Brian Listo. You're as fucking hot right now as the first time I saw you in that stupid writing class. All broody and deep, like some kind of Heathcliff stalking the halls at Herndon High. Women want you and you want them. It's no different with Melissa. Why should it be? The only person you truly love is yourself."

"I deserve that."

"You think you could've helped him, right? You could've cared enough to call or come home or ask him out there, right? Isn't that it?" Now she looked at me and I thought she hated what she saw. "You think you could've saved him if you'd woken up for five minutes the night he called."

"I wasn't home that night," I said.

"You were sleeping."

"I hadn't been home in a few days." I wasn't sure she saw me anymore. "I stayed at Meli's." I was going to be honest with her from now on.

"You saw his number on the caller ID and chose not to pick up the phone, didn't you?"

"No, I wasn't there."

"You figured you would call him soon and ask what had been so urgent at three in the morning on a Monday, why had he needed you then?"

"Kacie, I just said . . ."

"Maybe you'd come home that weekend and everything would be okay once you two could hang out for a while."

I walked closer to the bed. She was staring at the TV again.

"Kacie? Did he call you?"

The electronic snow was like a strobe light, flickering over her face, pale and streaked with tears. The computer monitor had gone to screen saver and a rainbow triangle floated across the screen, changing shape and size.

"Kacie?"

"Like an hour before he died," she said softly.

I sat down on the bed.

"I didn't pick up the phone." In a long exhalation, she said, "It was late and I hadn't been sleeping well anyway. So I didn't want to wake up, I'd never get back to sleep. The phone rang a few times and I saw it was Tony. He's called before, and I said to myself I would call him the next day and I did, around ten, and Rhonda answered the phone." She took a deep breath and the tears fell over her eyelids and poured down her face. "And Rhonda said he hadn't made it through the night. I asked if he had been sick and she said in a way and I asked her what happened and she handed the phone to Mac but I knew, right then I knew, and I just hung up."

I watched her hands, gripping the fold of the comforter. I reached for one but she pulled it away. "You can't hurt me anymore, Brian," she hissed. "You want to fight? Let's fight about Tony. You think he's a hero? I think he's a wimp. Had he waited just a few more hours, I'd have been there for him, but he didn't think about me, or about what time it was, or about how hard it was for me to not pick up that phone. He thought about himself, always about himself." She turned her face toward me and glared at me. "Just like you."

"How long had he been thinking about us before then? Years, Kacie." I remembered the letter in the notebook. "He told us."

I saw in her look that she knew I'd read it, but she swallowed the clump of tears in her throat and said, "It doesn't matter. I was his friend. I was," she said, jerking her thumb toward her chest. "I was a good friend." She shook her head and looked back at the TV. "By the time Jason called, I was already packed. I was just waiting for you to call me and tell me. But it was Jason." She ripped another Kleenex out of the box. "I don't deserve this."

"Neither did he," I said.

"Why did he do it?"

"He'd been hurting for a long time." I reached for her hand again, but again she pulled away.

"Do you remember the last time you were in this room?"

I nodded.

"You were so angry with me. You called me a whore."

"I had just found out about you and Jason."

"A *whore*, Brian, you called me a whore."

"I didn't mean it."

"It was the worst thing anyone's ever said to me. My father said it once when he found you in my house, and he hit me when he said it but when you said it, you kissed me."

I remembered. I remembered grabbing a handful of that golden hair and pulling her head back so that her lips were turned up to mine. I remembered kissing her long and hard, thinking maybe she wouldn't taste him anymore if all she could taste, all she could feel, was me. With every touch I thought about how he'd touched her and it made me sick inside myself, and yet I'd kissed her anyway. I'd treated her like the whore I thought she was. She had given herself to me, thinking I was forgiving her, but I wanted to punish her. I had made a lie out of us.

Kacie shook her head slowly. "That was the worst thing anyone had ever done to me. Until Tony called me Monday."

"I'm sorry."

"No, you're not," she said again. "You're not ever sorry for anything you do." She blew her nose into the Kleenex and crumpled it up. "You're the best at what you do, why apologize for that?" She laughed, short and raspy, and then stared again at the television. "Even if it does make you the world's biggest asshole."

"Kacie," I said, reaching for her hand. When she pulled away for the third time, I seized the remote from her and turned the TV off. The room was darker now, although still lit by the lamp on the desk, a candle on the nightstand and three on the dresser.

Her eyes met mine.

"It is not your fault Tony is dead," I said. And meant it.

"No more than it is yours," she said.

"No more than it is mine." But I wasn't sure I believed that.

I picked up the pack of M&M's and tore them open. Kacie held out her hand and I poured a few in. We each took one, mine red, hers orange, and sucked on the candy.

"What now?"

"Now you accept my apology." I reached for the vodka and the tumbler, pulled it toward us, and refilled it. I offered it to her. "It's the only thing I have. It has to be good enough."

She took the glass and drank some. Then she watched me for a second, seemed to read my eyes, my lips, and then said, "Okay." I was surprised to hear it. She seemed surprised to feel it and then she added, "You're not going home."

"No," I said. I took the glass from her, downed the rest of the shot, stood, and walked to the desk. I pushed the monitor button to turn it off and twisted the lamp switch. The room was dark except for the candles. I walked along the foot of the bed to the other side. Sat down, took off my shoes, and scooted backward up onto the bed beside her. Shoulder to shoulder with her against the headboard and poured more candy into my hand. When I reached for her hand, she let me have it. Then her head fell against my shoulder, and I kissed the top of it. I remembered her shampoo instantly. I sucked on another piece of candy to scrub the smell from my tongue.

Kacie closed her eyes and took a deep breath. "I remember these nights," she said softly. "I remember fighting late into the night and then . . ."

"Sex-till-sunrise."

"Yes, *making love*," she said. "Until the sun came up."

I thought about holding her. I thought about what would happen if I kissed her. I held a piece of candy in front of her mouth. She leaned forward and ate it from my fingers.

"I'm kind of drunk," I admitted.

"Me, too," she said.

"Why did you leave the bar early?"

"I didn't want to have this conversation in Uno."

"What conversation?"

She sighed and sat up, pulling her head away from my shoulder. "This conversation," she said. "I love you, Brian, I always have."

"I know that."

"I don't think you do," she said. "If someone knows that someone else loves them this much, how does that someone hurt that other someone so badly all the time?" She was finished crying now. She put the tumbler on the nightstand and collected the crumbled Kleenex in her hand, a wad of them.

"Maybe it's the loving that does the hurting. Like, if you didn't love so much, it wouldn't hurt so much," I said, still staring at the wall.

"Maybe," she admitted. "But an agreement? I mean, we were both cheating." She stood up and walked to the trashcan between the desk and the TV. "We pretended that was okay. But it wasn't." She dropped the used tissues in it and turned around to face me. "It took me a while to admit you didn't love me."

"But I did. I do."

"No, you don't. Not anymore." She wiped a stray tear from her cheek and tugged the cloth band out of her hair. She bent over, pushing all of her hair down and combing her fingers through her long locks. They bounced in space, catching the candlelight. She stood up, flipping the whole mane back like a wild animal. I thought I would lose my mind. Then she clasped all those tousled curls in her fist, twisted them, piled them on her head and secured the band around them. I thought it was the sexiest thing I'd ever seen her do.

"It was real love," I said. "We just didn't know what to do with it."

"So we beat the hell out of it?" she snorted. "Nice. No, I don't believe that. I don't believe even you are capable of that kind of abuse." She smiled a bit, looked right at me, seemed to be considering something about me and then said, "Someday you will love, Brian. You'll really love." She walked back to the night-stand, picked up the vodka, and said, "And I hope that girl fucks you over."

"Oh, that's great," I laughed, popping three more M&Ms into my mouth. "Thanks a bunch, Kace."

Audrey's bed had wrought iron head and footboards and leaning against the headboard was starting to hurt my back. I took the pillow Kacie had wedged between her back and the iron and shoved it behind me.

"Do you want me to stay?"

"Of course I do."

"But?"

"But it isn't like it used to be," she said. "Can never be again. Neither of us is who the other wants us to be." She put the vodka bottle down on the floor again, bent one knee on the bed and leaned toward me on one palm. She reached behind me, tugged the pillow out, and dropped it on her side of the bed. Then she lay down, turned on her side, away from me. I sat against the headboard again and it still hurt.

I had always been me, always been this guy right here, this guy sitting against the headboard, chocolate candy on my tongue, vodka racing through my veins. I slid my legs over the side of the bed and stared at Audrey's closet, my back to Kacie. My head was beginning to pound and I wished I had a bowl to smoke. I pulled my cigarettes out of my breast pocket, stood and moved toward a candle, and lit one with a deep inhale.

"Kace," I said finally, blowing the candle out.

"Hmmm?"

"Are you sleeping?"

"Yeah, right, with you still here? Not a chance."

I smiled to myself, doused the other two candles, and reached to the floor for an ashtray I remembered hidden underneath

Audrey's bed. Pulling it out, sitting down, and balancing it on one knee, I said, "Why not?"

"Don't do this, Brian," she muttered.

"You want me to leave."

"Of course I do."

I smoked quietly on one side of the bed while Kacie lay on the other. We stayed quiet for a while. A tree beyond the window looked skeletal in the moonlight and the shadow of it fell over the closet doors, out of which bulged piles of Audrey's clothes. I let myself remember better times in this room. Me waiting while Kacie got dressed to go out, flipping through magazines or channels on the TV. Me listening to her sing Cranberries and Natalie Merchant songs as the CD player changed discs, dancing around in her black panties and matching bra. In my head I narrated watching her twist her hair into messy knots and buns as the curls spring free, unruly, around her temples and chin.

I finished my cigarette, replaced the ashtray under the bed, and folded the M&Ms closed, tucking them into the breast pocket of my shirt. Then, slowly, I unbuttoned the front of my shirt and removed it, tossing it in the direction of Audrey's clothes. I sat in my t-shirt and jeans waiting for Kacie to move, to say something. She didn't. I stood then and unbuckled my belt and unbuttoned my jeans, dropped them to the floor and stepped out of them. Reaching down for a pillow that had been tossed aside, I crawled back into the bed with her, this time under the covers.

I lay on my back, staring at the ceiling thinking about burning skies and angel's wings for a few minutes. Kacie shifted a bit and I could feel her bare leg up against mine. Rolling onto my side, I propped an elbow up on the pillow and watched her.

She turned over and stared at the ceiling showing me the outline of her face in the candlelight from the desk.

"You torture me," she said softly.

"I know."

She turned her face to mine and we kissed, gently. She tasted like vodka, but her lips were soft as ever. My right hand crossed her belly, clasped her hip, and pulled her toward me. I kissed her again, this time a little harder, a little longer, until I tasted her. She whimpered a bit, and I broke my lips from hers and kissed her neck.

"You know this is not good."

"How can it be?" I asked, but I didn't stop. My fingers pinched the band that held her hair and tugged it out, tossed it aside, as I pressed my face into a tangle of curls.

"We shouldn't," she said, her cheek pressed to mine.

"No, we shouldn't." I slid my hand up under her t-shirt, cupped her breast and then traced down her belly to the edge of her panties.

She kissed my cheek, my ear, my jaw. My lips met hers again and she was pulling on the edge of my t-shirt. I tugged it over my head and tossed it to the floor, then did the same with hers and we were bare against each other, chest to chest, belly to belly. She was beautiful underneath me, her hair fanned across the pillow, her eyes like melted emeralds, and her skin soft and warm.

"I want you," I said, running my palm down the length of her arm and pushing my fingers into hers. Then I folded her arm over her head and held it there. My lips against hers, I touched my tongue to hers, and settled myself, heavy, between her legs.

"There's nowhere," in murmured breaths between kisses.

"Unless you're there," she whispered, closing her eyes and arching her back.

"All the time," I murmured. "All the way."

We smiled and teased each other into nakedness. Convinced that this was the last time ever, I wanted to remember the love we were told we had. The love I had thrown away.

When I pushed inside her, she cried out and fresh tears filled my eyes. She fit me, she always had. Each plane perfectly matched, each move perfectly met. My face buried in her neck, the scent of her filled me and we connected again and again as if there had never been another for either of us and there never could be.

I owed her. So, I made love to her slowly and tenderly, worshipping her. And she let me, took me, accepted me, came with me in trembling pulses of desperation and completion.

What I gave her was all I had left to give.

NEW YEAR'S EVE 1998

I lay back on the bed, staring up at the tapestries and listening to the music. It had been too cold to do anything today and we'd spent most of the afternoon in Tony's room fucking around and waiting for it to be time to go to the twins' house for New Year's Eve.

Tony was painting, a brush in one hand and a rag in the other. He'd dab the end of the brush in some paint, smear it onto the canvas, and then swizzle it in a jar to remove the color, wipe the end on the rag, and choose a different color. There was some kind of method to the layering of color, but if he'd explained it to me I hadn't retained it.

"This music is wearing me out," Chris complained from his seat by the glass doors.

Tony grinned. "I dig it," he said.

"Who is it?" Kacie asked. She was sitting on the bed, against the wall, her legs over mine. Her fingertips were absently stroking my thigh.

AFTER DECEMBER

"Fighting Gravity," Tony said. "They've been playing around here lately. Some gigs with G Love and Special Sauce."

"Bar music," I said.

"Mostly," he agreed.

"Don't you have any Dr. Dre or Jay Z?" Chris asked.

"311 close enough?" Tony said, but Chris rolled his eyes and shuffled the deck of cards.

I looked at Kacie and she smiled and I smiled back, but I had nothing to say to her and she didn't have anything to say either which was kind of weird. She had come to get me that morning with the intention of going to a movie, but we hadn't been able to agree on which one, and we'd gone to Tony's to seek his input and invite him along. Then we'd just stayed there until Chris showed up, too, and we were all just hanging out.

We'd packed a few bong hits and gotten pretty well stoned. The glass bong Tony had was tall and well-crafted and its shaft, when filled, delivered a single hit that would put me down for at least an hour. I couldn't remember when I'd moved last except to lay back on the bed and stare at the tapestries overhead.

Tony, though, hadn't sat still. He'd boxed up some books for Kacie, played a hand of cards with Chris, and then taken one of the canvases he'd prepped last night and begun this latest piece.

Kacie was now flipping through the pages of one of the books from the box and tickling my leg through my jeans.

Chris was playing solitaire on the floor.

"What time are we leaving?" I asked again for about the ninth time.

"I dunno. When did they say we should come?" Chris asked.

"Like eight," Kacie said. "Tabby is cooking a dinner for us before we really get into the boozing." She smiled. "Good to have a foundation, I guess."

It was like Tabby to want to do something adult-like on New

153

Year's. We'd have been happy with takeout or burgers but she'd make it some kind of special occasion.

"Man, I love that," Tony said. "Get all blazed and then eat a really good meal. Nothing better. Is she a good cook?" He was wearing a white t-shirt and jeans and he tugged at a belt loop just then, getting paint on the shirttail.

"Joel says she is," I said.

"Yeah, she is," Kacie said. "She made a couple of things for Thanksgiving."

"Will it be ethnic food?" Chris asked.

"No," Kacie said, but she smiled. "Well, maybe."

I caught her hand on my leg and she looked at me. "You had Thanksgiving with them?" I asked.

"Yeah, I told you that. My parents were gone and Audrey was with her boyfriend." She looked away and let her hair fall into her face. It was like a curtain between us. I reached forward and pushed it back so I could see her.

She turned her face into my palm but I pulled it away as soon as she did, not on purpose really, but it kind of felt that way.

"I'm sorry," I said.

She shrugged. "Nothing to be sorry for. It was very nice there. Got to see Mrs. Lincrest's parents. Didn't know it would be the last time. They're such sweet people."

Mrs. Lincrest's dad had died the week before and she was still in Nannyglow, Pennsylvania, on New Year's. The twins had been gone most of that time, too, but they'd come back yesterday and decided to have the Crew to their place for New Year's Eve. We would all sleep over and hit Amphora in the morning for New Year's breakfast, a tradition we'd started years ago.

I had stayed a little longer in San Francisco and been home just a week by that point. I usually came home for the full break and since I hadn't come home at Thanksgiving my parents were pretty pissed I'd waited till Christmas Eve to fly back. But I told them I had some job opportunities to look into which was about as true as if I'd said I had a cat to care for.

Tony stopped painting just then and grabbed his green velvet notebook off the television stand. He plopped down in front of the stereo and backed the disc up a bit. Then he listened to the song again and scribbled the lyrics in the book.

"Great stuff," he said.

Kacie was smiling at him, amusement on her face like she was watching a cute child or a cuddly animal do something precious.

She caught me looking at her, and we exchanged another pair of awkward smiles.

Moving an ashtray from the night stand to my belly, I lit a cigarette and lay there and smoked, exhaling in long cloudy streams toward the ceiling, occasionally puffing out thick rings.

"Play some Matchbox Twenty," I told Tony. "Something a little bit more lyrical."

"You mean something you know," he said and replaced the Fighting Gravity disc.

"That, too."

An hour later, Tony's canvas was full of colors, Kacie had left to change clothes, and Chris and I were packing another bowl.

Tony went into the bathroom to shower.

"You need a shower?" Chris asked me.

"Nah, but some air would be good."

We went outside and sat on the lounge chairs by the pool. We passed the bowl back and forth and got stoned again.

I remembered the summertime here, when the pool was open, and we'd all lay around in the heat and sunlight. I closed my eyes and thought of Kacie in her bathing suit, swimming through the clear water, diving under, and resurfacing.

It had taken me a long time to figure out how to be in a pool without doing laps and being angry. But she'd come to me in the water, pressed herself against me, felt me against her, and then swam away. I'd never tried to swim with a hard on before.

I didn't share this memory with Chris, and he didn't ask why I was grinning as I stared at the pool cover. He must have thought I was just high, which I was.

I was remembering hanging from the diving board when she wrapped her legs around me. I remembered swimming in the dark, the water picking up the moonlight and the house lights, but mostly being deep and dark and cool. I remembered swimming over to the seat dug into the concrete, sitting in it with Kacie straddled on top of me. In my head I narrated peeling her bathing suit away from her wet skin and kissing her hardened nipples.

I took a deep breath on the pool deck, pulled a cigarette out of my breast pocket, and lit it.

"You okay?" Chris asked.

"Erotic memories," I said.

He laughed.

"It's like that when I'm back. I can hardly be here, in the moment, because all those old moments are everywhere."

"It's homesick," he said. "You're homesick."

"Nah," I said. "I'm just horny."

He laughed again.

"Try not to do anything about that on my pool deck," Tony said, walking up from the basement stairs and catching the last bit of our conversation.

Chris handed him the bowl, but he waved it off.

"We about ready?" he asked. "Jason just called."

I looked up and saw Tony had his coat and backpack on and he'd turned the lights off downstairs and closed the door.

"What did he say?" Chris asked.

"He said not to eat anything, Tabby made dinner. It's ready in twenty minutes."

"Sweet. I'll be ready by then," Chris said, and grinned.

"Me, too." I stood up and faced Tony.

"Is Kacie meeting us there?" he asked.

I shrugged. "I guess so."

He tilted his head a little at me.

"What?" I asked.

"Could ya make an effort?"

I started to walk past him, but he stepped in front of me.

"Brian."

"I know, Tony. Shit. Come on. I'll call her."

I heard Chris ask Tony what that was all about as I went down the stairs and into his room. I didn't turn on the lamp, just lifted the receiver on the phone and dialed Audrey's house. The phone rang four times and no one answered. I hung up and went back out, slid the door closed behind me, and climbed the stairs.

I raised my arms to either side. "No answer."

He shook his head and turned to leave.

Chris followed him and I did, too, and we walked around the outside of the house to the driveway. As we approached Chris's car, Kacie pulled in behind it.

I walked to her passenger door and opened it, sat down in the seat and said, "Perfect timing."

"You guys leaving?" she asked.

"No. Well, yeah. But not without you."

"Right." She put the car in reverse and backed out of the driveway.

We drove to the Lincrests' which was just a couple of streets over. Tony's parents had moved over here when we were in high school but before then we had taken a path through the woods from Joel's house to ours. My parents' house was still beyond a thick cluster of trees from Jason and Joel's. I didn't think I could find my way through it now, the path was about a mile and half long, but it probably wasn't as dark as I remembered it. There were enough houses and street lamps to almost fully illuminate that cluster of woods. From Tony's we drove around it, but I could see a break at the end of the street where a path had been forged into the woods. It probably led by the old ramp we built back there. We used to meet at that ramp and skate until it got too dark to see. Once someone fell, we'd call it a night.

I smiled thinking about that ramp, how we'd built it from the scrap wood under my parents' deck and Tony's and how we hadn't told our parents about it because we were pretty sure they'd say it wasn't safe. Then the neighborhood construction had really gotten going on the other side of Reston Parkway and we could always find concrete cylinders meant for sewers and empty swimming pools to skate in. When we went back to that ramp in the woods, the weather had worn the wood through and other kids had found it and vandalized it. Riding past the woods to the Lincrests', I was so involved in that memory of the ramp that I didn't realize Kacie was speaking.

"I'd hoped we could talk," she was saying. "But I don't see how or when that's going to happen. There's always other people around. Or we're too fucked up."

"We can talk tomorrow," I said. "Let's just hang out with our friends tonight. Try to enjoy everyone." I hoped that would work and it seemed to for the rest of the ride over.

"Brian," she said, after she parked the car and we were about to get out. "Can we just . . . for a minute. I mean."

"Kacie, it's cold," I said. "And dinner's gonna be ready. Everybody's waiting." I leaned over the center console, kissed her, cupping her cheek in my palm. "It can wait. Come on."

Joel opened the door and pulled me to him for a big hug. Inside, the Lincrests' house was still decorated for Christmas.

"Man, it's good to see you," he said.

I clapped my hand on his back. "You, too, man. So sorry about your granddad."

Joel nodded, we separated, and he turned to Tony. "Thanks," he said as he accepted Tony's condolences and hug.

I stepped past Joel and met Jason coming into the foyer. He hugged me, too, a tight embrace in which I could feel just how much bigger he'd gotten since I'd seen him last summer. He took my coat from me and smiled.

"How ya been?" he asked me.

"I'm makin' it." I walked past him into the kitchen, where Tabby was standing over the stove with a spoon in her hand. She'd just licked it.

"Caught ya." I put my twelve pack on the counter and walked to her.

She wiped a bit of sauce off her lip. "Yep," she said. "Quality control."

I leaned in and kissed her cheek, sliding my arm around her waist for a half circle hug. She grinned and said, "Good to see you."

"You, too," I told her.

I turned back and watched Tony and Joel walk into the kitchen, one carrying beer and the other talking animatedly with his hands. Whatever he was telling Joel ended and they both laughed. Tony stepped past me to Tabby.

"Hey, pretty girl," he said.

I looked over and saw Chris following Tony and Joel through the door and beyond him, Kacie and Jason lingering in the hallway. Jason was taking her coat from her and they were speaking but I couldn't hear them.

"Brian, have a beer," Joel said, following my eye line toward his twin and stepping into it. He smiled. I smiled.

"Happy New Year," I said, tipping the bottle toward him.

He tipped his own bottle in and we clinked them together. "Of course," he said.

"It smells wonderful in here, Tabby," Chris said. "What are we eating?"

I stopped listening to the food discussion. Tony and Joel struck up a conversation about how cold it was. I wasn't listening to that either. I watched Kacie and Jason talking in the hallway.

She felt my gaze and looked up. She pulled her shoulders back, looked at Jason, said something that looked final, and walked toward me. I tried to read her face and when I couldn't, I looked over her shoulder to see Jason's. But he'd left the hallway, taking our coats with him.

"You okay?" I asked as she walked up.

"Of course," she said.

Joel draped his arm over her shoulder and hugged her to him.

"She's perfect," he said, and kissed the top of her head.

She blushed a little under his arm.

I raised my beer in salute and said, "I'll drink to that." Then took a long pull from the bottle.

As Tabby moved around the kitchen finishing prep, we slowly got pushed away from the counters. Joel set our twelve packs out on the back deck where it was cold enough to keep them chilled. I stood by the pantry door with Chris watching Tony and Kacie set the table, and when Jason came back in he paused in the doorway with us and watched, too.

"So how ya been?" he asked me again.

"Really sorry about your grandad," I said.

"Yeah, Mom's torn up about it." He had his hands on his hips which propped his elbows out to either side and made him look even wider. "It was unexpected." Then he rubbed a palm across his chest absently, like maybe the shirt was itchy or as a reference to his grandad's heart attack, and I could see he was firm, too, hard muscles under the shirt he wore. Next to Chris he looked like an Olympian. I wondered if Chris noticed.

"Chris, Tabby said you're going on a diet?" Joel said, walking over to us.

Chris rubbed his hand down over his belly. "Yeah," he said. "Gotta get back down to my boxing weight."

Jason rapped his knuckles against him in a small gesture. "Why don't you start running?" he said. "That'll get the weight off."

"Ya think?" Chris asked. "I gotta do something. Too much Southern fried food, I think."

I took a drink out of my beer and looked past Joel to where Kacie was laying silverware alongside a plate. She seemed focused on the task or lost in it.

Tony stood near her and when he spoke to her, it took a second before she stopped what she was doing and looked at him. He pointed at something she'd done and she looked back to the table, confused.

"Right, Brian?"

"What's that?"

"I said, cardio work," Jason said.

"Right," I said, nodding.

"That's your secret?" Joel asked.

"My secret for what?"

"Jesus, man, pay attention. Fuck." Chris laughed. "Let's go smoke."

"Well, that'll make cardio harder," Jason said.

"Sign me up for that shit tomorrow," Chris said. "Tonight, I'm just fat and happy. Good friends, good food, good booze. Couldn't ask for more."

"Right?" Tony agreed, stepping away from the table. "Let's smoke."

"Coats are in the living room," Jason said.

Chris and Tony headed toward the front door. I turned to Kacie. "Kace? You wanna come?"

"Oh, no thanks," she said without looking up. She was moving all of the forks to the other side of the plate and replacing them with the knives and spoons.

I followed Tony and Chris to the living room, picked up my coat, and then went with them out to the back deck. We stood in a semi-circle and smoked.

"So when does the job at Friday's start?" Chris asked.

"Monday. They make me work the prep and lunch shifts for like three weeks before I get a night shift." Tony was wearing a t-shirt, a flannel, and a ski jacket with the lift ticket still on it, all of which were open and he was shivering.

"Man, zip your coat. You're making me colder," I said.

He laughed. "I like it," he said. "Means I'm feeling something."

"Kacie's high," I said.

"Aren't we all?" asked Chris.

"No, I mean, she's coked up. Did you see the way she was putting the silverware out? She's fucked up." I took a drag off my cigarette and shook my head.

"She'll be okay," Tony said.

"Sure she will," Chris said. "She's with us."

I pulled another bottle out of my twelve-pack as we headed back inside. Tony laid his hand on my back and I held back a bit.

"Go easy on her," he said quietly.

"Yeah, I know," I said.

"Don't act like you know," he said. "Act like you love her."

"I do."

"Act like it," he said again.

I watched him walk past me and then I closed the back door securely. He stepped up into the kitchen and closer to Kacie. He pulled her to him and kissed her cheek. I watched her eyes close as she accepted it. Then she opened them and looked at me, standing in the dim family room near the back door.

"Did you smoke?" she asked. "I wanted to go."

"We're ready to eat," Tabby said.

"Oh, well, let's do that first," Kacie agreed. She took the basket from Tabby's outstretched hands and walked it over to the table. She squinted at me under the kitchen table light. "Are you going to come in?" she asked.

I smiled at her and walked up into the kitchen. Handed her a beer, she took it, and then pulled a chair out to have a seat.

We all sat down around the kitchen table and passed plates and shared the food Tabby had made for us. It was an Italian feast with a huge pan of lasagna, a basket of bread, and a wooden bowl with a ginormous salad. Tabby had poured wine into glasses at each seat. Tony handed his to Joel. Kacie sat next to me and Tony sat across from me. Chris sat next to him and Tabby and Joel sat at either end. Jason chose the seat on Kacie's other side. He sipped the wine, nodded, and said something about its flavor to Tabby.

"So what happens now?" Chris asked and Jason described the farm team process for selecting players. He described the practice and game schedule and the traveling and described road accommodations, hotels, and such.

"Except in Charlottesville," he said, "and Atlanta and Pittsburgh," he added, "where I get to stay with my friends."

"Cheers to that," Joel said, tipping his glass toward his brother.

Kacie's left hand went under the table and she slid it down my lap to my knee. She squeezed my leg gently and pressed her shoulder into mine.

"It's all a very slow process," Joel was saying. He was describing some kind of development he was working on with another web designer. They had an idea they were pursuing and thought it might really be something.

"When will you know?" Tony asked.

"Sometime early spring."

"But you're still in school."

"Oh, yeah, gotta get the degree finished," Joel said. "Should be done in May."

"By May," Chris was saying to Tabby. "That's if I can get this class I need. If not, I'll have to wait until the fall to take it."

Kacie's hand moved in slow circles on my leg and then slid up toward my zipper. I felt myself respond to her and tried to keep from laughing. She turned toward me, and I looked at her in my peripheral vision. She was smiling.

"Thanks for that," I said softly. "Now I won't be able to stand up for a while."

Across the table, Tony was still listening to Joel, but he was watching Kacie and me. I met his eyes and he smiled.

There was a slight pause in music while the discs changed and then a new mood came through Mr. Lincrest's old hi fi.

"So very sophisticated," Kacie said, after listening for a moment.

"It's this collection of discs with funny names," Tabby said. "Like they've rebranded the classics or something. Bach for Breakfast. Mozart for Your Morning Workout."

"Strauss for Stress Relief?" I asked. "How very clever."

"Dvorak for Dinner," Joel said.

"Beethoven for Beers?" Chris asked.

"Haydn for Hangovers," I said.

"Haydn," Joel said, "Nice pull."

"It's not Dvorak," I said. "You tuning into the college station out there at Pitt?"

"Right. Like the Pitt station plays classical music." He laughed.

"I started with the Victoria's Secret tapes," Tabby admitted. "Free with purchase. Full of Tchaikovsky. Swan Lake, Nutcracker, Sleeping Beauty. Stuff I'd heard on cartoons." She had the attention of everyone at the table. She pulled her glass to her in an elegant gesture, smiled gently toward Joel.

"Tchaikovsky for Children," Joel said.

"I like it when I study," Tabby said. "No lyrics to distract."

"I'll have to try it when I paint," Tony said. "Instead of Matchbox Twenty." He grinned at me. His blue eyes were clear, shining, and happy.

"They were also the cheapest CDs at Tower Records, remember?" Joel said. "So I could buy three of those or one Alice in Chains. Easy choice."

Then we all listened again for a moment, the clink of forks and wine glass stems to plates as they were set down and lifted in turn.

"Brian's mom plays classical music at dinner time," Kacie said.

Tony laughed. "Yeah, she does. Always has."

"Makes me hungry," Kacie said.

"That's the intention," I said, reaching under the table and folding her fingers into mine. I caught Tony's eye again and he nodded at me right before he shoved a forkful of lasagna in his mouth.

We finished dinner with a round of compliments for Tabby, and then we all stood up to help with the clean up and go outside to smoke. Chris and Jason and I starting clearing dishes to the counter, Kacie and Tony stepped outside. Joel helped Tabby at the sink and they rinsed all the dishes as we brought them and put them in the dishwasher.

When Kacie and Tony returned, they took over for me and Chris and we went outside to smoke. By the time we'd returned the kitchen was pretty much clean and Tabby was just gathering the napkins and placemats from the table. I helped her stack them and then followed her to the laundry room where she laid them on the washer.

Back in the kitchen, Joel was pulling the trash bag out of the trashcan and tying it off. I reached under the sink for a new one and shook it open. Looking around, I didn't see Tony or Kacie.

Chris was leaning out the back door to get another beer, and Jason had stretched out on a chair in the living room and turned on the TV.

"There's a bowl game on tonight," he said over his shoulder to no one in particular.

"Where's Kacie?" I asked Tabby.

"She went to the bathroom."

I put the trashcan back under the sink, grabbed my beer off the counter, and started toward the living room.

The hallway bathroom door opened and Tony stepped out.

I looked past him.

"Just me, man," he said.

"Of course," I said. We stepped into the living room together and flopped down side-by-side on the couch. Jason had found the game and we watched long enough to figure out the teams, the score, and the quarter. The second half had just started.

Chris took a seat next to Jason and when Joel came in from the garage, he and Tabby sat next to me on the couch.

"Oh, right, the Peach Bowl," Chris said. "Virginia and Georgia. Who's winning?"

"Twenty-one to seven, Cavs," Jason said. "Third quarter just started."

Tabby asked Joel which New Year's Eve broadcast he preferred. Tony and I were watching the game. Georgia tied it up then Virginia scored again, but the kicker missed the extra point. It was nearly the fourth quarter and Kacie still hadn't returned so I went to look for her.

I walked down the hall, past the powder room, the living room, and took the stairs up to the second floor. There was a mid-way landing then the staircase curved back, making the foyer tall, open, and dramatic. The upstairs hallway railing stretched above me as I climbed. At the top, I looked down to the right and saw the twins' rooms and the bathroom they shared. The door was closed and a light glowed underneath. I approached it and knocked gently.

"Kace?"

"Hold on," she said.

After a second, she opened the door, yanking on it to come unstuck from the frame.

"You okay?"

She nodded and motioned that I should come in.

I stepped inside and pressed the door closed behind me. It wedged into the frame again and the knob clicked.

"All that garlic," she said, and pressed her hand to her stomach.

I looked over at the toilet, but the lid was down.

"You okay?"

She reached out and touched my arm, dragging her palm down my sleeve, weaved her fingers into mine, and pulled me to her. When she kissed me, I kissed her back and her lips were cold like she's just rinsed her mouth out. She shifted and sat on the counter, her legs dangling to either side of me, heat at her center, against my belly. I groaned through the next kiss.

"You torture me," I murmured, threading my free hand into her hair.

"I know," she said, pressing kisses to my jaw. She released my hand to unbuckle my belt, but I stepped away after seeing myself in the mirror over her shoulder. My mouth was swollen and red. I pushed my hand through my own hair and shook off the arousal.

"Come on, Kace," I said. "Let's get back to the party."

"Something quick?" She was really skinny. Her jawbone was sharp and her cheekbones more prominent than they'd been over the summer. Her green eyes squinted at me. I hadn't smelled anything when I'd entered and now, with her so frisky and her eyes so pale, I thought the garlic thing wasn't true. Still, sex now was a bad idea for a dozen reasons.

I sat down on the closed toilet and looked up at her. She wore a long-sleeved v-neck shirt, black with ridges like it was meant to be long underwear or something. It fit her loosely, but I didn't think it was supposed to. Her jeans were baggy, too, with square pockets on the front that looked like they should have been on the back. She had left her shoes downstairs and wore black-and-grey striped socks over her feet that kicked against the cabinet.

"Kace," I said again.

She hopped off the counter and came to me, her belly at my eye level. I pressed my face into her and could feel how thin her frame was. She straddled my lap and sat down so that her face was nearly even with mine. I felt her back curve as she lowered her lips to mine.

We kissed and her hands were in my hair, on my head, holding me tightly to her.

"Kace," I said for the third time. "Are you high?"

"So," she said.

"So high or so what?"

"High," she said. "What?"

I held her shoulders and tried to pull her away from me. She squirmed and almost lost her balance; she put a foot down and then pushed against my chest.

"What?" she said again.

"Not here," I said. "Not now."

"What here?" she said. "What do you think is happening?" She ducked her head into my neck and kissed me, wet and tender, then biting and fervent.

"Ow, shit, Kacie. Stop."

"Stop?" she echoed.

I pressed against her shoulders; she was holding my head.

"Don't you want me?" The words were smeared together and came out as more of a whine than a question.

"What did you take?" I asked.

She leaned away from me, still holding on, and tried to focus on me. Then she let go and fell backward. I reached to catch her but not before she hit the floor.

"Ow. Shit," she said, then laughed. "Okay. *That* was sexy."

"Come on," I said. "Stand up. Let's go back downstairs." I took hold of her elbow and tugged a little.

"I got this," she said. One palm on the floor, she tried to stand again, but her feet got tangled together and she started to fall. She reached out, not for me, but for the shower curtain, and yanked it trying to hold herself up. The rod gave and the shower curtain, liner, and rings, all crashed to the floor. Kacie, too, only this time she smacked her head on the counter top.

I knelt down beside her. "Shit, Kacie," I said. "Are you okay?"

I could see tears welling in her eyes, but she swallowed them back, squeezed the lids closed, and took a breath. "I'm fine," she said, exhaling slowly.

She let me take her elbow and help her up. Facing the mirror, she put both palms on the counter to steady herself and looked into her reflection.

I inspected the shower curtain and rod tangled on the floor. Then lifted the pole and shoved the rings toward the middle, raising the curtain high above the edge of the bathtub.

Someone called up the stairs.

"That really hurt." Kacie pressed her fingertips against her head over her ear where she'd hit the countertop on the second fall.

"Shh," I said.

I heard the person call again.

"Open the door and tell them you're okay."

"I'm okay," she said but it was too quiet for anyone beyond the room to hear.

I put the shower curtain down, stepped over to the door, yanked it open and heard Tabby's voice again.

"Kacie? Honey, are you okay?"

"We're fine, Tabby," I said. "We'll be out in a minute."

I shoved the door closed again and stepped past Kacie to the tub.

"She's worried about me," Kacie said, still checking for damage to her head and widening and narrowing her eyes in her reflection. She tugged the cuff of her sleeve over one fingertip and wiped under her eyes at smudged makeup.

I didn't answer, just went back to re-positioning the shower curtain. I put one end up and got the other wedged in. Had to shove and shift so it would fit and stay. In frustration, I dropped my elbow and it made contact with something. When I turned, I realized it had been Kacie.

"Ow, fuck," she grunted, her palm on her cheek.

I'd elbowed her just below her eye.

"Shit. Are you okay?" I put my hand out to her, but she backed away and stopped up against the sink. "This is a small fucking room," I said, pulling her hand away from her face and looking at the spot where my elbow had made contact. "Why were you standing under me?"

"I was helping," she said in a pouty voice and she raised her arms lamely, as if pushing the curtain rod up. She moved slowly, hazy, and I could see her blink and try to shake it off.

I cupped her face in my palm, tilting her head.

"Kacie, what did you take?" I asked again, trying to look into her eyes.

She pushed my hands away and turned to the door.

"Let's go," she said. She tugged on the knob but the door wouldn't budge.

I reached around her and pulled, too, but the door was wedged again.

"You have to yank it," she said.

With another jerk, the door came free and slammed into her,

the bottom scraping her foot and the ridge smacking her in the forehead.

"Ow," she said for the third time. "Shit," we both said.

"We gotta get you outta this bathroom before it sends you to the hospital." I slid my hand down her hip and pressed my lips to her forehead, kissing her softly. "Jeez," I said, holding her up when she leaned into me, more of a wobble than affection.

She stumbled out into the hall rubbing her forehead. The light from the bathroom illuminated the upstairs but when I flipped it off, the darkness seemed to overwhelm her. She wandered toward the railing taking slow steps and looking around as if trying to figure out where she was.

"I thought you'd quit," I said.

"Quit what?"

"I mean I told you I had."

"You told me today."

"Easy there." I passed in front of her, held my hand near her elbow, but didn't touch her. She jerked away as if I had.

"God, Brian, is that why you came up here? To spy on me? Fucking judge me?" She headed toward the stairs. Her steps were unbalanced, but she held tightly to the banister.

"No, Kace, I'm worried about you. I can't do shit when I'm that fucked up," I stopped then because I could see Jason coming into the foyer from the living room. "Awesome," I said under my breath. I walked around her again, taking the top step before she could.

"God, you're really a piece of shit, you know that. Today, Brian. I can't just switch off like that. I need time." She staggered down the stairs past me, made it to the landing and turned back to look up at me. Her face was in shadows, her eye sockets dark orbs. "Okay?"

"What's going on?" Jason asked, flipping on the overhead

light and illuminating the foyer, staircase, and Kacie and me as
we descended.

"Nothing," Kacie said. "It's nothing."

"We heard a crash," Tabby said, and I realized she was right
behind Jason.

"I'm fine," Kacie said. "I'm fine. I fell. The curtain fell. The
counter top. Fucking awful." She was moving her arms, but they
were out of synch with her story. She didn't look directly at any
of us. "Then the door hit me. Stupid."

I watched her on the landing, like a small stage in the foyer,
trying to explain what had happened without saying what had
happened, trying to put the words together without really knowing the words to use.

"We're fine," I said, stepping down toward her.

Jason stood like a sentry at the bottom of the stairs and
reached up to help her down. She took his hand and started
toward him.

"What's this?" he said, cupping her jaw in his palm and looking at her cheek under her eye. From where I stood, I couldn't see
but it must have been red.

She brushed him aside. "I said I'm fine." She stumbled on
the last two steps, and Jason held her waist. Then Tabby stepped
forward and Kacie went to her.

"Honey, are you okay?" Tabby asked.

Kacie nodded and then shook her head. She reached up and
tugged the hair tie out of the low ponytail and shook her hair out
into a riot of golden waves.

"What was the loud noise?" Tabby asked in a tone used for
children.

"I fell. I pulled the shower and it fell, too. Then I helped but
I got hurt." Kacie turned back toward me. "Tell them, Brian."

Jason stood between me and Kacie. When she moved toward
me, as if she'd climb back up the stairs, he stepped in front of

her. He took her face, again, in his hands, and searched her eyes. She blinked and bit her lip.

"Did he hit you?" he asked.

"What?" I said, and my voice echoed in the open space of the foyer. "Are you joking?" I looked down the hall. "Tony!" I called, galloping down the last few steps.

The others came in. When I reached the landing, Jason said, "Just stop, Brian."

"Jason, fucking relax. I didn't hit her. Tell him, Kacie."

"He didn't hit me."

"You told him, right?" Jason said quietly.

Tabby moved forward. Joel stepped into the room behind her. "Kacie," she said. "Did you say something? Do something?"

Kacie wiped her fingertips under her eyes. "I didn't do anything," she said. "And he didn't hit me. I fell. Let's just let it go. It was nothing. Nothing's wrong."

I watched her pull away from Jason.

He turned on me. "Tell the truth for once, Brian," he said.

"What the fuck, man?"

Tony arrived, pushed past Joel to where Jason and I were at the bottom of the stairs. "I'm sure it's fine," he said. "Brian would never hit her."

"Of course not. Don't be a fucking idiot," I said to Jason. "She told you what happened." I came down two more steps. Kacie was an arm's length from me. I reached for her, but Jason knocked my hand away.

"She'd lie for you," he said.

"Oh, so now we're both liars?" I said. "Fine. Awesome. Anyone else wanna weigh in on what happened here besides the only two people who were actually there?"

"Kacie, honey," Tabby said. "Are you okay?"

"Yes," Kacie said, but her voice was dazed, kind of feeble.

She nodded slowly, not very convincingly, tugging on a lock of her hair. "I fucked up."

"You should go," Joel said to me.

"What?"

"Wait a minute," Tony said. "They just told us they're okay."

"Go?" Kacie looked up at me and lifted a lock of hair to her lips, sucking on it absently.

"Do you want to?" I asked.

She nodded and the curls bounced near her temples.

"Okay," I stepped down closer to her, pushing Jason out of the way. I went past Joel, who stepped aside, walked into the living room, and got our coats.

"If you told him and he hit you, Kacie, you can't go with him," Tabby said.

"I didn't. We're going to go. It's time." She leaned in, kissed Tabby on the cheek, and turned to Tony. He hugged her.

"Should I come?" he asked.

She shook her head and turned to Jason, but his jaw was clenched and she shrank away.

"What the hell, man?" I said, handing Kacie her coat and stepping between them. "This is some fucked up shit."

He shook his head at me. "If you hurt her again," he said, "you're gonna see some fucked up shit."

"I didn't hit her."

"I don't trust you."

"Well, she does."

"I need my purse," Kacie said from behind me, and she wandered toward the kitchen.

I turned to Joel. Tabby stood at his shoulder now, her hand clasping his waist.

"How could you even think I'd do that?" I asked.

"I don't know what you'd do when you're high."

"I'm not high."

Joel raised an eyebrow at me. His arms were folded over his chest, and he looked almost as big as Jason. I looked from him to his twin and saw identical anger.

"I'm not high," I said again.

"How are we supposed to believe that?" Tabby said. "Look at Kacie."

"Oh, fuck off, Tabby. I didn't give her whatever she took."

"Didn't you?" Jason asked from behind me.

"This is so fucked up," I said.

"You can't be trusted, Brian." Joel glared at me and I wondered if he really meant that; all I could see was the distance between where we were and where we'd once been.

"Joel, come on," Tony said. "Kacie even said they were fine."

"Seriously, guys, just relax," Chris said.

"No," I said. "It's good to know this is what they think of me."

I felt Tony's hand on my back. "It's okay, Brian," he said. "Kacie needs a ride home. We're all just sitting around waiting for midnight anyway."

Chris came forward and folded his hand into mine. We leaned toward one another. "See ya tomorrow, man. Happy New Year."

Tony grasped my hand after Chris let it go and leaned in to me. "It's okay," he said again. I nodded into his shoulder.

Kacie returned from the kitchen, her hair tied back into the band she'd been holding, and her purse slung across her chest. She stepped over to Chris for a kiss on the cheek. She gave Tony one, too, and then waved at Jason, Tabby, and Joel.

"K, bye," she said, dragging the last sound out in a childish whisper.

"Kacie," Jason said, trying again to step between us. I took her wrist, though, and pulled her gently toward the door. "You don't have to go," he said.

She nodded. "Yes, I do," she said. "I fucked up." And a tear dripped down her cheek.

"Honey, don't go," said Tabby.

Kacie smiled. "I want to," she whispered.

I looked at Joel again and the resolve in his face was something I'd only seen once or twice before.

"I'm sick of this shit," he said.

"Well, it's over now," I said.

And we left.

In the driveway, Kacie gave me the keys and I opened the door to the passenger seat for her. She fell in, the relief in sitting evident on her face.

"That was fucking crazy," I said.

I closed the door, walked around to the other side, got into the driver's seat, and started the car. She was slumped against the door, her cheek to the window.

"Seriously, Kace, what are you on?"

"Leave it," she mumbled.

I lit a cigarette, rolled the window down, and backed the car out of the driveway. Kacie's sister lives a short drive from the Lincrests', down Reston Parkway, toward the county recreation fields. But there are several lights and the car would lurch forward as we slowed down nearing them, and backward as I pressed the gas to move through them. Kacie was in full rag doll mode in the passenger seat, the inertia of the stops and starts pushing her body around.

We reached Audrey's and the clock on the dashboard said 11:15. I went around to the passenger door to help Kacie out, and she managed to stand upright without assistance and walk up the stairs to the front door without holding on to me. She did grip the rail but seemed to have gained more control.

I followed her inside and we went back to the kitchen where Kacie peeled her coat off and hung it on a chair, then poured herself a glass of water and drank it completely down. She filled another and started out. I reached into the fridge, grabbed a beer, and followed her up the stairs to Audrey's bedroom.

"Where's your sister?"

"She went to D.C. tonight."

"Will she be back?"

"No," she said. The hallway was dark and Kacie stopped at the bathroom, flipped the light on, and closed the door.

I went into Audrey's room. The moonlight in the window made everything shadowy so I reached for the switch on a lamp on the desk. There were clothes and towels on the unmade bed. I took my coat off, pulled the chair away from the desk, hung the coat over the back, and sat down.

After a few minutes, Kacie came in. She had changed from her jeans and black shirt and wore just a t-shirt that fell over her bare thighs. She had abandoned the band that tied her hair back and the curls fell like a golden mane. She'd washed her face and it was fresh and clean. She had no bra on, and I could see the curve of her breast and the fine point of her nipple under the t-shirt.

She put her glass of water on the nightstand and reached for the clothes on the bed, scraping them up into a pile, and tossing them aside. Then she sat down. It was a small room and our knees were close. I leaned forward on mine and reached over to touch hers.

She didn't pull away but she didn't look at me either.

"So what's the thing you have to tell me?" I said.

"Thought you heard that," she said. Her voice was a bit clearer, though she said each word slowly as if concentrating on it.

"It's so bad Jason thinks when you say it I'll hit you?"

She smiled weakly. "He's paranoid."

I sat back and took a drink out of the bottle I'd brought up with me. I hadn't gotten stoned for hours and only drank a few beers; I didn't feel at all fucked up. Not exactly the way I'd planned to spend New Year's.

The clock on Audrey's night stand said 11:40.

"Do you want me to leave?" I asked.

"You're going to want to," she said. "After."

"So tell me and then I'll go."

She was stroking her fingers in her lap. Thumb and forefinger like a pinch on her right hand, she ran down each finger on her left. Then the left hand pinched and the right was stroked. It looked like itching, or rubbing in lotion might look, except her hands were dry.

"I don't know how to say it so I'll just say it," she said. "I slept with Jason."

"You did what?"

"I was lonely," she said.

"When?"

"I'm always lonely," she said.

"No, I mean, when did it happen?"

She looked at the clock as if the time could be estimated in hours, not days or weeks. She said, "Thanksgiving."

I closed my eyes and tried to remember that I didn't really love her anymore and that I had been with Melissa in California. I tried to remember that she was here by herself and that she would have needed someone.

"Okay," I said slowly, opening my eyes and looking at her. She wouldn't meet my stare. "So you needed someone. I can understand that." I took a deep breath and then said, "You couldn't fuck some nameless guy in Charlottesville?"

"That would have been okay?" she said, as if, had she known, she'd have done it that way. She looked up at me, and her eyes were brimming with tears.

"No, but . . ." I struggled for words that weren't there.

Then she filled in saying, "Jason isn't the problem, Brian. It's us." Tears poured over her eyelids and streamed down her face and she finished, "We are fucked. There is something seriously wrong."

"The problem is that you fucked Jason," I said. "There was no problem until that one." But that wasn't true and I knew it and it came out sounding like a lie.

She stood up, wobbled a bit, and walked to the window. She flipped the light switch on a lava lamp and picked a candle up off the windowsill. She wiped tears off her cheeks with one hand and then the other, shifting the candle from palm to palm. Then she set it down on top of the television and pushed both hands, open and empty, down her hips and thighs, wiping her hands on her shirt.

I looked away, at the bed, the clock, the closed door, the computer monitor, the desk. My own legs, my own hands. Took a drink from the open beer. I heard the scrape of flint as she struck a match and looked over at her again. The glow of the fire was muted by the lamp behind me. I watched Kacie light the candle and then blow the match out.

She came back toward me, though she wasn't looking at me, and leaned over me. I felt her breast graze my shoulder, smelled her against my face. She turned the lamp off and then pulled back.

Before she could step away, I caught her in my arm. I held her to me.

"What are we going to do?" she asked.

"About what?" I pulled her against me and kissed her.

She kissed me back. I ran my hands under the shirt she wore, felt the edges of her panties, her belly, her breasts. She pulled at my shirt, tugged it over my head. She was standing between my legs; I was bare-chested in front of her. I pressed my face to her belly under her shirt, kissed her navel and the underside of each breast. Her shirt was on my face as I smelled her skin and dragged my tongue over her. Then she stiffened a bit, stepped back, and dropped her shirt back down.

"Come on, Brian," she said and put a hand on the back of my neck, dug her fingers into my hair, tilted my head back so I looked up at her.

"Tell me," I said.

She stepped away from me and put her knee down on the bed. She crawled on and for the slightest second I saw the curve of her ass below the edge of her panties. She would make me wild with that shit. She knew exactly what to do, what to show. She turned and faced me, her legs underneath her.

She reached for her glass and took a long drink. "What do you want to know?"

"Whatever you think you need to tell," I said.

"Mom and Dad went to Colorado for Thanksgiving. Audrey was with her boyfriend. It's the first time I've ever been alone on a holiday. I was really sad. Jason was home and said he wanted to see me. We all went out, Tony and Chris, too, and we ended up at Uno of course."

I thought of them all standing around the table at Uno, drinking beers, taking shots, not talking about how I wasn't there. Maybe not even noticing.

"Then Jason brought me home."

"Here? He brought you here?"

She shoved her hand into her hair, gently shaking it above her ear and the curls bounced and danced in the dim light of the candle and lamp.

"And what?" I said. "You invited him in? You brought him upstairs?"

She looked down at her hands. Her hair fell in a curtain around her face.

"He took your clothes off?"

Her shoulders sagged.

I stood up, walked to her, stood over her. She didn't look up and I didn't touch her. The room was dark and the colors of her shirt, her hair, her skin, and the bedcovers were all gray and shadowy. She was kneeling in front of me. Then she leaned slightly and her forehead rested against my belly.

I heard a breath like a gasp. She was crying again.

"It was a mistake," she said and started to tremble. "You weren't here."

"So you found a replacement?"

"That's not fair, Brian," she said, taking ragged breaths between sobs. "It isn't just that. Look at us."

I put my hand under her chin and raised her face so I could see it.

"Look at you," I said.

She put her hands on my hips, trying to steady herself. Her cheeks glistened with tears and her face was starting to swell. She bit her lip and closed her eyes.

"Get off the coke, Kacie. That would fix us." I let go of her jaw with a tweak and stepped back. Then I turned away and reached for my shirt. I tried to remember we were kissing a minute before. I tried to remember it was okay. She was okay. I tried to treat her like I loved her, like Tony told me to. I tried to remember I loved her. But I couldn't even look at her.

"I didn't mean to," she said.

"You fucked Jason," I said. "Were you high?"

"You got me to."

"To fuck Jason?" I clenched my fist around my shirt.

"No, to get high. You got me high." She shook her head. I

could hear her breath oscillating with the motion. "I can't do this. I don't know what's happening."

"You're a whore," I said finally, as if realizing it suddenly. I turned back to her. Waited for her to dispute it.

She looked up at me, disbelief in her eyes.

I was looking at her, but all I could see was him. Him in this room, with her, over her, on her. I squeezed my eyes shut to block out the image. I felt her hands on me. She was pulling me to her.

"Don't say that," she said.

She was up on her knees on the bed. She took my wrist, twisted my shirt out of my fist and tossed it away. She put her hands on my hips, just above my jeans, and pressed them down.

I folded and knelt on the floor in front of her.

She pulled my head into her belly.

I let my hands slide up her hips, under her shirt.

She pulled her shirt off and threw it aside then bent over me, pressing her breasts into my mouth.

I took each one, gently at first and then hungrily. I remembered Tony telling me to act like I loved her. I climbed up on the bed, pressed her back into it, and shoved my hand into her hair at the base of her neck, lifting her face to mine. I kissed her salty cheeks. I kissed her trembling lips. I kissed her throat where her pulse throbbed. We were chest to chest, my belt buckle grinding into her belly, I was hard and she was hot, and I wanted her.

"No," she said suddenly. "I'm fucked up, Brian, stop." She turned her face away from me. Her hair was in my eyes.

I closed my eyes and stopped moving, just held her still, waited for her breathing to calm down. I lightly kissed her ear.

She stared at the ceiling. Then she twisted underneath me, jerked away, and sat up. "Why do you always have to push too far?" she said.

I rolled over onto my back. "What do you want from me, Kacie?" I said.

"This is what I always get," she said.

"It's all I have left to give."

"Is it?" She curved her shoulders in, put her face in her hands.

I reached out and dragged my fingertips up and down her back. Then I saw it, a tiny butterfly, orange and black, tattooed on her shoulder. I sat up to get a closer look. She felt me move closer and pulled away.

"What's that?" I asked, pressing my fingertip to it.

She scooted away and started looking for her shirt; she was on her knees but leaning toward the floor.

I reached for her and took her arm.

"Don't," I said.

She lay down and I shifted so I could lay behind her. I cupped her shoulder in my hand, my thumb on the butterfly. I almost covered it, rubbed at it as if I could wipe it off. Then I pressed myself against her, leaned in and kissed it, ran my fingers along her arm, her belly, her breasts. She moaned quietly. Her breathing had slowed. I heard her lips part and put my hand on her jaw, my thumb to her lips. They were wet as were her cheeks. She turned her face away from my palm and though she was settled against me, she didn't press herself back into me, or arch into my hand on her breast.

"It's not enough," she said, finally.

"I know."

We lay there, quietness around us. The clock on Audrey's table said 12:20. I stroked her back, her side, her belly, with the tips of my fingers. Her breathing deepened and evened out. She had fallen asleep. I rolled to the other side of the bed and stood up. Stepping past the candle and lava lamp, I blew out the flame on one and switched the other off. In only the light of the moon,

I found my shirt and pulled it on. I looked down at her, tugged the covers up over her, grabbed my coat off the chair, and left.

When I got to Tony's the neighborhood was dark. I saw his parents' cars in the driveway and parked Kacie's behind them. I cut the engine, checked to be sure I had my smokes, and headed around back to the pool. The night sky had cleared, and a large moon hung high above. My breath made puffs of steam, and I pulled my jacket tighter as I turned the corner of the house.

Tony was stretched out in a lounge chair.

"Man, it's fuckin cold," I said. "What the hell are you doing?"

His head rolled toward me and he grinned.

"Back already?" he asked.

"What?" I got closer to him and saw his jacket and shirt were hanging open. "Come on," I said. "Let's go inside."

I draped his arm over my shoulder and hoisted him off the chair.

"I'm cool, dude," he said. "I can walk." He pushed away from me and stood. Then he raised his hands to either side and shrugged. "See?"

The moonlight fell over his face casting shadows around his eyes. His short hair was spiked on top and mashed down in the back. He'd felt cold to the touch.

"How long have you been out here?"

"Pshhhh," was all he said, and stumbled by me, toward the stairs. He took them quickly and I was unsure if that was intentional or a controlled falling until he slammed against the glass door and I realized he was falling.

I walked down after him, looking up at the house to see if any lights were on.

"Where's Chris?"

"Left."

The sliding glass door slid open and Tony stepped in. He turned to me and put a finger to his lips. "Shhhh." He started laughing. "Just kiddin', man. It's cool."

I leaned toward the lamp and twisted the knob to turn it on. Golden light spilled into the room. I watched Tony head for the bathroom and closed the glass door behind me.

Through the open door I saw him fall to his knees in front of the toilet and hang his head over the bowl. His frame lurched and he vomited.

"Shit," he grunted.

I walked to the doorway and watched as he retched into the commode.

"How ya feelin'?"

"Fucked up." He gurgled and then spit into the bowl. He sat back on his heels, closed his eyes, and then leaned forward again, another spray of vomit spewing forth.

I felt my own stomach churn as the smell reached me. I turned on the faucet for water. Grabbed a damp washcloth off the counter and shoved it under the stream.

Tony boosted himself up to the handle and flushed the toilet. A fresh wave of vomit odor floated toward me and I gagged.

He lowered the lid and then rolled over on his hip and sat down, his back against the bathtub, and stretched his legs out in front of him. He had his eyes closed and he was facing me, ski jacket still on, flannel and t-shirt underneath.

I turned the water off and tossed the wet washcloth at him. It landed on his neck. He startled, his blue eyes opening slightly, and then he grabbed the washcloth and wiped his face and mouth and chin and neck with it.

I sat down in the doorway, my back against the cabinets under the sink.

"Did you fuck her?" he asked.

"Who?"

"Melissa."

"I've been fucking her, Tony. You know that."

He nodded. His eyes fluttered like he was trying to keep them open, but I think, actually, he was trying to keep them closed. I watched his chest go up and down as he took deep breaths.

I pulled a cigarette out of my pocket and lit it.

"That's fucking cool," he said.

"I just whiffed your vomit, dude. Don't give me shit about cool."

He laughed then. "Yeah, this was some good shit."

"What did you give her?"

"Who?"

"Kacie. What do you mean who? Is this the same shit you gave her?"

"Why? Did she puke, too?"

"Pretty sure, though she didn't let me stand over her while she did it."

"I woulda sold tickets for that shit," he said. "Make a fucking Just Say No commercial out of it or something." Another laugh. "Fuck me."

"Answer the question," I said.

"I've been fucking her," he said.

"What?"

"You said you've been fucking her like I knew that."

"You knew."

"Yeah I did," he said. "Everybody knows."

"Kacie?"

"Is she part of everybody? Then yeah. Shit."

"She fucked Jason," I said.

"Everybody knows that, too."

I reached over my head and tapped ash into the sink without

really bothering to see if I'd hit the counter or the basin. Tony hadn't moved. I leaned over and shook his foot. His eyes opened and he grinned at me.

"So did you get laid tonight?" he asked.

"After she told me? Come on."

"You're the kind of asshole that gets guilt pussy," he said. "She felt really guilty."

"Is that why she got high in Jason's bathroom?"

"Did you hit her?"

"What? No. Fuck you, man."

"They think you did."

"They also think I gave her the drugs."

Tony laughed again.

"Why did you let them think I gave her the drugs?"

"Fuck it. It doesn't matter." He pulled his knees up and looked like he might stand. Then he crossed his arms over them and bowed his head.

We sat like that for a while. Him by the toilet, against the bathtub, the shower curtain open behind him, the bathtub dirty and dry. The crown of his head toward me, his spiked hair flattened on the back. His forearms folded over his knees, each hand clasping the other elbow. His feet still in his Timberlands, untied and muddy, his cuffs bunched over the laces. I stretched up to ash again and pulled my arm back down.

"What did you give her?" I asked.

"What I always give her," he said. "What you always give her. Just what she asks for." He was speaking into his arms but the whole place was so quiet I could hear him fine.

"What the hell does that mean?" I asked.

"Fuck it. It doesn't matter," he said again.

"Are you sure it doesn't?"

"Pretty sure," he said. Then he put his palm on the floor, turned toward the toilet, and hoisted himself up, holding on to the bathtub and then the sink. His palms went flat on the sink and he leaned toward the mirror.

I looked up and watched him examining himself.

"I'm all smeary," he said.

"Fucked up."

"Yeah it is. It's all fucked up." He looked at his reflection and I imagined what he saw. His blue eyes looked watery and blood-shot. His jaw was covered with a day or so of beard he probably hadn't noticed before. Those stupid dog tags were around his neck. From where I sat beneath him, I could see the silver beads on his throat below his shirt. He looked big, but it was just the ski jacket. He shoved his hand through his hair and it feathered back up. He rubbed both palms up and down his face, breathing heavily through his nostrils and mouth, a combination of snort and sigh.

"What are we doing?" I asked.

He shook his head. "Fuck if I know." He looked down at me.

"I love her."

"I did, too."

"I didn't know."

"I think you did." He looked away from me, lifted the tap on the faucet and ran water into the sink.

I put my left hand on the floor and shoved myself up, still holding my cigarette in my right hand. I reached around him, tapped ash into the sink, and turned and left the bathroom. I saw him cupping water in his hand and pouring it over the top of the sink basin. Then he raised a cupped hand to his mouth and slurped water out of it.

I walked into the bedroom and crushed my cigarette into an ashtray sitting on his nightstand. I stood in front of the canvas he'd been painting that afternoon. The swirls of red and gold reminded me of a valley we'd seen once. Autumn tree tops, that's what they looked like. I stared at it as if seeing it for the first time.

"So that's it?"

"That's it," I said.

"You just left her?"

"What was I supposed to do?"

"Work it out, fix it. I dunno." He came out of the bathroom and I saw his reflection in the sliding glass door as he came toward me. "Give her a chance at least."

"Right."

"This isn't like you, Brian."

I turned and looked at him. He was still fucked up. His eyes were swollen now and the front of his shirt was damp from where he'd slurped handfuls of water. He stood across from me, my best friend, kid I've known my whole life, and we were like strangers. I tried to recognize myself in him. He was always the best of me. But I couldn't see anything but my worst.

"Thank you, Tony." Me, sarcastic and mean and he, wincing. "But I know what I'm doing."

"Always do," he said. He grabbed the edges of his coat like he'd peel it off, but he didn't, just tugged on them and the fabric strained and straightened against him. He was looking around. "Treetops," he said absently, gesturing to the painting.

I turned away. "Yeah, I recognized them."

"Wanna go up to the valley in the morning?"

"It is morning." I heard him laugh a little.

"After some sleep," he said.

"Sure. Come get me?" I started toward the door.

"All right. How?"

"Kacie's car is outside."

"How are you getting home?"

"Gonna walk. Feel like I need the space."

"I could use a walk."

I looked back at him. He looked dirty, confused, and lonely.

"Nah," I said. "You need sleep."

"Right. Right, that's probably better."

"K. See ya in a while." I walked to the glass door, shoved it to the right, and stepped through. I turned to close it and saw him through it. He lifted his hand and I lifted mine. Then I turned away, walked up the steps, and around the house to the front.

I realized I still had Kacie's keys in my pocket. I opened the car door and dropped them into the driver's seat. Looked up and saw the moon high above. The stars around it looked tiny and fragile. I raised my fingers, squinted one eye, and pinched the air, closing my fingers around the moon and its companions. Then I walked home.

SATURDAY

I woke to pale sunlight drizzling through the window and onto my skin. Neither warm, nor bright, its only purpose, it seemed, was to tell me it was now Saturday. Five days since this nightmare began. One hundred hours since Tony was alone in his bathroom, bloody and sad. Before I opened my eyes, the hours between me and him felt immediate. I could hear them. Count them. The distance between us greater than it had ever been. Soon those days would be weeks. But not yet. My head really hurt. Knowing what I had done made it throb even more.

Kacie lay next to me, sleeping quietly, breathing and not moving other than that. I could see the tiny Monarch butterfly on her shoulder, the curls piled up around her head, and the sheet pulled tightly around her bicep. The clock on her side of the bed said 8:30. One hundred one hours and thirty minutes since he'd taken his own life. The breath in my chest was heavy, suffocating.

I slipped out from under the covers and dressed quickly in the cool morning air. My belt jingled against the button of my jeans. The folded pack of M&Ms crinkled in the breast pocket of my flannel. I walked around the bed and found my shoes by the desk, sat in the chair, and pulled them on. Reaching for the bag that held the Gatorades, I let the plastic snap as I tugged on it and stood up. When I took my keys off the desk near the computer, they rattled. I looked over at the bed. Kacie's eyes were closed and I wished she would open them. She didn't stir so I set one bottle of Gatorade on the nightstand and left.

I drove home in the sunlight without sunglasses, squinting the entire way, and parked my father's car in the garage. Mom's car was gone, I assumed carrying her to one of her Saturday appointments like hair or nails or spa but Dad wasn't home, either, I discovered, as I entered the house and seeing everything turned off and quiet. A note on the island in the kitchen said they'd gone to run errands, they'd be back later, and Melissa called twice.

I went upstairs and fell onto my bed. I decided to call California, though it wasn't even six a.m., and crossed my fingers her answering machine would pick up.

On the third ring, before I could feel relieved she'd not answered or wonder where she was, the line picked up.

"It's not yet six," she said.

"Sorry. Just got back. Forgot about the time change."

I heard her moving and I closed my eyes, imagining her shoving the pillow under her cheek to prop herself up, pinning the receiver to her ear. Her eyes would still be closed. The room would still be dark.

"I'll call back."

"Where have you been?" she said.

"Virginia."

"Brian."

"Here. Sleeping."

She let out a stream of air like a sigh but with more frustration.

I listened for a moment, waiting for her to say something else. Then I rolled over onto my back and kicked my shoes off. I stared up at the ceiling, the phone cord across my chest. Closed my eyes.

"You're okay?" she asked.

"Yesterday was tough," I said. "I'm sorry I didn't call."

"I said I wouldn't ask about it."

"Okay."

"But you need to tell me about it."

"Which part?"

More quiet and then enough shifting that I knew she had sat up. I imagined her rubbing sleep out of her eyes, maybe taking a drink out of a water bottle on the nightstand. Screwing the cap back on.

"I hit a guy last night," I said.

"Someone you know?"

"Someone Tony knew. His dealer. Fucking douche named Eric Waters. Said Tony didn't know when to say when. So I decked him."

"But it wasn't an overdose."

"No."

"And you're dealing with that?"

I shrugged, realized she couldn't see me, and said, "Trying to."

"How?"

"Drinking mostly. Some weed."

"Coke?"

"No."

"Sex?"

"No."

Quiet. The quiet of three thousand miles and my dishonesty stretching like a spider's web thread between us.

"Okay," she said finally.

"Let me call you later?"

"Will you?"

"Probably not."

"See you tomorrow," she said and hung up.

I put the phone back on the cradle on the floor by my bed, rolled over into the unmade covers, and fell into a deep sleep almost immediately.

After I left Tony's on New Year's Eve I had walked the length of his neighborhood on the sidewalk. The moon was bright and round in the sky and everything was clear and visible despite it being nearly one a.m. I found the break in the woods that led to the path stretching between Tony's old house and Joel's. I kept walking to the extension path that wound into the thickest of the trees, toward my parents' neighborhood.

It was colder than it had been and I kept my hands shoved into my pockets, making fists with them and then releasing them, trying to stay warm. I reached the old ramp, though it was only a collection of boards in a pile, and almost tripped over a few scattered around. It was much darker than I'd expected it to be. I squinted through the trees toward the edge of the neighborhood and saw a few backyard lights glowing. I should have realized it would be too late for deck lights or window lights. Out in the open, the moon had made it seem near daylight, but in the trees, it was much darker.

I had walked slower than I wanted to in the cold, asking myself if it had been a stupid decision to walk, and then rationalizing that it was New Year's Eve and I probably would have run across a DUI checkpoint on the street anyway. I think it took about thirty minutes, which isn't really that long, but to have gone only about a mile-and-a-half as the crow flies, it seemed pretty slow.

When I made it to my parents' house, I walked around the fenced backyard and stopped on the porch to smoke a cigarette. I knew inside would be warmer but I felt a certain amount of punishment, beyond the long walk in the cold and dark, was warranted.

On the porch, I had gone over and over the moment in the

Lincrests' foyer when Joel told me to leave. I'd reviewed the words between Jason and me after he accused me of hitting her and then relived that breathy confession when she'd said she'd slept with him. I focused on the moment when she'd peeled my shirt off my back. After sitting there for some time, I decided to go back to San Francisco right away.

I stubbed out my cigarette, let myself into the house, and locked the door behind me. In the upstairs hallway, before I reached my door, I was blinded by the overhead light. My eyes burned with its brightness and red and blue dots floated in front of me.

I stopped and turned toward my parents' room, blinking, and trying to focus.

My dad stood in the open doorway. He had looked at me for a moment and then, without speaking, had turned around, walked back into his room, and closed the door behind him.

I flipped the hallway light off, let myself into my old bedroom, removed my coat and shoes, belt and pants, and dragged my shirt over my head. It smelled like her. I pressed it to my face. Then I threw myself onto the bed and slept.

Six weeks, two cross-country flights, one funeral, and several hours of Saturday morning sleep later, my mother knocked quietly on my bedroom door. The sunlight was heavier in the room as I let myself be stirred from sleep.

"Brian? Kacie's here."

"Send her up," I said, rolling over and folding a pillow under my cheek. Through the window I could see the backyard trees, naked limbs stretching in early afternoon sun. The branches seemed to glisten, as if iced. I rubbed my eyes and Kacie came through the door.

Walking around to the side of the bed by the window, where I could see her, she looked fresh and clean, although a little tired.

"Feel rough?" she asked and sat down, cross-legged on the floor in front of me.

"A little. Fucking vodka." I smiled and she did, too. "What time is it?"

"After noon."

"My folks are home, obviously," I said more to myself.

"That was a shitty thing to do this morning," she said.

"The sex or the leaving part?"

"The leaving part," she said. "The sex was fine."

"Just fine?" I rolled onto my back, still rubbing sleep out of my eyes.

"Just fine," she echoed softly.

"I'm sorry about Tony calling you," I said, staring at my own blank ceiling. "I don't think anyone knew anything about that."

"I didn't tell them."

"How come?" I turned my face and saw her hair was loose over her shoulders, waves of yellow curls, and the window above her giving a halo effect. In a baby blue sweater, a white headband, and pale pink lip gloss, she looked like some teenager out of a movie.

"Thought they might think I could have helped him."

"Because that's what you think?"

"Not anymore, not really. I may have helped him put it off another night but ultimately . . ." She dropped the sentence there.

"He'd have done it anyway," I finished for her with a sigh that ended in a cough. I realized suddenly how uncomfortable my clothes had become.

She leaned her head back against the windowsill and looked around the room.

"Didn't tell Jason?" I asked as the thought occurred to me, not bothering to weigh how she would react or what sort of fight it would start. I reached into my pocket for my cigarettes and extracted one from the box. I offered her one and she took it. I pulled my own ashtray out from under the bed, thinking about how it was hidden like Audrey's.

Kacie propped herself on her knees and pushed the window behind her partially open. I slid off of the bed and leaned my back against it, facing her and the window. I lit my own cigarette and then handed her the lighter.

For the first time, I saw she had two bottles with her. She handed me a Sprite and uncapped her own Diet Coke. We sat there taking sips and smoking cigarettes for a minute.

"So are you with him?"

"No," she said then considered for a minute and added, "not that anyone can really be with Jason. He's got this pedestal thing he does where he puts you up there and waits for you to screw up. I already know I'm not what he's looking for." She shrugged. "No big deal. Last thing I need is another long-distance relationship."

That made me smile and I said, "It's because of his mom, you know."

"Yeah, I know."

"But, hey, if it worked out, he'd be the lucky one." I meant it, too. I wasn't ready for it to work out, but whomever Kacie picked would be lucky. I meant that part.

"Thanks," she said.

I took another drag on my cigarette and she exhaled one off hers and we didn't make eye contact. I pulled my knees up and rested my arms on them. She dropped her head back against the wall.

"I didn't know him," I confessed. "I thought I did, but I didn't, not really anymore." I bit my lip, tearing at a peel of chapped skin.

"Because if you knew him you would have seen it coming?"

"I just stopped listening to him. He would call at all these random times and it became harder and harder to keep up with what he was saying." I closed my eyes and laughed a little bit. "I was not a very good best friend."

Kacie shook her head. "No, things would have come around again. All friends grow apart for a while; the good ones come back around." She smiled. "He did love you. He used to talk about you all the time."

"Eric Waters said he'd never mentioned me."

Kacie frowned. "Eric Waters is a user and a drug dealer. He wasn't Tony's friend. It's ridiculous that he thought Tony was his." She took another drag and then crushed her cigarette. When she exhaled, she tilted her head back, arched her neck, aiming for the open window, and I thought she was perfect.

"You're not using anymore?" I asked, unfolding my legs and stretching them beside hers.

She shook her head and sighed dramatically, as if there was a long story to tell and she didn't know where to begin. "I started going to this church in Charlottesville and I liked it and after a few weeks . . . partying became less important."

"You're going to church?"

"You don't believe me?"

"No, I mean sure. Just why?"

Kacie shrugged. She was beautiful when she did that. "You need something to believe in, don't you?"

"I guess. I don't know. Whatever keeps you sober."

"I keep me sober," she said. "Or off the coke anyway. I wasn't a very good addict." She took an interest in her fingernails, and I watched as she considered them one at a time. "I never could stop caring totally. Which was the point of it, right? To stop caring?" She dropped her hands and looked at me. Her legs were straight out, her hands rested on her thighs, her jeans' cuffs bunched over a pair of canvas shoes.

I pinched the end of one of the laces and tugged on it but she'd double-knotted them and it didn't give. I took a drag off the cigarette and exhaled, wondered what watching someone else smoke was like. My exhale drifted past her through the open crack in the window and dissipated.

"I keep thinking all those things they told us are wrong and we got sold a bill of goods." I realized my cigarette had burnt down to the bottom and put the rest of it out in the ashtray. Took a drink from the Sprite she'd brought me.

"You're cynical these days," she said, but she was smiling. "It's charming." She wagged her feet back and forth and the nearest one bumped my hip. "What do you see in my future, oh oracle of doom?"

I closed my eyes and put my fingertips to my forehead. Scrunched my face as if trying to peer into the future.

"Three more years in Charlottesville at law school," I said, opening my eyes and dropping my hand. I reached over to where hers rested on her thigh and tickled her fingertips.

"Of course." She looked down at our hands.

"And someone to love who will love you back."

"Here's hoping," she said, raising her Diet Coke in a mock toast.

"We all have a future, don't we? All of us except Tony."

"Nothing you can do about that," she said.

I figured those words were about to become our mantra and suddenly wished I had those stupid dog tags he'd worn. They belonged with him, of course, he'd worn them everywhere, even during summer league swim meets, since we were twelve. I think he'd started to believe they were lucky or something. I sometimes saw him kiss them before a half-pipe drop-in or while sitting on the Clerk of Course benches waiting to race.

"Did you know he got his stupid dog tags at the Smithsonian?" I bent my knees again and pulled them to my chest, folding my arms over them and peeking over my elbow at her.

"Oh yeah?" Kacie asked, she laid her head back against the

window sill again and closed her eyes. I thought maybe she was envisioning his dog tags.

"We'd seen them in the gift shop on a class field trip, but we couldn't stay long enough to get them made." I remembered the drive into D.C. seeming so long, like going to another state. It was just as far as the burning valley, only in the opposite direction. For some reason, though, when we were with the school and went, and we went every year, it took all day. But with our parents, and later, when we went on our own, we could just pop over to D.C. for lunch without it being the all-day-mission those annual field trips had been.

"The American History Museum," I said, "had an exhibit on Vietnam and Tony talked Mac into going back that next weekend to see it. He was obsessed. He had to have a set of dog tags. I don't know if he thought they made him look like a soldier or what."

"Could be," Kacie said without opening her eyes.

Dog tags are supposed to display legal name, blood type, inoculations, and religion. Pretty much the unchangeable stuff as far as the military was concerned. But the souvenir ones printed at the Smithsonian had a character limit and couldn't fit all that. Tony never went by Anthony Michael Williams, so he'd had just "Tony" on his. He didn't know his blood type or that they had a specific abbreviation they used, so he'd just put "B Positive." Where he ought to have put Presbyterian, he put "Have Faith."

He'd come home and shown me and he was so excited. Maybe I was jealous or just a mean kid, but I hadn't given him the satisfaction he'd wanted. I'd sort of sneered at them and called them his "stupid dog tags" after that. Sneaking in and out of the house and they'd rattle and I'd say, "Shh. Hold your stupid dog tags." Watching him throw himself into flips off the diving board and surface with them choking him, I'd say, "Take off your stupid dog tags. You'll drown."

On the floor in my room between the bed and the window, on that February Saturday with the sunlight blazing through the glass, I would have given anything to take those moments back or to hold those stupid dog tags in my hand.

"It's all like a bad movie," I said aloud, stretching my legs out again, my socked feet pressing against the wall at Kacie's side.

"No," she said, head still back, eyes still closed. "It's a love story and someday you'll tell it. But be nice when you write me," she added, looking up finally and smiling that perfect, healthy Kacie smile.

"My parents are moving," I said. "To Arizona."

"Seriously?"

I nodded. "Told me yesterday. Expecting to be gone late spring."

"It won't be the same," she said, looking around the room. "But I guess it's not supposed to be."

"Your parents have been gone a while."

"Two years, yeah."

"But you come back."

"Well, Audrey is here. And Tony was. And you."

"And now?"

She raised her knees in front of her and wrapped her arms around them. "What are you going to do?" she asked and it was sort of rhetorical, like just dealing with it.

But I responded, "Go back to San Francisco, try to become a writer." I looked at my white socks, dingy from the inside of my boots.

"What will you write?"

"I'm supposed to start a novel for Don." I let myself laugh thinking about his suggestion, but Kacie looked confused so I said, "Dr. Kittering, a professor. He wants me to stay on as his student for a master's degree. The novel should be my thesis."

"See? Someone has faith in you."

"Don't you?"

She shook her head. "No, Brian. I've been let down enough."

"It won't be our story," I told her. "We're not over yet."

She smiled but it was a sympathetic kind of thing. I wanted to memorize it, her chin on her folded arms, her eyes like liquid gems.

"I wanted to wake you this morning," I said.

"But you didn't."

We sat still for a few more minutes until she asked, "What made you hit Eric Waters last night?"

"He said Tony didn't know when to say when."

Kacie laughed out loud. "None of us do." Then she rested her cheek on her forearm and closed her eyes again.

We had all been returning to that place time after time, expecting it to be the same every visit. We had all refused to acknowledge the changes in each other for fear that those changes might force us apart. We had all refused to grow apart. But we had, without meaning to, we had grown apart and Kacie, smiling at me, sitting on the floor under the window, seemed to say that it was okay.

"So should we talk about the last page in the green notebook?" I asked.

She lifted her head and then shook it, slowly, pressing her lips together in a small smile. "That was a long time ago," she said.

"We're not who the other wants us to be," I said, remembering her protest from the night before.

"And never will be again."

"And that's okay?"

"Sure, we can be friends."

I laughed. "I promise to be a better friend than a boyfriend."

"You were an okay boyfriend." She reached her hands out to me and I pulled my knees up and grasped her fingers. We both pulled and rose together. When we stood, we were inches apart.

It was a trick we had been doing for a long time. She stepped back quickly, though, leaned down to retrieve her Diet Coke, and headed for the door.

I glanced around but didn't see her jacket and guessed she must have left it downstairs.

"You should shower," she said over her shoulder as she left the room.

I walked behind her, down the hall, as far as the bathroom door. Before I stepped inside she said, "Remember not to set off the smoke detector." Then she winked and disappeared down the stairs.

When I called Chris a half-hour later, I was clean and dressed and smoking another cigarette, sipping on beer number one to kill what was left of my hangover. When he answered, he was out of breath.

"What are you doing?" I asked him.

"Just came back from doing it," he answered.

"What's that?"

"Running."

I started laughing involuntarily. I could sense him frowning on the other end of the line. "Why would you do a thing like that?"

"Needed to clear my head, that's all."

"You running alone?"

"Nah, Jason's here."

"Ah, the jock put you up to it." I laughed again at the thought of Jason dragging Chris down a residential street in some worn gray sweatshirt turned inside out and a sweatband around his head.

"Something like that." He held the phone away and I could hear him coughing. "Talk to Jason," he gasped.

"Brian?"

"Yeah, man."

"You got home okay last night?"

"Yeah," I said, not bothering with the details. I pressed my shoulder to the phone to pin it to my ear as I pulled a sock on over my foot.

"What's the plan?"

"I need food," I said.

"It's like one-thirty," Jason countered.

"So?"

"Nothing. Okay. I have to shower. Chris does, too, he's saying. How about Bistro in an hour?"

"Make it thirty, I'm starving. Oh, and not Bistro. Let's hit Santa Fe so we can shoot some pool." Jason agreed and I hung up the phone. I finished putting my shoes on, stubbed out my cigarette, and then made up the bed, tucking the sheet in under the mattress so that it would be tight and cool when I slipped in later that night.

I bounded down the stairs, shoving my wallet in my back pocket and lighter in the front one. I dropped a full pack of Marlboro Lights into the breast pocket of my flannel and turned the corner into the kitchen. Dad sat alone at the kitchen table.

I paused for a second and then said, as cheerfully as I could, "You okay, Dad?"

"Yeah."

"Wanna go shoot some pool with me and Jason?"

"Jason and me," he said.

"No," I said with a smile, "Jason and *me*."

"I don't think so." Dad's hair had begun to gray around his ears and temples. He wears it military short as if the haircuts just happen, once a week, without anyone actually planning to have it done. I never remembered him getting a haircut, I just remembered it was always neat. He sat staring at his hands, which were splayed on the table before him, the tips of his fingers going white from his downward exertion on the wood surface and then regaining color as he relaxed his grip.

"Dad?" I said after a moment. "Are you all right?"

"Take the car," he said absently.

I stood awkwardly against the counter for a minute. "I'm starving," I said finally. "I was thinking I'd get some food down at the Cue Club. Wanna come and eat?"

"Not really," he said. "There's a lot to do here." He was still watching his hands, pressing and releasing, pressing and releasing.

I started to leave, taking his keys from the counter near the laundry room door.

"What do you suppose Mac is doing today?" His question stopped me in place.

"I don't know. Why don't you call him? Or I could call him and invite him along to Santa Fe with us. Then would you want to go?" I stared at him for a minute, trying to figure out what this was all about. I heard Tony remind me to act like I love.

"No," he said finally and looked up at me. He was hurting and, I thought, wondering what to do about it.

I walked toward him but stopped when he stood. Then he closed the distance between us and hugged me and I let him.

Two firm claps on the back and then he pulled away, ducked his head, and said, "Dinner later?"

"Sure thing. Around eight?" I was already heading for the door.

"Your mother wants to go out."

"Great. I'll call at seven and we can meet somewhere."

Then I left. Pool and beer and a sandwich would help me to move on and moving on was what it was time to do. It had been five days since Tony had taken his own life and I was ready, I thought, to let the healing begin.

I took Baron Cameron Road into Herndon and sat at the light at Herndon Parkway. I looked down toward the high school, thinking that the trees growing in the median used to be much smaller than that and would probably be much bigger in two months when the leaves come back. The median trees were a vain attempt to make the parkway look like a country road. All of the new roads were that way, four lanes with a median that grew vegetation as if some deal had been struck with environmentalists. The area continued to develop beyond its capacity and each time I was home it seemed further disfigured, nearly unrecognizable.

The snow that had littered the ground when I arrived on Wednesday was completely gone now. Even the stubborn piles against the curbs and in the parking lot of the strip mall where Santa Fe Cue Club was had melted into the pavement. I parked near one of the puddles and locked the doors before closing the driver's side behind me.

Jason and Chris hadn't gotten there but I asked the server for a table and she led me back to the far corner and, after asking what I would like to drink, sauntered off in search of a pitcher of Killian's. I racked a game of nine-ball. The room was empty except for some Latino guys at the table near the dartboards. They spoke in Spanish to one another but didn't look my way. The music was low, and I could hear a muted version of Billy Joel coming through. When the server came back I would ask her to turn it up, I thought.

I put the triangle up on top of the low hanging lamp and bent down to shove the unused balls, still in their square tray, below the table. I pulled my keys out of my pocket and tossed them on the railing on the wall where there was an ashtray and a few crumbs from someone else's food. I guessed it was just a lazy

Saturday afternoon and the server probably didn't really want to work that day.

As if the thought had summoned her, she returned with the pitcher and set it on the rail. She wiped the crumbs away with a frown and set two frosted glasses down; she had carried them, stacked, in her right hand.

"Can I get you anything else?"

"We'll need a third glass and could you turn the music up a little?" I asked. "It's at that annoying level where you can make out what the song is."

"But not the lyrics," she said. "I know, it's been that way all day and every time I think to change it, I get busy doing something else." She laughed in spite of herself. "Short-term memory I guess. It's pretty busy today, huh?" She surveyed the near-empty room with all of the low lamps and the empty tables with green felt. Fourteen tables in all. Just two of them in play.

"I probably could have put you up front," she said but didn't really seem committed to it. She was slight with pale brown hair and thin shoulders. She looked undone and careless, more than a little tired and distracted.

"This is fine," I said. "I'm Brian. My friends Jason and Chris will be here soon. I guess just send them back." I gave her one of the smiles then, one of the ones I knew would make her think I was flirting.

Tony had once told me I was a player and I had agreed at the time, taking pride in the idea that women wanted me, and I could have them. Meli and Abby had teased me in California for being exactly what they expected someone who looked like me to be. Watching the server walk away, I considered how much of my flirtation was rehearsed and how much was natural. I wondered if I really was a player and if I had a right to be. But the real me, I thought, was a totally different person.

With Kacie, I had always been smooth until Saturday. I had

been romantic, passionate, and dramatic. I had been complimentary and doting early on, and challenging and demanding in the end. But until Saturday, I had never been honest with her. It was hard to be. I worried I was growing out of the person she had fallen in love with.

I was different in San Francisco. For one thing, I drank red wine and coffee and Kahlua. I knew Shakespeare and Thoreau, read more than I wrote, and counted my friends on two hands, mostly new hippies like Meli and Abby and gay men like David, who completed our foursome.

In Virginia, I consumed beer by the pint, pitcher, and twelve-pack and let televised sports substitute for conversations I didn't want to have. I hung out only with the guys I'd known my whole life and I pretended they knew me, too.

Jason entered the bar halfway through my game of nine-ball. He walked to the back, thanking the server for the direction and dropped his keys beside mine on the rail. I followed through on the shot I was taking, then walked around the table to the rail where he stood.

I extended my hand and made eye contact with him. He shook it, smiled, and said, "The traffic in this place kills me. It's Saturday for God's sake!"

"No kidding," I said. "I sat through the Parkway light twice." Then I pulled my cigarettes from my pocket and lit one. "What happened to Chris?"

"He'll be around. Had something to do first." Jason poured himself a beer, checking his watch as he did so. "I think we may have a long night ahead of us."

"You heading back tomorrow?" I asked.

"Yeah, I gotta hit the rink tomorrow night, try to work off some of the beer I've consumed the last few days." He took a big gulp and smiled again.

"Cool of them to let you off."

"I'm playing third line so I don't see a lot of time anyway."

"Isn't third line the thug line? Put in just to injure the other team's starters?"

Jason laughed. "It looks that way sometimes, yeah. Mostly, though, it's just a bunch of anxious rookies who don't have skills so they take it out on the checks."

"And that's you," I said. "I noticed at New Year's you'd gotten bigger."

"Did you invite me here to talk hockey, Brian?" He put his pint glass back on the rail and squared his chest with mine. "Because we can avoid the Kacie thing all afternoon if you want to."

I stared at him for a minute, not sure what to say. Then I looked away and smoked my cigarette. "Rack 'em," I said.

Jason stepped over to the table and circled it. He retrieved all the balls I'd sunk and pulled the triangle off of the lamp where I had left it. He worked at putting them into the nine-ball diamond shape for the break.

"I never hit her," I said.

"I know that now."

"She told you?"

"No. Tony did. But I knew then, I think."

"So then, why the drama?"

He stood up and the lamp was between us. I couldn't see his eyes, just a headless torso on the other side of the green felt table. He stepped around the lamp to make eye contact with me.

"I was angry with you for the way you treat her."

"You accused me of hitting her because you were *angry* with me?"

"What am I supposed to say? I wanted her. I've always wanted her."

"And you had her."

"When did she tell you?" he asked.

"New Year's Eve. *After* you assumed I'd probably hit her and called us both liars."

"I'm not proud of that night."

"Me neither." I crushed my cigarette in the ashtray on the rail and swallowed back the last of my beer.

He took a cue stick off the wall and picked up a blue square of chalk. I watched as he went through the motions of chalking the end, surveying the balls, and lining up his break shot. Then he leaned over the table, set the cue ball on the mark, and aimed. The stick went through his splayed fingers with ferocity and the cue ball smacked the other nine with a loud crack.

"I didn't give her the drugs, either. Did Tony tell you that, too?"

He shook his head, still watching the balls scatter across the table. "He only talked to me about you, and she wouldn't respond to me at all."

"She said it happened once over Thanksgiving."

He nodded and stood upright. He was hidden again, behind the low-hanging lamp.

"But that's not the truth, is it?" I realized suddenly that the server had made good on the music promise and the overhead radio was playing some light rock song I remembered from my orthodontist's office. I wondered if Jason had heard me. I watched the balls roll over the table and the blue two ball drop into the side pocket.

He moved out from behind the lamp again so he could see me and stopped, a few feet away, on the same side of the table where I stood. His arm fell away, the cue stick angling out from his body, his stance wide. He pulled the arm back in and then pushed it out again, like a paddling of some kind.

"What do you want me to say?" he asked.

"I don't want to lose either of you as friends."

"How are we still friends, Brian? We never see each other and when we do it's bullshit conversations like that one about hockey. I know you don't watch hockey in San Francisco. Tony said you hardly watch sports at all." He shook his head.

"What else did Tony say?" I reached for the pitcher and poured the last of the Killian's into my glass. Then I took another cigarette out of my pack and dropped the box back into my pocket.

Jason surveyed the table looking for a shot on the one ball. After a minute, he turned and looked at me, and leaned against the table. "Tony always said there was a side of you we didn't know and that all of us were just pretending."

"Pretending what?" I asked.

"How the hell should I know what that crazy fucker meant? He said shit like that all the time. Like you and Kacie hadn't been true to one another since high school, and she had no business doing what she was doing to try and keep you." He wore a white sweatshirt with the word Frostburg across it in red plastic screen print. He jerked at one of the cuffs, raising it up his forearm.

"I didn't want to stop being friends," he said, "even when Joel said you were probably too fucked up to notice." He shifted the cue to the other hand and jerked at his cuff on that side. Now both sleeves were up near his elbows and the extra material made his biceps look humongous.

"So we can't be friends?" I asked.

"What makes us friends? The past? That's weak."

I agreed with that, I knew I did. I was trying not to get defensive, but I did. "Tony."

"He's dead."

His words were sharp, and they cut a bit.

"What have you and Chris been talking about since you got back?" he asked.

"Tony. High school. Getting high."

"And?"

"That's pretty much it," I admitted. "Except he's been telling me what Joel was up to. Turns out I had no idea he had started a business." I shrugged.

"Seventy-five cents worth of conversation," he said bitterly.

We were quiet for a while. I lit the cigarette in my hand and took the box out and offered him one. He waved it off. He looked around for the server and I did, too, and when she looked over at us, I lifted the empty pitcher off the rail.

Finally he said, "I didn't sleep with her to get back at you." He stepped closer to me and looked directly at me, forcing me to look at him. "I've always loved her. I knew you had other women in California and wherever, but I never said anything. I watched her start with the cocaine to be near you, to be with you. I watched it and, yeah, I got angry."

The guilt flooded me like tears burning my eyes and I had to look away.

"And the shit thing was, Brian, when she finally did sleep with me, she needed someone to take care of her, to love her, and you were so incapable of it that she ended up in my bed." Jason is taller than I am. He's probably more handsome, too. He's genuine and honest and while I know he had a few flings, he respects women like no guy I've ever seen except Joel. I figured he probably hated me then.

"More than once," I said.

"What do you think?"

I remembered calling her a whore and felt a rush of shame.

"I knew you'd go over there last night," he said. "I tried to get her to let me stay but she knew, too, and she chose you. She sent me home because she chose you." He walked away from me, found the one ball and lined up a shot. I watched him lean over the table, shove the cue stick through his splayed fingers, and knock the yellow ball into the side pocket.

The waitress reappeared with a fresh pitcher and poured our glasses full. She also had the third glass, though Chris had yet to show, and she didn't fill it. I thanked her and watched her walk away.

"I'm not good for her," I said. "And I'm not a very good friend."

"That's where you're wrong." He walked back over and grabbed his beer from the rail behind me. "You're the best friend we have. You remind us of how invincible we once were. When we're with you, we feel like we used to feel."

"Whatever," I said.

"It's true, Brian. When have we been to San Francisco? Never. Tony once. Me? Joel? Chris? Never."

"I've never been to Detroit," I said.

"Chris has. Tony has, Joel and Tabby, Kacie has, too."

"What does that have to do with me?"

Jason sighed and waited for a minute until I guess he'd gotten his thoughts together and then said, "You're the only one pretending you've never changed. And you pretend we've never changed, either. Which is why it came as such a shock to you that Kacie and I might have anything in common."

"What do you and Kacie have in common?" I asked.

"She was in Detroit interviewing for a job."

"What kind of job?"

"She wants to be a sportswriter."

"But what about law school?"

"She hasn't wanted to go to law school for two years, Brian."

I thought back to our conversation that morning and how I had said she'd be in Charlottesville for three more years getting her law degree. She hadn't corrected me. The anger hit first and then the embarrassment. I said, "Why didn't she tell me?"

"Did you ask her?"

I never had. On the way from San Francisco to Virginia three days ago, I was so sure that I was the only one who had changed. I stood there, the fool, in Santa Fe Cue Club.

He stared at the table for minute and then said, "Are we cool now?"

"I'm not sure," I admitted.

"Me neither."

"It's still your turn."

Jason drank another half of his beer, said, "This is going down too easily." He walked around the table to where the cue ball lay and lined it up with the red three ball and took another shot. This time the ball hit the rim and rolled away from the pocket.

I stepped over to the cue ball, lined up a shot and leaned down to take it. I managed to sink the three, four, and five balls before bouncing the six ball off the rail. I stepped away from the table so Jason could take over.

I felt confused. My own replay of the week streamed by like a montage. I thought of the conversations I could recall, what my perceptions had been of them, and then what this new information transformed those exchanges into. I thought about Chris and me telling Mac about the redheads. But Kacie said it wasn't all redheads, just one. I thought about Tabby telling me I was selfish and that everyone put up with it because they considered me the Captain. I realized what that meant. I thought about the conversation Joel and Chris and I had the second night we were back. I had told them about Tony calling me on Sunday. Then I told them about my freshman year roommate's girlfriend whom I'd fucked. I called her a whore and we had laughed about it.

Just minutes before Joel walked into the men's room that night, I had stood in the stall with my cheek to the metal wall, breathing deeply and wishing I could just say all of the things I was thinking to the people who were supposed to be my friends. Then when Joel asked me to tell him, I had shut down. I didn't have that kind of relationship with him, I had reasoned. Besides, after New Year's Eve, and with Tabby and Kacie as close as they were, I wasn't sure he was still my friend at all.

I had been stoned. I felt like a fool.

I played nine-ball with Jason, quiet for a long time and thinking back on the week and all that had happened. I thought about that last page in Tony's notebook and the message he'd written to me and Kacie.

"Tell me something," I said. "Why am I still around when you all have moved on and I haven't? I mean, why not just leave me out?"

"That's easy. Tony wouldn't let us." Jason knocked the nine ball into the pocket, winning the game, and leaned his cue against the wall. He took the pitcher off of the rail to pour himself the last of the Killian's. "Tony kept telling us about what you were doing in San Francisco, classes and writing and all. He said you were busy. He said you were really talented."

"He didn't know shit about writing," I said.

"I guess it was his way of saying you were building a good life for yourself."

"Without him?"

"Without any of us." Jason grinned, which made me flinch. "Don't take it so hard, Brian. You're still the Captain." There didn't seem to be any regret or remorse in his voice at all. It was all very matter-of-fact the way he put it.

I was confused again and the beer wasn't helping to clarify anything.

Chris arrived, walking past the server, not ordering another pitcher even though we needed one. He came to the table, set a stack of pamphlets on the rail, and clapped hands with both Jason and me. Then Jason went for more beer.

I looked at the pamphlets, saw they were home-buying guides and new construction brochures. Walking over to the lamp, I pulled the triangle down to re-rack the game.

Chris watched me.

"You okay?" he asked. "You look like your dog died."

"Apparently I have been distant and neglectful of all of my friends," I said, "and while you've all grown together, I've cut myself off from you."

"So?"

"So? What do you mean 'so'?"

"You just figured this out?"

"Jason told me."

"Wish he'd have let you figure it out." Chris pulled a cigarette from his pack and lit it, dropping his keys, lighter, and box of smokes on top of the stack.

"Was there some sort of conference on this?" I asked.

"No, just some speculation, mostly on Tony's part. He would tell us to be patient with you and all that. No big deal."

"No big deal?" I repeated.

"Nah. Don't stress over it."

Jason returned and looked at the two of us. "Who's playing?" he asked.

"I'll play," Chris said, then added, "I thought you were starving. Where's the food?"

Again, as if summoned, the server appeared with the fresh pitcher of Killian's and a menu.

"Did you want something to eat?" she asked.

"Yes," I said and took the menu from her outstretched hand. I glanced through it quickly and placed an order for a Donnie's Inferno chicken sandwich with fries. She offered the menu to Jason and Chris but they waved her off.

We shot pool until about six thirty. We had five rounds of beer, cashed out the day server and welcomed a new one on shift. I was feeling kind of drunk before the whole thing was over. Joel showed up around five and it was nice to finally be back together again, just the guys, without hiding in the men's room.

He picked up the brochures, sliding Chris's keys and cigarettes onto the rail. "South Riding?" Joel asked, holding one up.

"Yeah," Chris said. "Really building up out there."

I stepped over to where Joel was thumbing through floor plans and picked up one of the brochures. On the cover was a four-story corner unit town home with a double garage on the bottom floor and a tall concrete staircase leading to the front door.

"Home ownership?" I asked.

"Possibly," Joel said. He put the stack back on the rail and said, "What's your place like in San Francisco?"

"It's a loft. Small." I thought about the bay window and the sunlight falling through and the boxes against the wall and said, "It's mine."

"Tell me about Melissa," he said.

"Not much to tell."

"How long have you known her?"

"A couple of years," I said. "We were friends for a long time."

"That's a good place to start," Joel said, probably thinking about Tabby.

"Does Kacie know?" Chris asked.

"Yeah," I said. "I think she's known for a while." Tony had told her. She would have said she thought I was distant the last time I was home and why hadn't I wanted to come home for Thanksgiving? Tony probably would have said I was busy with school or working on some really important project, and Kacie would have known it was a girl. Then she'd have asked who the girl was and Tony would have had to tell her, because as it turns out, he had really loved Melissa and I had stolen her right out of his memory and put her in my bed.

"Tony really loved her," I said to no one in particular.

"Who?" Chris asked.

"Melissa. Kacie said Tony really loved Melissa." I thought

about how that sounded for a minute and then said, "If I had known, I wouldn't have taken her."

"Yeah, you would have," Chris said with a weak smile. "Only then you would have kept it from him, too."

Joel said, "He was here, and she was there. He gave up his claim."

"Doesn't matter now," I said.

"Not much does in the long run, Cap'n," said Chris and that was the first time any of them had called me that in years.

Chris and Joel talked some more about getting a townhouse. Chris said he'd buy the place if Joel could just help him with the mortgage payment. Then, when it was time, Joel could move out to be with Tabby. They talked about South Riding and Joel asked if Chris's stepmother, Angela, who was a real estate agent, could help them. Chris said he was thinking about getting into real estate, too, so they could just wait and see.

"Will Tabby move here?" I asked.

Joel shook his head. "Her whole family is in Pittsburgh. I'll go back there after I get things set up here. What will you do when you've finished?"

"I'm going to Spain for six months to write. Hemingway's stomping grounds in Barcelona. Maybe go over to Madrid for a few nights." I shrugged.

"Tough life," Jason said.

"Yeah, well, I'm starting an MFA and I have to write a novel for my thesis. I figured what better way to do it than to hang out in Spain?" I took my turn on the table and finished off my glass of beer.

"Send postcards," said Chris.

"I figured you to come back here after graduation," said Joel.

"Alan and Joan are moving." I hadn't called my parents by their names before, not the way Chris and Joel and even Tony did. Hadn't seen them as apart from me. Until now.

"When?" Chris asked. "Where?"

"Soon. Arizona." I took another turn, sunk another ball, and said, "Won't have any reason to come back and won't have anywhere to stay."

"Ouch, man," Chris said, real hurt in his voice.

"Us," Joel said, "you'll stay with us."

I felt a little drunk from the beer, and I wasn't holding myself in my normal Virginia posture anymore. All I'd ever felt about Herndon was wanting to get the fuck out. As far away as I could. I looked at each of them. My reasons for coming back.

"Brian," Jason said. "I think Spain sounds great." He put his palm out and I folded mine into it. He pulled me against him for a slight hug. I turned my cheek into his shoulder.

I pictured the wrought iron chairs of a sidewalk café in Barcelona as the flaming ball of fire set in the west and the long shadows of stucco buildings crept across the ground and over my lap. I tried to see the three of them around the table. The thought made me smile. They smiled, too, and I wondered if they saw what I was seeing.

"Not going to Spain," said Chris, as if reading my mind, "but we'll be here when you get back."

At seven I called my parents and Mom said she and Dad were coming over to Hard Times Café, the chili restaurant attached to the Cue Club. I knew they were coming to get Dad's car before I tried to drive it home.

Joel and Jason left to drop one car at their mom's and pick up Tabby who had been trying to get in touch with Kacie when Joel found us. Chris declined my invitation to stay for dinner and met my parents at the door. He said he'd be back in an hour to get me.

Mom told the hostess they wanted non-smoking and we followed her to a booth against the wall in the back near the jukebox. They sat on the same side across from me, an arrangement we'd adopted when I was in high school.

"What errands did you run today?" I asked.

"We sent flowers to the Williamses, went to Lowe's for some hardware and screws for the towel rack in the guest bath. What else did we do?" Mom said.

"Checked on the car."

"What car?" I asked.

"We may buy a new car for your father," Mom said.

"What kind of car?"

"A Jeep Cherokee. We want the four-wheel-drive for when we go skiing," Dad said.

They talked like that, finishing each other's thoughts, answering questions that were asked of the other one. It was a great act that I was used to, but Tony always said it freaked him out. His own parents were rarely in the same room and when they were, his mom did most of the talking.

Dad ordered a Killian's and Mom got a glass of wine. I asked the server for an ice water.

"What did you do today?" Mom asked.

"Slept for a while, hung out with Kacie for a while."

"How was that?"

"Different," I said. She had asked but they were both listening. I sat up a little bit, putting my elbows on the table. "I've never thought of her as a friend before but today we really talked like friends."

"That's good?" Dad asked.

"Yeah, I think so."

"Did you call Melissa?" Mom's fingers tugged at the cocktail napkin below her wine glass, shifting it a little, fidgeting.

I nodded. "Talked to her this morning. Came here and shot

pool with Jason and Chris and Joel. That was enlightening." I smiled a little bit and said, "Do you think I keep my friends in a box?"

"Why?" Dad asked.

"Jason says they've all grown up and still know each other, but I haven't changed to them or let them change to me. Do you think that's true?"

"I don't know," Mom said. "What do you think?"

"I kept thinking nothing had changed but I knew that I had. Then I didn't change here, I was the same here, but California it's different, ya know?" My head was a little fuzzy and as much as I wanted to work this all out, I was having trouble deciding if I wanted to work it out with them in the room. That indecision made me stutter a bit.

"What will you order for dinner?" Dad asked suddenly.

"Can't decide."

"You seem tired," Mom said. "You don't have to figure all this out right now," she added, and reached for my hand, squeezing it gently across the table.

I noticed that the jukebox had quit playing and the room was filled with the noises of a restaurant, the clinking and scraping of silver and plates, the voices of cooks and servers. Then the hostess stopped by the jukebox, pushed some numbers, and it roared back to life with a country music tune. I thought of Tony and wondered if he'd have known this song.

"So what time's my flight tomorrow?" I asked Dad.

"Late. Four forty-five."

"Good. I'd like to go by and see Mac on the way out."

"Sure," Dad said.

"We'll all go," Mom agreed.

I asked them how long it would be before they completed the move to Oro Valley. I let them tell me again about the community and their plans to ski in the winter and play golf until it got too hot. Mom told a story about her sister-in-law trying to get an Arizona driver's license. Dad reminded her to gather the required documents before going to the DMV so she wouldn't have to make multiple trips like Deb did.

We ordered our meals, and when they arrived I tried to convince myself that I was hungry. It had only been a couple of hours since I'd eaten, but I knew more food would be needed to get through what Jason had predicted would be a long night.

Sometime into our meal, after another round of drinks arrived for my parents, I said, "Let's talk about what happens in San Francisco."

Alan and Joan exchanged a look. I took a long drink out of my ice water.

"Okay," Dad said. "What's the plan?"

"I've been asked to stay on for graduate school."

"That's wonderful," Mom said.

"Is there a salary?" Dad asked.

I laughed. "Yeah, Dad, it's paid. Not much, I'll still need help, but I think it's the right thing to do. Right now I think that."

"But?" Dad said.

"But I'd like to take a break first."

"What kind of break?" Mom asked.

"I want to go to Spain this summer and stay until Christmas."

Dad lifted his burger to his mouth and took a bite. After a slight pause, Mom went back to eating her chili mac.

I ate a couple of French fries I'd soaked with vinegar. I'd learned to eat them that way at Camden Yards. Joel would get a cup of fries and douse them all; he said his dad ate them that way. I had wondered, at the time, what I'd gotten from my dad. He liked cracking peanut shells at baseball games and took sunflower seeds with us when we went fishing that time. But I wasn't overly fond of peanuts or sunflower seeds.

"We can talk about Spain," Mom said and took a drink from her wine glass.

"Let's talk about it now," I said.

We went to Europe when I was a teenager. We took Tony with us. We saw Paris and the French countryside, stayed in a villa, and went to several vineyards. Tony had been inspired to paint and, lacking real materials, had done several charcoal drawings on a parchment tablet Mom bought him in a gift shop. Mom and Dad always said it was cheaper to take Tony on vacation than to have raised another kid. I was proving to be rather expensive, but still less than another kid my age or younger would have been.

"What will you do in Spain?" Dad said finally.

"Are you any good at bull fighting?" Mom smiled over the rim of her glass.

I smiled back at her. "I've taken up Flamenco dancing," I said.

"Do you have a partner?" Dad asked, raising his beer to his mouth.

"No," I said, "but Jason may come over to bum around during the off season. So there's a possibility." I wasn't even sure what Flamenco dancing looked like and in my imagination, Jason and I looked more like a pairs figure skating duo with costumes that resembled wrestling singlets and bore Kandinsky-like paint splotches. "We'll start with some basics; he doesn't have my experience. Cha-cha, tango, that sort of thing. But he's a good athlete. I think he'll catch on." I let myself laugh at the image and could see my parents' amusement, too, at the idea of Jason and me ballroom dancing.

"And when you're not setting the Flamenco dance scene on fire with your talent, what then?" Dad asked.

"I'll write," I said. "Try to make a go of that. Get ready for graduate school. I'll have to complete a novel or a story collection as a thesis in the MFA program."

"MFA?" Mom asked. "That's three years."

"It's a terminal degree."

Mom looked over at Dad, then they both looked at me.

"All right," Dad said. "I think we can work that out. Just put a plan together," he added. "Place to live, work, a show of progress. Aside, of course, from your blue ribbons from the dancing."

I smiled. "Of course," I said. "The dancing will just be a hobby."

"Literary magazine submissions or agent queries or whatever," Mom said. "Whatever the thing is serious writers do." She wiped her hands on her napkin and laid it on the table. "Make a real commitment to it, okay?" she asked.

"Okay," I said. "I'll write up a plan."

"Okay," Dad said. "And after you give it a go, you should expect to get a real job."

I grinned. "Of course, Dad."

Chris came to get me. My parents had finished their meals but ordered another round of drinks and were people watching in the restaurant.

I told them both goodnight and kissed Mom's cheek. Chris said goodbye and we left.

We drove over to the high school again but this time we didn't get out of the car; we just sat in that shadow of the bleachers and listened to Mazzy Starr.

"You and Kacie work things out?" Chris asked me.

"I think so."

"How about Jason?"

"Yeah, it's okay I guess."

Chris tapped his fingertips on the steering wheel. "Brian, I just want you to know that I don't blame you."

"For what?"

"For wanting to keep things like they were. I mean, they were great, ya know?"

"I guess."

"Did you understand what Jason was saying today?"

"Yeah. I've been pretending nothing had changed. But I thought all of you were pretending, too."

"We were. To you, anyway."

"Treat the Captain with kid gloves. He's mad," I said.

"Feel like there's been a mutiny?"

"Sort of." I laughed. "Then I feel sort of relieved, too. Like I don't have to keep up the act anymore, ya know?"

"What kind of act?"

"I don't know. Sometimes it all felt fake."

Chris and I were quiet for a while and then he said, "It's all good."

"Yeah, I guess it is."

While we passed the bowl back and forth, headlights appeared in the distance of the parking lot. We rolled all of the windows down, and Chris put the car into drive. Pulling slowly out of the space and heading toward the exit, we pulled up alongside the patrol car, having rolled three of the windows back up.

"Good evening, officer," said Chris through his open window.

"Evening," said the cop, scoping out the two of us, the car, and the placement of our hands. Chris had one arm on the window and one arm on the wheel. I had one arm on my window and was turning the radio down with the other hand so he could see it.

"You guys have business around here?" the man asked.

"No, sir. Just a couple of high school buddies reminiscing, talking over some stuff before this guy flies back to California tomorrow," said Chris, gesturing to me.

"Have a safe trip," said the cop. Then he nodded and pulled away.

Chris crept slowly toward the exit and turned his headlights on. I turned up the radio a bit and started laughing.

"Close as hell," said Chris, "motherfucker."

Thinking Chris may have lost his buzz in that conversation, I packed another bowl for us to finish before we got to Town Center.

I missed Tony then, I know I did. Nothing was the same without him around. He was home and without him, it was just Virginia.

The light on Bennet Street changed and Chris turned out onto Dranesville Road. We passed the cemetery where we'd left Tony yesterday. Neither of us spoke and I don't think Chris even looked, but I was staring toward the grave, trying to see if the Greene Funeral Home tent was still up. It wasn't.

Then Chris turned onto Herndon Parkway and we left the cemetery behind and followed the tree-lined median toward Baron Cameron and Reston Town Center.

We parked in the lot outside of Uno and Chris smoked another bowl while I finished a bottle of water. I was high and ready to start drinking again. I followed Chris into Uno where we found the Crew sitting at the table we'd all occupied the night before. I looked over at the bar to see if the pretty cheerleader bartender was there. She smiled at me and waved.

I turned back to my friends.

Kacie sat in a chair up against the window, sipping wine out of a tall glass. I watched her fingers wrap around the glass, lift it to her lips and set it back down. She slid her fingertip over the rim where her lips had been and then put the tip of her finger to her tongue. She still wore the blue sweater and white headband and she looked like a celebrity. As I watched her, she glanced over and caught me staring.

I smiled. She smiled back.

"Beer?" Chris asked me.

"I'll get it," I said and went to the bar. I waved off the first bartender, waiting for Ashley. She turned around and came toward me.

"Hello again."

"I'm here to pay up," I said.

"You haven't even started a tab yet," she said.

"On last night's promise."

She smiled. "Let's just see how the night goes, okay?" She looked over my shoulder at the Crew and then leaned in close to me. "Neither of those girls is your girlfriend?"

"Not one of them," I said. "Not even the one in the gray underwear," I added, referring to Chris who wore a three-button Henley that looked like long johns.

Ashley laughed. "Beer?"

"Old Dominion draft?" I held up two fingers.

She filled a pair of tall glasses from the tap. "Do you want your own tab?"

"Yeah," I said. "That would be great." I was taking her home tonight, I decided right then. And maybe I was feeling reckless or maybe I was just high, but the decision made me wink at her as our fingers touched.

Back at the table, I slid Chris's beer in front of him and took a long drink from my own.

"That buzz wear off?" I asked Jason.

"Started to. I hurried over here for some CBR."

"CBR?" Tabby asked.

"Cold Beer Rejuvenation," Jason said with a grin. Tabby rolled her eyes, but I laughed because I was high and it was funny.

The Caps were playing on TV, tied 1-1 with the Sharks going into the second intermission. Jason predicted Gonchar, who'd scored the Caps' tying goal, would get another hat trick.

"He's the best in the game right now," he said.

"For sure," I agreed though until yesterday I'd had no idea who he was. I took the chance to rib Tabby, though. "He's already got as many goals as your whole team last night."

She glared at me but at least this time it wasn't about Kacie or me flirting or Joel being drunk or me being high. It was just sports. An easy substitute for the real talk we were all tired of. Four days, one funeral, a fist fight, and a slew of shots and nobody had the stamina for anything more serious. Not even Tabby.

Jason laughed out loud. "No shit. Gonchar has as many goals as the entire Pittsburgh roster. Six to one? Pens got beat down last night."

"Care to place a wager?" Tabby asked. "I bet the Sharks win."

"Shots on the loser?" I said.

"Deal." Jason stuck his hand out.

"Buyer's choice," Kacie added.

Jason and Tabby shook hands across the table and we all lifted our drinks to toast the wager. I felt a shared grin and more than a buzz. I felt at home.

"Told my parents about Spain," I said to Joel.

"What about Spain?" Tabby asked.

"Brian's planning to go Hemingway on us for a while," Joel said, a grin causing wrinkles at the corners of his eyes.

"You know he drank himself to death," Tabby deadpanned.

I lifted my glass for a long drink before I succumbed to a rude retort.

"How'd your dad take it?" Kacie asked.

"I think he wants me to work for it," I said, lighting a cigarette and blowing the first exhale toward the ceiling. "I know this guy in San Francisco who worked on the docks in Barcelona for a year to pay his way to the States."

"Where's he from?" Jason asked.

"South Africa."

"Must be an interesting guy," Joel said.

"Yeah, his parents own a sugar cane plantation and paid his way to Wales and he just bummed around Europe for two years. Got the job in Spain and made enough to come over here. He works down on the docks in San Francisco. He says the language of docks is universal."

"Really?" Chris asked. "What's the language?" He took a long drink from his tall draft beer and set the glass back on the table."

"Hard work, good pay, great hours," I said. "Luke said he and his buddies would work from around five a.m. until about eleven and then have the afternoons off."

"Five a.m.?" Joel asked.

"Well, I swam at five a.m. every day for twelve years. I think I can get back to it." I smiled. "If it comes to that."

"Will Melissa go with you?" Kacie asked.

There was a shift of the others at the table, a kind of exchange of glances as if this would become a fight.

"No," was all I said. Just then a shot arrived from the bar. I looked over at Ashley who drained one just like mine and I followed her lead. When I turned back to the table, Tabby had crossed her arms over her chest and sat back into her chair. So much for the sports diversion.

"Did you want one?" I asked.

Her eyes narrowed.

I looked at Kacie but she was letting Jason light her cigarette before he lit his own.

"About time to quit these I guess," he said.

"What's the likelihood you get picked up by the Wings?" Chris asked.

"Slim," Jason said. "Or at least that's what I keep telling myself so that I'm not thirty and still playing minors hoping the Wings will come to their senses. I figure a few more years and if it doesn't happen, oh well."

"What will you do?" I asked him.

"My old coach said there's a place for me here, helping with the little kids. I guess I'll start with that. Maybe coach high school or assist at a college somewhere. I know I want to stay in hockey. I may need to finish my degree at some point."

"Chris may need a roommate in that new house," I said.

Chris looked from me to Jason and said, "Sure, after your brother bails."

"You're buying a house?" Kacie asked.

Chris shook his head. "It's just an idea."

Tabby looked at Joel.

"It's just an idea," he repeated, and took a long drink out of his glass.

I looked from him to Tabby and she was glaring at me again.

"What?" I asked.

"The Crew goes to shoot pool for a few hours and suddenly everyone's got a plan," Kacie said. "Wish I'd been in on that brainstorm session." She winked at me.

Tabby still had her arms crossed and the look on her face was accusatory. I would have told her I didn't have anything to do with the townhouse-buying plan, but I thought it was better to take whatever blame she wanted to assign me. After a second, she reached for her purse.

"Bathroom?" she asked Kacie.

They slid off their stools and headed toward the ladies' room. Kacie had her cigarette in her hand and I watched her raise it above her head as she went so as to not burn anyone. Then the crowd swallowed them and I turned back to the guys.

"Why does she hate me so much?" I asked Joel.

"She doesn't hate you. She just doesn't know you."

"And what she knows isn't all that good." Jason stubbed out his cigarette, wasting another one after two drags. At least it wasn't one of mine.

"Guess not," I admitted.

"Don't worry about her," Chris said. "She'll come around. They all do. The ladies love Listo." He jerked his chin toward Ashley who was, just then, smiling at me.

"So, a dock worker, huh?" Joel asked.

I laughed. "Can you see it?"

He shook his head. "Hard work? For you? Nope."

"You wanna hire me at your company?" I asked.

"Can you write code?"

I shook my head. "Man, I don't even know what that means."

When we skated, Joel was the best of all of us. They all thought I was because I pulled hard tricks. I skated without fear, they said. But Joel was clean. He landed everything. He didn't go for the big air, but he didn't land on his knees, either. Starting a company was like going for big air and I was more proud of him than I knew how to say. So I just clinked my glass to his and took a long drink.

I turned and saw Chris had pushed his way through the crowd. He was ordering from Ashley and talking to a guy sitting at the bar and they both turned and looked toward our table. I knew him. Chris came back with a tray of shots, seven square glasses filled to the brim and a plate of lemons coated with sugar.

"Vodka," I said. "Good man."

The girls returned and we all situated ourselves as standing or sitting around the cocktail table by the window. Just like last night and the night before.

"Vodka," Kacie said, taking a glass and a slice of lemon. "Good man." She raised her glass toward Chris who was the only other person with a shot in his hand.

"Let's do this," Jason said.

We all grabbed a shot, leaving the seventh one on the tray.

"To being a good man," Joel said. "Cheers."

We all raised the shots and then drained the glasses of vodka.

Kacie, Tabby, Joel, and Chris shoved lemons in their mouths. Jason made a face but chased the shot with his beer.

Chris moved closer to Jason to let someone else into the circle. I looked at the newcomer, who now stood shoulder to shoulder with me. Christian Heilman.

"Hi, everyone," he said cheerfully. Though he was the same age as us, he had always looked older. Acne scars and a persistent deep tan made him look like a middle-aged real estate agent. Rumor was he hadn't been carded for cigarettes or beer as long ago as eighth grade. He'd played lacrosse with Chris and Joel. I stepped back to let Joel move closer so they could talk.

The bar music swelled and I took advantage of it to lean in close to Kacie and say, "You look hot."

"You're an idiot," she said in response. She reached past Tabby and took her wine glass. Jason watched us but she didn't meet his eye. She had an unlit cigarette in her hand.

"Didn't you just have one?" I asked.

"You're not the boss of me," she said and stuck her tongue out at me then lit the thing. She blew the first exhale at me and I pretended to cough in response.

I stepped back and took another drink out of my glass, realized it was pretty empty, and turned around to see what the best way to get to Ashley would be. I pushed through the crowd and got a refill.

When I returned, Christian Heilman had moved around Joel and was talking to Kacie. I watched for a minute, from a few feet away, until he leaned in toward her, as I'd done, and said something in her ear. When he pulled back, I caught a glimpse of Jason across the table. The look on his face was murderous.

I stepped between Kacie and Christian, putting my fresh beer on the table, and held out my hand.

"Christian," I said. "Been a long time."

"Hey, Brian," he said. "Sorry about Tony."

My fist clenched at my side. "Thanks," I said tightly.

"I was just telling Kacie I saw him not too long ago. Wasn't he working over at Worldgate?" Christian and I are the same height, and when I looked him in the eye I could see the dilation I knew to be coke-induced.

I managed to smile, clap a hand on his shoulder, and say, "Yep. What've you been doin'?"

He said something about a job at the U.S. Geological survey and then added he was hoping Joel would hire him and looked over his shoulder when he said it. Joel wasn't paying attention, though. He was having a silent conversation with Tabby across the table.

"You still out in L.A.?" Christian asked me.

"San Francisco."

"Oh yeah?" He shoved his hands into the pockets of his khaki pants and leaned back on his heels. "Used to be L.A.. That's right."

"Nope. Used to be San Francisco."

"No, you went to UCLA."

I laughed again. "Pretty sure I didn't."

"Right. Okay, so, you're in computers, too? Bay Area, Silicon Valley, all that shit?"

"Not even a little bit," I said.

"He works on the docks," Joel said, clapping Christian on the shoulder and moving him to the side so he could get back to Tabby.

I looked over at her as she pushed her hair over her shoulder and adjusted her shirt.

"You leaving?" I asked.

"Nah, just going up the block. Tabby's bored," Joel added.

I looked up at the hockey game. The Caps were up 2-1.

"Come back soon," I said. "You'll owe us a round of shots."

She pretended not to hear me, but I saw Jason grin out of the corner of my eye.

I moved out of the way and Joel took his coat off of the back of Kacie's chair. Tabby slid off her stool and squeezed behind Kacie. She had her coat and purse in her hand.

"You'll need that," I said, pointing at her handbag. "Joel's balls are in it."

"Very funny," he said.

Tabby glared at me, turned with a swish of her long black hair, and stormed off, down the steps to the hostess stand and into the vestibule.

I looked back at Kacie. She didn't look amused. But when I looked past her at Jason, he was laughing.

"I really don't know what I did to piss off your sister-in-law," I told Jason.

"Don't call her that," he said. "I like her and all, but none of us is there yet."

"Amen," Kacie said, sliding over into the chair Tabby had vacated.

I turned to see if Chris was listening but he was talking to a petite, dark-haired girl at the next table. She had a moon-shaped face and smallish features. She looked like an elf but in a pretty, pixie-like way. She wore a black lace choker with a thick silver chain over it.

"What's with the dog collar?" I asked of no one in particular.

I turned to Kacie and Jason and they were watching Chris and the pixie, too.

"It's a Tiffany necklace," Kacie said.

"It looks like K9 hardware," I said.

"Don't be mean."

"I'm not trying to be," I said.

"Is anyone gonna take that?" Christian Heilman asked and I

turned and realized he was still there. He reached for the seventh shot glass, still sitting in the middle of the table.

Jason put his palm over it.

Christian pulled back, looked at each of us, but getting no explanation, said something I didn't hear, and walked away.

I watched him go.

"So this is fun," Jason said.

I turned back to where he and Kacie were sitting side-by-side with an empty stool next to her. I sat down on it and felt her stiffen. We all looked straight ahead.

"Nope. Still too weird," I said, and stood up and walked away without looking back.

"Hey, Brian," Kacie called after me.

I turned.

She raised Tony's shot to me in salute and then took it.

I smiled at her and pushed my way into the crowd in the direction of the men's room.

It wasn't empty like it had been on Thursday. Uno was packed and there was a line about six guys deep. I wished for a minute I'd brought my beer, and then thought about what I would do with it while I pissed and decided it was best left on the table with Kacie and Jason. I imagined Kacie dropping a roofie in it. The idea of that made me smile. I amused myself thinking through a story where the guy's ex-girlfriend and new boyfriend drug the guy and take pictures with his body like *Weekend at Bernie's* or something. The idea of the corpse, though, reminded me of Tony, and I remembered what he looked like lying in that satin and then I really wished I had something to drink.

I started counting the number of beers and shots I'd consumed, looking at my watch to see the amount of time we'd been here. I thought of the hours on the dock and wondered if they passed as quickly as the hours in the bar. I wondered why I'd told them about Luke and the docks when working there was really unlikely. I wondered why they hadn't asked how I met Luke. Funny story, I thought to myself, standing in the men's room line. He was David's boyfriend for about a month once he found out I wasn't gay.

The line moved forward, and I walked into the bathroom only to find the urinals were all full. I pushed on the first stall door, the one I'd been in Thursday. It was locked. Then someone stepped away from a urinal and I took his place.

Through the mirror to my right I saw the line moving and saw Jason enter. Then the door to the first stall opened and Christian Heilman came out. The two moved around each other and exchanged words. I finished at the urinal and stepped away. Jason and Christian were chest to chest. The music throbbed outside and flooded the room as the door opened.

"What's going on?" I asked Jason.

"This fucker was talking about Kacie."

"What did you say?"

"Just that I heard she likes to party," Christian said. He rubbed his nostril with the forefinger knuckle on his right hand. "And that I'd hit that."

Jason grabbed Christian and shoved him up against the stall door.

The room was crowded and some guys backed away, shoving others into the urinals and sinks. Two guys we didn't know tried to peel Jason off Christian, and the guys trapped in the stalls in the commotion pounded on the doors.

Jason came away, cussing at Christian and fighting his captors, but not really. He was bigger than them and he was only halfway into the fight anyway.

"All this for a strung-out whore?" Christian said.

For the second time in as many days, I decked a guy. I landed my fist right across his eye just as the bouncers came through the door to the men's room.

"You fuck!" Christian shouted from the floor.

The bouncers were as big as Jason and they shoved him and the other guys out of the way and grabbed me. I didn't fight them, just let them drag me out into the bar. The crowd parted and I saw Kacie turn, still perched on her stool, blue sweater, white headband.

I thought she was smiling but if she had been, she wasn't after she saw me.

The bouncer dragging me didn't bother to stop at the coat rack. He just shoved me out onto the sidewalk. When I turned, Christian was being shoved out, too. Once he righted himself and the bouncers went back inside, he turned to me.

"What the fuck, man?" he said.

I started laughing.

"You dick," he said.

"Get outta here, man," I said. "I was in a fight here last night. I'm pretty sure I'll be forgiven."

Chris came through the door then with my coat and stretched it out to me. "I told Ashley we'd settle up after they close," he said.

Jason and Kacie came out next.

"What the hell happened?" Kacie asked.

"There she is," Christian said.

Jason stepped between them. "Get the fuck outta here," he said.

"It's a free country, Lincrest," Christian sneered. "Besides, she's Listo's whore. What do you care?"

Then Jason hit him.

"Jesus, Jason," Kacie said, but she didn't look away.

This time Chris laughed.

Christian staggered toward the street, cussing us all. I watched him on the crosswalk, shoving his trembling hands through his hair, spitting blood onto the concrete and finally jerking open the door at Bistro Bistro. He looked back at me and flipped me a bird.

I returned the gesture. "What now?" I asked Chris, shoving my arm into my coat and pulling it over my shoulders.

"What the hell is wrong with you guys?" Kacie asked.

"Just drunk," I said.

She pulled her coat tighter around her. It was the pink ski jacket she'd been wearing on Wednesday, and I remembered her telling me to stay away from her.

"Don't be mad," I said.

Jason stepped toward her, reached for her, but she turned away.

"Come on," she said over her shoulder. "Put your coats on. Fucking assholes. Let's go to Market Street." She started up the sidewalk not waiting for us to follow her.

Jason flipped his coat over his head, like we used to do when we were kids, and shimmied into it. He managed to smile. Chris laughed again, looked at me, and I shrugged.

"Is that where Joel and Tabby went?" I asked.

"Not sure," Jason said. He looked after Kacie, and his smile slipped away.

"Don't worry about it," I said. "She's drunk, too."

The walk to Market Street was the inner sidewalk of Reston Town Center, past Gap, Victoria's Secret, and Sam Goody, past the courtyard and the ice-skating rink, the fountain and the white wire chairs. We passed Clyde's and as we did, the revolving door rotated slowly and Tabby and Joel came out.

"Perfect timing," Kacie said.

"Where are you guys headed?" Joel asked.

"These assholes got us kicked out of Uno." Kacie jerked her head toward us. Her hands were still in her pockets. The arms of her coat and the pink puffiness of the down made her look like a Valentine.

"Another fight?" Tabby asked.

I grinned. "Not much of one."

Tabby pushed her arm through Kacie's and said, over her shoulder, "We're going to Bistro," and headed back toward that end of the street.

"No, you're not," Jason said.

"Why not?" Tabby demanded.

"Because the motherfucker Brian and I just had to hit is there."

"You?" Joel asked.

"*Had* to hit him?" Tabby asked.

"You didn't have to hit him," Kacie said.

"He called you a whore," I said.

"So did you once."

"We're back to that?" I raised my arms to my sides. "Come on, Kace, give me a break."

She shook her head. "We're done, Brian. All this shit, it's done."

"Kacie," Jason said, stepping between us, and I let him. I stepped back.

"You, too," she said. "You two." She shook her head.

"Let's go," Tabby said. But she didn't walk toward Bistro. She walked toward the center of the courtyard where a taxi was idling as some people in the backseat climbed out.

"Perfect timing," Kacie said again, and she and Tabby climbed into the cab.

Joel ran over to the car and leaned in. He said something to the girls and then closed the door.

"So now what?" Jason asked, as we watched the taxi pull away from the curb.

"Market Street," Chris said.

The four of us fell into stride side-by-side and walked past the ice rink toward the Hyatt and the bar on its ground floor, Market

Street. It was one-fifteen and we had enough time for a round of beers and another round of shots, with one extra, which Joel took, calling it his doghouse shot.

When I went to piss at Hyatt, I walked by a long wall of pay phones. After a minute to think about it over the urinal, I came back through and lifted one of the handsets. I dialed Melissa's number.

"Please deposit three dollars and thirty-five cents," said the voice of the operator.

"Man, whaddya doin?" Chris asked, stepping up next to me.

I hung up.

"We're ready to go," he said. "You okay?"

I nodded and followed him back into the bar. Then we paid that tab and walked back down to Uno.

The bar had closed and people were filing out. We stood on the sidewalk waiting for the place to empty out. Chris and I smoked cigarettes, and Joel and Jason kept their hands shoved in their pockets. We didn't see anyone else we knew. Joel asked Chris if he was okay to drive and Chris asked the same of Joel and we all sort of agreed to say yes and just be careful.

Jason asked me when I'd be coming back to Virginia and I told him I didn't really plan to. Chris said I would have a place to stay after my parents moved, and I said I knew that was true.

Chris looked through the window and nodded at me. Inside, we found Ashley and closed our tabs.

"What time's your flight tomorrow?" Joel asked, shoving his wallet back into his pocket and pulling his jacket back down over his pants.

"Four forty-five," I said, putting my own wallet away.

"Breakfast? Amphora?"

"Like a New Year's Day do-over?" I asked.

He grinned. "Sure," he said. "Why not?" He held his hand out and I folded mine into it and let him pull me in for a hug.

"I sure have missed you," he said quietly.

I pressed my cheek into his shoulder and nodded.

A few more hand clasps and half hugs between Jason and me and Jason and Chris, and then the twins went through the Uno vestibule and set out across the parking lot. Chris and I watched them through the window and then I turned back to the credit card slip in front of me. I added a tip and totaled it up and then signed my name.

"Brian Listo," Ashley said. "I thought I recognized you the other night, but I wasn't sure." She poured a fresh beer and put it on the bar for me. "Stay a while."

I looked at Chris and back at her and she nodded and poured him a drink, too.

"Wanna tell me what this whole thing's been about?" Ashley said, taking the napkin holders and straw containers down from the counter one at a time and storing them on a shelf on the other side. She took steaming glasses out of the dishwasher and stacked them together, placing them in the cooler in front of her.

"This whole thing?" I asked.

"Well, most people come into town twice a year, summer and Christmas break, to see their high school buddies and fight with old girlfriends. It's not summer yet and Christmas was a while ago," she finished.

"Yeah, it was," I agreed.

"So?"

"So, my best friend killed himself and we all came back for the funeral."

"Shit," she said.

"I told you the other night, but I was really drunk and a little bitter, trying to cope, ya know?" I pulled my cigarettes from the breast pocket of my button-down shirt. "Chris said you probably wouldn't remember."

"I remember," she said. "I guess I was hoping you were just drunk."

"Can't get drunk enough to make it not true," I said with a weak smile, "but I've tried." I took another swallow of beer, lit the cigarette, and exhaled a stream of smoke.

"What's with the fighting?"

"It's not usually my thing," I said. She cocked her head and looked skeptical. "Last night a drug dealer said the wrong thing and tonight some douche who went to Herndon with us said the wrong thing."

"Christian," she said.

"You know him?"

"I graduated with you."

"Really?" I asked. "Did I know you?"

"Nope. Hey, let me take these glasses. I'll be right back." She lifted a huge tray of upside-down glasses and walked out of the bar in the direction of the kitchen.

I stared up at the television.

"She came in late junior year," Chris said.

"Really?"

He nodded, tapping ash off his cigarette. "Some kind of trouble at Paul the Sixth."

Ashley returned then and we just drank our beers and smoked. She cashed out our credit card slips, taking the tips out of the drawer, and said, "Thanks."

"So, you were at Herndon," I said. "That's how you knew about the ex-girlfriend?" She nodded and lit a cigarette for herself.

"Would I have known you at Herndon?"

"No," she said. "I kept a low profile." She continued her closing work, folding the mats into the washer, wiping down the trays they'd sat in, and taking occasional drags off the cigarette she left perched in the ashtray we were using. The other bartender returned from the back, where he'd been since we'd come back in, and handed her a wad of cash.

"Thanks, Dan," she said, shoving the money into her pocket. "So, I'm almost done here," she said to me. "Can you give me five minutes and then we can go?"

"Go where?" I asked.

"To my house. My roommates aren't home, or if they are, they're cool."

"Female roommates?" I asked, looking at Chris who was still staring at the TV.

"Two of them." She disappeared into the kitchen to finish whatever it was she had to do. I figured she'd invited Chris to come over so I wouldn't have to spend the night if I didn't want to, or if she didn't want me to, once we got there.

Ashley told us how to get to her place and I told her I'd ride with Chris in case he got lost, but really it was so we could get high again. She lived down West Ox Road, an area I was familiar with from summer league swim meets. We drove over the toll road, through a stoplight and took a right, following the Mustang she drove that I felt certain her parents paid for. She turned again at a stop sign and sped up the road before turning into Bradley Farms. She pulled into the driveway, but Chris parked on the street.

She waited for us on the front walk and we followed her up the stoop to the front door. It wasn't locked and I figured her roommates must be home. Inside, she tossed her keys on the staircase in front of the door and put her purse on the counter in the kitchen.

"Hello?" she called down the stairs. It was just after three a.m. "Hello?" she called again.

"Hey, Ash," came first one voice and then another, both female.

"Brought company home," Ashley said. Then she headed

down the stairs, having not looked at me even once since we'd gotten there, and I followed her, feeling like more of a stranger every minute. Chris tugged on my sleeve and I stopped and looked at him. His eyes widened for a minute and then he choked on a laugh. He was really stoned.

"Come on, asshole," I said.

"Hey, Ash," said one of the girls with long black hair and deep black eyes. She looked at me for a minute and said, "Do we know him?"

"I don't think so," I said.

"He's Brian Listo," the other girl said, and I looked at her for the first time.

She had short auburn hair and was smiling broadly.

"Do I know you?" I asked.

"I dated Tony. Briefly. I think you were in California. How's Tony doing?" she asked.

"He's dead," I said dully.

"Excuse me?" the black-haired girl asked.

"I'm sorry," I said. "I don't remember you." I was still looking at the red-haired girl, wondering if what Kacie had said could possibly be true with the evidence of Veronica from last night and now this girl claiming she'd dated him.

"We haven't met," she said. "I'm Tara."

The black-haired girl said, "Did I know Tony?"

"Yeah," said Tara. "He was the cute guy that delivered pizzas that one summer, remember? This is Nell." Tara made the introduction as if I gave a fuck what the black-haired girl's name was.

"Oh, yeah, that dude," said Nell. "He's dead?"

"This week," I muttered. "He died this past week. Ashley," I said, turning to my host, "can I get a glass of water?"

"Sure, upstairs," she said. "I need to shower anyway." She led the way back up to the kitchen and then turned back toward the hallway. "I'll be out in a minute," she said over her shoulder, and I heard her run up the stairs.

Chris had followed us to the kitchen.

I found the glasses and poured one full. "This is a weird house for three girls to live in," I said. "It's like someone's parents' house."

"No shit," Chris said. "You gonna get with Ashley?"

I shrugged and then said, "Not sure."

Chris opened the refrigerator and looked inside. "That doesn't look like someone's parents' house," he said.

I glanced down. He'd stepped aside to show me. The shelves had names: Ashley, Tara, Nell. There were Styrofoam boxes and beer, condiments, yogurt, and cheese slices.

"What are we doing here, man?" Chris closed the door and straightened up. The kitchen got darker.

I shrugged. "Not ready to go home." I gulped down half the glass of water in my hand.

"Are you really going to Spain this summer?"

"For the last half of the year, I hope," I said. "Can't see anything really keeping me here."

"Not Melissa?"

I shrugged. "Don't you think I'm about to fuck that up with the girl upstairs?"

"Why do it, man?"

"Not ready to go home," I said again. Then I poured the rest of the water in the glass down the sink and looked out the window into the back yard. I saw some lawn furniture stacked near a fence and a tarp covering a pile of chopped wood. Looking left, inside, past the kitchen, I saw a wood-burning fireplace at the far end of a darkened family room.

"Why do you think Christian said what he did about Kacie?" I asked.

"Man, I don't even know what he said," Chris said. "I was

asking Kacie about that interview in Detroit and then she was smacking me telling me to help you and the bouncer was chucking your ass into the street."

I laughed, thinking about what being flung out of the bar must have looked like. I shook my head, remembering Christian falling out the door after me. I heard the flick of a lighter behind me and smelled Chris's cigarette. I turned back around to face him and leaned back against the sink. I pulled my own cigarettes out and stuck one in my mouth.

"This place is so fucked up," Chris said. "It's like being in a circus whenever I'm here. I keep expecting someone to run by chasing a wild animal or look up and see the bottom of an elephant's foot smashing down on me." He looked up at the kitchen ceiling.

I laughed.

"What?" he said.

"And you wanna move back?"

"Well, yeah. I guess. It's home, ya know?"

"Motorcycle-riding grizzly bears and all?" I said. "No, I don't know."

I glanced at the clock on the stove, decided not to smoke, and said to Chris, "I'm gonna go see if this will happen. Shouldn't take long."

He nodded and I sauntered down the hallway toward the front door, turning to the left to climb the stairs. I stepped over Ashley's keys and looked up to the darkened hallway above. With each step, I named something I would stop thinking about once I reached the top.

Chris and the roommates downstairs.

Whether or not I should have brought a beer up with me.

Whether or not I should have brought a glass of water with me.

Whether or not I should have brought a condom with me.

Kacie leaving Town Center in a taxi.

Christian calling her a whore.

Me calling her a whore.

Halfway up, I paused and listened for the shower. I could hear the sound of it down the hall to the left and then it cut off. I listened for the clang of shower doors or the skittering rush of curtain rings. I may have imagined those things. I took another step and got back to naming the things I wasn't going to think about.

Sex with Kacie last night.

Not calling Meli even though I'd told her I probably wouldn't.

Whether Jason had gone to Kacie's tonight.

Whether she had let him in.

Whether Tony fucked both the roommates or just the redhead.

When Tony had told Kacie about Melissa.

I reached the top and walked down the hall toward the master bedroom. A light glowed from under the crack in the door. Closing the bedroom doors behind me, I turned toward the bathroom. A few quiet, uncertain steps later, I leaned against the door jamb, and pushed the door open a bit. I looked at her through the mirror. She had a towel on her head and a t-shirt on. It was damp in spots and I could see the edge of it tucked into the hip string of her panties. They were yellow bikinis and just below the strap was a tattoo, a ring of dolphins nose-to-tail.

"Thought you might have left." Ashley was clean and the room was steamy. She tugged the towel off her head and her hair fell down, slick and wet, over her shoulders. "What now?" Her smile didn't reach her eyes and I guessed she was tired and maybe a little sorry she'd invited me over.

Determined to make her less sorry, I walked into the bathroom, stepped up behind her, and moved the damp ropes of hair aside. My lips pressed against her neck. My arm slipped across her belly, under her shirt, and I pulled her to me so she could feel me against her back.

She moaned a little as my hand caught her breast. "Yeah, okay," she said, as if she had been debating, too. "This could work."

"I can go." But I didn't back away, instead pinching one nipple lightly between my fingers so she caught her lip in her teeth and hissed.

"Don't go." She stepped forward, out of my grip, and tossed the towel on the floor. Then she turned and brushed past me and I barely moved. She hooked her finger in my half-open palm and tugged me with her as she backed out of the bathroom. I followed, flipping off the light switch as we left the steam behind.

In the bedroom, I watched her walk the perimeter, a slink in her step and a sway to her hips, tugging the strings on the blinds and opening them. The room filled with a silvery glow of moonlight and streetlight.

"How long have you lived here?" I asked.

"Since tenth grade. My parents left the country eight months ago. They didn't want to sell the place because they'll be coming back in a year or two so I got a few roommates and we stayed. They pay rent."

"And you don't?"

"Don't have to. Parents cover the mortgage." She walked around a tall bureau, the kind with wide, deep drawers and I wondered what was in them. Several half-melted candles sat on top. She opened the blinds near the bed and then turned toward me.

"So, did we have any classes together in high school?" I asked, the distance between us making me feel awkward again.

"I don't expect you to love me," she answered.

"But I could, you know," I lied.

"Sure, you could," she answered and grabbed the tail of her shirt, tugging it over her head. She stood in front of me, bare except for yellow panties. "What's not to love?" Her voice had a bitterness I hadn't heard before. She spread her arms wide.

"What do you want from me?" I walked closer to her, angling around the bed, toward the windows, and took in the way the light and shadows made her appear sharp and angular.

She dragged fingertips up her thighs and hips.

"Just the experience of you," she said, and lifted a shoulder like a shrug.

I wondered just what the fuck that actually meant. Then added that to the list of things I wasn't going to think about. I reached for her and she took my hand. Our arms hung between us. I raised her hand to my lips, turned it over, and kissed her palm. Pulling Ashley to me, I tilted her face upward with my fingers on her chin and kissed her softly first then a bit more firmly. She wrapped her arms around my neck and shoved her tongue in my mouth.

I lifted her against the wall and pressed in to pin her there while I dug my hands into her ass. Her lips were on my mouth and her hands were in my hair and she was new and hot and the decision had been made as long ago as Thursday night, I realized. Now I was just agreeing to let it happen. I let her down and she pulled her face away from mine with a sexy, breathy moan. She turned toward the wall and slid her palms up it. I slipped my hand under the strings of those yellow panties and pulled them over her ass, going to my knees behind her with light kisses on her naked skin before slipping my hand between her legs. She was hot and slick and pressed her ass into me and groaned.

Then she stepped out of the panties, shoved me away, and strutted over to the bed where she climbed up to the center, palms down, on all fours, and looked at me over her shoulder.

"This is my attempt to seduce you," she said.

I looked at the curve of her ass, the moon spotlighting that ridiculous dolphin tattoo, and moved as if tugged on a string.

Belt unfastened, then button undone, and the jeans shoved to the floor. I tugged my shirts, both of them together, over my head, and tossed them into a heap, finally crawling onto the bed behind her. Her skin felt cold and damp like a girl I used to fool around with in the locker room after swim practice. Before Kacie.

I told Ashley how beautiful she was and meant it. I told her how good she tasted and how warm she felt despite the numbness the condom caused. I kissed her when she turned her face to me and clutched her breasts and her ass. I kissed under her ear and dragged my tongue down her neck. Finally, after she'd faked one orgasm and actually had another one, I finished up, kissed her jaw and cheek, asked her if she felt okay, and then pulled out of her, dragging the condom with me. I grabbed my boxers from the floor and tottered into the bathroom to dispose of the evidence.

I flipped the bathroom light on and its brightness stung my eyes. The door swung closed behind me as I stepped over to the toilet, cleaned myself up, and flushed away the condom in a wad of toilet paper. When I looked up and saw myself, naked, holding my boxers, in the strangely wide mirror of the bathroom of some random girl's parents' house, I blinked at my reflection, the bloodshot eyes, the rope necklaces, the swollen lips and dry tongue. I glared at who I saw and left, flipping the switch on my way out.

She was curled up on her side, with the blanket tucked around her waist and her shoulders bare. I stepped back into my boxers and jeans and then sat on the bed behind her. I ran my fingertips across her bare skin, still clammy, only now from exertion. She withdrew from my touch.

"I used to only have sex with people I loved," she said quietly.

"And now?" I asked.

"Now I don't think it matters."

I stood and buckled my belt and grabbed my shirts, standing

in the moonlight, trying to figure out if she'd really meant that. Then I decided not to care, pulled my shirts over my head, and left the room, closing the doors behind me.

It was quiet downstairs and when I looked into the kitchen, I could see Chris's back as he leaned against the counter where I'd left him. I stepped closer and saw, in the reflection on the stove across from him, Nell kneeling in front of him.

With a smirk, I backed out of the kitchen into the hallway, turning the corner of the staircase and sitting on the third step, putting my feet on the bottom one, to wait. After a few minutes, I kicked Ashley's keys and they rattled. The sounds of running water, murmured voices, what might have been a kiss, then footsteps approaching.

Nell sauntered through the hallway, turned the corner to the stairs, and stepped wide of me.

"Goodbye, hot black guy's cute friend," she said. Her voice was dreamy, stoned. She climbed the staircase and disappeared.

I crept back up the hallway to the kitchen and found Chris gulping water out of the glass I'd left there before.

"So now you're 'hot black guy'?" I asked, stifling a laugh.

He turned, saw me, and poured the rest of the water into the sink. When he strode past me, I followed him through the foyer and out into the night.

Chris staggered down the front yard hill to the car, a jerky pace that looked almost like a run. He opened his car door and then looked back up at the house.

I crossed to the other side of the car and faced him over the roof.

"That place had a weird brothel vibe to it," he said.

"It's her parents' house."

Then we got in and Chris started the engine. He drove straight down the street, deep into the cul-de-sac, and made the U-turn.

As we passed the house on our way out of the neighborhood I said, "Did you get the full package or just the blow job?"

"Nah, didn't have a condom on me," he said. "First time any girl hit her knees just because I'm black, though."

I fired up a bowl and passed it to him. The streets were dark and empty and Chris drove slowly, looking for policemen and minding the yellow lights. Across the toll road, past Town Center now dark except for the lampposts, over Baron Cameron past the old Hechinger's Hardware, and toward the Giant shopping center with the Baskin Robbins.

When he left me in my parents' driveway, it was four-thirty in the morning. I was tired, drunk, and stoned again.

I looked up at the house and considered going inside. Then I walked around the outside of the house and into the woods. I found the path I'd followed home on New Year's and followed it deep into the trees. It had taken about thirty minutes before so I picked up the pace as much as I could without stumbling. The small clearing where the ramp had been was still littered with piles of boards. The moon was bright, though not full, and the woods didn't seem as dark this time as they had been last time. I emerged into Tony's neighborhood and walked down the street like it was the most normal thing in the world to be doing at nearly five a.m.

Five years ago, I would be sitting outside of the Herndon Community Center right now waiting for my coach to arrive and open the door. Well, not right now, I reminded myself. Today was Sunday. Nearly a week between me and Tony's death.

I stumbled down the steps and caught myself against the glass door to Tony's room. I tugged on it and it opened quietly. Stepping inside, I felt a surge of grief.

"Tony? Wake up, asshole," I said. Then I closed the door behind me and stepped over to his bed. I took off my coat and tossed it aside. I lay down, my face in his pillow, and closed my eyes. In the memory that came to me then, we were in my room, not his.

"Brian?"

"Yeah, Tony?" I hadn't wanted to look at him. He looked like I felt, like he hadn't slept, like he hadn't even tried to. His coat was still on, the zipper hanging open, the ski lift ticket crumpled, dirty, and still glued to the pull. Underneath, a flannel, a t-shirt, and those stupid dog tags.

"What does your heart tell you?" He had said it so softly I almost didn't hear it. Standing in the corner of my old bedroom, he watched me shove items into a duffle bag.

As usual, I deflated his point by taking him literally. "I feel a strange grumbling, but I think it's my stomach telling me I'm hungry." I rolled last night's jeans and shoved them in under the t-shirt that smelled like Kacie.

"How often do you hear your heart?" I mumbled. "Fucking stupid." My heart didn't have a voice. I had never heard it.

He took the yellow ball cap off his head, ran his hand through his short spiky hair that was now matted not only in the back, but on the brow, too. I heard him expel a long stream of air like frustration with me or just exhaustion, or maybe the last of the high he'd been on when I'd seen him a few hours before.

"What do you want from me?" I had stopped moving and sat down, avoided looking at myself in the mirror over the dresser.

"I told her about Melissa," he said.

"Jesus, Tony. What'd ya go and do that for?" I asked. I looked at him through the mirror. He seemed to cower in the corner but I thought it was probably just the drugs.

"You two are killing me with this shit," he said. "I mean, fuck, Brian. Listen to your heart, man. It's gotta be breaking for her."

"How often do you hear your heart?" I asked again.

"Every time there is an important decision to make."

Eye contact, his blue ones and my greys. His pupils so tiny

they were like pinpoints, his lids half-closed, his lashes fluttering. My eyes bloodshot from lack of sleep. Wide, incredulous, demanding.

"Is this one of those?"

"You tell me," he mumbled. Then his fists came up and scrubbed his knuckles against his temples. He shifted the hat on his head, the script R looked crooked and he seemed to wobble a little. He was looking at the floor, then the doorway, and down the hall. He was the same Tony as every other day for our whole lives.

"I don't know what this is," I said.

"Have you thought about what you're doing?" he said, his voice hoarse with the thickness of hangover and too many cigarettes. Weak from no sleep. High.

"Since she told me." I stood up again and tugged the zipper around the edge of the duffle bag, smacked it, and the noise echoed between us.

"Time to leave?" he asked.

"Seems like it's always time to leave," I had said, and hoisted the bag onto my shoulder.

I rolled onto my back on his bed. What I wanted to do was sob into his pillow, curl myself around the aching I felt in my belly, break wide open and let everything from the last five days spill out. But I rolled onto my back and looked up at his tapestries. Burning skies and angel's wings. I squeezed my eyes and one tear slid out. It dripped down my temple and into my ear. I raised my hand and rubbed it away.

"You could be good to her," he had said. I couldn't shake the image of him facing me in my room on New Year's Day.

"It's too late for that," I had replied, thinking about leaving her sister's house before. I had looked at him again and wondered how he'd gotten to my parents' house.

"Did you drive her car over here?"

He nodded.

"Jesus, Tony," I said, for the second time. "Now she'll have to come and . . . shit. Fucking go. Just go."

I didn't think about him driving high though he probably couldn't focus. I didn't think about how I'd said we'd go to the valley, though that was probably why he was there. I didn't think about what he had been doing since I left him four hours ago.

I only thought about having to see her again. And Jason thinking I'd hit her. And Joel thinking I'd given her the drugs.

"Just go," I said again.

"This isn't her fault," he had said.

"No," I had agreed. "It's yours."

Sunday

"Brian, son, wake up." A gentle shake on my shoulder.

I opened my eyes. Mac was standing over me and for a second I thought I must be dreaming.

"Shit, Mac." I pushed myself up. "I'm sorry."

"It's okay." He was dressed for church in grey suit pants and a white shirt. Down his chest hung a purple tie with swirls of pink and green; the Jerry Garcia tie Tony had gotten him for Christmas some years ago. He was clean-shaven and smelled like cologne.

I leaned my elbows on my knees and dropped my face into my hands.

"You all right?"

"Just hung over." I looked up and smiled weakly at him.

"Yeah, I smell that on you." He looked around, shoved his hands in his pockets, and rocked back on his heels. "The Crew is here," he said. "Upstairs."

"Everyone?"

He nodded. "Except the girls."

I pushed my hand through my hair and smacked my lips. Then saw a glass of water on the nightstand.

"That's yours," he said. "Thought you might need it."

I took a long drink from it.

"I'm sorry, Mac."

"I'm glad you're here. You forgot to take this with you Friday." He reached behind the easel, removing a canvas. When he pulled it out into the space between us, he turned it so I could see the painting.

It was the burning valley.

Tears swelled into my throat. I stood up, staggering a bit, and threw myself at him. He caught me with one arm and held me. Over his shoulder, I looked up at the ceiling. The tapestries hung still and dim with the watery light from the door. I felt as if I were trapped underwater staring up at the surface. A hot surge of tears dripped over my eyelashes.

"Why aren't you mad at me?" I asked, my voice caught in the back of my throat.

"You're just a kid," he said.

"But Tony . . ."

"Was just a kid, too." He squeezed me tighter and I held on. "You'll be okay," he said, his voice seeping into the skin behind my ear.

"When?"

Then, like Friday, he set me away from him with his palms on my shoulders. I pressed my hands to my eyes, digging the heels in and willing them to crush my skull.

His eyes were wet and he said, "You need to go."

He handed me the painting. I felt its weight and size in my hand. The auburn, crimson, maize, and gold burned against the canvas. The layers of the paint gave the image depth and made the thing heavy. It was big, about thirty inches wide and forty inches tall. It looked like he'd set fire to the trees himself.

I met Mac's gaze over the top edge of it.

"Come back soon," he said.

I nodded. But I wouldn't.

Upstairs, Chris said, "How the fuck did you get here?" He was standing by the bathroom and looked like he might have just blown chunks.

"Did you sleep?" I asked.

"It's ten o'clock, Brian." Joel's tone was cold and he had his arms crossed over his chest. They all wore coats and Jason's cheeks were slightly flushed.

"Come on," Jason said gently. "Let's go. Mac and Rhonda are going to church."

"Rhonda's gone," Joel said. "Bad enough Mac found your strung-out ass passed the fuck out in Tony's room."

"I'm not strung out." My voice was hoarse. "Just hung over."

"No drugs?" Joel looked at the painting in my hand but didn't say anything about it.

"No sleep," I said.

Jason and Joel were closest to the door. They turned and opened it and we all walked out onto the porch. I looked back into the foyer, but Mac hadn't followed me up the stairs. Closing the front door, I trailed my friends down the front walk and out to the driveway.

"Chris went to pick you up and your mom said you never came home," Joel said.

"That's not entirely true," I said. "I went home. I just didn't stay there."

Jason and I walked around to the far side of Joel's SUV. We opened the doors and climbed into the seats. Chris and I were in the back. He was chugging a bottle of yellow Gatorade. I slid the canvas across the floorboard. He pressed it against the front seats and looked at it. I could see recognition in his face.

"So, breakfast?"

"You stink," Joel said.

"Been getting that a lot this week," I said.

"Burning skies," Chris breathed.

I turned my face to the window and felt fresh tears drip down my cheeks.

Breakfast didn't take very long. We slid into seats at Amphora, ordered coffee and pancakes, toast and omelets, a Sprite for me, and lots of water. There was a crowd and half of the people were wearing church clothes and the other half wore the remains of last night, like us. I saw a pair of runners in Spandex pants and sneakers getting coffees and bagels at the bakery counter.

"So, did Tabby make you sleep on the couch last night?" Chris asked Joel.

"She'd gotten over it by the time I got home."

"Which is code for she'd passed out," Jason said.

I finished the first Sprite and asked for another one.

"Where did you guys end up?" Joel asked.

"Bradley Farms," I said.

"The bartender?" Jason asked.

I nodded. "Even Chris got some."

"Twice," he said. "I went to Sara's after I left you. Ran into her Thursday night coming out of Bistro and she said I should come by and I thought why not?"

"At four in the morning?" I asked.

He shrugged. "No big deal."

"How long has it been since you've seen her?"

"We hooked up last summer. But not since then." Chris smiled. "Last time I saw her was the weekend that Tony and I tripped and went to Scott's Run all day. That was a blast."

I glanced at Joel. He was adding another sugar packet to his coffee. He shook his head but didn't say anything.

Chris didn't notice Joel's look. He was too busy grinning over whatever he remembered of Scott's Run. I remembered the path he was talking about; we'd shroomed out there a few times. Chris put both hands around his glass, his fingertips met on the far side.

"Tony slipped and tore a hole in these Hawaiian shorts his mom had bought him for his birthday," he said.

"Hawaiian shorts?" Jason grinned, bacon grease making his lips look glossed.

"Not sure what's weirder. Him having them. Or him wearing them." Chris laughed.

We were all quiet for a few minutes and I thought we were all probably thinking about Tony until Joel said, "You guys gotta cut all that shit out."

"We have," Chris said.

"Mostly," I said.

"I'm serious, Brian. Look what happened to Tony."

I felt Chris shift next to me, sit up a little straighter.

"That wasn't an overdose," I said.

"But it wasn't Tony either," Jason said.

I thought about Tony on the floor in his bathroom puking his guts out, laughing and coughing and then crying a little with the confusion and misery of it all. Years and years of headaches, medications, addiction, and helplessness. Somehow, I'd thought he'd just figure it out. And he had, finally, in the worst possible way.

Our food arrived and we ate in silence.

"You don't get another chance in this life," Joel finally said.

"Are you going to lecture us all morning?" Chris said.

"Are you going to quit with that shit?"

"I told you we have," Chris replied.

"Sober people don't stay up until four in the morning."

"Lighten up, Joel, Christ," Jason said. "Can't we work on one fucking terrible thing at a time. They get the point." He crushed his napkin in his hand, wiping bacon-greasy fingers on it. He glanced at me and then at Chris and picked up his water glass.

"I hadn't talked to Tony since New Year's," I said, and my voice was a little louder than I expected it to be. I thought strangers turned and looked but it may have just been the Crew staring. Chris had a piece of toast in mid-bite and Jason's hand stopped mid-air with his water glass. Joel sat across from me, coffee mug in his hand, brown eyes still wearing a flash of anger from the drug remarks.

"Are you serious?" Jason said.

I nodded slightly and tried to meet their eyes, but I couldn't. I could barely even look at their faces. Could barely even stand that they were sitting there. That any of us were.

"Brian," Chris said, "what the fuck?"

"Six weeks, man," Jason said.

"Didn't seem like that long," I said softly. I pushed my plate away and picked up the glass of Sprite. I took a drink, closed my eyes, felt a spin, and opened them again. Put the glass back down.

"He told us to forgive you," Joel said. "He told us you hadn't done anything wrong."

"He acted like he'd talked to you," Jason added.

"He acted like he was the only one who had," Chris said.

I shook my head. "He hadn't talked to me. He'd called."

"You're a real dick," Jason said.

"You think I don't know that?" Then I did look him in the eye. "You think that hasn't been made clear to me?"

"Don't," Joel said. "Just don't."

"Anyway, it doesn't fucking matter now." I thought about the canvas of the burning valley in the backseat of Joel's SUV. I thought about the green velvet book lying on the nightstand in my room. I thought about the phone ringing and me not answering it. I thought about the caller ID saying, "Help me," and me ignoring it.

"I can't ever get it back," I said. "And right now, I'd give any-thing to get it back." I put my elbows on the table and my fore-head against my thumbs. I stared into the drying yolk on my plate, the broken toast and severed pancakes, the nubs of sausage links and the crystals of sugar in the syrup.

I guess they must have looked at each other. I guess they must have decided something. I guess something happened while I sat there just trying to breathe. But I only know that nothing else was said for a while. They moved slowly, I could see that much, and when I lifted my head finally, I saw they'd gone back to eating, so I did, too.

More breakfast, quiet chewing, avoiding eye contact, drink refills. The sounds of the restaurant, clinking plates and quiet conversations, rattling ice and coffee brewing, the radio playing oldies and the servers calling across tables to one another.

"Where's the burning valley?" Chris finally asked.

I swallowed the bite of pancake in my mouth. "Harper's Ferry."

"Will you take us there?"

"Today?"

"Next time."

"Sure," I said.

"When will you be back?" Jason asked.

I shrugged.

"You'll have a place to stay," Joel said quietly.

I looked up at him and his eyes were clear, his face softened, the sharp angles of disapproval and blame gone, and the dude I remembered under the banner on the hill at the skate park sat across from me. He'd taken a flat white sheet from his mom's linen closet and spray paint from his dad's garage and painted "The Crew" in tall black letters. Then we'd each signed it with red permanent marker. He'd hung it every time we competed. We were a team. We had a name.

"It should have been you," I said. "At the X Games. You were better than me."

Joel's chin came up a bit and he said, "Slides and plants aren't exactly gold medal tricks."

In team competitions, they had always let me go last. Joel usually went just before me and we'd almost always have already won the whole thing before I even went. I threw big tricks, but he had the cleanest blunt to fakie of anyone in town. I'd never told him that.

"You would have practiced," I said. "You would have taken it seriously and skated without making any mistakes."

"Everybody makes mistakes," he said.

After we'd paid the check and walked out into the morning sunlight and given the same folded palms half-hugs as outside of Uno the night before, Jason pulled the canvas out of the backseat and handed it to me. Then the twins climbed into Joel's SUV, and Chris and I got back in his Civic.

"Smoke?" he asked me.

"Thanks," I said. "Trying to quit."

He grinned and drove me home.

Chris and I said goodbye in front of my parents' house. He drove away and I watched until his car disappeared before going inside. The garage door was open, and Dad's car gone. The house was quiet, but I could hear Mom in her bathroom as I climbed the stairs. I didn't go into her bedroom. I went instead to mine and propped the painting against the dresser mirror.

I dragged my hanging bag out of the closet and put it on the bed. While I rolled up last night's flannel shirt and shoved it into the suitcase, Mom walked into my room. "So, they found you. You okay?" she asked.

"Not sure," I said. "Stayed at Tony's last night. Saw Mac this morning."

"What did he say?"

"That I'm just a kid and I'm gonna be okay." I turned around and sat on the bed, staring at the canvas.

Mom came deeper into the room and stood beside me, looking at the painting, too, and our reflections in the mirror around it.

"You know, Brian," she said. "Your father and I, we loved Tony very much." Then she started to choke on the words and the tears and stopped for a second.

"I know you did," I said and took her hand.

She sat down on the edge of my bed next to me. "We love you, too," she whispered.

"I know you do."

"We might not always see eye to eye, we might not always do the right thing for you, but we mean well."

"I know you do," I repeated.

"We're concerned about you going back to San Francisco. Maybe that's not the best place for you."

I could smell her, that scent I remembered from before I even knew what it was. I could feel her warmth and also her hesitation. Through the mirror, I smiled at her.

"I just need to finish up there, and then I'll come back before I go to Barcelona."

"You can't postpone grief." She took my hand and held it. I let her. We stayed like that for a minute and then she said, "Melissa called again."

"Are you going to take my furniture to Arizona?"

"No."

"Then I should probably say goodbye." I squeezed her hand and turned to look at her. She was a little shorter than me and she smiled, cupped my cheek in her hand, and then stood up.

"Right," she said, taking a step away and then paused at the door. "Did you hear me about Melissa?"

I nodded. "Probably oughta do something about that."

When she was gone, I walked over to the side of the bed where I'd hidden the phone and picked up the receiver. Then I thought better of it and headed into the bathroom to shower.

I closed the door, ran the hot water into the tub, pulled the stopper to shift the stream to the shower head, and then stepped away from the curtain. I looked up at the rod and the memory of Kacie falling in Jason's bathroom came back to me. I shook my head and stepped over to the sink. Too many fucking memories in this place. It was like living in a jigsaw puzzle and trying to make the pieces fit, turning and matching, and pressing them into place but mostly being a disconnected scattering of fragmented memories. I scrubbed my teeth, staring into the mirror and watching the edges of it fog over. The steam overtook my reflection. Then I got in the shower to wash off the night before.

When I came out of the bathroom, I closed the door quickly so as to not set off the smoke detector. I walked down the hall to my room with a towel around my waist, and my jeans and shaving kit in my hand. I pulled the belt from the loops and rolled the jeans up, shoving them into the suitcase beside two button downs. Reaching into the closet, I extracted my one suit, my funeral attire, and laid it beside the suitcase.

I dug for clean shorts and dragged them up under the towel. Then I pulled the towel free and tossed it toward the door. Sitting down on the edge of the bed, facing the window, my back to the door, I stared out to the backyard at the tree. Its branches swayed in what must have been a cool breeze. The naked limbs bumped against each other, cracking, and splintering.

I imagined spring coming to Virginia, waking up one morning to find it was nearly sixty degrees outside: the trees showing blossoms ready to burst, the sun casting a warmer glance in my direction, driving around with the windows down, the first patio happy hour. Spring was still some six weeks away.

I leaned over and shoved the window open. Then I walked

back to the suitcase, extracted a clean pair of jeans, and stepped into them. Reaching for the box of cigarettes on the dresser, I slipped one out and stuffed it between my lips. I grabbed the lighter and set the flame to the end of it, walked back over to the window, and sat down on the floor.

With the first inhale, I thought about my San Francisco apartment with the wood floors and large windows, the windowsills with candles on them, and the bare white walls with shadows dancing across them. With the exhale, I thought about how Kacie had never seen those walls, never been to my flat, never even been to California, though I'd lived there three and a half years. I thought about Tony sleeping on the futon couch, blankets twisted around him like a cocoon as we watched Red Dawn and Star Wars and Rocky late into the night. I thought about how the television made the room glow blue.

I thought about Tony holding my glass bong between his legs, packing the bowl, lighting it and taking one good pull. He'd cover the top of the cylinder with his palm and tilt his head back, then expel a long stream of smoke into the air above him.

I remembered him smiling there, in my San Francisco flat, and imagined for one minute that he'd be there when I arrived later today. I looked over at the canvas leaning against the dresser. From where I sat, the light from the window made it look like it held specks of gold in the maize and rubies in the auburn.

The phone rang and I picked it up.

"Where have you been?"

"Hi, Meli." I expelled a long stream of air. "Santa Fe Cue Club, then Hard Times Café, then Uno and Market Street."

"Bars."

"Mostly."

"Where did you sleep last night?"

"Tony's."

"Jesus."

"Melissa, listen."

"And the night before?" she asked.

"I thought we weren't going to do this."

"That was yesterday."

"Meli, this place is crazy. It's like a circus," I said, stealing Chris's line.

"Are you making me the clown?" she asked bitterly.

"No, come on, wait." I closed my eyes. How to tell her. What to tell her. I didn't think I had the energy for this. "I don't know where to begin."

"Try," she said. I imagined her sliding down the edge of her own bed and sitting on the floor. Narrated her in my head. She'd fold her arms over her chest and pinch the phone between her shoulder and her ear. She'd glance over at the floorboards, maybe see a cobweb she hadn't noticed before, and reach over and snag it, rolling it up in her fingers. She'd be waiting for me to say something.

"Tony loved you," I said.

"What?" Now she was probably holding the receiver, her arms unfolded, her back straight. Now she would twist the cord around her hand. "He didn't even know me."

"That's what I thought, but no. He was in love with you and he was pissed at me about you. He told Kacie about us." I took a drag off my cigarette and blew smoke toward the open window. "It was a whole thing that happened over New Year's," I added, feeling the chill from outside.

"New Year's?"

"Yeah, I'll tell you about it when I get home."

"Tell me now."

"Meli, please, it's been a shit week. I need a little space on this."

"Space?"

"Wait, that's not what I meant. Fuck."

She was quiet for a minute and I was, too. I heard the doorbell ring downstairs. I shoved the cigarette into the ashtray and
crushed it out. Then I waved my hand to push the last of the
smoke out and nudged the ashtray under the bed with my foot.
I folded one leg under me, sat on the bed, and faced the door.

"We drank all night," I said. "Chris and I. Then I didn't want
to be alone, so I walked to Tony's."

"You know that sounds crazy, right?" she said.

"I feel crazy," I said.

Then Kacie appeared in the doorway. I felt myself smile at
the sight of her. She wore that same pink ski jacket and she gave
me a little wave and then stepped into the room.

"It's been hell here, Meli."

Kacie looked up at the name and I met her eyes. She nodded and then turned away. That's when she saw the painting and
she moved toward it. I watched her face in the mirror until she
stepped in front of the canvas and I couldn't see her reflection
anymore.

On the other end of the phone I heard Meli's breathing stag-
ger a little. "I think you've done something really bad, Brian."

"What? Why would you think that?"

"And I called wanting to know what it was," she continued.
"But now I don't want to know." I heard her breath catch in
her throat between the phrases, and the last word sounded high
pitched.

"I haven't done anything wrong," I said.

Kacie looked over her shoulder at me.

I thought of Ashley turning her back on me this morning.

"Is she there?"

I closed my eyes and imagined Melissa standing up now, walking toward the front window of the room with the phone's cradle
in her hand and the handset to her ear. I imagined her long red

hair, the way it seemed to catch fire in the sunlight. I looked past Kacie to the burning valley painting.

"Tony left me some stuff," I said. "One thing is a painting I think you'll love. It's of this place we went one time."

"Is she there?" Meli asked again.

"No," I said. "No, Meli, she's not here."

I heard her break then, the air choke out, the tears bleed through. I knew well enough what that flood sounded like to imagine what she looked like just then.

"I'll be home today." I closed my eyes.

"It's over."

"Meli, wait."

"Goodbye, Brian," and she hung up.

"Fuck." I slammed the phone down on the cradle. And then slammed it three more times just for emphasis.

When I looked up, Kacie was watching me.

"Need eight bucks for a cab?" she asked.

"Very funny," I said.

"Come on, Brian." Her hands were in her pockets and she spread them like a shrug and her coat looked like pink bat wings.

"I'm going back today," I said. "I'll go see her. We'll fix it."

"What did you expect?" Kacie asked. She had on a grey sweater with a white shirt below that. A long pink scarf hung around her neck.

"Not this." I stood up facing the window and then turned toward her. She looked amused and it irritated me. "Are you here to apologize?"

She laughed. "Fuck off," she said. "You first."

"Get in line." I was bare-chested and it was getting colder in the room. I leaned over to the window and shoved it closed.

"Your mom let me in," Kacie said. "I won't stay. I'm here for the book."

I pushed a hand through my hair, tugged on the necklaces

for some breathing room, and managed to smile at her. Stepping closer I said, "Joel said Tabby forgave him."

Kacie laughed again. "Of course she did. She's got a lot of good advice for how I should handle you, but Joel's a fucking saint." She turned back to the painting. "So, you went and got it?"

"Mac gave it to me this morning. I sort of slept there last night." I reached for the suitcase and dragged it toward me. Shifted things around, looking for a fresh shirt, but everything seemed crumbled and worn.

"The book, Brian," she said, and her tone had changed, got ten sharper.

I picked up the green velvet book from the nightstand and held it out to her.

She snatched it from me.

"What's wrong?"

"Did you fuck the bartender?"

"Who told you?"

"That's what you want to know? Who told me? You really are an asshole."

"Why are you so angry?" I asked. "We got drunk, we smoked, Chris and I went to her place. It was weird but it wasn't a thing really."

She closed her eyes and hugged the book to her chest. "I guess Melissa heard it, too."

"Heard what?"

"Your obvious guilt."

"I don't know what you're talking about."

"You said you read it." She held up the green book between us.

"I did." I found a shirt then and shook it out, pressed it to my face and sniffed it. Then I shoved my arms into it and pulled it over my head.

When I looked back at her she was watching me. The Kacie

I'd met in my bedroom yesterday, the one who'd said we could be friends, the one I was willing to defend with my fists last night, she was gone.

"Look, it wasn't that big a deal." I stepped around the corner of the bed but she backed away and squared herself to face me.

"You're broken," she said quietly.

"It's not like I impregnated her."

She slapped me. Hard.

"Shit. It's not you, Kacie."

She slapped me again.

"What the fuck?" I said, rubbing my cheek. "I said it isn't you. What do you care?"

"You're the whore. You sell parts of yourself. You expect payment. But you don't *give* anything. Not to anyone."

I stared at her face; her eyes hardened and her lips trembled. She held the book up between us. "It had *my* name on it," she said, her voice so quiet I thought I hadn't actually heard her speak, the words had just been in my head.

She turned around to leave, and I remembered her looking like a Valentine last night.

"Kace," I said. "Don't go."

But she didn't bother responding. I watched her stride down the hall, turn right, and descend the stairs. Once before I had chased her out, but this time I just watched her go.

I looked at the painting again.

"This isn't her fault," Tony had said. I could see him, standing in the corner, trying to make it right, trying to fix what we'd fucked all to hell.

"This isn't her fault," he'd said.

"No," I said aloud, in my room in my parents' house. "It's mine."

The thing about Tony carrying that green book with us every-where was true. He was always catching things he liked and put-ting them in there, phrases and poems and quotes, and they could come from anywhere. I always figured he would use them some-how in his art, like those decoupage word art pieces I'd seen on the walls of the coffee shops in San Francisco. I expected him to paint lyrics into trees somehow or lace an angel's wings with a poem in script. But he'd just left them in there, flipping through them now and then, always smiling and remembering where he'd been when he caught it. The notebook was like a photo album for him that way, or a scrapbook. But when I'd looked at it on Thursday, I hadn't seen what he'd seen. I was glad to have given it back to her. It felt like too much of an albatross, all his memories in those pages.

I stared forlornly at the painting of the burning valley. That would be anchor enough.

Reaching into the closet for my suit, I spotted the Jeff Grosso board leaning against the closet wall. I tossed the suit on the bed and grabbed the skateboard. My hand clasped the trucks and the feel of the chopped-up metal scraped the skin on my palm. Lifting it, I eyed the deck, the grip tape, and the plies. If I took it back to San Francisco with me, it wouldn't get chucked with the yearbooks Mom was sure to throw out when they moved. I reasoned the board would be safer with me and laid it flat across the bottom of the hanging bag, tucking the edges in around it. Maybe I'd even take it to FTC and get it cleaned up for use. Maybe I'd ride it again. At some point.

I took the copy of *The Catcher in the Rye* out of the inside pocket of my suit and left it on the dresser. I hadn't made much progress packing, but it seemed like a while that I was working on the memories that swirled around me, when Dad stepped into the room.

"Your mom said you were saying goodbye to the furniture," he said.

I nodded. "I was gonna just leave a note, but . . ."

"The nightstand can't read," he supplied.

"And the dresser always makes it about her."

"Well, try not to get too sentimental. I wouldn't want to have to explain your leaving to the headboard." He clapped my shoulder and then turned to go. "What's that?"

I knew he meant the painting. "The burning valley," I said. "A place out near Harper's Ferry Tony and I went once."

He nodded. "How you gonna get it back to California?"

"Haven't worked that out yet."

"We'll have it shipped," he said. "Tony did it?" When I nodded he said, "It's good."

"Take it to Arizona. I'll get it from there."

Then I felt him leave and all this time I had been shoving clothes into my bag, stacking rolled shirts on the Rosso deck. I carried my suit back to the closet and hung it up next to my letter jacket and an old ski coat. I picked up the lift ticket and turned it over in my hand. *Wisp!* it said. *Full Lift Access. December 27, 1998.*

I dropped it, closed the closet door, and turned back to my suitcase. I zipped the bag closed and carried it to the doorway of my room.

"Goodbye, nightstand," I said. "Goodbye dresser. Goodbye, bed."

Dad didn't bother with the radio and we rode in silence the few miles to the airport. Out of the neighborhood, down Reston

Parkway over Baron Cameron and past Town Center to the Dulles toll road. I watched the landscape race by, heard our breathing synchronize, felt my heart beat like it would break if I let it.

"You're going to be okay," Dad said, but it was more like a question than a reassurance. "Your mom and I will come to help pack."

"Don't worry about it."

"I'd like to see the apartment I've been paying for."

"Fair enough," I admitted. "I'll find someone to sublet while I'm in Spain."

Then silence again for a few miles.

"Send the details of that, okay?"

"Sure. Like where to stay, that kind of stuff?" I flipped the lid on the center console in Dad's car and pulled out the pack of spearmint gum. I shoved a stick in my mouth and chewed slowly.

"Like cost of flights, plan for submissions, work if there is any."

"Ladies who will accept favors for cash?"

"Or meals," he said.

"Or cigarettes."

He frowned. "Right. Look, after something like this, there can be a little bit of depression," he said. "It may set in kind of late and you might need . . ."

I could tell he wasn't sure where he was going with this as he stalled a bit and then said, "Someone to talk to."

"Sure," I said.

"Just know that," he stalled again, and I thought this must be another one of those moments he could become my best friend. There had been several of them over the years.

My senior year in high school he'd taken me skiing for three days and I'd dragged him on more black diamonds than he would have liked, leaving him bruised at the end of the day. We drank canned beer in the motel room and had talked about March Madness coming up soon, but we hadn't mentioned college or San Francisco even though those choices had already been made and my leaving was just six months away.

"I'll understand if you need someone to talk to," he said, but it wasn't an offer. "Just send me the bills, you know. I don't think student insurance covers that sort of thing." That was more along the lines of what I'd expected.

It was the best he could do so I said, "Thanks," and looked out the window.

He parked in the hourly parking and said, "I'll walk you in."

Dad and I went to the counter, got my boarding pass, and checked my bag through to San Francisco. We filed through security and once on the other side, we walked into a sports bar and took seats in front of a television showing downhill skiing. We ordered draft beers and I lit a cigarette and he pretended not to mind.

"We used to come here when you were little, remember?"

"Sure, before trips."

"No," he said. "When you were like three and four I used to bring you here to watch the planes take off and land."

I looked around. "Here?"

He laughed. "Well, not here, but the observation deck. They had a big one here. But I don't think many people knew about it because it was just us a lot of times."

"I don't remember that."

"Then the Challenger exploded and you didn't want to watch take offs anymore."

It was three p.m. on Sunday. One hundred fifteen hours and twenty-seven minutes since I'd heard that Tony was dead. I'd come back to the Crew. We'd drunk and we'd seen his parents, then we'd drunk and we'd buried him, then we'd drunk and I had sex with one girl and we'd drunk and I had sex with another.

Then this morning they'd found me passed out in Tony's bed and we'd all gone for breakfast. Then Melissa had somehow figured everything out and Kacie had decided not to forgive me after all and I was sitting in the bar, shoulder to shoulder with my dad.

"I don't have to come back," I said.

"No," he said. "You don't."

"Thanks for that."

At five thirty p.m. on Sunday I asked the flight attendant for a beer and she made change for my ten-dollar bill and moved past my aisle. I sat back into the seat, wished I had smoked another cigarette before leaving, changed my watch to Pacific Time and stared into the clouds beyond my air-tight window.

The sky stretched onward and the passengers shifted in their seats. I felt tired but not sleepy, worried but not anxious.

It was two p.m. Pacific Time, one hundred nineteen hours since I'd been told Tony was dead and the breath had escaped my lungs.

"Brian?"

"I'm still here, Dad."

"You okay?"

"Yeah, Dad."

He had taken a breath through the phone and said, "I'm sorry, son."

"I know."

I had worked all week to go through the motions of grief and regret. I secured my tray to the seat back in front of me and tilted my chair out of its upright position. I closed my eyes and waited for that noise of machinery to cease.

Tony is dead. He killed himself Monday night.

There's nothing I can do about that now.

On that Sunday evening flight, it felt like it had been a year since I'd seen him, even longer since I'd heard his voice.

"Fucking magnificent," he'd said, spreading his arms out wide to either side. "It's like it's burning."

That's when the real sadness found me, right there over Omaha. It overtook me like the San Francisco fog.

The Green Velvet Notebook

Page Six

Inside each of us there lives another person, concealed to those who would glance only once, but obvious to those who look below. It is in our deepest essence that our duality thrives.

—Kerry Halpern, 9th grade Earth Science, first period, Herndon High School, 1991

Page Nine

I love you.
Not only for what you are,
But for what I am when I am with you.
I love you.
Not only for what you have made of yourself,
But for what you are making of me.
I love you
For the part of me that you bring out;

I love you
For putting your hand into my heaped up heart and passing over
All the foolish, weak things that you can't help dimly seeing there,
And for drawing out into the light
All the beautiful belongings that no one else had looked quite far enough to find.
I love you because you are helping me make
Of the lumber of my life
Not a tavern but a temple;
Out of the works of my every day
Not a reproach but a song.
I love you because you have done more than any creed could have done
To make me good,
And more than any fate could have done
To make me happy.
You have done it
Without a touch,
Without a word,
Without a sign.
You have done it by being yourself.
Perhaps that is what being a friend means
After all.

—Roy Croft, "Love", found in <u>Best Loved Poems of the American People</u>, edited by Hazel Felleman, published by Doubleday, 1936

Page Eleven

"If you don't mind, it don't matter."

—Duana, Fatz Café bartender, talking about her best friend, Todd, who drew her unicorns

"*How can you miss what you have forgotten?*"

—Tami, Acropolis waitress, giving advice to another girl about an ex-boyfriend

Page Sixteen

It's easy to love something when you don't have to work at it. It's harder when it asks something of you.

—"Act V: The Truth" Nike ad, Vanity Fair, October 1996

I believe you possess a goodness few can see and even fewer can comprehend. I feel fortunate that I can see it and can call it what it is.

—Bar Napkin Poetry, Charlottesville, 1996

Page Seventeen

She was a Broad Street girl in a wedding march.
She would turn her head as the tourists gawked.
Never broke a stride when she walked.

—Backyard Green, "Charleston Song"

Dignity is pride even when there is very little to be proud of.

—Bar Napkin Poetry, Charlotte, 1997

Page Twenty-One

As the flags would unfurl, they'd call my name in the street, all the
love in the world lying there at our feet.
I miss the days when we were young and beautiful.
I miss the nights when I was invincible.

—Backyard Green, "Invincible"

Page Twenty-Three

Twilight is a black light across the summer sky.
All bodies move in shadow forms. Nameless, faceless, shadow forms.
And all words are whispers lost in absent wind.
Then what is white tends to glow on hair, around lips, around eyes.
All ghosts are illuminated and purple patches quilt the arena where
tigers pace to pounce, irritated as the black light brightens white
stripes and their camouflage is lost.

Page Twenty-Eight

We thought we'd be famous. Fame was what we knew of as great
achievement. We pretended to appreciate hard work and family, but
we craved fame. We were raised on it. Told to want it.

—Bar Napkin Poetry, Herndon, September 1998

Check reality and illusions come to surface as twilight sucks the day
into darkness.

—Bar Napkin Poetry, Reston, August 1998

Page Thirty-Two

Dear Brian and Kacie,

I'm sorry. I'm not sure at what point I lost that thing I knew and started operating without it, but I'd lost it, sure enough. This morning I think I found it again. I remembered what it was like before and I wanted to remind you.

Love is such a gift. Such an amazing gift. We think it's work and we treat it like a burden. We take it for granted and we trade it for other things that are maybe shinier or sexier. But love is a gift. It's the most precious thing we could ever know.

I know you both think the love between you is dying. I know you think it's run its course. I thought that, too. But this morning I remembered my grandfather's poetry book and the thing he said the day we buried my grandmother, "Love is not a single thing that we discover and pass between us. It's a changing, growing, learning process. If we'll allow ourselves to be changed, love will make us the people we are meant to be."

You are not the people you once were. But you don't have to be. You don't even have to be in love. You'll both make it just fine without the other.

That thing I'd lost that I was operating without? It was my certainty that your love, first love, only happens once. It cannot ever be again. We shouldn't want to escape it or be angry with it for making us hurt or bend or feel broken. We should be grateful to it. It was the first time love changed us. All of us.

I'm sorry for being the weight and the wait.

I ought to have been the light.

I love you both more than I could ever say. If ever you loved me, too, then love one another for what you are, not for what you have been.

Love, Tony
January 24, 1999

02/02/02

I always thought Pittsburgh was an industrial city. I envisioned pipes and steam and dirt and sweat. Like a coal mining village or a mill town. But it's not. It's actually rather sleek and sophisticated. Clean, classic, and well-tended like D.C.

Joel had told me that the exit from the Fort Pitt Tunnel would make me feel like I had "popped out" into Pittsburgh and he was right. The skyline nearly took my breath away and I had seen several impressive ones by then. The cab driver wasn't the chatty sort and he didn't bother to point out landmarks, but I knew Three Rivers Stadium and recognized a few other places with readable signs.

The cab had let me out in front of the William Penn Omni Hotel on Thursday. It's one of the oldest hotels in Pittsburgh and apparently ranked as a best wedding site by some authority. A bellhop took my bag and I followed him inside.

The lobby of the William Penn is impressive: marble floors, spectacular archways, and a proscenium balcony running the length of one side. A grand piano sits in the middle of the room, as if at any time some visiting maestro will simply wander by and take a seat.

I'd checked in, made it to my room, showered and changed,

and gone to the hotel bar to see if anyone else had arrived a day early. That was Thursday.

Friday had been more reunions and the rehearsal.

Today I was in the lobby in my cold-weather running gear waiting for Chris and Jason to shake off their hangovers.

"You really are a masochist," I said to Chris, as he came in off the street.

"Where's Jason?" he said.

"Speak his name and the Devil appears," I heard from behind me and turned to see Jason walking toward us. He was as cheerful as he had been in Vegas three weeks ago. He wore a wool beanie, a turtleneck, and black gloves. He looked like a cat burglar.

"Where's your better half?"

"He's Tabby's better half now," Jason said, grinning.

I checked my watch. Eight-thirty. "In about nine hours anyway."

"I should warn you, assholes. I've been marathon training and usually do about seventeen miles on Saturdays." Chris leaned down into a deep hamstring stretch. "Luckily, I already got ten of them out of the way this morning."

"Fuck you," Jason said. "When did you get up?"

"I didn't close the bar last night like you clowns," Chris said.

"I should warn you," I said, mocking Chris with a stretch of my own: raising my arm over my head and my leg behind me, in a silly arabesque. "I run about three miles and stop for a beer."

Jason put his hand to his stomach. "Not yet," he said.

"Give it a few miles," I said. "You'll be ready."

Chris stood up. "Hash House Harriers-style, huh?"

"Are we gonna do this, or what?" Joel asked, striding over from the elevator hallway. He had on a hat and gloves. "It's fucking cold out," he added.

He'd been excited to show us Pittsburgh and since we were only here for a few days, he'd suggested a run this morning as a kind of tour. I expected Jason and Chris to leave us behind and Joel and me to stop and read landmark signs. But the kinds of landmarks he showed us were stadiums and sandwich places, bars he'd puked in, and the best place in town to watch a game. Chris and Jason held the pace back so Joel and I wouldn't struggle, though we picked our pace up a bit like we usually did when we ran with them. When I ran on my own, which was irregularly, I kept it under five miles.

Joel directed us around corners and through intersections on a thirty-minute loop that may have been just over three miles. We finished the run at a bagel shop where we got coffees and some fresh-baked breakfast and then walked back to the hotel.

We didn't hang around the lobby, just made plans to call one another when we were ready to do the next thing, and then rode up to the seventh floor where our rooms were.

I shoved the key card into the door lock and stepped inside.

"I really didn't think you'd go," she said lazily from the bed.

"I told them I would." I tossed the paper bag at her. "Breakfast." Then I stepped into the bathroom, closed the door, and turned on the fan.

The rehearsal had been at four the day before so I'd flown in Thursday. Kacie had, too. We met in the hotel bar and after some awkwardness around being in the same place together, not just talking on the phone or by email, and after a few glasses of wine, we'd decided to have dinner. Kacie took me to an Italian restaurant that Joel and Tabby had taken her to when she'd come in town for dress shopping over the summer. It was walking distance and had a cozy European feel to it, reminding me of a place I'd dined in Vienna not too long ago.

"I'm ready to actually eat something," Kacie had confessed. "I've been dieting for weeks."

She looked perfect, though, and I said, "To fit the dress?"

"It's rather unforgiving." She held up two fingers to the

hostess and we were shown to a back corner and a small table lit by a single well-melted candle in a glass globe. I helped Kacie remove her jacket and passed it to the hostess with my own. She hung both coats on a nearby hat rack.

"What did you order last time?"

"Veal marsala," she said. We opened the menus and perused the options. I chose a wine from the list and ordered a bottle when the waiter appeared. He named the specials. I chose one and Kacie chose the other and we surrendered our menus to him. With nothing to hold between us, we had stared at one another through the candlelight.

"Hi," I said.

"Hi." Her green eyes were bright and happy.

"It's nearly eleven," I said. "Doesn't feel that late."

"No, but we're still on Pacific time, right?"

"I'm glad we have tonight," I confessed. "Before everyone else gets here."

"Me, too," she said. "It's good to see you."

The waiter returned and poured the wine for us. We tasted it, agreed to it, and when he'd walked away Kacie said, "I always hated wine presentations. I used to make my bartender come out and do it for my tables."

"When was that?" I asked.

"Small restaurant in Charlottesville," she said. "Worked there over the summer after Tony died." She ducked her head then and I felt a small ache.

I raised my glass and she lifted her eyes to mine. We clinked the wine goblets and took small sips. There was still that between us, that piece we were reluctant to completely let go of. We'd been healing, working on our own and together, but there was still that. There was before Tony died and after Tony died. Our timelines forever altered by that event.

"This place reminds me of Da Domenico," I said.

"Me, too." She smiled with a fondness I'd like to bottle and keep forever. Da Domenico was the Italian place in Tyson's Corner I'd taken her to for our first date all those years ago.

After dinner, we walked back to the hotel and when we reached the elevator, I had let her step in by herself. I didn't know what floor she was on and I didn't ask. It was after midnight. I wandered out to the terrace and smoked a cigarette in the cold Pittsburgh night by myself.

Friday morning, I slept in and then lay around the hotel writing a few impressions and thoughts from the night before in a marble composition notebook the edges of which were worn and fraying. I tried to capture the Fort Pitt Tunnel experience and the cab driver's disinterest. I thought about Tony's sketches of the French countryside and wished, not for the first time, that I could draw.

On Friday, Joel came over to the hotel and picked me up for lunch around eleven thirty.

"Kacie's here," he said.

"I saw her."

"Last night?"

I nodded. "We had dinner together. Villa Romano."

"We love that place."

If he had any curiosity, he kept it to himself. I didn't tell him anything else and he didn't ask. We went for brats at a bar down by the stadium. He told me about bringing Chris there for the Backyard Brawl and the two of them making a bet with some WVU fans. I guessed that was reason enough for him to love the Pitt quarterback who'd won the rivalry game for them that year. But apparently the guy threw a 72-yard touchdown pass in the bowl game, which Joel described over lunch as if it were the most epic football play ever.

"Did you win?" I asked.

He shook his head sadly.

"Good thing that wasn't the game you had the wager on." I raised my glass and took a drink, looking around at the clientele of the restaurant. It was a weekday and most everyone was in business attire, though being Friday, some wore jeans. The sharply creased button-downs and employee badges hanging from their belt loops, though, tipped me off that many were still working. That and the ice-water-with-lemons on the tables in front of them all. Except me and Joel who each had a tall Yuengling draft.

"I love drinking when other people are working," he said and grinned.

"Tabby didn't think I'd make it," I said. "She told me I'd need to fly out yesterday."

"We're finally used to it. Whenever we think Brian, we think California."

"Surf shack, babes in bikinis."

"Right," Joel agreed. "Board rentals and bonfires."

"Pacific Standard Time."

"For now," he said. "Now that we're used to it, you'll probably go off somewhere again." He said it without malice or jealousy, just the observation of a guy who was living in the one place he knew he'd always be.

"Man, I'm glad you're here," he said.

"Wouldn't miss it."

When we'd returned to the hotel, Chris was in the lobby checking in to his room. He'd sent the bellhop up with his bag and flopped into a chair beside me.

"I'm still recovering from Vegas," he said.

I laughed. "Old man."

"I can't hang like you anymore," Chris complained.

"Hey, hey, Hemingway!" Jason crossed the lobby in three strides.

I stood and hugged him.

Chris did, too, and we passed around some Vegas remarks.

"Is it happy hour yet?" Jason asked, making a point of looking at his watch. It was two o'clock. I'd had two beers at the stadium bar with Joel and nodded in response.

"Not for me," Joel said. "Tabby's got me on lockdown until Sunday."

"Well, there are photographers around," I said. "Probably wise to keep even."

"Shit, this ain't my wedding," Jason said.

"That's good enough for me," I said. "Chris?" But he begged off, saying he had to call his girl and check in with his office before the heavy drinking started.

So we'd been in the bar when Kacie found us and reminded us the rehearsal was starting upstairs soon. She looked really pretty in a black turtleneck and slim charcoal grey pants. She'd come in without me noticing, but Jason stood and took her into a big hug.

I looked over my shoulder and saw them, saw her pull back and look him in the face, saw them hug again, and I smiled.

"Have a seat, Kace," I said, using that one-syllable version of her name that I'd earned back the right to.

She looked at her watch and then agreed, but she didn't order a drink. Jason got us a fourth round of beers. After some discussion around flights and what time we'd all arrived, Jason asked me if I knew why Chris hadn't brought Sara with him.

"He's dating Sara again?" Kacie asked.

"Yeah, been about a year I guess," I said.

She laughed. "I guess some things come back around again, huh?"

I raised my eyebrows at her and she shook her head. Jason grinned.

"That's what he gets for moving back to the circus," I said. Chris and Joel had made good on their plan to share the townhouse. Chris was still living in it, but Joel had been in Pittsburgh for the last year. Jason hadn't moved in with Chris, instead, Chris had found a roommate from a group of friends he and Joel had made. Now when we got together, Chris was saying things like, "Guess who I saw?" and naming random people we'd gone to high school with. Though not nearly as frequently as Tony used to.

"It's about that time, best man," Kacie said.

"Guess that means I win?" Jason teased.

"Nah, Joel wins this weekend," I said.

"Aw, look who's all romantic," Kacie sang.

I tilted my head at her and delivered one of my smiles. She rolled her eyes and stood to leave. Jason and I followed.

I told the bartender to put our drinks on Joel's tab and we followed Kacie out into the lobby and up the elevator to the mezzanine with our bottles in our hands. We met the other participants and shook hands all around. The coordinator and minister walked us through the motions of the ceremony and where to stand and what would happen when.

Joel's mom hosted the rehearsal dinner at The Terrace Room and it was the kind of place prom dates go, but it was February so it had mostly politicians and anniversary couples. Joel's groomsmen were me and Chris with Jason as best man and Tabby's bridesmaids were Kacie and her two sisters. Her eldest sister was her maid of honor. The three of them looked very similar and Kacie stuck out when they posed for pictures. I smiled across the room at her. Between the rehearsal and dinner, she'd changed from the turtleneck and pants into a cocktail dress. She wore small black heels and black pantyhose.

I met Joel's freshman-year roommate and former business partner and his wife, and Joel's mother's new husband. I met Tabby's parents and younger brother and her grandmother Rose who was ninety-two and hard of hearing. Tabby told me to ignore her; she mostly spoke Tagalog. In my travels, I'd learned a few phrases I tried on her; they made her blush which prompted Tabby's mom to laugh and accuse me of flirting.

Chris and I refrained from ordering shots. Jason and I took turns telling stories about cities we'd been in that were the same or different or better or worse than Pittsburgh. Joel escaped to our corner of the room a few times, sneaking long pulls off beers we left sitting within reach for him. Once he found us out on the terrace smoking and stole a few puffs off Chris's cigar. I'd offered Chris a cigarette but he'd declined and made some excuse about marathon training and not inhaling on a cigar.

It was mostly like every other time we'd gotten together in the past three years. Atlanta. San Francisco. Dallas. Nashville. That time Joel met me in Paris, and the week Jason and I spent in Barcelona. We ran up large tabs at the best bar we could find. Sometimes we went for a run to survive the hangover. Sometimes we went to a game or a concert. Sometimes one of us was working and the others would just drink. Once we played golf in Arizona. We always ordered a fifth shot for Tony. We usually reeked of smoke and booze.

On Saturday, that would change. We would lose Joel to matrimony and where his first company's success and the house in the Pittsburgh suburbs hadn't really aged him, marriage would. Kids couldn't be far behind, we figured, and so this milestone meant a little more than the other trips had.

I should have been hurting Saturday morning but I really wasn't and the run had been good. Cold but surprisingly fresh for a city route. When I got out of the shower, the room was empty and the bag with the bagel gone. I dressed in khakis and a button-down shirt with the TV streaming CNN.

I called Chris and he reminded me that we had pictures at three. "Lunch?"

Seated across from one another in a sandwich shop around the corner from the Omni, Chris asked if I'd decided to buy my loft in San Francisco and I said I had not. He said he knew a good mortgage broker if I did decide.

Jason asked if I was planning to go somewhere else and I said not until the MFA was done, which would be May at the earliest.

I asked Jason if he'd invited Kacie to have lunch with us and he said he hadn't seen her since last night and added that she was probably busy with prep stuff, anyway.

We finished lunch and split up to return to our rooms for naps. Then, at three o'clock, we met in the hallway in front of Joel's room, dressed in tuxedos.

Chris and Jason looked sideways at me and I stood up straight.

"Damn, Hemingway," Jason said. "You wear the hell out of a rental."

"Seriously," Chris said. "You're such a fucking asshole."

I laughed. "Fuck off."

Joel let us in and handed me his bow tie. "Who doesn't rent clip-ons?" he asked. Later, in the receiving line, when Tabby asked him who he got to tie it for him and he said Brian, she would raise an eyebrow and look over at me with that same Tabby skepticism.

The ceremony took place in a small ballroom in which the wedding coordinator had erected a center stage with an arbor and arranged seats on all sides like theatre in the round. Tabby's parents and Joel's mom sat in the front row. Her brother was an usher along with her cousin; they were both in high school.

Chris and I stood outside of the room waiting to be invited in.

"A few more of these," he said, "and I might as well buy a damn tux."

"Oh yeah?"

"Pretty much everyone I know except you and Jason."

"And you."

He smiled and looked at his shoes.

"What? You got something you're not sharing?" I asked.

"I'm going to ask Sara," he said.

"Really? Man, that's awesome," I said. "Congratulations." I hugged him and then, over his shoulder, saw Mac walking up the mezzanine hallway.

He looked smaller somehow, like he'd lost weight. His hair was fully grey and he wore a dark blue suit with a striped tie. He had a woman with him, but it wasn't Rhonda.

I let him come to us and then I hugged him.

"We're late," he said.

"We'll talk later," I promised.

Chris opened the door for him and Tabby's brother walked his date to a seat in the fourth row. Mac followed.

"Have you seen him?" I asked Chris.

"Not since Tony," he said. "I'm glad he's here."

About that time Jason and Joel came down the hall, looking more like twins than ever in their identical tuxedos. It was remarkable the way they'd stayed so alike for all those years. The four of us stood outside of the ballroom door and looked at one another.

"So it's time?" Jason asked.

"It's time," Joel said. And we went inside to marry the guy off to the first girl he'd ever loved. We stood near the arbor, our hands in front of us, looking backward for the ladies to enter.

A string quartet began "Jesu, Joy of Man's Desiring" and Kacie floated in first in a long grey satin dress that looked like a nightgown. The straps were thin over her shoulders and she had a transparent shawl that didn't look like it would provide any warmth at all but made her look as though she were made out of shiny silver snow. Her hair was piled on top of her head, with ringlets hung around her ears and temples. She wore diamond earrings and a diamond pendant necklace. Tabby's two sisters followed, each as pretty as the other, and then Tabby, looking like a snow queen in a long white gown.

The ceremony was as perfect as Tabby would have expected it to be. After Joel kissed his bride and they charged down the aisle, the guests were shown into a containment area with cocktails and hors d'oeuvres while the bridal party posed for pictures. I kept myself between Jason and Joel, tried not to stare at Kacie, and when I caught myself doing so, I'd feel a thrill at the new strand of memories we'd begun writing.

While the bridesmaids and groomsmen followed the crowd into the cocktail area, Joel and Tabby were directed away for more strategic pictures and a grand entrance into the reception. I followed Kacie into the crowd and leaned to grab her hand and pull her to me in a dark corner. She giggled and tugged away and before I could give chase, I was facing Mac.

He'd seen the exchange with Kacie and he was smiling.

"You two back together?" he asked.

"It's new."

"Tony would have liked that."

I nodded. "I think so." I looked past him and said, "Where's Rhonda?"

He looked around, too, saw his date at a safe distance, and said, "We didn't make it." He shoved his hands into his pockets.

"I heard you sold the house," I said.

"She never came back from Stacey's."

"I'm sorry."

"Me, too." He smiled, though, and said, "What can ya do?"

"Not a damn thing." I clapped him on the shoulder, noting how thin he'd become since I saw him last in Arizona over the summer.

Chris walked up then with a few bottles and handed one to each of us. We toasted and took long swigs.

"You're a dog," he said to me, then he looked over at Kacie.

"What?"

"How long has that been going on?"

"A couple of days," I said, and it was the truth. Sort of.

Jason came over and hugged Mac. "Man, it's been too long."

"Yeah," Mac said. "It has been a long time." His date walked over and he introduced her to us. She worked in his firm, he said, and she was from Pittsburgh. She said she couldn't pass up the opportunity to show Mac the city. I got the feeling they didn't plan to stay through the reception.

The crowd began to move. We were being ushered into the reception area and Chris and Jason and I had to join the bridesmaids for introductions.

Chris held his elbow out for Tabby's younger sister and she grinned. She may have been all of nineteen and I think she was indulging herself in a crush. I let Kacie walk over to me, mischief in her eye. She held out her arm and I slipped mine through it. Jason escorted Tabby's eldest sister and they entered last.

The D.J. called our names and we entered and stood, in pairs, on the dance floor. Then he said, "And, for the first time, Mr. and Mrs. Joel Lincrest," and the spotlight shone on an upper walkway. Joel and Tabby appeared as though standing on the clouds of heaven. Tiny white confetti fell from the ceiling and it seemed to be snowing in the room. Joel and Tabby descended, Sophie B. Hawkins' "As I Lay Me Down to Sleep" played and there was murmuring and clapping and "aww-ing" all around.

I looked over at Kacie, who was now holding my arm. Her face was lit from within with a smile I remembered from a long time ago.

"You're beautiful."

She looked at me, her green eyes about to burst with tears of joy and said, "Thank you, Brian."

Then Joel and Tabby came by us like the cake topper on parade and we all gave them hugs and kisses and brushed confetti off one another's cheeks and shoulders. The D.J. queued their first dance song and we all took our partners in our arms.

I pressed Kacie against me, rested my hands on the satin of her dress, and buried my face in her neck.

Once I'd found her and gone to her, she'd been reluctant to see me. Then, in her living room in Seattle, after a painful exchange about how long it had been, she had said, "What do you want?"

It was then that I described where I'd been. I hadn't spared any imagery. I would have written it, I'd said, but, until recently, I didn't have the vocabulary for it.

I described the bay in Montenegro and the island with the abbey and how it reminded me of Alcatraz, just a different kind of prison. I described hiking the mountain in Dubrovnik and hearing the gunfire in neighboring Serbia behind me while the Adriatic stretched its sapphire brilliance before me.

"In Barcelona, in Portugal, in Rome, Paris, there was only you," I had said.

"Why are you doing this?" she'd whispered.

"I finally felt that spiritual cooling that Tony found. I could feel myself healing on the inside. I wanted you to know."

When I reached as far back as Barcelona, just eight months after Tony's death, she'd fled to her bedroom. I'd chased her there and thrown myself on the floor at her feet.

"Hear me," I'd begged. "Every day the sun would wear me down. I would work until my hands were raw and my back was broken," I said. "I would strip off my stinking clothes in the outdoor shower in the crowded courtyard of the Spanish villa where I lived. I would step inside, lean my head to the post, pull the chain, and let the cold water pour over me."

I was on my knees in front of her. She was sitting on the edge of the bed in the room she'd been renting for about five months.

I told her how I'd knelt at Santa Maria del Mar and lit a candle and prayed even though I didn't know how. I told her she'd been with me from the beaches of the Mediterranean to the jagged rocks of Big Sur. I told her I'd been seeing it all but I hadn't really seen anything except her.

"Go away," she had cried.

"There is nowhere," I had said, "unless you're there." It was a line from the Bryan Adams song, "Everything I Do" and we'd been quoting it to one another since we'd lain on my parents' couch in the dark watching *Robin Hood Prince of Thieves* on VHS with my hand up her shirt under the blanket and my breath on the edge of her jaw under her curls.

"Just go," she replied.

Then I'd stood and left. I'd gotten out of her city, gone back to mine, begun putting the pieces together. I scribbled the stories on every scrap I could find, filled marble composition books and spiral-bound journals. I submitted and was rejected and I submitted again. I attended class and graded freshman comp papers for my advisor. I read deep into Rough South Literature and American Realism. I studied and I wrote.

When next I reached her, it had been several months. I finally had a story accepted and I sent her the complimentary copy of the journal with which they'd paid me. I stuck a Post-It on the front and wrote her name on it. She called after she got it.

"Brian. It's perfect."

"Thank you."

We talked for a while. I described my MFA program in San Francisco and the work I was submitting to literary magazines. I described the rejection letters and how I'd begun burning them and scraping the ashes into jars and how I was on my third jar and I laughed and said that was okay, it meant I was a real writer.

She apologized for Seattle and said she hadn't been ready and would I like to try to meet again, maybe on neutral territory and I told her to come to San Francisco. But she didn't.

Then one night several months later she called and said she had been thinking about sending me back the notebook and would I like to have it. I said yes and when it arrived, I expected to weep over it, but instead I flipped through it and felt an odd disconnection.

I called her.

"It's here," I said, "so thanks. But it's missing something."

"I know."

"I can't feel it anymore."

"Me neither."

I had been sitting at the bar counter in my flat, the same one I'd been coming back to for the past five years from Virginia, from Spain, from Arizona, from everywhere I ever went. I held the cordless phone to my ear waiting for her to speak again.

"So that's it?" I asked.

"Maybe," she said.

Then we were in Pittsburgh and we'd been living these parallel lives, she visiting Tabby to help with wedding prep, and me with Joel and weekends in Vegas among other places.

He and Jason had made it out to San Francisco and the first thing he'd said was, "It's fucking cold here."

Joel had been to Arizona on business, and I'd gone down to Oro Valley and had him to Mom and Dad's for the weekend. We'd poured three shots in front of the painting of the burning valley, which my parents hung in their living room over their new deep orange suede sofa.

Joel's company made a ton of money and he sold it. He was now on to some new thing, a serial entrepreneur he called himself. I listened to how he talked about Tabby. I listened for whether she was on his side or against him. I listened for him making plans and including her. For him responding to her plans.

Kacie and I had been keeping close to Tabby and Joel and watching them grow up together. We watched love change them.

When I'd last talked to Kacie she had said, "You'll have to fly out Thursday."

"I know," I had said and told her what Joel told me about the Fort Pitt Tunnel. She had confirmed the description and then said she'd have to go early, too. She had moved down to Eugene by then, working the varsity beat for the University of Oregon. She'd been making a good run as a sports journalist but had confided she was anxious to find something more meaningful to do.

I had asked her some time ago about Jason, but she said they'd made their peace and he was in a different world than she. I knew he was still playing hockey, though, and that he'd been interviewing for coaching jobs at the University of Minnesota and the University of Montana. I expected he might try Oregon, too. But Kacie denied it, saying there was no reason for him to move out there for her.

In Vegas, three weeks before Joel's wedding, Jason confirmed Kacie's assertions and when I asked him about Pittsburgh, he said, "It'll be good to see her again," with no sign of anything but friendly affection. I expected they'd been thrown together at the shower Tabby's family had at Christmas time, since Kacie had said she was going there before seeing her parents in Denver. But she hadn't mentioned much else about that trip other than her flight was delayed heading to Tempe for the Fiesta Bowl. I went to Oro Valley and asked if she wanted to spend New Year's Eve together but she declined.

She called after Vegas but before Pittsburgh and said, "I'll meet you in the hotel bar."

There we were, two days later, dancing so slowly we may have been standing still. Her breath on my cheek and my face in her neck, pressing kisses gently on her collarbone like the ones I'd covered her in the night before.

After the rehearsal and the bride and groom had gone to their separate quarters, we had gone back to the hotel bar and ordered shots, five of them. Kacie, Jason, Chris, and me, and Tony's shot sat on the table until we'd told all of our stories and filled in all the gaps. Then Chris went up to bed, and Jason ordered another round of beers.

The three of us sat and brainstormed about their lives after sports. Kacie wanted to write about politics, and Jason wanted to coach for the Olympic team. I told them about my short story collection which would be my master's thesis. Jason described my San Francisco flat to Kacie, and I told her about the time we all met in Dallas when he'd played hockey on Saturday night and we'd seen the Redskins play the Cowboys on Sunday.

Then the bar closed and we'd all gone up to the seventh floor. Jason and I had gone to our separate rooms and Kacie went to hers, and my phone rang before I'd even gotten my shirt unbuttoned.

"What do you have to give?" she asked.

And that was how she ended up in my bed again.

Beneath the blankets of the William Penn Omni king-sized bed, holding her against me where she'd always fit so perfectly, I'd threaded my fingers through hers and pressed her arm over her head, into the pillow.

"There's nowhere," I murmured, laying gentle kisses on her lips and jaw. "Unless you're there."

"All the time," she'd replied. "All the way."

She let me make love to her in that slow and satisfying way we had when we remembered our first love that would never happen again.

The next night I held her on the dance floor, our friends surrounding us, and imagined a day when she would be the one in white and I would be the luckiest man in the room. Tonight, though, it was Joel and Tabby's first dance and Billy Joel sang, "I don't want clever conversation, I never want to have to work that hard. I took the good times, I'll take the bad times."

And all of us, the Crew, sang, "I'll take you just the way you are."

Then I leaned back and looked at her, those eyes I knew so well, and kissed her lips with the frosted lip gloss and the sweet honey taste. I pressed Kacie closer to me and whispered, "I love you," thinking, feeling, like maybe I'd finally earned the right.

THE END

THE You-KNOW-WHO-You-ARES (YKWYA)

This book has literally grown up with me. Its first iteration was in 1989 when the Fanning family moved to Aptos, California and I sat in my window seat scribbling in spiral notebooks. Because it grew up with me, it grew up with a few other people, too.

Thank you to Kristen for being my first beta reader and always saying "Yes," when I asked if I could read a scene out loud to you.

Thank you to my mom and dad for supporting my weird scribbly suchness and letting me spend hours in front of the computer typing up the first version of this book that turned my handwriting into text. And my other moms and dads who love me and believe in me (YKWYA).

Thank you to Clemson University and my roommates there (YKWYA) for letting me play Pink Floyd at all hours while I hunt-and-pecked my way through the version of this novel that took all the grief and anger I had at 19 and found a place for it.

There were writing professors who warned me away from this bleeding-on-the-page career and who contributed great lines to Brian's development. (YKWYA: "My friends say I'm lucky and they're right.") My Nana and Papa who meant so much to me. My bartenders and musicians (YKWYA) who helped me tell my stories one bar napkin at a time.

Thanks to my friends who encouraged me: Tami, Josh, Jessica, Kevin, and Damaré, even if they didn't fully understand what this whole writing thing was about. And friends who totally got it like the South Carolina Writers' Association Columbia II Chapter members (YKWYA). They hate Brian, so they don't get their names listed here (Yep. I'm spiteful like that.)

Thanks to my very supportive network including a filmmaker, a local pub, and a crowd of early reader-reviewers (YKWYA). All those starry-eyed-smilers who said, "That's awesome!" and then bought a copy, shared the marketing stuff, and told their friends about the book.

My editor and bestie Jonathan Haupt who has serious writing chops and let me show off mine a little bit at a time. Anything I can ever do for you, my friend, just ask.

My publisher, Alexa, who never blinked after saying, "Yes," and has been the most amazing friend and partner in this endeavor. Oh, the places we will go!

My first two heartbroken beta readers, Preston Taylor Stone who told me he "literally cried about Butterscotch when I didn't even know the dog existed the page before." And Jodie Cane Smith who pushed me to explain why Brian would answer the phone on page one and a dozen other places where she made me better. Thank you both.

Finally, this book grew up with me, but I grew up with Charlie Whitener. Thank you for believing in me. For loving me. For being the best friend to me and dad to our Hollie you can possibly be. I didn't forget you, HB, you taught me what real love is. I hope I earn it from you and your daddy every day.

TAKE ME TO YOUR BOOK CLUB. I CAN BE TRUSTED.

I have a great relationship with book clubs. I've been kicked out of three. Twice I've had the chance to speak to Book Club Conferences (Pat Conroy Literary Center and Fairfax County Public Library) and both times I delivered: "Read Like a Writer: How to Get Kicked Out of Book Club." FYI, if you read like a writer, you'll be asking your wine-sipping, John-Grisham-loving neighbors and friends to go too deep.

Thanks for picking this book. Contact me at kasie@clemsonroad. com or through the website www.AfterDecember.com to let me know what your group thought. I'm glad to appear via video conference in the meeting where you discuss this book.

Here it is, in gradually-getting-deeper order, the Book Club Guide for After December.

1. Brian is our only point of view in this book. How did you like his perspective? Would you have rather heard from someone else? Why do you think his is the only voice? What are the limitations of this first-person narrator?

2. The chapters are organized by the days of the week Brian spends in Northern Virginia. Did this organization work for you? Why or why not? How else could the book have been arranged?

3. The section titled "New Year's Eve 1998" comes after a turning-point scene between Brian and Kacie. Why do you think the author put this scene between Friday and Saturday of the current week? Why not start the book with that exposition?

4. As Brian returns home, he is assaulted by the places and landmarks of Northern Virginia, those memories he only allows himself to revisit occasionally. Why do you think Brian tries to forget Virginia when he's in California?

5. Kacie rejects Brian's assertion that they had "an agreement" when they were apart. Brian is convinced she was cheating, too. Do you think she was? Or did she just let him believe that? When she cheats with Jason, was it casual? Circumstantial? Or intentional?

6. Brian is unwilling to forgive Kacie and Jason at first. How is Brian as the injured party a position "that has the most stability (p. 39)," when he admits that it is "a complete farce (p.39)"? What does his willingness to pretend in the first night back with his friends tell us about how he treats them?

7. Are Brian's parents neglectful? Do they seem disinterested in him? Unwilling or unable to connect? Why does he claim that they are?

8. The twins are witnesses to their mom's abusive relationship with their father. How does that fuel their suspicions about what happens between Brian and Kacie upstairs on New Year's Eve?

9. On Saturday night Brian remarks to Chris that he's about to ruin his relationship with Meli by hooking up with the bartender, Ashley. What does his reason, "Not ready to go home," (p.246) tell us about how Brian deals with emotional complexity? Why do you think he chooses to go through with the hook-up with Ashley?

10. The Crew formed a competitive skateboarding team in their teens. How does their history of competing together fortify their relationships? What do they expect of one another as best friends and teammates?

11. The final scene, 02/02/02, reunites the Crew in the most grown-up thing they've done since Tony's death. Does ending the book on a wedding provide closure for you? What about what Mac witnesses between Brian and Kacie ("it's new," p.295)?

Get more from www.AfterDecember.com including interviews and blogs with author Kasie Whitener and alternate scenes narrated by other characters.

COMING SPRING 2021:
BEFORE PITTSBURGH

Barcelona 1999

Dear Kacie,

Last night I went out with Marco and Paulo, two of the servers at that coffee shop I go to a lot. They wanted to take me to a club and I haven't really been out in a long time so I agreed.

I dressed up, for me anyway, a silver button-down shirt with short sleeves and an open collar and black jeans that fit a little too snug. Probably all the dock work making my legs bigger. Even so, I was less conspicuous than either Marco or Paulo. They slick their hair back, wear jewelry, and flash rolls of cash when they pay cover charges and bar tabs.

I'm not used to paying cash and only a little bit more familiar with the currency here. In the first week, I had a cab driver look at my wad of bills and pluck one from my hand. Probably overpaid for that ride. Haven't taken a cab since. Bakeries and coffee shops are less criminal in their transactions. Even so, I worked pretty hard to learn the currency.

All that said, Marco led the way last night and Paulo followed up in the rear to keep me from falling behind or getting taken for another ride. The story goes like this:

Marco knew some girls at the first club but none of them spoke English. They were all excited to meet me but my poor Spanish didn't make the situation much better. Then we had about four rounds of shots and one of them stuck her tongue in my mouth and I felt like we maybe had gotten past the language thing.

I begged off dancing but the making out was just fine.

We left that crowd and went on to the next bar, Marco promising them we'd meet back up and then telling Paulo and me he had no intention of doing so. He reminds me a lot of me.

The next bar was one I'd been to before but Marco knew the bartender and Paulo greased the door man so we got in ahead of the line and only paid for about half of our drinks.

We didn't know any girls at this place but some found us, approached us, and introduced themselves. One of them, Anna, was an American. She's on exchange from a high school in Pennsylvania and when she said high school I quickly put her on the do-not-touch list. It was nice to talk to an American, though, and since she'd just arrived I could show off a little about what I knew of the city.

She asked why I was working on the docks and I pretended I hadn't heard the question.

Punishing myself for my best friend's suicide didn't seem like a bar-night kind of response.

Finally Marco said the crowd there was too young and we left. I told Anna to come by the dock and we could get lunch sometime. I forgot how bad I smell after work but I didn't expect she'd show up anyway. She knew I was too old for her and I think she got the sense that I was hiding something. She was much more cautious at the end of our conversation than she had been at the beginning.

The third bar was nearer to my house in Vila de Gracía. It's inland from La Segrada Familia, near the Avinguda Diagonal. I've been staying there since I arrived and the communal courtyard, bath, and kitchen facilities have grown on me. My roommates are all guys like me, working their way through studies. A pair of guys from Saudi Arabia are in their thirties and two kids from South Africa are just out of high school.

The bar was filled with foreign nationals, drawn to the area by the promise that it was full of locals. The primary language, though, was heavily accented English. I liked it, even if it was rather dim and dingy, less posh than the Olympic area or less flashy that the club scene we'd just left. It felt a little bit like how I imagined Seattle.

Marco ordered our drinks and Paulo secured us a table. I hit the john. The single door had a hook-and-hoop lock and gave a few centimeters of visibility while I stood at the urinal.

I looked at the wall above the porcelain commode and read some lyrics from an old Counting Crows song. They made me smile and then ache a little.

I remembered them from the Green Velvet Notebook. Which you still have. Because you took it back the morning I left.

So very far away from Virginia and yet still haunted in innumerable ways by all that happened after December. Anyway, back to the story:

When I left the john, two girls were blocking my way out of the back corner of the bar. I was a little drunk by now.

"Your friend said we should come get you," the taller one said. "Or you might get lost."

"Coming back from the john?" I asked.

The shorter one winked. "Want to?"

I looked past them to Paulo who was grinning at me.

"Um, ladies, thanks, but I'm just with my buddies tonight."

"You don't *have* to just be with them," one of them said.

"You know Lara, don't you?" the other one said.

I thought back to my first weekend here and the girl who'd shown me around Barcelona and introduced me to the dock manager. She was dark-haired and creamy-skinned and I'd enjoyed her but she had been off to another adventure further south.

"She's not from here," I said.

"She told us to look you up," the shorter one said, dragging her fingertips down my arm.

"She told us," the taller one leaned close to me, her lips on my ear, "About the courtyard."

I closed my eyes and felt myself responding to the two of them, the touch, the warmth, the promise of something. I needed it.

"Move," a harsh Russian accent.

I looked up and one of the mean bastards from the docks was there.

The girls shifted closer to me to get out of his way.

Wrapping my arms around them, I pulled them close.

"You need both?" the Russian grunted. "Greedy Americans." Then he barreled his way into the john and I let the girls kiss me.

The shorter one nipped at my neck, her hand on my ass. The taller one kissed my mouth, her hand sliding down the bulge in my jeans. I needed this, I told myself.

Then, over the tall one's shoulder, as she kissed my ear, I saw the Russian pissing through the crack in the door, watching me with the girls.

"We should go," I said.

Then the door burst open and the Russian was there. The girls flinched and he had his hand around my throat, shoving me against the wall.

"Paulo!" one of the girls squealed.

Then my friends were shoving their way into the darkened corner of the bathroom hallway and the Russian was shoving me toward the back door. We fell through, his hand still on my throat, my feet barely on the ground. Outside was a ramp down toward a parking lot and a railing behind which was a closed dumpster. The Russian shoved me and let me go and I tumbled backward over the rail onto the lid.

A backwards somersault, the light of the parking lot, the building's hard edges, then I was falling onto my knees on the asphalt. The Russian leapt the rail, feet first onto the dumpster and then to the ground beside me as I was getting to my feet.

"Come on, then," he said, and then something in Russian.

"Guy, wait, I'm not gonna fight you."

"Yes, you are."

"But I don't want to." I looked up to the rail for Paulo and Marco.

"Woah, big guy," Marco's accented English voice came through the noise bleeding out of the bar's open back door.

"You don't want to fight," he said. "You're just drunk."

"Am not. I've been ready to kick this little shit's ass for weeks."

"What the fuck did I do to you?"

"Shut up, Brian," Paulo said.

"You work but you don't need to. Fucking Americans taking jobs."

"From Spaniards. Kind of like your immigrant asses," Marco said. "Maybe I oughta kick your ass on behalf of all of Spain."

"Bravo," Paulo said.

"Fuck it, Marco. He wants me, let him have me."

The Russian pushed past Marco and charged. I took a swing as he came near and caught his jaw with my fist. He was hard, though, and the punch glanced off without much impact other than to infuriate him and make my hand throb.

"Fucker!" he shouted in a voice heavy with throat-trapped saliva.

"Ivan!" He turned at his name and I landed another punch,

this time on the other side of his jaw. He reeled and stumbled back.

His friends were on the rail now and they watched as he righted himself and came back at me. His eyes burned with hatred but I could see something else there, too, an unfocused glaze that made me think he was drunker than he'd admitted to being.

"Ivan," the friends from the railing called again.

I squared my hips and decided to go for body blows this time.

"I'm going to make you pay for that," Ivan said.

"Let's have it then."

He took a swing and I ducked. He reeled and stumbled again. I dug a punch into his stomach and he doubled over.

Then his buddies were on the asphalt, too, and one of them had grabbed me and the other landed a punch across my face. Blood spurted from my nose.

"Hold the fuck up," Marco said, diving into the fray and engaging the guy who'd hit me.

I broke free from the one holding me, turned and swung at him. He ducked and hit me in the ribs.

"Everyone, everyone, wait." Paulo was trying to get us to stop fighting without getting into the fray himself. But his efforts were wasted as Ivan stood back up and lunged for me, his buddy held me and Ivan landed a punch in the gut. I groaned.

Marco and the other Russian were trading swings.

"Paulo!" I shouted. "Get in here."

"Enough, enough," he was saying.

Finally, the back door opened again and the bar manager and two bouncers streamed out and down the ramp toward us. The Russian let me go and followed Ivan and the other guy as they fled down the alley. Marco and I stood catching our breath while Paulo explained to the manager that we'd been brutally attacked.

I looked up and saw the girls in the doorway. I'm sure my

face and shirt were ridiculous, covered with blood. They came back to the villa with me, though, and peeled my shirt off in the courtyard and stepped me into the shower and washed me clean.

Then the three of us went to bed and I decided to work on the sex demon tomorrow.

Along with the fighting demon.

It had been a long night and I'd earned the tenderness of strangers.

I'm sorry. But not really.

Love, Brian

About the Author

DR. KASIE WHITENER writes GenX fiction. At her core is fantasy romance and not-quite-getting-over-the-90s. She serves on the board of directors for the South Carolina Writers Association and is a member of the South Carolina Council on Humanities Speakers Bureau. Dr. Whitener has presented workshops for the Bowling Green State University's Winter Wheat Literary Festival, the Pat Conroy Literary Center, and Fairfax County Public Library. Her short story "Cover Up," won the Carrie McCray Prize in 2016 and other stories have appeared in Spry, Kairos, and The Petigru Review. She is founder & President of Clemson Road Creative and a lecturer at the Darla Moore School of Business at the University of South Carolina. Happily married to her best friend Charlie and crazy-proud mom to the one-and-only Hollie, Kasie reads voraciously, plays golf, and cheers for the Clemson Tigers.